# Yesterday's Girl

*Also by Anna Jacobs:*

THE GIBSON FAMILY SAGA
Salem Street
High Street
Ridge Hill
Hallam Square
Spinners Lake

THE KERSHAW SISTERS
Our Lizzie
Our Polly
Our Eva
Our Mary Ann

THE IRISH SISTERS
A Pennyworth of Sunshine
Twopenny Rainbows
Threepenny Dreams

THE SETTLERS
Lancashire Lass
Lancashire Legacy

THE STALEYS
Down Weavers Lane
Calico Road

THE PRESTON FAMILY SAGA
Pride of Lancashire
Star of the North
Bright Day Dawning
Heart of the Town

STAND ALONE NOVELS
Jessie
Like No Other
Tomorrow's Promises

ANNA JACOBS

# Yesterday's Girl

HODDER

First published in Great Britain in 2008 by Hodder & Stoughton
An Hachette Livre UK company

2



A CIP catalogue record for this title is available from the British Library

ISBN 978 0 340 840818

Typeset in Plantin Light by Palimpsest Book Production Ltd, Grangemouth, Stirlingshire

Printed and bound by
Mackays of Chatham plc, Chatham, Kent

Hodder & Stoughton policy is to use papers that are natural, renewable and recyclable products and made from wood grown in sustainable forests. The logging and manufacturing processes are expected to conform to the environmental regulations of the country of origin.

Hodder & Stoughton Ltd
338 Euston Road

In loving memory of my father, Derrick Sheridan,
who passed away in December 2006. We all miss you
very much, Dad, and 87 years weren't nearly long enough.

# PART ONE

## September 1916

# I

Violet Gill was walking home with a bag full of spoiled fruit and vegetables that she'd got cheaply from the market. She'd just turned a corner when she saw some lads snatch a loaf from an old lady, who was hobbling painfully along. They'd started running towards Vi before they noticed her and tried to swerve, but she didn't hesitate for a minute. Dropping her shopping bag, she flung herself sideways at the lad carrying the booty, shoving him so hard he bounced off the wall and let go of the loaf.

She grabbed him by the neck of his ragged shirt and gave him a couple of good clouts about the ears. 'Don't you *dare* steal anything again, Frank Pilling, or I'll hand you over to Constable Tucker! And you can be sure I'll tell your mam about this.'

His two companions in crime stopped further along the street to watch.

'I'll be telling your mams too!' she shouted at them, still holding the young thief by his shirt front. 'I know who you are. Brave, aren't you, to steal an old woman's food!' She gave her captive another thump for good measure and then let go of him. She knew how short of food the lad's family was, but it was no excuse.

He half-raised one hand to hit her back and for a minute all hung in the balance.

'Don't – you – dare!' she said softly, and although she wasn't much taller than him, something in her tone made him shrink away. With a yell he ran off down the street towards his companions. Only when the trio had disappeared round the corner did Vi turn to the lads' victim, who was leaning against the wall looking pale and shocked, and put one arm round her.

'You all right, love? See, I've got your loaf back. It's a bit dusty, though.'

'Thank you.' The old woman patted her chest. 'Eh, it give me a right old shock, that did. Made my heart pound. Be all right – in a minute.'

Vi waited patiently for her to pull herself together, then gave her back the loaf and watched her walk slowly and painfully away. The town hall clock struck the hour just then and she clicked her tongue in annoyance at the delay before picking up her own bag and retrieving one or two apples which had fallen out. Hurrying up the street, she turned the corner into the Backhill Terraces, twenty or so narrow streets clustered round the town's two big cotton mills on a slope that led up to the moors. It was here, in the poorest area of Drayforth, that her family's corner shop was situated.

She always enjoyed her outings to the markets, where the stallholders knew she'd pay them for bruised or overripe pieces and saved them for her. She paused at the door, sighing. She didn't enjoy being shut up in the shop all day. But what choice did she have? What choice had she ever had from the minute she finished her schooling? Her father left most of the running of the shop to her mother and herself, and her mother had been ill for a few years, though she'd been a lot better in the past year, thank goodness.

Vi had been needed while her mother was ill. Without her the shop would have failed.

The two ladies who had stopped to watch this incident from further down the street began walking again.

'Well done, young woman!' Lady Bingram said softly. 'Who is she? Do you know, Freda?'

'I think she works in one of the corner shops. I've seen her when I've been visiting the slums.'

'Can you find out more about her?'

'I suppose so. Why?'

Daphne Bingram grinned, an urchin's grin for all she was in

her mid-sixties. 'I'm looking for more young women to join my Aides. The government finds my little group so helpful in the war effort that it's asking me to find more of them, and is even giving me some money towards the costs. I certainly couldn't afford to support a bigger group myself.'

'Surely you don't want women of *that class* in your group?'

'Snobbery won't win the war, Freda. There are plucky women in all classes, and that's the only sort I want working for me.'

Her companion sniffed. 'Well, rather you than me. Some of those women from the Backhill Terraces have no moral fibre. The things I've seen in my charity work!' She frowned. 'I'd have thought you'd want younger aides, though. That one must be well over thirty.'

Daphne stopped trying to reason with a woman who had always been a snob and a stick-in-the-mud, and wasn't likely to change now, war or no war. The trouble was, she needed the money her companion was raising to help buy the necessary cars and motor-bikes for those women from her group who were acting as couriers to various offshoots of the War Office. It was so good to be able to contribute to the war effort. It gave a meaning to her life she hadn't had for a long time. She'd do anything she could to keep her Aides going, even be nice to Freda Gilson.

As they were parting company on the main street, she reminded Freda of her promise. 'If you can find out about that young woman for me, I'll be very grateful. I have to get back to London soon.'

'You're still coming to lunch tomorrow, though? The Lady Volunteers are looking forward to meeting you and hearing what you do with the money we've raised.'

'Of course I am. That money is being put to very good use, I promise you. You've done really well.' She'd never liked Freda, who was the daughter of a now-dead friend, but war made for strange bedfellows.

Vi arrived home to find a queue in the shop and her mother telling one impatient customer she'd have to wait. Her father was nowhere to be seen. Grimly, wondering what his excuse would be this time, Vi carried her purchases through to the back room, tied on a pinafore and began serving.

When she went to the till for some change, she was surprised at how few coins there were and looked across at her mother, who flicked her a quick glance then avoided her eyes.

During a lull between customers she asked bluntly, 'Has Dad been at the till again?'

Her mother hesitated then nodded.

'Why didn't you stop him?'

'I tried to. He pushed me away.'

'Oh, Mum!' Vi bit off further protests. Her father was a big man and her mother, like herself, was barely five foot tall. 'How much did he take?'

'About ten shillings.'

'Then I'm not providing him with any food at teatime for the rest of the week.'

'He'll only take ours.'

'Just let him try. We'll eat when he's not there.' Lips pressed together grimly, Vi went to sort out a few greengroceries for themselves from the stuff she'd brought home then set up a small box holding the rest on top of a packing case just outside the door. The less provident women would buy these pieces one or two at a time and she'd make a small profit on what she'd paid for them at market. Every penny helped.

And she wouldn't allow her father to steal any more of her hard-earned money for his drinking.

When the teatime rush had passed, Vi left the shop in her mother's capable hands again and went to seek out her brother. She wasn't particularly close to Eric, well, no one was. He kept his thoughts to himself, always had done. He took after their father in looks, but was much cleverer. Though he no longer lived at home, Eric thought the world of their mother. Vi hoped he'd help them in this constant battle to stop their father drinking away the profits she and her mother worked so hard for.

She found her brother standing by the bar in The Drover's Rest pub. She didn't like going inside, but needs must. 'Could I speak to you outside for a minute, Eric? Me and Mum need your help.'

He set his glass of beer down on the bar and looked at the landlord. 'Keep an eye on that, Den.'

The landlord nodded and placed the half-empty glass on the back shelf.

Outside Eric cocked one eyebrow at her, waiting.

'Dad's been at the till again. If he goes on like this, the shop will fail because we won't be able to pay our suppliers. Could you persuade him to leave the shop money alone? Mum was that upset today.'

Eric nodded. 'Dad's a stupid sod. Can't think beyond the next drink. You were right to come to me. I'm not having our Mum upset. I'll pop round tomorrow after tea and have a word with him.'

'Thanks.'

He nodded and went back into the pub without even a goodbye.

He was like that, their Eric was. Didn't waste his time on chat or politeness, just went straight for whatever he wanted. He worked for Mr Kirby, helping Sully, who was in charge of collecting rents and looking after the many houses Mr Kirby owned. Eric must be earning decent money because he had good lodgings and never seemed short of a bob or two.

If anyone could stop Dad ruining them, it was Eric.

The next evening Vi waited impatiently for her brother, beginning to grow anxious when time passed with no sign of him. He turned up eventually at nine-thirty, waited for the last customer to leave and locked the door behind the woman.

'We don't close for another half hour, love,' his mother said.

'You do tonight. I've got something to say to Dad.' He studied her face. 'You're looking tired, Mum, working too hard.'

'We can't lock the door yet. Your father's not back from the pub.'

'I'll go and fetch him. Where's he drinking these days?'

'He usually goes to The Drover's Rest.'

'Not since I started drinking there, he doesn't.' He patted her arm. 'Don't worry. I'll soon hunt him down. And don't open the shop again. You look tired. If those silly bitches can't remember to buy their food earlier, let them go without.'

May went into the back room and Vi followed Eric to the shop door. 'Thanks.'

He shrugged. 'I'm not letting him do that to her.'

Ten minutes later there was shouting in the street and someone hammered at the door. When Vi opened it, one of the men who worked with Eric shoved their father through and Eric followed him inside.

'Lock up again,' he said curtly as he guided the drunken man through into the back room and pushed him down on a chair.

When Vi went to join them, she found Eric going through his father's pockets and dropping the coins he found on the table.

'Only four and twopence. No, here's another penny.' He slammed his father against the chair back. 'Damned well stay where you are, you!'

Arnie subsided, scowling at his son.

Eric smacked one hand down on the table so hard everyone jumped. 'This is the last time you take money out of the till, Dad. The very last time.'

Arnie was pot valiant still. 'It's my shop, my money.'

'It's Mum and Vi who work in the shop, so I reckon it's their money. You're a lazy sod an' you hardly lift a finger. I don't know how Mum's put up with you all these years.'

'I do my share.'

'You've never done your share.' Eric leaned forward and poked his father in the chest. 'I meant what I said.' He waited a moment and added in a softer voice that was nonetheless chilling, 'If you do pinch any more money from the shop, I'll see you get the beating of your life.'

Arnie shrank away. Eric had a weak heart, so he didn't get into fights himself, but if he said he'd arrange a beating, he'd do it. He never made threats he couldn't carry out. Arnie glared at his wife and daughter.

'Even if Mum doesn't tell me, I'll find out,' Eric gathered up the money and looked at his mother. 'How much did he take?'

'About ten shillings.'

'Here.' He added five shillings out of his own pocket and put all the money into her hand, clasping her fingers round it. Hesitating a moment, he gave her a quick, almost furtive kiss on the cheek and left without another word.

'You went and told him,' Arnie threw at his daughter.

Vi stared back defiantly. 'I certainly did. An' I'll do it again if I have to. We need that money. Takings are down because of war shortages.'

He spat into the fire and heaved himself to his feet. 'I'm going to bed. It's a fine lookout when a daughter's as ungrateful as you. It's me as provides the roof over your head and don't you forget it. Children! Bite the hand that feeds them, they do . . .'

When he'd gone up the stairs, still grumbling, Vi looked at her mother. 'He's getting worse.'

'Yes. I don't know what's got into him lately.'

'You go up to bed, Mum. I'll check the shop and bring the takings in.'

It was another half-hour before Vi got to bed, because she liked to leave things tidy. She rubbed her aching forehead and climbed the stairs to the bedroom she now had for her own. It seemed a long time since she'd shared it with her older sister. Beryl had been married for the past eighteen years to a nice fellow who did what Beryl told him and seemed happy with that state of affairs.

Vi sometimes wished she'd found a fellow to marry, because she'd have liked a family of her own. But what would have happened to her mother if she'd left the shop? Her mother had had several years of ill health, though she was much better these days.

Anyway, no one had asked her to marry them, had they? A couple of lads had asked her to walk out with them when she was much younger, but she hadn't been fussed whether she did or not because they weren't up to much. Her mother said she read too many magazines and books, real men weren't like the heroes in those stories, nor was real life. But if it came to a choice between staying a spinster and marrying someone like her father, Vi would rather stay single any day.

They were dead now, those two lads, poor things. Both killed in the first year of the war. A lot of the fellows she'd grown up with were losing their lives in this dreadful fighting and all she could do was serve in the shop. She'd have liked to make a contribution, join the VADs or something, but her mother had needed her. And anyway, the sight of blood turned her queasy, so she didn't really want to nurse anyone.

But the years of her life were passing so swiftly it shocked her sometimes. What had become of yesterday's lively girl? She was thirty-five, had done nothing, gone nowhere. She was far too old to marry now, though she didn't feel old. Why, her hair wasn't even going grey yet. She had nice hair, her best feature her mother always said, but who was there to notice that now? All the men her age were either away fighting or long married with several children.

The following day Daphne Bingram was driven to Freda Gilson's house for lunch, her last engagement locally before she returned to London. She pinned a smile to her face as the group of women fluttered and fussed over her because of her title. Silly things! She'd come from a much poorer home than theirs. But they weren't too silly to raise money.

During a lull in the conversation she turned to Freda. 'Did you find out about that young woman?'

A sour expression crossed her companion's face. 'Not so young. She's thirty-five.'

'And . . . ?'

'Her family runs a corner shop, a mean little place. She and her mother do most of the work and it isn't thriving because the father is a drunkard. So you see, she's really not suitable to join your Aides.'

Daphne held back a protest and pulled out her little notebook. 'What's her name?'

'Violet Gill, but they call her Vi. I abominate nicknames, don't you?'

'And the address of the shop?'

'Corner of Reservoir Road and Platts Lane.'

'Thank you.' Daphne put the little silver propelling pencil into its holder and slipped the notebook back into her handbag. She endured another half-hour of inane chit-chat, thanked the ladies again for their wonderful contribution to the war effort and took her leave.

'I need to visit someone in the Backhill Terraces,' she told her elderly chauffeur.

After stopping to make enquiries, they pulled up outside the shop and Daphne studied it with a grimace. It looked very run-down, though of course paint was in short supply because of the war. But the window was clean and had a neat little display of tins of food in it.

That young woman had stayed in her mind for the past twenty-four hours. Daphne's instinct about people rarely let her down. 'Wait for me here.'

She got out of the car and stopped at the entrance to the shop, watching for a moment or two as Vi served an awkward customer, jollying her along. Then they both turned round and gaped at the sight of Daphne, who knew she looked like a creature from another world in her elegant clothes, so moved forward, smiling.

The customer stepped hastily back and Vi looked at the newcomer enquiringly.

'Do finish serving this lady first,' Daphne said. 'Then I wonder if you could shut the shop for a few minutes. I'd like to talk to you.'

'I'll come back later,' the customer said and scuttled out with another nervous glance at the newcomer.

Vi followed her to the door, locked it and hung up a sign saying, 'Back in ten minutes'. Then she turned to her visitor and waited.

'Is there somewhere we could sit down for a minute or two?

What I'd like to talk to you about is rather important, to do with the war effort.'

'Come through into the back.' She led the way and introduced her mother, who was sitting at the table, weighing quarter pounds of sugar on the kitchen scales and pouring it into triangular blue paper bags.

Daphne held out her hand. 'Pleased to meet you, Mrs Gill. I'm Daphne Bingram.'

'Pleased to meet you too, Mrs Bingram.'

'It's Lady Bingram, actually, but I don't like to stand on ceremony.'

Vi pulled out a chair for their visitor then sat down herself. 'How can we help you, your ladyship?'

Daphne explained about her Aides. 'I saw you in the street yesterday, dealing with those louts and retrieving the old lady's loaf. I knew at once that you were the sort of woman I want in my group. Would you like to come to London and work for me, help win the war? I pay a pound a week all found, and I provide the uniform.'

It was the mother who spoke. 'Eh, that sounds wonderful. You should do it, our Vi.'

'How can I, Mum? I'm needed in the shop.'

May frowned in thought, 'I think I could manage now. I'm a lot better and this is a good chance for you, love. It'd mean a lot to me to give you a better chance than this place. You deserve it.'

Vi stretched out one hand to her and they smiled at one another. Lady Bingram was moved by their obvious closeness, wishing yet again that she'd been blessed with children.

'I reckon Tess Donovan would jump at the chance to help in the shop, Vi. She did all right before when you were helping our Beryl after she miscarried. With her husband away in France, Tess is desperate for money. She's a good worker.' May waited and when her daughter didn't speak, added, 'And now that our Eric's keeping an eye on your father, I'll be all right. Eric won't be going anywhere after failing his medical.'

Daphne nodded approval. 'Well spoken, Mrs Gill. It *is* a good chance for your daughter to see a bit of life and help win the war.'

May turned to her. 'You'll – look after her properly? She's never been away from Lancashire before. I wouldn't want her to be lonely or unhappy.'

'She'll live in my house and as there will soon be twenty other Aides, she definitely won't be lonely.'

They both turned to Vi, who was looking stunned.

'Well?' Daphne asked gently. 'Do you want to come with me?'

Vi opened and shut her mouth then swallowed hard and looked at her mother. 'Are you sure?'

'Yes. I'll miss you, but it'll make me that happy to see you get a chance like this.' She reached out for her daughter's hand again. 'Do it, love. Don't let this opportunity slip by.'

Vi turned a face glowing with excitement towards Daphne. 'Then I accept, Lady Bingram. And thank you.'

Daphne stood up. 'Can you be ready to leave tomorrow?'

Vi gasped then nodded.

'I'll pick you up tomorrow morning about eight o'clock, then. I'm driving down to London and you'll probably find it easiest to come with me.' She turned to May Gill. 'Thank you so much for letting me have your daughter. I can guess what this will cost you.'

The two older women shook hands.

Vi stood there like someone frozen to the spot till her mother nudged her, then she moved forward to show their visitor out.

After her ladyship's car had driven away, they made no attempt to open the shop. Going back inside they locked the door, then looked at one another.

With a sob, Vi flung her arms round her mother. 'I don't know how I'll ever thank you for this.'

'It's your big chance. I couldn't bear you to turn it down.' May held her daughter at arm's length and studied her face for a moment as if memorising it, then gave her a little push. 'Now, there's a lot to do. You'd better go and fetch Tess to help out. Her mother will look after the little lasses and the son's in school. Then you'll have to do some washing and bring down that old trunk of mine from the attic. It's still sturdy enough, even if it is scratched. And—'

Someone hammered at the shop door and May moved towards it. 'I'll serve in the shop and if there's a rush, they'll just have to wait their turn. It'll take you all your time to get ready.'

For once, Vi let someone else tell her what to do. Bemused, still not believing this could be happening to her, she left the shop and hurried along the street to her friend's.

Tess opened the door and smiled at Vi. 'You don't usually come calling at this time of day, love. I hope nothing's wrong.'

'Something's come up – it's good news, though – and we need your help.'

Tess held the door open and Vi walked in. Her friend's little daughter was playing on the rag rug and a baby was crawling nearby. The whole place was immaculately clean, if sparsely furnished.

Vi didn't waste any time but explained what had happened, ending, 'I can only do it if we get someone to help Mam in the shop. Do you want the job?'

Tess gaped at her for a minute. 'You're going to London?'

'Yes.' She gestured to the children. 'Can your mother look after them for you?'

Her friend beamed. 'Yes! We could do with the money an' I like working in the shop.'

'You couldn't start today, could you?'

Tess gave her a cracking hug. 'Give me half an hour to get my mam.'

Vi walked out, feeling as if the world had turned upside down. After a moment's hesitation, she went to find Eric and share the news with him. He was just as important as Tess in her new plans.

He stared at her, lips pursed, then nodded slowly. 'It'll be a good thing for you, that. An' I'll keep an eye on Dad for you, don't worry.'

'Thanks.'

He nodded and walked away.

She smiled as she watched him go. You'd think words cost money, he was so sparing with them. But it didn't matter. He'd look after their mother and keep their father in check.

She hurried off to call on her sister Beryl and let her know what was happening. Not that Beryl would be much use to Mam, because she and their father didn't get on and she refused to have anything to do with him. But still, it was only right to let her know. Vi didn't see her sister very often because the shop kept her busy till all hours but they'd always been fond of one another.

Joy flooded through her and she stood for a moment beaming at nothing, still unable to believe her luck. She was going to see the world she'd only read about before.

# 2

Sergeant Joss Bentley sat in the dugout shelter in France and frowned at the letter that had just been handed to him. He didn't recognise the handwriting, but it was from Drayforth, his home town. He tore it open quickly, hoping nothing had happened to his family.

Inside was a short note with no address or signature.

*Your wife is messing around with other fellows. You want to get home and give her a good thumping.*

He stared at it in shock then screwed it up. Whoever had sent this was lying. Ada wouldn't . . . couldn't possibly . . . would she? No, of course she wouldn't. It was all lies.

But something made him bend and pick up the letter, smoothing it out and shoving it in his pocket.

'Bad news?' the man next to him asked.

Joss shrugged. He wasn't sharing this with his men.

'You all right, Sarge?' another asked.

'Mind your own bloody business.'

He pulled the letter out several times that day and reread it, though he knew it by heart. But still, there was something about seeing the words that made you wonder if they were true.

In the end he forced himself to throw it away, telling himself it was someone trying to stir up trouble.

But in the next few days he received three more such letters, all in different handwriting and on different sorts of paper – though that didn't prove anything. And each one said the same thing. Not one of them named the man, though.

He couldn't sleep at night for worrying and when Captain

Warburton asked if anything was wrong, he hesitated, then showed him the letters.

'You're due some leave, Bentley. Put in for it – I'll OK things – then go and sort this muck out. It's probably all lies. We'll see if we can get you on to a quick course while you're over there. There's a new thing for sergeants, preparing them for promotion to officers, which you richly deserve.'

Perry Warburton was a good bloke, Joss thought, not for the first time. He was lucky to be serving under a captain like him.

It wasn't until a month later that Joss was able to go home and during that time he received several more anonymous letters, all short and all making the same point. He burned them. He wasn't having anyone else but the captain finding out about this.

Joss didn't tell anyone he was coming back on leave. When he arrived in the evening, he walked straight home from the station, not pausing to drop in and say a quick hello to his parents, as he would usually have done, but walking straight past the family shoe shop and along to the neat terraced house he rented a few streets away.

He found his mother sitting in the kitchen, toasting her feet at the fire and knitting something khaki.

'Joss, love! Why didn't you let us know you were coming?'

He gave her a quick hug. 'What are you doing here? Where's Ada?'

'Out with some friends. The poor lass was getting moped, sitting at home on her own every night.'

He took a deep breath but held back his angry response. What better thing could his wife have to do than stay at home and look after their children? If she was lonely, she could go and visit his parents, or her mother, or his brother and family.

'How are the kids?' Roy was only six and Iris three, and he hated the way he was missing their childhood.

'Fast asleep. Go up and have a peep.'

'I'd rather wait and— Do you know where Ada is?'

'At the Crown. They have a ladies' room now. She'll be in

there with her friends. Why don't you go and surprise her? I'm not in a hurry to get home. Your dad's doing some shoe repairs tonight.'

He bent to kiss her. 'Thanks. I will go and find Ada, if you don't mind staying a bit longer.'

At the pub he looked into the ladies' room and saw no sign of his wife, only a group of older women he knew by sight, most of them widows. He didn't like the way they nudged one another and stared at him.

Turning he went into the main lounge area and saw Ada at once, laughing and happy, sitting at a mixed table. He stood and watched her, furious at the way she was smiling at the fellow next to her.

He threaded his way across the room. One of her friends saw him coming and nudged Ada, who looked up, her mouth falling open in surprise. If he'd ever seen a guilty expression, he was seeing one now, he thought grimly.

Mindful of the people watching them, he tried to force a smile to his face, but couldn't, just couldn't manage it.

'Joss! Why didn't you say you were coming home on leave?'

'It all happened suddenly. I thought I'd surprise you.' He took her arm. 'Let's go home, Ada.'

'Stay and have a drink first,' one of the other women urged.

'No, thank you. Ada?'

She got to her feet, dropping her handbag and getting flustered as she tried to pick up the bits and pieces, and nearly fell over. *She was tipsy!* He pulled her to one side and picked up her things in silence, stuffing them into the handbag anyhow. Nodding to the group, he took her arm and propelled her outside, keeping hold of her when she stumbled. Let alone he didn't like to see women drinking in the public rooms, to see his own wife the worse for drink sickened him.

Outside, Ada smiled at him and tried to throw her arms round his neck.

He took a step backwards. 'What the hell are you thinking of, going out drinking with that lot?'

Her smile vanished and a shrewish look replaced it, a look she saved for him alone, he sometimes thought, because she was always smiling and friendly when other folk were around.

'I'm not sitting in that house every night on my own. I've a right to a bit of enjoyment.'

'What about the kids? Don't they have a right to someone to look after them?'

'They've got your mother. *She* understands my feelings and she doesn't mind coming round every now and then.'

'No wonder you've been asking me for more money, if that's how you're spending it.' He dragged her arm through his and began walking, not letting her pull away.

'You don't know what it's like in Drayforth now, Joss. Boring, dull. No one talks of anything but that stupid war. I'll go mad if I don't get out with people who know how to have a bit of fun.'

Before the war, he'd sometimes felt he'd go mad if he had to sit and listen to her silly gossip. Later, her total misunderstanding of the war and the wider world had made matters worse, so that they hardly had anything to talk about. Each time he came home on leave they seemed further apart.

He didn't know how he was going to face living with her after the war. He'd married one woman, he sometimes felt, and gone home from church with another. She was as selfish as her mother, but without her mother's ability to manage money and a household.

But he'd stayed faithful to her. *He* hadn't gone out drinking with other women, had he? 'It's one thing for you to go out with other women, Ada, but you were out with men as well. What will people think of that?' And how had those men avoided conscription, which had come in earlier in the year? They looked fit enough to Joss.

She wrenched her arm away from his. 'I was sitting at a table in full view of everyone. What could I be doing to upset you?'

'You're a married woman. You shouldn't be out with other men in the first place.'

'So are some of my friends married. But our husbands are away so we go out together. We're not doing anything wrong.'

'Well, people are noticing. I've had letters about you, accusing you of—' he broke off, hating even to say the words.

She gaped at him, her mouth wide open in shock. 'And you believed them?'

'I didn't know what to believe, did I, stuck out there in a trench?'

She started walking fast and he had to hurry to catch up. 'Why will you not believe that I've done nothing wrong?' she threw at him.

During the next two days they quarrelled several times. She wouldn't promise not to go out with her friends and he knew there was no way he could make her stay at home, not when he was in France and she was in Drayforth. He couldn't ask his mother not to look after the kids, because he wouldn't put it past Ada to simply leave them alone. At least they were safe with his mother.

When he got back to France after finishing the course, the letters from Ada stopped altogether, though his mother still wrote regularly. Things were serious enough in his sector for him to set his worries about the accusations aside as he struggled to keep himself and his men alive in this mayhem and madness.

At first sight, London terrified Vi, as well as fascinating her. They drove through streets crowded with more people than she'd ever seen in her life before. There were so many vehicles the traffic got into tangles and Lady Bingram's car had to slow down to walking pace sometimes. Vi was glad of that because it gave her the chance to look round.

Eventually, the big black car pulled up in front of a grand house four storeys high, part of a row of similar residences. She smiled. A bit different from the Backhill Terraces, this. It was late at night now but there were lights showing inside the house still.

'We'll get something to eat before we go to bed, shall we? Albert will bring your trunk in.' Lady Bingram took her silence for agreement and led the way across the big square entrance hall to the rear of the house.

Three women were sitting chatting in a room just off the kitchen. They greeted her ladyship with pleasure, which didn't surprise Vi, because she'd found for herself today how pleasant and approachable her benefactor was. But she was startled when they all called a titled lady by her first name.

She drank a cup of cocoa and ate a hot, buttered crumpet, listening to the chat. Two of the women were just going on night duty and the other had recently come in. The latter took Vi up to the bedroom she'd share from now on with three others.

She was so weary after the long drive, so sated with new sights and sounds that she could hardly put one foot in front of another.

'Bewildering at first, London, isn't it?' her companion said with a sympathetic smile as they climbed the stairs to the second floor.

'Yes, very.'

The bedroom was so large it didn't seem crowded, even with four single beds. The other three were occupied and although one woman roused enough to give her a quick smile before turning over, the others didn't even stir.

Vi didn't bother to unpack her trunk, which was waiting at the foot of her bed, just took out her nightdress and visited the bathroom along the corridor. How wonderful to have an indoor lavatory and a bathroom where you could just turn a tap and get hot water running into a fixed bath. Everything was so luxurious and there was even electric light upstairs and down. How easy, just to switch a light on! She couldn't believe it was real.

Yawning, she walked back to her bedroom and fell quickly asleep.

The next morning someone shook Vi awake and she looked up in shock at a stranger's smiling face. It took her a few seconds to remember where she was.

'I had to wake you or you'd have missed breakfast. Of course, you could still have got something to eat, but it's nice to meet the other women, isn't it? And soon after, we've got an appointment to have a uniform made for you. Can you be ready in ten minutes? Good. I'll come back for you.' She paused at the door to say, 'I'm Livvie, by the way, short for Olivia.'

The other beds were empty. How had she slept through three people getting up? Vi wondered. Livvie had a very posh accent, but she'd been as friendly as her ladyship.

Downstairs Vi ate a hearty breakfast, listening to the others chat. It didn't take her long to realise that this was a very happy group of women, all proud to be members of Lady Bingram's Aides and doing their bit for their country. Most of them were wearing brown uniforms and looked very smart. She felt ashamed of her shabby clothes.

'Are you always so quiet?' Livvie teased, smiling, as she was buttering another piece of toast.

Vi felt herself blushing as all eyes turned in her direction. 'It's all so new to me. I'm just – enjoying listening.'

'Tell us about yourself,' another called down the table. 'How did Daphne find you?'

So Vi told them about chasing the boy with the loaf and then her ladyship coming to her family's shop. In return she heard about rich girls who'd been living on their family's estates, other women who were clearly from superior homes to hers and others who, like her, came from poorer backgrounds. They all talked about it cheerfully, no one seeming to look down on another. It was – marvellous. She'd have so much to say when she wrote to her mother.

By the following week, Vi had her uniform, a beautifully cut set of garments tailored to her size. She'd never had anything that fitted so well. The outer clothing was made from wool which was so soft she couldn't help stroking it from time to time. There was also a set of pretty yet practical underwear, including three lace-trimmed bust bodices – not that her bosoms were all that big, but she'd never had lace-trimmed underwear before either, let alone one of these new bust bodices. All she'd had was a cotton camisole. She was so proud of the uniform she was afraid of seeming vain, but couldn't resist lingering in front of the mirror in their bedroom when no one was around, to admire her smart new appearance.

She worked in the house all week, cleaning or helping with the cooking and clearing up. This work was organised by a sensible woman of fifty called Esther who managed the house and all its inmates, including her ladyship.

The following week Vi was to start learning office duties, because she'd always kept the accounts at the shop and was good at figures. Lady Bingram had a position in mind for her already and she felt a bit nervous about that, because it would mean working with a group of men under a Major Warren, about whose unit her ladyship was rather vague. Vi still didn't dare call her Daphne, or even think about her by her first name.

But a permanent posting wouldn't happen for a few weeks, because the unit was still being formed, apparently, and in the meantime Daphne wanted her to gain as much experience as she could. So she was sent to a bewildering number of offices, spending a week or two in each and trying to learn as much as she could and not make a fool of herself.

Her main form of relaxation was a weekly letter to her mother, and she got one back every week in return. She saved her money, amazed to have a pound a week all to herself, and after the first couple of weeks, opened up a savings bank account. But gradually the other women talked her into spending a little. She went to the cinema, a luxury she'd rarely been able to indulge in before, or out for walks round London. As soon as she'd saved enough, she bought one of the new, shorter, fuller skirts, with a matching jacket and two blouses, simple but flattering. It felt extravagant to buy so many brand-new things, but her friends insisted she couldn't wear the uniform all the time and her own clothes were so shabby she was ashamed of them.

Daphne had formed a sort of club for rankers on leave who had no family or friends in London and wanted somewhere quiet to meet people, instead of a noisy, smoke-filled pub where they often had to stand up to drink. There were suitable clubs for officers, Daphne said, but not much for the ordinary soldier. So now there was a meeting place on the ground floor and the Aides were asked to go and talk to them sometimes.

Vi had never had much to do with men and was shy at first, but gradually she began to enjoy herself as she realised that what these fellows craved most of all was to spend time with decent women, not street walkers, to have a little fun and above all, forget about the war. They were always very respectful towards the Aides.

In fact, she had never enjoyed life so much, still felt she might wake up from this wonderful dream. And her mother's letters said everything was going well.

Tess Donovan was enjoying her new life, too. She loved working at the shop and the money made a huge difference to her family, not only herself and her children, but her widowed mother, whom she paid to look after the children. What with the money the Army sent her from Joe's wages, she'd never been so comfortable.

On market day, Mrs Gill went off to market and left her in charge. Tess was kept busy at first, then during a lull, managed to make herself a cup of tea and tidy up the shop.

Arnie Gill came in and smiled at her. 'Just need a shilling from the till, Tess.'

She remembered the warning Vi had given her. 'Mrs Gill didn't say anything about giving you money.'

He drew himself up, towering over her and making her feel nervous. 'I'm the owner of this shop. I don't need to ask the hired help if I can use my own money, thank you very much.'

'Mrs Gill won't be long. We can sort it all out when she comes back.'

He cursed and shoved Tess out of the way, holding her at arm's length while he opened the drawer. Taking two shillings out he slammed the drawer shut. 'If you try to stop me again, I'll sack you.'

She watched him walk away, feeling guilty that she hadn't been able to prevent him, because she knew he shouldn't have done that.

When Mrs Gill came back, Tess explained what had happened.

'Oh, no! I didn't think he'd dare start again. Our Eric will throw a fit.' She hesitated. 'Perhaps it's just this once. I really don't want to cause trouble between them.' She began to fiddle with the edge of the counter, biting her lower lip and looking so miserable, Tess couldn't help giving her a hug.

But Mr Gill did the same thing the next market day, only he took three shillings this time.

His wife sat down and wept when she found out. 'I can't manage if he goes on doing this. He has his own money every week. Five shillings. I could make five shillings last a week and still have some left over. I'd not spend it all on booze. I'll give Arnie a good talking to but he doesn't listen to me lately.'

Tess put her arm round her, not saying anything. She knew it'd be up to her to do something, as Vi had warned her, but she wasn't as good as Vi at telling people what to do. Mrs Gill was a lovely person, but since her illness she was a bit too soft for her own good and Arnie never paid any attention to what she said.

After work Tess went down to the Drover's Arms and looked for Eric Gill. He was there, standing by the counter. She didn't like to walk through the crowd of men, so gave a lad a penny to ask Eric to come out and see her urgently. She stood waiting in the shadows to one side of the pub, twisting the ends of her shawl round and round her fingers.

When she saw Eric come to the door and look round, she took a deep breath and moved forward. 'It's about your mum.'

'Oh?' He waited.

Tess couldn't help her voice wobbling, because she was a bit frightened of Eric Gill, who was gaining a bit of a reputation in the terraces as a man not to be crossed. 'Your dad's started taking money out of the till again. Vi said I should tell you if he started doing that.'

Eric seemed to swell and a vein began throbbing in his forehead. She could see it quite clearly by the light of the gas lamps burning brightly outside the pub.

'I hope I did the right thing, telling you, I mean?' she faltered, suddenly afraid of him.

He lost the fierce look and gave her a quick smile.

'You did, Tess. You definitely did. And you're to tell me if it happens again. Leave it to me now. Wait!'

She swung round.

'You must have paid that lad to fetch me out of the pub. How much?'

'Just a penny. It doesn't matter.'

'It does.' He slipped twopence into her hand and turned away.

She walked home worrying about what he'd do, worrying about what Mrs Gill would say when she found out who'd told on her husband, worrying most of all that she might lose her new job. Her husband teased her about being a worrier but she couldn't help it.

The following night Arnie reeled home from his local pub, helped by his son.

'I found Dad in an alley next to his pub. Someone had beaten him up.'

'Who could've done that?' May gasped.

Arnie glanced sideways at Eric. May followed his gaze and saw her son smile slightly. But it was a smile which put the fear of God into you, not one that comforted you and she guessed what had happened. Eric never did anything violent himself, but there was a man called Fred who accompanied him on his rounds and sometimes did the necessary. It upset her that it had been necessary this time.

'We'll never know who did it, will we, Mam? Dad didn't see them, did you?'

May watched Arnie open his mouth and shut it again, then shake his head. 'It were too dark.' He let his wife bathe his wounds, avoiding her eyes and his son's, then said he'd go to bed.

May watched how he winced as he moved. 'I'll sleep in Vi's bed, Arnie. You won't want anyone bumping into you in the night, you poor thing.'

He grunted.

'I'll leave you now, Mum.' Eric stared at his father. 'Better be more careful in future, eh?' Then he walked out.

When May came back from locking the shop door, her husband was already upstairs.

She collapsed on to a chair. Eric had done this, she knew, even though she'd not let on that she'd guessed. He'd done it for her. Tess must have told him and Vi must have warned Tess about Arnie's thieving from the till.

And the worst of it was, she was glad, because it was hard enough to manage the shop without Vi, however willing Tess was. May was better, of course she was, but she wasn't her old self. Well, at sixty you didn't expect to be. Only Eric could stop Arnie stealing from the shop. And she'd let him, whatever it took, because she didn't want things to go wrong while Vi was away. Her younger daughter had given up so much over the years, but now she was going to get her chance in life, whatever it cost May.

For a long time she sat staring into the fire, feeling sad. When you got married, you promised to love and obey your husband, didn't you? But she didn't love Arnie any more, hadn't for years. And as he'd done nothing worthy of her respect, she wasn't going to obey him, either.

Sighing, she went up to Vi's room, glad to be sleeping alone for once. She lay down and closed her eyes tightly but tears still leaked out. This incident wouldn't cost her Arnie's love, because he didn't love her, never had. He'd needed a wife to help him in the shop after his mother died, so had courted her because she was a hard worker. She'd heard him boasting about that to someone once.

But he'd not been nearly as bad then. And he'd given her children, which was the biggest comfort of all.

Of their three children, Beryl was safely married to a nice man with a steady job as a carpenter, Eric was making a good life for himself in spite of his weak heart, and Vi was in London having an exciting time. That thought gave May a lot of pleasure. Three good 'uns, they were, her children.

Next thing she knew, it was morning again and Arnie was cursing the knocker-up, who was rapping at the front bedroom window and would continue to do so until May called out to him.

# 3

Vi felt sick with nerves the day she first went to work for Major Warren, with whom Daphne said she'd be working for the foreseeable future.

She arrived at the address, straightened her broad-brimmed brown felt hat, taking courage from how smart her uniform was, and walked quickly inside. It was a big building and she was told to wait on an uncomfortable bench in the foyer. It was ten minutes before someone arrived, a young fellow with an ugly limp.

He came across smiling and shook her hand vigorously. 'Glad to have you with us, Miss Gill. I'm John Deavers, Captain. They tell me you're good with figures. I've been doing my best, but accounts aren't my thing. The Major's busy at the moment, but he said to make you welcome and show you round.'

His accent was so posh she'd have been even more terrified if his smile hadn't been so wide and friendly.

'Our unit hadn't long been together and they're going to settle us in a house somewhere. In the meantime we're camping out in three rooms.'

The three rooms were in chaos. The Captain and Major Warren shared one and the other two were full of desks and people, none of them women, Vi noted at once, feeling a little overwhelmed. There was one office boy, an eager lad who looked at the soldiers with envy. Don't wish yourself old enough to be killed, she thought. But he would, of course. Most lads his age were dying to be old enough to fight and many lied about their ages in order to enlist.

When Captain Deavers showed her the new account books, she relaxed a lot, because he'd made an absolute mess of setting them up. She began to question him carefully about the unit's finances and expenditures. It had a huge amount of money at its disposal – well, it seemed huge to her, more than she'd ever handled before in her whole life put together. But it still came down to figures and she was good at them, always had been.

By the time the Major came back from his meeting, she had worked out several headings, subject to his approval of course, and was assigning the expenses roughly to them, starting to go through the piles of receipts. The Captain had collected those conscientiously, at least.

'We've got a house,' the Major announced, beaming round at the room. 'We can move in tomorrow, though there'll still be a lot to do to get it habitable because it's been unoccupied for a few years.'

The men in the room cheered.

The Major's eyes fell on Vi and he smiled even more warmly. 'I see we've got our newest recruit. Miss Gill, welcome to the unit. Lady Bingram has told me how efficient you are.'

She could feel herself blushing.

'Come and have a cup of tea with me, tell me about yourself.'

She followed, surprised at how old the Major was.

He gestured to a seat and sat down behind the desk with a gusty sigh of relief. 'Not as young as I was. I'm sixty-eight and came out of retirement to help the war effort.'

She found herself telling him about her family, relaxing, realising that he was like Daphne Bingram, easy to talk to with no hint of snobbery or condescension.

'Think you can sort out our accounts? Poor old Deavers hasn't a clue.'

'I think I can, though I may have to go and ask advice about some things.'

'You do that, and if you need me to grease the wheels for you anywhere, just say.'

'Well, I worked in an accounting company's office last week and I think they'd be happy to help me, since it's for the war, so I can probably manage. I'll go in my lunch hour and—'

'You'll go during working hours, because it's work. Lunch hours are for resting. I'll be working you hard, but I'm a firm believer in taking a proper break in the middle of the day. And you don't need to ask permission to go anywhere. If you have to see someone, just leave a note on your desk saying where you're going, and go. If you need bus fares, take the money from the petty cash and make a note of it somewhere. It's one of the things you'll be setting up, the expenses accounts.' He saw her surprise and added, 'I'm a great believer in trusting my staff to get on with things – unless they give me any reason not to.'

'I'll never do that, sir.' She was won over at once, knew she had fallen on her feet.

And nothing, during the next two years ever made her change her mind about that. The work was hard and very hush-hush, sometimes involving long hours of overtime, but the Major knew how to create a team and no one ever said anything to disparage her because she was a woman.

Anyway, they couldn't have done without her, because she proved her worth with figures and with other jobs, too.

The men in the unit came and went, but Vi and Major Warren stayed on in the tall narrow town house.

In France, Joss was relieved when the anonymous letters about his wife stopped. But they started up again a few months later, two or three of them a week. It was as if the writers knew one another and were working together to keep the pot boiling. His wife was still going to the pub, had been seen out alone after dark. He should come home and give her good thumping. As if he'd ever hit a woman!

Why could they not leave him in peace? He told himself to leave the letters unopened, but couldn't. It was the only way to find out what was going on . . . if they were telling the truth. It wasn't something he could mention to his parents. All he could do was worry about it.

He began to dread the post arriving and couldn't even talk about this latest onslaught to the captain.

One night, when his company was on a week's rest behind the lines, he got a letter in which the writer described seeing Ada kissing a man down the back alley and then going off with him. Why did they never name the man?

Sickened, suspecting it was true, knowing his wife's need for someone to lean on, he shoved the letter in his pocket and tried to drown his worries. The next thing he knew, someone had picked up the letter, which had fallen out of his pocket, and was reading it aloud, a chap he'd always hated.

Red rage filled Joss and he went for the fellow, taking huge satisfaction in giving him a good thumping.

He lost his stripes for that and would have been put in prison if Captain Warburton hadn't found out what caused it and intervened.

As a private, Joss was earning less, so he cut Ada's allowance and told her why he'd lost his stripes.

She didn't reply to his letter. In fact, she hadn't written to him for months.

He had one quick visit home, but he slept on the couch and spent most of his time with his children or his family. He and Ada hardly said a word to each other. He couldn't accuse her of sleeping with someone without proof. All he really wanted to do was sleep in the blessed quiet of a near-normal world with no guns pounding away night and day.

The only bright spots in his life were when Captain Warburton made time for a quiet chat, not saying anything about the situation back home, but encouraging him to hope for a corporal's stripes again and simply being with him. If it hadn't been for the captain's support, Joss would have gone mad, because the letters had begun again, still telling him things he didn't want to know, yet had to know.

In the end he put one inside an envelope, addressed it to his wife and sent it off. Let her see what he was receiving.

The anonymous letters stopped. That puzzled him greatly. How had she managed to do that? It couldn't simply be coincidence.

He didn't know whether to be glad or sad that no more letters arrived. He still wondered what Ada was doing and who with.

And the war went on . . . and on . . .

It was at one of the meetings with soldiers at Lady Bingram's club that Vi met Len Schofield, who was recovering from an injury. He was a quiet man but had a straightforward friendliness about him that made her enjoy his company more than that of the other men.

They all went to a Lyons Corner House the next evening to 'give the boys a little treat', paid for by Lady Bingram. Vi still wasn't used to such gigantic eating places, where hundreds of people could have a meal at any time of day. She shuddered at the thought of how much washing up all these customers would be creating. *She* wouldn't like to be doing it, that was for sure. But the Nippy waitresses were very cheerful and smart, in their black and white uniforms, and they were always so obliging, nothing too much trouble.

Len had one arm in a sling, so someone had to cut up his food for him and she was sitting next to him, so it fell to her.

At the end of the outing, as the men were walking the Aides back to Lady Bingram's house, Len pulled her behind the others. 'Can I see you again, please, Violet? Just you.'

She stared at him, shocked rigid by this. But he looked so anxious as the silence lengthened that she said hastily, 'I suppose so. If you really want to.'

'I do. You – haven't got a fellow back in Lancashire, have you?'

'No. I've never really had a fellow.' She clapped one hand to her mouth. What had made her tell him that?

'They must be mad in the north.' Len looked at her earnestly. 'I hope you don't think I'm too forward, but there isn't time to court lasses properly these days and I really like you.'

'I don't mind at all. I like you too.' She could feel herself blushing hotly.

He made arrangements to see her the following evening.

She went to bed glowing with pleasure at Len's compliment

and looking forward to going to the cinema with him. But she was surprised that someone would want to take a plain Jane like her out.

Len asked her to marry him the following week, the sixth time he took her out. And by then she felt so comfortable with him, she said yes. She knew all the arguments about wartime marriages, but she didn't care.

'I don't know where we'll live, though,' he confessed. 'My mum and dad died when I was a lad and I've no brothers or sisters to take us in.'

'I don't care where we live, but I wondered . . .' She hesitated then said, 'I thought I'd talk to Lady Bingram. They're letting married women go on working now, because of the war, and when you go back to France,' she had to take a deep breath here, because the thought of that filled her with dread, 'well, it'd keep my mind off things if I could go on working. Besides, the Major says he can't manage without me now.'

'You talk to her ladyship, then.'

So after she got in, Vi went to tap on Daphne's door and confess the whole to her.

'What wonderful news!' Daphne said cheerfully. 'And of course you must go on working after you're married. Let me think.' She frowned, then looked at Vi. 'There are a couple of rooms above the old stables in the mews at the back of this house. We could have them whitewashed. They don't have electricity or any of the amenities we have in the big house, but there's water and a bathroom of sorts that grooms used. Bring Len round tomorrow night and we'll inspect them. There wouldn't be any rent, because the rooms aren't needed for anything.'

'You're so kind to us.' Vi blinked her eyes which had filled with tears at this generosity.

'You're a hard-working woman. You're serving your country just as much as the fighting men do. How could I not help you?'

'I know it's wartime, but I've never been as happy in all my life,' Vi confessed.

When she'd gone, Daphne sat on, staring into the fire, hoping desperately that Len Schofield would survive the war. From the fragments of information Vi had let fall, the poor girl had had a hard life with not many chances of happiness. Please let her keep this man, Daphne prayed.

In a large house on the ridge overlooking Drayforth, Phyllis Warburton read the latest letter from their brother, who was a captain in the Army, serving in France, then went to find her sister Christina. 'Perry's coming home on leave for a few days.'

'Oh, no! He'll find out. We can't hide it from him.'

Phyllis nodded and fumbled for a chair. She felt so weary today and her brain seemed dull. 'What are we going to do, dearest?'

'What can we do? See if we can find a woman in the town to do some cleaning and open up the drawing room again.'

'But we've so little money. It seems a waste and Perry won't mind using the little sitting room, I'm sure.'

Christina frowned in thought. 'Maybe we can make it seem because of the war that we're without help? If we did that, made it fun to eat with Cook in the kitchen, and didn't let him know we'd got his bedroom ready ourselves . . . ?'

Maybe it'd work.

And for the first day after Perry returned, it seemed as if he believed them. Then, on the second evening, he put some more wood on the fire and leaned back in his chair, staring at his two elderly sisters. 'What really happened to the servants?'

Christina sighed and didn't even try to lie to him. 'We couldn't afford to keep them. We've got Cook and a woman for the washing, plus a woman to do the rough cleaning every week, so we manage very well and—'

'What happened to that little diamond drop and gold chain you always used to wear, Phyllis, and those pearl earrings that Father gave you for your twenty-first birthday, Christina?'

They fell silent, each avoiding his eyes.

'Why didn't you tell me things were this bad?' he asked gently. 'I could have sent you some of my money.'

'You need that money to keep up your position, Perry dear.'

'I don't, actually. There is no such thing as position in the trenches, just mud and blood. I'll make arrangements the minute I get back. Who sold the things for you? And how much did you get?'

They told him.

'That fellow cheated you. Don't go through him any more.' He sighed and stared into the fire for a few moments. 'I was extravagant after Father died, wasn't I? And then I invested unwisely. I'm sorry, my dears, so very sorry to have placed you in this predicament.' He looked from one to the other. 'In the meantime, you and I will go into Manchester, Christina – I don't think you're well enough for a lot of walking, Phyllis. We'll find a decent jeweller's, so that you have some money for the next few months. We've a storeroom full of things we're never going to use again. You must help me choose one or two to sell.'

He and Christina went the following day, taking the train into Manchester and walking arm in arm along Deansgate and Market Street, looking in the shop windows.

They got more for their grandfather's pocket watch than she'd expected and for an oval silver platter. It was with relief that she put the money away safely when they got back to Drayforth.

'I won't be extravagant any more,' he whispered to Christina as he said goodbye. 'Look after poor Phyl. She doesn't seem at all well.'

Christina could have told him that what ailed their sister was as much low spirits as anything physical. They couldn't afford to return hospitality, so had stopped accepting any, and life was very dull.

When he got back to France, Perry continued to worry about his sisters. One evening when he was on watch with Bentley, they got talking.

'Had any more of that family trouble?' he asked. 'Only I couldn't help noticing that you started getting extra letters for a while.

Tell me not to pry, if you like, but it sometimes helps to unburden yourself.'

Joss shrugged. 'It was the same old thing, saying she's been unfaithful. They didn't say who with, but they made it sound worse than last time. I sent one of them back to her and suddenly the damned letters stopped. I don't know what to make of that. I can't ask my family if they've noticed anything. My brother's got enough on his plate keeping the shop going and anyway, he's too nice to notice such things, always thinks the best of everyone. And my parents are quite elderly, so I don't want to worry them. All I can do is wait for this damned war to end. Who'd have thought it'd still be going in 1917?'

They stood in silence for a few minutes, both appreciating a more peaceful evening, with no bombardment going on.

'You've been looking a bit worried yourself, sir,' Joss ventured.

'Mmm.' Perry looked sideways at him then said quietly, 'It's my sisters. They're older than me and I've mucked things up for them, made some unwise investments and left them short of money. They've been selling their jewellery, not telling me. And if anything happens to me, I don't know what they'll do, how they'll manage. I've been a fool about money, a bloody fool.'

After another silence, he said abruptly, 'Bentley, you live in Drayforth. If anything happens to me, will you go and see my sisters and . . . keep an eye on them as much as you can?'

'Surely there are other family members, someone of your own class?'

'No. We're the last of this branch of the Warburtons and the other branch emigrated to America some decades ago. We've lost touch with them.'

'You've got to convince yourself you'll survive, sir, or else you won't.' Joss firmly believed that, as did several men he knew.

'I can't. I've got a feeling that . . . well, I've not got long to go.' Perry heaved a sigh and stared into the distance for a moment or two, then looked back at Joss. 'So if I do cop one, will you go and see them for me? Do what you can? They're a lot older than me.'

'Yes, sir. Of course. I'll try my best, anyway.'

'They've no one, you see, absolutely no one else in the world. And I trust you. If I live, I'll see you get made up to sergeant again.'

What did you say to that? Joss wondered. He wasn't in a position to help two impoverished elderly ladies, because he wasn't flush with money and was never likely to be with a spendthrift wife like Ada. And anyway, he had his own troubles.

But his promise seemed to satisfy the captain.

Vi and Len made a visit to Drayforth the week before their wedding. They went there to introduce Len to her family, and everyone met at her sister's. Things went well between Len and everyone except her father, who seemed grumpy and disapproving from the very start, muttering quite audible remarks such as 'At her age' and 'What does he see in a scrawny old maid like her?'

Colour heightened, she tried to ignore him, but Len wasn't having it. After hearing yet another muttered remark, he dragged her father to one side, ignoring Arnie's spluttering protests, and said very loudly and clearly, 'If I hear any more remarks like that about my Violet, I'll forget who you are and punch you in the face.'

Eric, who was standing to one side, grinned and nodded approval.

Vi's mother tried to fill the silence that followed but the gathering remained uncomfortable until she and her husband had taken their leave.

After their parents had gone, Eric went across to Vi's fiancé. She tensed, but her brother only held out his hand and shook Len's. 'She's a good lass, my sister. You were right to stand up for her.' After that, he left.

On the train going back to London, she took Len's hand and said in a voice choking with emotion, 'Thank you for telling my father to stop.'

'I very nearly punched him. What sort of fellow runs down

his daughter like that? I feel sorry for your poor mother, I do that. She's a nice lady.'

'She's really pleased about us getting wed.'

He grinned at her. 'So am I.'

They were married in London a week later, with Daphne and some of the Aides attending. It wasn't a fancy wedding, but it was fancy enough for them and made Vi blissfully happy for a few days.

Then Len went back on duty and she began a life where happiness was laced with an acid dose of worry about his safety.

At first he was posted somewhere on the south coast and as soon as she heard that, she felt better. He was even able to take leave a few times and they spent golden weekends in their rooms above the stable. The place was sparsely furnished but a cup of cocoa and a quiet chat with the man she loved were more than enough for Vi, far more than she'd ever had in her life before.

They even began to make plans for after the war. Brought up in an orphanage, Len had never had a real home of his own and they spent hours planning each room of a little two-up, two-down house in detail, window shopping together for furniture.

Then Len was posted back to France and Vi found out what real worry was, a pain that gnawed at her, tormented her in the dark stretches of the night, never went away.

# 4

Six months after her marriage Vi received the telegram every soldier's wife dreaded. Lady Bingram brought it round to the unit and the captain beckoned Vi into his office to read it. She knew what it was before she opened it, of course she did, but still she read every single word.

*It is my very painful duty to inform you that a report has been received from the War Office notifying the death of . . .*

Then there were black lines on the page, empty of print, filled in by fancy italic handwriting. She touched Len's name, written so beautifully, and went on to the final paragraph:

*By His Majesty's command I am to forward the enclosed message of sympathy from Their Gracious Majesties the King and Queen. I am at the same time to express the regret of the Army Council at the soldier's death in his Country's service.*

A note was enclosed saying that Len had been buried with full military honours together with some other men from the same regiment. After the war, she would be able to go and visit his grave. His possessions would be forwarded to her.

She felt as if she'd been turned to ice. When Daphne put her arms round her, Vi looked sideways, unable to speak. But there was no comfort to be found anywhere, not even in tears.

'I'll drive you home, dear,' Daphne said.

Vi moved away and considered this, head bent, then looked at them both. 'No. There's nothing to do there. I'd just – sit and mope.'

'Are you sure?'

'Yes. I knew – Len and I both knew – this might happen. But I'm still glad I married him.' Her voice broke for a moment and she had to swallow hard before she could continue. 'He was a wonderful man and we had a few months' happiness. We'd have had a good life together after the war, just the two of us, that was all we needed, one another.'

She looked down at the piece of paper again, then across at the Major. 'Can I keep on working, sir? I'll go mad if I have to sit and think. It's not as if I have a funeral to arrange—' her voice broke again and she finished in a near whisper, 'or anything like that.'

He came to lay one hand briefly on her shoulder. 'Of course you can. But if you change your mind, if you want to go home, you only have to say. My car's at your disposal.'

'I shan't change my mind, sir. But thank you anyway.'

Everyone was very quiet as they went about their work and they left Vi to tot up her accounts in peace. She found the figures vaguely soothing, whereas overt sympathy would have destroyed her.

When she got home that evening, people would know, she was sure. She couldn't face the other women's sympathy, not yet, so went in the back way and lit one lamp to show she was there, before sitting alone in the room she'd shared with Len. It was dreadful to think he'd never come through the door again, beaming at her.

The gong rang for the evening meal, but she wasn't hungry.

Later, Daphne came across with a plate of sandwiches covered by an upturned dish and a pot of tea.

Vi thanked her, but couldn't eat anything. She disposed of two sandwiches surreptitiously so that they'd think she'd eaten something and not pester her to swallow when her throat was choked with unshed tears. Then she went back to sit by the window, turning the lamp off so they'd not bother her again, sifting through the memories of her time with Len.

She had his trunk, which contained all his worldly possessions. Poor lad, he hadn't had much. But she'd treasure his books and the other things. It was a pity she'd not had a child. They'd have liked one, but it had never happened. Well, she was a bit old for child-bearing.

It was well after midnight before she really went to bed. She wept for a while, stifling her sobs in the pillow, but wouldn't let herself go on crying. It wouldn't solve her problems.

She was certain of two things. She didn't regret marrying Len, because his love and the time they'd spent together had been precious beyond belief. And she wasn't going to stay here over the stables. This room held too many memories. One night of grieving, that's all she'd allow herself.

She'd ask Daphne if she could move back into the house tomorrow. It'd be better to share a room with someone than sit and mope on her own. And besides, Len had forbidden her to mope if the worst happened.

'A lass like you,' he'd said, 'will be bound to marry again one day. You'd have my blessing for that. You're a treasure, Violet, my love, a real treasure. And I'm the luckiest man on earth to have found you.'

She was certain she wouldn't remarry. There was only one Len in the world. And no one else but him and her mother had ever considered her a treasure. Her mother wrote her the loveliest letter when she heard about Len. Her sister wrote a quick note.

And that was it, the end of her marriage. Life went on.

Lacking a maid, Christina Warburton opened the door to Gerald Kirby herself. She didn't care for the man and had always avoided him socially, not that she and her sister had much social life these days. She didn't invite him in because she didn't want him in her home. 'Can I help you?'

He smiled at her, a practised, insincere smile which didn't reach his eyes. 'I wonder if I might have a word with you and your sister?'

She hesitated but there was no avoiding it. Reluctantly she opened the door. 'Come this way, please, Mr Kirby,' she said loudly, to give Phyllis warning. She showed him into the small parlour, saw him glance round as if he could tell at a glance how poor they were. Taking a seat next to her sister on the sofa, she waited till he'd sat down. 'How can we help you?'

'I've written to your brother but haven't heard back from him.'

'Oh?'

'I've offered to buy this house and land. As I told him, I'm prepared to give you a very substantial price for it. You'd live comfortably on it for the rest of your lives.' Again, his glance flickered over the shabby room. 'I wondered if you'd heard anything from him about it?'

'We haven't heard from him for a week or two.'

'So he's not told you about my offer?'

'No. But I'm sure he won't be interested in selling.' Kirby had offered once before and Perry had said very forcibly that he'd never, ever sell to such a man. And anyway, why should they sell their home? It was where they lived, where they were happiest.

'I'd like to talk to you about it, Miss Warburton, Miss Christina.'

Phyllis stood up, surprising Christina by the sharpness of her tone. 'I'm afraid we couldn't do that, Mr Kirby. The house belongs to my brother.'

'But surely he'd consult you and—'

'Christina dear, I'm feeling rather tired. Would you show Mr Kirby to the door, please?'

'Certainly.'

He stood up, scowling at them now.

'This way, Mr Kirby.'

Christina closed the door on him with relief then went to peer through the net curtains in the drawing room. He walked part way down the drive, then stopped to study the house.

She heard footsteps and her sister joined her.

'Perry would never sell to *him*!' Phyllis said scornfully. 'He's a dreadful, vulgar man.'

'Maud Renson didn't think so.'

'She was left penniless, married Kirby for his money.'

* * *

Three months after Len's death, there was a German air raid on London. These raids had started with the Zeppelins, though the huge inflated airships were too dependent on the wind and often went astray. But since the Hun had started making Gotha aeroplanes, the number of air raids had not only increased, but they'd killed more people too, because planes were much more manageable.

There was a lot of agitation in the newspapers and elsewhere for the government to do something to stop it, though what they could do apart from sending British planes up to fight the Hun in the air, Vi didn't know.

At first the raids had taken place in the daytime, but lately the planes had been coming over at night, which felt worse.

Vi and a few others were working late on a special job one night, though she'd nearly stayed at home because she'd eaten something that had disagreed with her. She hadn't felt well all day and had made a lot of hasty visits to the outhouse. When the warning sounded and everyone began to make their way down to the safety of the cellar, she hesitated and whispered to the Major, 'I have to go to the outhouse, sir. I've got a bit of an upset tummy.'

'You should really stay in the cellar.'

She clutched her stomach. 'Sir, I *can't* wait.'

'Well, hurry up, then, but you'll have to go across in the dark because it'd be foolish to show a light. We're a bit out of the main path for bombings here, so you should be all right.'

She hurried to the outhouse, whose door opened awkwardly inwards. It was dark inside but she didn't light the candle kept on a little shelf because of the raid. The stomach gripes weren't nearly as bad this time, thank goodness. Maybe the worst was over.

When she heard the sound of a plane overhead, she froze. Should she run for the house? No, better to stay where she was. She didn't want to be caught out in the open.

The explosion was so sudden and so shockingly loud she thought her last hour had come. The ground rocked beneath her feet and the outhouse door was blown off its hinges, falling in on her and knocking her sideways off the seat. Fortunately, it then acted like a shield as pieces of masonry hit it, mostly a patter of small sounds but also occasional thuds that shook the door. She stayed where she was, huddling in the corner on the floor. The outhouse was at right angles to the house and quite a distance away. Even so, plaster rained down on her from the ceiling and she could hardly breathe in the dust-filled air.

As the crashing sounds and rumblings that had followed the explosion died down, she stayed where she was for a few seconds, taking stock of her situation. Apart from a few scratches and a covering of grit and dust, she was unhurt. She pushed the fallen door to one side and stood up, hastily pulling up her French knickers and buttoning them, then righting her clothing.

She peered out. The house looked to have received a direct hit, as far as she could tell in the moonlight, and only the length of the back yard had saved her, she was sure.

A neighbour came running in from the alley at the rear, carrying a lantern. He stopped when he saw her. 'Are you all right?'

'Yes. I was in there.'

'You were lucky.' He turned to look at the house, holding up the lantern. 'I can't see how anyone could have survived.'

But even as he spoke, a man's voice called out for help from the ruins.

'By jingo! I'd never have believed it.'

'Oh, thank goodness they're not all dead!' Vi felt tears of relief run down her dusty cheeks. She tried to smear them away with one shaking hand, but more tears followed.

The man patted her shoulder. 'You stay here, love. I'll go and see if I can help them.'

But she followed him towards the house, ashamed of her moment's weakness, concern for her workmates overcoming her own reaction to the bomb. As she picked her way through the debris, the moon appeared suddenly from behind the clouds, its light giving everything an unreal air, with everything in blacks, whites and greys, like a film at the cinema.

Voices were coming from the basement and two other neighbours joined them, wearing overcoats on top of their pyjamas. Everyone stood looking down into the paved area below ground level which led to the basement, then one of the men said gruffly, 'Can't leave our lads in there, can we? What if the gas main blew up? It's bound to have been fractured.' He climbed carefully down and another followed.

The door was blocked by a fall of masonry, but the rescuers managed to clear a path to the window and smash it open with one of the fallen bricks. The two men who'd been calling for help climbed out.

Stan was helped out first, cradling what looked like a broken arm. Captain Deavers followed, bleeding profusely from a wound to his scalp, but insisting he was all right. The blood looked more like black, sticky tar in the moonlight.

'Have you seen the Major?' Vi asked.

'He and Sergeant Mills had just gone down to the cellar with some important papers. Stan and I were gathering the rest of the files together when it happened. They may still be alive but I doubt we'll get through to them without expert help. Half the house has fallen in, I think.' He looked backwards at the rafters and beams exposed by the blast and the roof, which had half its tiles ripped off.

A policeman came striding up, making flapping gestures with his hands. 'Keep back, *h'if* you please, madam! This is no place for a lady.'

Vi stayed where she was. 'I work in that house and I know my way around, Constable, so I may be able to help. There are people trapped in the lower cellar.'

'Well, you leave getting them out to the men who know what they're doing, missus,' he said at once. 'This isn't women's work. The Army will send some soldiers along as soon as it can. This isn't the only house that was bombed tonight, you know.'

'But the Major may need rescuing now. He may be injured.'

'We still have to wait. Rash behaviour won't get us anywhere.'

Before she could answer there was another yell and the sound of wood splintering and smashing. One of the rescuers took the lantern from the neighbour's hand and clambered back down into the basement area, angling the beam of light through the broken window. It showed Sergeant Mills clambering across the heaps of rubble inside. His uniform was in tatters and his face was streaked with blood.

They tried to help him up the basement stairs, but he refused to leave. 'The Major's trapped in there,' he said. 'I can see him but I can't get through to him because there's a ruddy great beam fallen across the doorway. The opening was too narrow for me to get through and I didn't dare try to make it wider in case I brought more stuff crashing down on him. But he was conscious, told me he was bleeding. You've got to send someone in to help him, someone small.'

'I'll go,' Vi said at once. 'I'm the smallest here.'

The men looked at one another, then at her, shaking their heads.

'Sorry, missus, but I can't allow you to put your life in danger,' the policeman said. 'Though it's very good of you to offer, I'm sure.' He glanced down at her hand. 'Your husband wouldn't thank me for sending you into danger.'

'You're not sending me. I'm going of my own accord.' Vi looked at the men she worked with. 'We can't leave the Major to bleed to death, we just – can't.'

Her words hung in the air for a moment or two, then Captain Deavers cleared his throat. 'The Major's rather important to the war effort, Constable. If Mrs Schofield can help him, then I think she should do. As long as she's not in immediate danger herself, of course.'

Against the Constable's protests they helped her down into the basement and then Captain Deavers went with her to the top of the cellar steps, holding the lantern to light up the area below. 'Are you sure about this, Vi?'

'Of course I am.'

'Good woman!' He grinned at her, his teeth white in his dirty face. 'Well, what's left of the roof *looks* stable enough, for what that's worth, though you can never be certain. But you're right: we can't leave the Major. I'll go down first. If you hear any movement above, get out as fast as you can.'

They went cautiously down the cellar steps, their way partly blocked by a fallen beam they had to climb over. Luckily it was securely lodged in a pile of rubble. The cellar was littered with debris and fallen masonry. At one spot the moonlight shone down through a hole in the celing three floors above them.

'Wait!' he said sharply, holding out one arm to bar her way. He shone the lantern round. 'I don't like the looks of that hole in the roof. We need to check first that there's not an unexploded bomb lying around. One bomb has definitely exploded and caused all this damage, but there may be another one still. If there is, you're getting out of here at once, Vi, and no arguments.'

'Yes, sir.'

But there was no sign of a bomb, just debris and another beam blocking the way into the front cellar.

The captain knelt and shone the lantern through the gap to one side of the doorway. 'I can see him, I think. Sir! Sir, are you all right?'

But there was no answer.

Vi pushed him aside. 'Hold that lantern up.' The gap was much wider at the bottom of the door. 'I think I can get through it here if I get down on my stomach.'

He held her back for a minute. 'It's risky, Vi. One of those beams looks unstable. Wait a minute and I'll see if I can find something to prop it up with.'

But the thought of the Major bleeding to death on his own in the darkness upset her so much that when the Captain turned away, she dropped down and began to wriggle through the gap.

'What the hell— Vi, stop!'

But she was out of his reach. 'Shine the light in,' she called.

A final wriggle took her into the cellar. Everything was pitch black except for the glow from the lantern the Captain was holding behind her. As her eyes grew more accustomed to the darkness, she could make out the Major lying on the ground with a dark trail of blood beside him. She fumbled for a pulse, her hand trembling, and to her relief found one.

'He's still alive. Go and get some candles and matches, then poke them through to me,' she called back to the captain. 'I need to be able to see more clearly. There seems to be a lot of blood.'

The lantern light faded, leaving her in the dark, which suddenly felt suffocating. She swallowed hard and told herself not to be silly. Just because it was pitch black didn't mean you couldn't breathe. After a few deep breaths to prove that point to herself, she began to feel the Major's body gently. There was a large wound in his side from which fresh blood was still flowing.

It seemed important to stanch the blood, so she stood up and wriggled out of her petticoat, folding it up and pressing it against the wound. How was she to hold it in place? It took her a moment or two to work that out, then she slid down her garters and took off her stockings. Tying them together, she passed them round the Major's body and used them to hold the makeshift pad in place.

After that she could only wait.

The Major groaned suddenly and tried to move.

'Lie still, sir. You've been hurt.'

'Mm? Can't see. Is that you, Mrs Schofield? What's happened?'

'A bomb exploded and you were hurt. We're in the cellar. They'll get us out when they can, but I need to keep this pressed to your wound.'

'What is it?'

'My petticoat. I've tied it in place with my stockings, but you'll dislodge it if you move.'

There was a rusty chuckle, which surprised her.

'Daphne told me you were enterprising.'

It was three hours before they were rescued. The Captain brought back some candles and matches, pushing them through the narrow gap tied to a long thin piece of wood. Vi lit a candle, feeling instantly better when she'd banished that terrible blackness. But time passed very slowly and she felt desperate to get medical help for the Major.

In the end a party of army engineers cleared a path and got them out, insisting Vi go first.

To her surprise, it was starting to get light outside. She stood for a moment, breathing the fresh, clean air. She felt tired and muddle-headed, wasn't sure what to do next, but a woman wrapped a blanket round her and they insisted on taking her to hospital for a check-up.

When they got there, Vi was more interested in the cup of strong, hot tea someone gave her – and in finding out how the Major was. Once they'd washed her scratches and made sure she didn't have concussion, they dismissed her from the hospital and told her to get some rest.

Daphne herself came to drive Vi back. 'You're quite a heroine, my dear.'

'Nonsense. Anyone would have gone to the Major's help.'

'Only a brave person like you would have done it. And the nurse told me the doctor said you did well to stanch the blood.'

Vi opened her mouth then shut it again, embarrassed by all the attention she'd received since she'd been rescued. She wasn't a heroine. She'd just been doing her duty, helping a gentleman who was making more difference to the war than she ever could.

In France, a heavy bombardment began at dawn and Joss expected at any minute to be blown to kingdom come. Instead, a bomb fell just along the trench from him and when he turned, he saw the captain crumple to the ground, blood spurting from a deep wound to the belly.

'Stretcher!' he yelled.

'They can't get through till this stops,' a voice called back.

He knelt beside the injured man, cradling Warburton's head on his lap.

'Told you – I'd not – survive,' the captain said.

He didn't seem to be in pain, which surprised Joss, because his companion was losing a lot of blood, but he'd heard that shock sometimes did that to you. He looked round. Still no sign of stretcher-bearers.

The captain tugged at his arm. 'You won't – forget your promise?'

'About your sisters? No, sir. Of course not. But you'll be seeing them yourself soon. This has to be a Blighty one.'

A faint smile crossed the captain's narrow, well-bred face. 'It's more than that. I can't feel my legs and I—'

As suddenly as that he was gone, dying with a faint smile on his face.

Joss bowed his head for a minute or two, then looked round. The bombardment was easing. Only he and three others were still alive.

'Sod the buggers,' one of the men said, then his eyes went to the still figure beyond Joss. 'Has he copped it?'

'Yes.'

'Pity. He was a good officer.'

It seemed a long time until the stretcher-bearers arrived.

The following day Joss wrote a letter to the Captain's sisters. For once, he was telling the truth when he said their brother had felt no pain and had died quickly.

He was made up to Corporal again the following week, and got a lecture about controlling his temper from the new Captain. As if he cared about that, especially from such a snob of a man.

He didn't care about anything much, actually, could only exist from one day to the next, always surprised to find himself alive in the morning.

What was happening back in Drayforth seemed totally unimportant now. Not only another world, but another sort of world.

Two weeks after Perry's death, Mr Kirby knocked on the front door of Fairview again.

Christina, who had heard footsteps on the gravel drive, peeped through the drawing-room window, her heart sinking when she saw who it was. With immense reluctance she opened the door.

'I was sorry to hear about your brother.'

Kirby and his wife had sent them a letter of condolences. They'd thrown it in the fire.

'Might I have a word?'

'If it's about the same subject as last time, it'll do you no good. We don't wish to sell the house.'

'My dear lady, you're not thinking clearly. You can't hang on here without money. The place will fall down about your ears. Anyway, I gather it's your sister who owns Fairview now, not you, so I'd like to speak to her.'

'We're in agreement about everything, Mr Kirby. Good morning to you.'

He put his hand out to stop her closing the door. 'You really ought to hear what I have to say.'

'We are *not* interested in selling.'

He stepped back, tipping his hat then strolling down the drive.

She shut the door and rushed into the drawing room to keep an eye on him, make sure he really had gone. Halfway down the drive he stopped to stare back at Fairview, an assessing, possessive sort of look. Christina watched until he had got into his car, which was waiting for him in the street.

When her ailing elder sister came in, she summoned up a wry smile. 'Dreadful man, isn't he? Won't take no for an answer.'

'I heard what you said to him and you're right. I shan't sell,' Phyllis said firmly. 'But tomorrow we'll go and ask our lawyer to draw up new wills. I want to make sure that Mr Kirby can never get his hands on the house – even after we both die.'

They were silent for a few moments then Christina asked, 'Do you think this war is ever going to end?'

'Oh, yes. And we'll win. We must. Perry can't have given his life in vain.'

And then they were both weeping in each other's arms.

# 5

Joss was with the new Captain when the messenger arrived.

'No need for a reply, sir.' The man gave a quick salute and set off again without waiting for permission, which was unusual. The sound of a motorbike echoed and faded into the distance.

Joss watched his officer open the despatch and gaped in shock as the man, who was so wooden and unemotional they called him Old Oak behind his back, blinked furiously then looked at Joss with tears leaking from his eyes.

'It's over,' he said in a voice that sounded thick and strange. 'This damned war is over . . . at last. Or it soon will be. Oh, hell.' He smiled through the tears and held out the message. 'Go on! Read it!'

*Received radio message from Marshal Foch this morning. Hostilities will be stopped on the entire front, beginning at 11 a.m., November 11th (French hour). The Allied troops will not proceed beyond the line reached at that hour on that date until further orders.*

The two men stared at one another. Joss felt his own eyes smart. When the Captain held out his hand, he shook it solemnly.

'Does that mean we stop shelling now, sir?'

'No. But it means I don't have to send anyone else out to be butchered, and I won't. We'd better continue to fire until that time, just for appearances' sake. We don't need to hit anything, though. I don't know about you, but I've had enough of killing.'

When Joss didn't move, the Captain said more quietly, 'Go and tell them the news, Corporal.'

Joss went to spread the word.

The men's reactions were mixed and sometimes strange.

Some stood silent, looking so dumbstruck, he wondered if they understood what he'd said.

Others looked towards the enemy as if they'd never seen the lines before.

One said, 'Won't Sarge be sorry to have missed it? What a time to get wounded!'

'You'd better all fire a few shots in the air,' Joss said. 'You don't have to hit anything now.'

'Well, I'm still going to try to kill as many of those bastards as I can,' said a man whose best friend had been blown to pieces the week before.

Joss opened his mouth to protest, then closed it again.

It seemed a long time until eleven o'clock.

'Cease fire!' he yelled. 'It's over.' Then he closed his own tear-filled eyes and whispered, 'Over.'

There were no celebrations because many of the men believed the Armistice was only temporary and the war would soon start up again. They weren't prepared to let down their guard in any way.

But during the night it began to sink in what peace would mean. Everything was so quiet. They weren't used to that. And the Captain said they could light fires. They weren't used to that, either.

One man suddenly began to weep and couldn't stop.

Joss just wanted to be left alone, so moved backwards into the darkness.

He hoped the war wouldn't start up again, though. The Captain said it wouldn't. But it felt so strange not to be fighting that he couldn't quite believe in peace.

Vi was working when she heard the news. The Major gathered them together and explained that as from eleven o'clock the war had ended, and as soon as that hour had passed, he was letting them go home.

'You'll want to celebrate,' he said. 'The streets will be full of people, as they were after the relief of Mafeking.'

Vi didn't feel like celebrating. Oh, she was glad the war had ended, but coming here to London had given her so much, especially meeting Len, even if he had been taken from her again. All she could wonder was what she was going to do with her life now. She wasn't going back to work in the shop, though, whatever anyone said or did – not even for her mother's sake. That was her yesterday. Today she was a different person, looking for a different future.

She walked slowly home through streets that were filling up fast with smiling people. She smiled back at them and allowed a few strangers to hug her, a few soldiers to spin her round in a clumsy, joyful dance. When she got home, she didn't join the others, but went round to the back and up into the rooms she had shared with Len.

'Well, your death wasn't in vain, at least, love,' she told him. 'But I do wish you were here.' She sat on a chair and tried to get used to the idea that the war was over.

No one missed her and when it got late she slipped into the kitchen as if she'd just come in from the streets. She got herself some bread and jam and went up to her bedroom. Later she heard the other women come in, but pretended to be asleep. She wished she could sleep. But somehow, all she could think of was how much the war had cost ordinary people – their loved ones' lives were such a high price to pay.

She carried on working at the unit, which she would do until they forced her to leave. The Major said he didn't want to lose her, but she knew they wouldn't keep volunteers like her on for longer than they had to. Already some people were insulting the women who were working on the buses and trams, telling them to get back home and leave those jobs for the men. That made her furious. Everyone had been full of praise for women who did such jobs during the war, and yet within days some people were treating them like pariahs.

Phyllis and Christina heard the good news from their cook, who'd heard it from a cousin who worked nearby and sometimes popped in.

'We must celebrate,' Christina said at once. 'I shall open a bottle of wine from Father's cellar.'

'And I'll set the table properly, with the good china.'

But before they did this, they looked at one another sadly.

'If only it had happened a few months earlier, we might still have Perry with us.'

Neither could hold the tears back and they didn't bother with the wine, after all.

The war might have ended but the influenza epidemic got worse and worse, paralysing the whole country. No one had seen anything like this and there were as many deaths as there had been in the fighting.

Because so many people were ill, Vi was still needed in the unit, which postponed her decision for a while.

Lady Bingram had set up the house and some Aides had volunteered to help people recovering from the influenza, those who had no families to look after them after they came out of hospital, where beds were needed for the acutely ill.

Vi went to chat to the invalids sometimes in the evenings, not afraid of falling sick herself, because she didn't care enough.

She felt as if she was waiting . . . but she didn't know what for.

It was a lot harder to get out of the Army than it had been to get into it, Joss thought gloomily. When the Captain summoned him and he saw papers spread out on the desk, his spirits lifted briefly. Rumour said that men with families would be the first to be released.

But the papers were to transfer him to a training camp in England which had been badly hit by the influenza. Sarge was on light duties there until he had fully recovered and it turned out he'd recommended Joss for these special duties, which earned those who undertook them a bonus. Their job was to help care for the sick men, because there simply weren't enough trained nurses.

Joss felt angry about that, worried too. He hadn't survived the war to die of the damned Spanish influenza, surely? What would Iris and Roy do if their father wasn't there to provide for them?

But he had no choice about it. It was a long time since he'd had a choice about anything. And when he saw how ill the poor sods were, how many died in spite of all their efforts, he forgot his anger and concentrated on the task at hand.

It was there that the letter from his mother found him, telling him Ada had died – not of influenza, but in childbirth. He gaped at it for a moment. Childbirth! Then as the words sank in and he understood what she'd done to him, he screwed the paper up and cursed, ignoring his companions' questions. He went to stand outside the hut for a moment or two, not sure what to do, only knowing he couldn't bear to talk to anyone.

'Joss?'

'Not now, Sarge. *Please!*'

He strode away, making for a quiet spot he knew, and to his relief Sarge didn't follow him.

Sitting down, Joss smoothed out the paper and reread the letter, feeling as if someone had punched him in the guts. No, he hadn't mistaken what it said: his wife had died in childbirth.

*Only he hadn't touched her for well over a year.*

Rage filled him and he wanted to hit someone, anyone, but he held back the red flood of fury till it ebbed slowly, leaving a simmering fire in his chest. He'd learned his lesson about giving in to anger, learned it the hard way by losing his stripes.

Who the hell had fathered this baby?

How could she have done this to him?

And why had no one told him Ada was expecting?

It took only a minute to work out the answer to that: because his family thought he already knew, assumed she'd told him. The cunning bitch! He'd wondered why he'd not heard from his mother lately, not that she'd ever written to him frequently. And Ada herself hadn't written to him since his last visit home.

He scanned the letter again. The baby was a girl, healthy and bonny. They'd called her Nora when they didn't hear from him and hoped he liked that name, which had been Ada's choice.

His sister was looking after the baby for now, but Pam was expecting herself and near her time, so couldn't carry on doing that for much longer. His father was ill as well, so his mother couldn't take Nora on, either. They hoped the Army would release him quickly, so that he could sort things out.

He did a quick calculation and worked out that the baby must have been conceived around the time of his last visit. Unless the real father came forward to claim it, how would he ever prove it wasn't his?

He shoved the letter into his pocket and buried his face in his hands. What the hell was he going to do now?

The letter was waiting for Vi one rainy afternoon when she got home from the unit. It was postmarked Drayforth, the address ill-spelled in big rounded letters, like a child's. She stared at it a minute before opening it. Her father. Why on earth would he be writing to her? He never had before.

Terror clamped an iron band round her heart and for a moment she couldn't open it. Then she forced herself to tear the envelope with fingers that trembled.

*Dear Vilet*

*Sorry to tell you yore mother passed away a couple of weeks ago. The Spannish 'flu, it was. She was alrite in the morning, dead by midnight. We buried her next to her parents. Wasn't time to get you here.*

*One of Beryl's kids died of it too.*

*I need you at home. Now.*

*Arnie*

Vi stared at the letter in horror, then burst into tears, sobbing so loudly and incoherently someone went running for Daphne.

It was a long time before Vi could control her grief and when she did, she found herself in Daphne's little sitting room, with no memory of going there.

It was so unfair! Her mother had been a lovely woman, hadn't deserved to die. Vi had been looking forward to living near her again, spending time with her, trying to make her life easier – even if she didn't intend to work in the shop again.

Now she'd lost both the people she'd cared about most in the world.

Spent by her weeping, she allowed herself to be persuaded to go to bed and eventually fell asleep.

The next day, for the first time ever, she didn't go to work at the unit. She needed to come to terms with this second loss before she could face her friends' sympathy.

She didn't even like her father, didn't feel close to Eric, and Beryl was so busy all the time with her family that they only saw one another now and then. Well, there was even less reason now for Vi to go back to work in the shop, whatever her father said or did.

Even her work would end soon, now that the war was over. What would be left for her?

Nothing, that's what.

She'd give herself this one day to grieve and feel upset. After that she'd get on with things as best she could. At least she still had a job in London, for a few weeks anyway, because the Major had asked for an extension of her employment. That'd help her get through this.

Life could be hard, though, very hard. She felt a million years old today, so tired of all the deaths and killing, so very weary.

# PART TWO

# February 1919

# 6

The final post was delivered to the unit late one afternoon at the beginning of February. The Major was out at one of his many meetings and Vi was hoping for an early departure today, unless the post was late. She had instructions to open Major Warren's mail in case any of it was urgent, but when she saw that the official envelope had her name on it, not his, her heart sank.

She could guess what it was. One of the other Aides had received a letter like this last week. Vi signed for it without a word and waited until the postman had left before opening it.

*Dear Mrs Schofield*

*It is with regret that I write to terminate your employment.*

*Please be assured that your contribution to the War Effort has been much appreciated by His Majesty's Government.*

*I am enclosing a service certificate in formal acknowledgement of your efforts.*

*If you will kindly clear your office on Friday afternoon, your place can be taken by a returned soldier from Monday onwards.*

*I wish you well in your return to a more normal life.*

The signature was an illegible scrawl, two little curved lines, as if the person who'd penned it couldn't be bothered to sign properly.

She clutched the piece of paper to her chest, fighting tears.

*Return to a more normal life!* What was 'normal' after the past few years?

And who would look after 'her' families now? One of her favourite parts of the job had been making sure the families of men who'd been killed were all right. She couldn't even tell them what their husbands had been doing and their distress always brought back her own sorrow about Len. But even so, she derived great satisfaction from helping them in practical ways: finding and inspecting new accommodation for those who needed it, often somewhere closer to the rest of their families, seeing they had enough money to eat and to clothe the children properly, dealing with numerous worries or small problems.

She hoped the man who was taking over from her was good at coping with weeping women, but she couldn't see a man feeling the same sort of sympathy she did. Luckily there were no more men out there being killed, but there were still some who were badly wounded and not expected to live.

A man might be all right dealing with landlords, though, she could hope for that at least. Some landlords would do anything rather than maintain their houses properly and that wasn't good enough for people whose menfolk had given their lives to help win the war.

Well, no use standing here like a lost soul. She put on her hat and coat and was just about to leave when the Major returned.

'Do you need anything else, sir?'

'No thanks, Vi.' He studied her face. 'What's wrong?'

She fumbled in her handbag and held out the letter.

He glanced at it, sighed and handed it back. 'I'm sorry. I asked for another extension, told them you were invaluable to me, but they were adamant. All voluntary workers are to leave as soon as possible, now that the influenza epidemic is dying down. Will you be all right? You've a family to go back to, I know, but have you –' he cleared his throat and avoided her eyes – 'enough money to manage on until you find a new job?'

'Yes, sir. I've managed to save quite a bit, so I'll be fine.' And Len had had money, too, nearly a hundred pounds in the savings bank. It was a fortune to someone like her, who had always been so short.

The Major laid one hand on her shoulder. 'I'm going to miss you, Vi, not just for the work you've been doing, but for your cheerful presence.'

'I'll miss you too, sir.' He'd been like a grandfather to them all. 'Well, I'd better be going.' She walked out, head held high. She wasn't going to weep all over him. She'd done with weeping.

On the afternoon of January the 3rd, Vi tidied up the major's office for the final time then went to set her own desk to rights. She couldn't resist going over to stand by the window for a final look at the busy London street. She was going to miss the animated scene below, had often stood here for a minute's break.

Pedestrians were always there in abundance, hurrying, dawdling, pausing to chat. At the moment a tangle of vehicles was rumbling slowly past: horses and carts, impatient motor cars, elegant carriages and lowly bicycles, all held up by a man pushing an overloaded hand cart. A slow-moving omnibus came into view behind them, an Old Bill. A lot of these buses had gone to France to take part in the war, making it hard for civilians to get around at home, but they were coming back now and the London General Omnibus Company's services were starting to improve.

Some young soldiers were sitting quietly on the open top deck of the omnibus, grinning lazily down at the passers-by, seeming oblivious to the cold. She felt her spirits lift a little at the sight of them. At least these lads weren't going off to die in the trenches. They would have as good a chance as anyone else of a happy life, would probably marry and have children to love. Ah, how she had longed for children! Every time one of her friends produced one, she'd had to hold back her jealousy, but it sometimes came back to her in the small hours of the morning, to sear her.

It was over a year now since her Len had been killed. Where had the months gone?

With another sigh, she turned away from the window, took one last look round the office to make sure everything was tidy then reached for her hat. She skewered it in place with two hatpins instead of her usual one, because it'd been quite windy this morning and the wide brim caught the wind. Then she put on her winter coat, a three-quarter garment in warm brown wool with a double row of silver buttons. Today she had on a matching mid-calf skirt and a knitted cardigan jacket over her cream blouse. This sort of skirt was much more comfortable for walking than the long skirts everyone used to wear and some older ladies still wore. She wasn't going back to them.

Walking out of the office she frowned, wondering where everyone was. She didn't want to leave without saying goodbye to her friends so walked down the corridor looking for them. As she turned the corner, someone grabbed her from behind and a hand covered her eyes. She reacted instinctively because all the Aides had been trained in self-defence since they had to go out alone at night. Grabbing her attacker's arm with both her hands, she dropped quickly to the floor, catching the man off balance and pulling him down with her. As he let out a yell of shock and fell beside her, she recognised his hair. Only the major had such silky, silvery hair.

'Oh, sir! I'm that sorry!'

They were lying pressed as closely together as any pair of lovers and she blushed as she tried to disentangle herself. But Major Warren threw back his head and let out his famous roar of laughter.

'Violet Schofield, you may only be five foot tall, but you're a dangerous woman.'

He was up with a nimbleness belying his years, pulling her to her feet after him, still smiling. 'Are you all right, my dear?'

She nodded, righting her clothes, straightening her hat as well as she could by feel and picking up her handbag.

Then the other men were crowding round them, laughing at the incident, all trying to explain at once that they'd arranged a surprise party to farewell her.

The major bowed and offered his arm, leading Vi into his office, where she found a spread of food the like of which had rarely been seen during the recent years of shortages: not only a huge plate of sandwiches with all sorts of fillings, but a cream-filled sponge cake and some small iced fancies. The tea urn from the canteen was bubbling away merrily in one corner.

She was escorted to the seat of honour and everyone else from the unit crammed in, smiling and joking as they found places round the edges of the room, perching on desks, or leaning against the wall. They were good lads, all of them, and she'd enjoyed working with them.

Clearing his throat, Major Warren waited till everyone was silent. 'We're here to say a reluctant farewell to one of our colleagues. I'm very sad indeed to be losing our Mrs Schofield. No one will be able to replace you, my dear lady.'

There was a chorus of 'Hear, hear!'

'And I'll never forget that you saved my life when we were bombed out of our other offices – at some risk to your own. You were very brave, a real heroine.'

She blushed and stared down at her hands, then realised from the expectant silence that they were looking at her, waiting for a response, and summoned up a smile. 'I'm going to miss you too, every single one of you. It's been a privilege to work here and I wish you all well.'

To her relief they didn't try to make her say more. She was too afraid of crying, didn't want to embarrass them or herself.

The captain bowed and gestured to the table. 'After you, my dear.'

Relieved that the formal part of the party was over, she went to collect a plate and put food on it. Not that she was hungry – she was too sad to have much appetite – but someone had gone to a lot of trouble and you had to show your appreciation.

When it was all over, they refused to let Vi help them clear up and Major Warren insisted on driving her home in his motor car. He wouldn't take no for an answer and she enjoyed her final ride in the comfortable vehicle. It'd be Shanks's pony from now on. Good thing she was an energetic walker.

Outside Lady Bingram's house, the Major shook her hand and kept hold of it in both his. 'Vi, my dear, you've got my written testimonial about how good a worker you are, but if you ever need references or help of any sort, you know where to find me.'

She nodded, unable to speak because once again tears threatened. He seemed to understand that, letting go of her hand and stepping back to square his shoulders and give her a smart military salute. He turned to wave through the rear window of the Bentley as he was driven away and she waved back till the car turned the corner.

She knew he would only be working for a few more months, then would be going back to a lonely existence in retirement, his wife having died ten years previously and his only son having been killed during the war. Life could be so cruel.

Vi stood in the street for a few minutes longer, staring blindly into the distance. She was going back to Drayforth, in spite of her mother's death, because all her remaining relatives were there, and family was important. If she couldn't be a mother herself, she could at least be an auntie to Beryl's children. Eric hadn't married and she wondered if he ever would. He was a strange man, her brother, but he'd looked after their mother when Vi was in London and she knew he'd help her too if she needed anything.

Since the letter from her father informing her of her mother's death, she hadn't received any other letters from him. Which of her sister's children had died? Vi had written to offer Beryl her condolences, but her sister hadn't replied.

She'd written again to let her father know she was coming and asked him to tell the others, but hadn't had a reply to that, either. Typical of him!

He'd be expecting her to take over the shop again and she wondered how he had coped on his own. She didn't know what to expect when she went back, she really didn't.

Daphne Bingram heard the front door open and someone walk briskly along the tiled hallway. She peered out. 'Ah, it's you, Vi. I can always recognise your step. Could I have a word, please?'

'Yes, of course.'

'Come in and warm yourself by the fire. It's a very chilly evening, isn't it?' She waited as the woman who was one of her favourites among the Aides turned obediently and followed her into the cosy sitting room.

Vi looked quiet, not her usual self, Daphne thought. Well, she was feeling rather sad too. She wasn't sorry the hostilities were over – no one could be – but she was very sorry to say goodbye to her 'girls'.

It had made Daphne feel so *useful* running the Aides and given her the companionship she'd been lacking. Her husband was an invalid now, declining steadily and grumpy with it. Everyone faced death differently. Arthur was doing it by staying angry – at her as well as at fate. If only they'd had children! Now what would she do with her time?

She pulled her thoughts together. 'Sit down, my dear.'

Vi took a chair, clasping her hands in her lap, looking neat and composed. In fact, that was the first thing you noticed about her, Daphne decided, the neatness not only in dress but in everything she did.

'I know you're leaving on Monday, so I wanted to have a private chat with you. You've made a real contribution to your country, my dear and I'm very proud of you.' She held back a smile at the telltale red that stained her companion's cheeks. Vi had always been uncomfortable with being praised, insisting she'd only done what anyone else would have.

'I know you told me your plans, and that you have money, but I want to stress that if you need any help . . .' She saw that stubborn twist to Vi's lips. 'No false pride, my dear. We've been through a lot together and I shall always be there to help my girls. I shall be popping up to Lancashire now and then, and hope we can meet and chat about old times.'

'I'd like that.'

'My husband hasn't long to live and afterwards the house will go to a nephew. I shall then go back to live permanently in Clough Lodge, which I've always liked. Why my husband moved down south, I'll never understand. The War Office has now moved out all the injured men who were living in Clough Lodge, so I can start putting it back to rights.' She paused. 'My dear, *promise me* you'll ask for help if you need it! If you don't, I shall worry.'

Vi looked back at her, lips pressed together.

Daphne cocked one eyebrow and waited.

Halfway between amusement and annoyance, Vi said, 'All right, I promise – but only if I'm truly desperate, Daphne.'

Once the influenza epidemic slowed down, Joss was given his discharge from the Army on compassionate grounds. He hadn't applied for that but it seemed his sister had written to the War Office just before Christmas to explain how badly he was needed at home now that his wife was dead.

The authorities gave him a new suit of civilian clothes – and it wasn't bad, either, a nice dark navy and fitted him quite well. There was also a pair of medals and some money, the equivalent of a few weeks' wages. That would help tide him over, at least.

On his last evening, the men in his platoon dragged him down to the pub for a farewell drink as soon as it opened at six, in spite of his protests that he was tired and had an early start and a long journey ahead of him the next day.

Even though it was now against the law to treat anyone, someone else bought his glass of bitter. Joss sipped it slowly. Weak stuff it was compared to the pre-war beer, but it quenched the thirst.

They tried to persuade him to drink more quickly, eager to line up other half-pints of beer for him, but tonight he couldn't pretend he was in the mood for a booze up. In the end he thumped the table. 'How many more times do I have to tell you? One glass will do me tonight.'

There was a moment's silence, then they began talking again. Most of them were drinking fast, eager to get a few pints down before the pub closed again at nine.

Later, on the excuse of relieving himself, he slipped outside and started walking back to the barracks with a sigh of relief.

'I guessed you were skipping out.' Sarge fell into place beside him.

'No need for you to give up your evening just because I've got a bit of a headache.'

'There'll be other evenings, but this is the last one I'll be able to spend with you. What's wrong, lad? And don't try to tell me it's a headache. You've been like a bear with a sore head for the past two months.'

'Look, Sarge, it's private. Nothing to do with the Army.'

'Joss, we were once sergeants together and we've been through some hard times together. Who else do you have to talk to about your troubles but me?'

He shrugged. Talk! Talk was easy. His wife had never stopped talking and look where that had got her.

Sarge let out a soft chuckle. 'Put it this way, then: have you ever known me give up when I want to find something out? I'll stay up nagging you all night if I have to. I'm worried about you, lad.'

This was spoken in the usual mild tone, but the threat behind it was very real and suddenly Joss did want to unburden himself. Just this once. After all, he'd be gone tomorrow, so he wouldn't have to face someone who knew his shameful secret. And he could trust Sarge not to tell anyone, he was quite sure of that. 'Let's find somewhere quiet, then. But it's to stay between you and me.'

'That goes without saying. I know a quiet, sheltered bench in the park. Come on.' He led the way down a side street and they both climbed over the railings.

'Damn sight easier than getting through the bloody barbed wire in France, eh?' Sarge jumped down nimbly in spite of the permanent limp from the leg wound that had sent him back to Blighty before the end of the war.

Regular soldier, Sarge was, and would be staying in the Army till he retired. For a moment Joss envied him the certainty of that life, but he didn't envy him the rules and regulations. When they were sitting on the bench, Joss bowed his head, not knowing how to start. He wasn't used to baring his soul to anyone. The moon was so bright he could see every detail of his clenched fists as they rested on his thighs, every detail of the gravel path below his feet, too. He wished he could see his own path through the next few months equally clearly.

'Is it because your wife's dead, lad? It must be hard to face going home without her, let alone there's a new baby to look after.'

'No. Ada and me weren't getting on all that well. I'm sorry she's dead but I shan't miss her, quite the opposite.' Joss took a deep breath and said it baldly, because there was no way of varnishing this particular truth. 'If you must know, it isn't *my* baby. I hadn't so much as touched Ada for a year or more before it was born. And . . . I'd had letters saying she'd been seen with another fellow. So I've been lumbered with someone else's child.'

Anger made his cheeks burn as he added, 'The trouble is, she was my wife and I was home around the time it was fathered, though we never . . . So you see I've no way of proving it isn't mine.'

Sarge let out a long, low whistle. 'That's a right old bugger, that is. Why didn't you say anything when you found out she was expecting?'

'Because she didn't tell me. When they wrote to say she'd died, they thought I knew all about the baby. And then . . . well, I didn't like to blacken her name, not after she was dead.'

'That's a rotten mess! What are you going to do about the child?'

'Damned if I know.'

Silence fell for a few moments then Joss jerked to his feet and shoved his hands deep into his pockets. 'I told you it was no use talking about it. You can't help me. No one can.' He turned slightly, staring up at the moon, his breath clouding the chill air. 'I don't want the baby. The real father should be the one to look after her, only I don't know who he is. Someone must have seen him and Ada together, though, to write those letters, and by hell, I'm going to find out who he was.'

'Well, don't do anything that'll rebound on your own head. You keep your temper in check, my lad.'

'Don't worry. I've learned my lesson there.' Besides, Joss could guess what had driven Ada to seek comfort elsewhere – the loneliness. He'd felt sorry for her when he left, irritating as she was. She loved company, pretty clothes, admiration. Her widowed mother had spoiled her rotten. As a wife Ada been a poor manager, always running out of housekeeping money, not keeping things tidy, falling behind with the washing – though she'd been a loving mother to Roy and Iris, he'd give her that.

'What if the fellow's already got a family, doesn't know about the child, won't believe you?'

'He must know. She'll have told him. She never could keep anything to herself. And he'll have seen her around, swelling belly and all . . . unless he was a soldier on leave when it happened . . . No, I don't think he could have been, because she'd have wanted the company, you see. That's why she'll have done it. Always had to have a man to lean on, Ada did.'

More silence, then Sarge said thoughtfully, 'It'll cause a lot of talk if you give the baby away.'

'Aye. That's what has me puzzled.'

The hand was still there on his shoulder and Joss didn't move away from its comforting warmth for a minute or two. It was no use fooling himself though. He was trapped, well and truly trapped. He'd struggled in the mud of the trenches, but the mud of his life seemed a lot deeper.

# 7

Early on the Monday morning one of the other aides drove Vi to the station in Daphne's car. She'd come to London with one trunk and a small suitcase, but now needed two trunks to hold all her things – not just what she'd acquired but some of her husband's possessions that she wanted to keep.

At the station she found a porter who helped the guard put the trunks into the luggage van for her. She tipped the men twopence each, which was more than enough in her estimation. She could see the porter had expected more and wondered why. Perhaps it was because she looked quite smart. She'd learned to make the most of her clothes by watching how the Aides who came from better-class families dressed. For travelling she was wearing the brown coat and skirt again, though with a pale green blouse this time. She'd sewn new buttons on the coat so that it didn't look like a uniform any longer but had kept the silver ones as a memento.

In London Joss had to run to catch the train, because the local milk train that had brought him to the capital from the army camp had been late. Ignoring a porter shouting at him to stop and some soldiers hanging out of a window further up the train whistling and cheering him on, he raced for one of the rear compartments, kitbag over his shoulder and suitcase in one hand.

To his relief someone opened the door just before he got there and he was able to sling his suitcase inside and leap aboard. Panting, he leaned out to yank the door closed, then turned to the person who'd given him such timely assistance, surprised to find only a woman in the compartment. 'Thank you. That was a big help.'

She smiled and he was surprised at how attractive her rather plain face suddenly became. Laughter lines crinkled the corners of her dark brown eyes, which twinkled at him in a most engaging way.

'It was dangerous jumping on board like that, but you must have needed to catch this train, so I thought I'd help.' She settled into the corner seat opposite him.

'I did.' Which was a lie. He'd run because he couldn't have borne to wait around for the next train. Now that he was on his way, he wanted to get the next few days over with and put some order into his personal life. He hoisted his case and kitbag up into the string luggage rack and sat down opposite her. 'Going far?'

'To Drayforth eventually, but I have to change at Manchester.'

'I'm going to Drayforth as well.' He held out one hand. 'Joss Bentley.'

'Vi Schofield.'

As she shook his hand, Joss looked down. His own, big and scarred, made hers look like a child's hand. It was soft and clean, the nails well-kept, as neat as the rest of her. 'I don't recognise you or the surname, though I know most families in Drayforth.' Most of the respectable ones, anyway, and she was clearly respectable. 'My family owns a shoe shop in the Market Square.'

'Bentley's Fine Footwear.'

'You know it?'

She smiled ruefully. 'I've never been inside. I wore second-hand shoes when I was a child and later I bought them cheaply at the markets. Even when they pinched, I couldn't afford to throw them away.'

'Not good for the feet. It makes such a difference if shoes fit properly. No corns, for a start.'

She looked down at her feet with another of those warm smiles. 'I take more care choosing my footwear now, I promise you.'

His eyes followed hers to the lace-up shoes worn with cloth

gaiters over them for warmth. 'Those look well made. Good leather.'

'Lady Bingram provided them for all us Aides.' Whether from wealthy or poor backgrounds, they'd all been dressed the same when on duty.

There was shouting and laughing along the corridor and the group of four soldiers who'd watched him leap on board pushed into the compartment, clearly the worse for drink. Joss frowned at them. Let alone he didn't like to see men drunk during the daytime, there was a woman present.

He didn't try to continue his conversation with Miss – he glanced down at her left hand – no, Mrs Schofield. Well, it'd have been impossible with the racket the youngsters were making. He'd seen a lot of high spirits since the war ended, but that was no excuse for bad manners.

A couple of hours into the journey Mrs Schofield leaned forward and asked in a low voice, 'Would you mind keeping an eye on my suitcase for a few minutes?'

'I'd be happy to.'

When she'd gone, the others commented on her appearance in a manner that made Joss's blood boil and he couldn't hold back. 'You should be ashamed, saying things like that about a decent woman.'

'Who are you to tell us what to do?'

He was about to answer when she returned and to his relief they did shut up. But soon after they began singing, and not always the politest of songs. He looked at her and she gave a shrug, but he still felt ashamed of them. It was a relief when the train pulled into Manchester. He wasn't surprised when their travelling companions tumbled out, not waiting for the lady to go first, and made a beeline for the exit. No doubt they were off to look for a pub.

He got Mrs Schofield's suitcase down. 'Need any help?'

'I've got two trunks, so I'll need a porter to take them to the next train. I've got twenty minutes, plenty of time. Thanks anyway.'

Brisk and composed she picked up the suitcase and nodded

farewell, then signalled to a porter, who retrieved the trunks with the help of the guard. With a feeling of faint regret, Joss strolled away, sorry the young soldiers had come into their compartment. He was sure he'd have enjoyed a chat with Mrs Schofield. She looked so neat and decent it did his heart good.

Their train was already waiting. Joss stopped, scowling, as Gerald Kirby strode along the platform and got into a first class compartment. Kirby might be one of the richest men in Drayforth, and he often bought shoes at their shop because he made a big show of patronising local businesses, but Joss disliked him. No one should look at the world in such a sneering way, as if he knew he was superior to those around him. Well, he wasn't, however fancy the clothes he wore or the motor car in which he was driven round.

And Kirby hadn't always been rich, nor had he been entirely scrupulous about how he made his money. Some of the houses he owned were the worst slums in town. Kirby might have come up in the world, but everyone knew the county set didn't invite him to their parties, however much money he splashed around.

Joss's father always fawned on the fellow, though, treating him as if he was royalty. Well, he'd not get that sort of treatment from Joss – if he went back into the business. His brother Wilf had been working in the shoe shop for a few years now, ever since Joss volunteered, because he had a gammy leg and hadn't been fit to fight. Maybe the shop would no longer support both families. A lot of businesses had suffered because of the war and consequent lack of goods for sale, and . . . Ah, let's face it, Joss didn't want to go back to selling shoes. He didn't actually know what he wanted to do with himself, but he'd better think fast now. He had a family to support.

Out of the corner of his eye he saw the porter and guard loading two trunks into the luggage van. Mrs Schofield dropped some coins into their waiting hands and began walking briskly along the train. Joss had just opened the door to an empty compartment and on an impulse he gestured an invitation to his former travelling companion to join him again.

She hesitated then did so, murmuring a quiet thank you. Lovely voice she had, the northern accent he'd missed, but spoken in a low, musical tone. He hated shrill voices.

By the time he'd put their cases in the rack and sat down in the window seat opposite her, he was wondering what the hell had got into him today. 'I thought if we travelled together, I could help the guard unload your trunks at the other end. Unless Drayforth has changed greatly there won't be many porters around.'

'That's kind of you, but I'm sure I'll manage. There are usually lads with handcarts to be found near the station.'

'Then I'll find one for you while you keep an eye on your trunks.'

She looked at him in surprise, her cheeks flushing slightly. He remembered the smile that had lit up her face earlier and wished he could make her smile like that again.

'Thank you. Just demobbed, are you?'

'Yes.'

'I've been involved in war work, too. I'm going to miss it.'

'What were you doing?' He was curious now. She was about his own age, as far as he could judge, with a few grey threads in her dark hair at the temples. She didn't look like a Land Girl or a VAD, though.

She explained briefly about the Aides. 'It was such interesting work, different for everyone in the group. We went wherever we were needed. It felt good to be making a difference.'

'Your husband didn't mind?'

She looked down at her left hand, her face twisting with sorrow. 'Len was killed over a year ago.'

'I'm sorry. My wife died three months ago.'

'Influenza?'

'No, childbirth.'

'I'm sorry. And the baby?'

'It's alive.' He didn't elaborate and was relieved when she didn't pursue the subject. He heard her sigh softly as she stared out of the window, and now that he knew her situation, he could recognise a fellow sufferer, so said without thinking, 'You don't want to go back to Drayforth either, do you?'

'Does it show that plainly?'

He nodded. 'It does to me because I feel the same.'

'You're right. My father has a corner shop, but I'm not working there again, not now my mother's dead. He's not – efficient, so you can never improve things. With the way he works, it's a struggle just to keep the shop running. There must be something better to do with your life than that.'

'I'm the same. I feel as if I'll go mad stuck inside a shoe shop all day, measuring people's feet, bowing and scraping to the richer folk. I shouldn't complain, though. At least it's a job.'

She nodded. 'Ah, here we are at Drayforth.'

In the bustle of getting their suitcases out and making sure her trunks were unloaded, then finding a lad to wheel them home for her, Joss somehow forgot to find out where she lived. He didn't know why he wanted to, it was no business of his, but he did.

He watched her walk away down the street chatting to the lad and was reminded of nothing so much as a bright-eyed sparrow. He was sorry when she disappeared round the corner.

Well, he'd no doubt run into her again. This was a small town. Schofield would be her married name. He wondered what her maiden name had been. She didn't look familiar and there was something rather striking about her upright figure, for all her lack of height, that would make you remember her. He frowned again, remembering the route she'd taken. Surely a woman like that hadn't come from the Backhill Terraces?

Then it began to rain and he forgot about everything but getting to shelter. Picking up his bags, he hurried off to meet his family for the first time in over a year.

Hell of a way to start a new life, saddled with someone else's baby.

The lad stopped the handcart outside the little corner shop, sheltering in the lee of the house wall as he waited for further directions and his money. Ignoring the rain, Vi examined her old home with distaste. The shop looked worse than ever, the paint peeling and faded, the glass in the display window dirty and a few goods piled there haphazardly. You might not be able to get paint because of the war, but there was no excuse for a dirty window. That wouldn't tempt customers inside.

She'd have to spend a night or two here, she supposed, or her father would take a huff, but she didn't want to. She turned to the lad. 'Wait there. I'll just check that there's still a spare room for me.'

Inside she stared in surprise at the woman behind the counter, someone she didn't recognise and who clearly didn't know her. Where was Tess?

But the customer gave her a smiling nod. 'You're back, then, Vi.'

'Hello, Mrs Jones. It's been a while.'

'You look that smart. London clothes, those.' She turned to the other woman. 'This is Arnie's daughter Vi.'

The woman studied the newcomer, as if she wasn't happy to see her, then nodded. 'Welcome home.' She forced a smile but it didn't reach small eyes set deep in a plump face.

Vi looked at her, trying to remember who she was. The woman might have been pretty when she was younger, but she'd grown stout now and a dewlap of soft flesh filled the gap between her chin and neck. And her hair was definitely dyed red because the brown roots were showing. 'Do I know you? I thought Tess was working here.'

'It's for your Da to tell you.' Going to the door that led into the house, she yelled, 'Arnie! Get yourself out here. Your Vi's arrived.'

There was silence, then someone came slopping towards them in ill-fitting slippers. Oh, how clearly Vi remembered that sound! Her father leaned against the door frame, staring at her. He'd always been a big man, but now he was much thinner, his eyes sunken and his cheeks gaunt. He didn't say anything, but continued to eye her up and down.

She knew he would be calculating the cost of every item she was wearing. She was suddenly glad she'd put most of her money into the savings bank and for a moment wished she hadn't even come back. Which was silly. He was her father. This place was all the home she'd ever known.

She looked round. The shelves were half empty. Was he still stealing money from the till and going off drinking? Well, there'd be no one to stop him now that her mother was dead, would there?

During the war, her father had tried to cadge money off her when she went back – and had tried it on her husband too, she'd found out later. Only Len wasn't daft enough to give him anything.

'Still wearing them fancy clothes, I see,' Arnie said at last. 'What happened to the silver buttons? Did you sell 'em or did she take 'em back? They'd be worth a bit, them buttons.'

She couldn't help wincing as he coughed and hawked till he'd worked up a gob of phlegm and spat it on the floor. Her mother would never have let him get away with that. 'Lady Bingram gave the uniforms to us.' She touched the coat lovingly. 'There's years of wear in this yet, but the buttons weren't right for peacetime.'

'What happened to the job, then?'

'Now the soldiers are coming home and the influenza epidemic is passing, her ladyship's disbanding the Aides.'

'Good thing. Made you look down your nose at us, that did. Nor I don't like to see women doing men's jobs. It's not right.'

The woman cleared her throat and looked at him meaningfully.

His expression was suddenly guarded. 'This is Doris. Me an' her have got wed. You remember her from the Navigation?'

Vi froze. Now she knew who the woman was. Doris had been a barmaid and if rumour was correct, she'd not been averse to earning a little extra on the side after the pub closed. How could her father have married a woman like this, and so soon after her mother's death?

Doris smirked at her and linked her arm in Arnold's. 'Your poor

Da couldn't manage on his own with you off in London and your poor mother gone.'

'No, I suppose not. I – um – wish you both well.' This solved one problem at least. He wouldn't expect her to work in the shop now.

The lad poked his head through the door. 'What about these trunks, missus? D'you want them bringing inside or not?'

'You'll be stopping here, Vi?' Doris asked quickly. 'It'll allus be your home an' me bein' married to your Da won't change that.'

Vi couldn't see how to refuse the offer without giving offence and setting tongues wagging about her relations with his second wife. 'For a day or two, if that's convenient? Is there still a spare bedroom?'

'Yes. We had to sell the bed, but we can make you a shake-down on the floor. There's some clean sacks in the back.'

*Sell the bed?* He must be in trouble financially, then. Had her brother stopped keeping an eye on things after her mother died? Probably. Eric only did what he wanted to. 'Thanks. Just till I find myself somewhere to live. I don't want to be a nuisance. Is there room for my trunks in the storeroom, Dad? Or should we take them upstairs?'

Doris bustled forward, towering over Vi. 'Your Da's not been well. You an' me can manage if we help the lad. It'll be easiest to put the trunks in the storeroom, though. Them stairs are so narrow, they're a bugger to get stuff up.'

The three of them manhandled the trunks into the storeroom, which was half-empty, like the shop. From the speculative way her father had been eyeing them, she was glad she'd got strong padlocks for them. After she'd paid the lad, she followed Doris up the stairs into the back bedroom, which smelled stale, as if the window hadn't been opened for a long time. She looked round for a mattress and saw nothing, not even blankets. 'Maybe I should find a boarding house. I can't sleep on the bare boards.'

Doris scowled at her. 'It'll look bad, you not staying here.'

Vi stifled a sigh. A couple of nights on a hard floor wouldn't kill her. 'You said something about sacks. And I'll need blankets, too.'

'I've got a couple somewhere. An' there are some sacks in the storeroom. They're clean enough to lie on.'

Doris went and poked among the piles of rubbish at one side of the room, coming out triumphantly with two ragged blankets, which would probably be as dirty as the rest of the house. 'There y'are. You can fetch your own sacks. You'll know where Arnie keeps things. I heard the doorbell so I'd better get back to the shop.' Doris turned away, clearly at the end of her efforts as hostess.

Vi made sure her suitcase was locked then went downstairs again. Her father was sitting in the back room and there were voices in the shop. 'What happened to Tess?'

'Had to look after that husband of hers when he come back. He got gassed, poor sod. He's in a bad way. So I hired Doris.'

'Did you have to marry her as well?'

He scowled at her. 'A man has his needs, as you should know, you being a married woman now. Any road, it was a good thing I did wed her. Saves paying her any wages and she's a hard worker. But we need *you* to sort the place out for us, make it like it used to be. You allus was good at them fiddly details. You take after your mum there.' He avoided her eyes as he added, 'Things have got a bit run-down because I've not been myself lately, but I dare say you can lend us some money to buy new stock. We'll pay you back once we're on our feet again and of course I'll not charge you for the bedroom.'

Charge her for the bedroom, indeed, when all she had to lie on was sacks! 'I don't have any spare money.'

'You must have summat tucked away, unless you've changed, an' don't tell me different.'

'I've none to *spare*, though.' He'd never paid her back the other money he'd borrowed and she was sure he'd not even attempt to do so this time – if she was stupid enough to give him anything, which she wasn't.

He hawked up another gob of phlegm, saw her disapproving look and aimed it at the fire this time. 'We could get some fish and chips for tea, only I've no money. *Can't leave the till empty, can we?*'

'I'll buy tonight, my treat because I've come home.'

He brightened visibly. 'An' a jug o' beer?'

'No. I've no money to waste on booze, only enough to tide me over till I find another job. London's an expensive place to live.' She looked at the clock then at the window. 'I've got some blankets in my trunk. I'll get them out then, if the rain holds off, I'm going out for a bit of fresh air. I'll bring back some fish and chips later.'

She strolled up and down Halifax Road, the main street, which was lined with shops and other little businesses in the town centre. She crossed to the other side to pass the shoe shop because she didn't want Joss Bentley to think she was a nosey parker, but she couldn't help slowing down and staring across at it.

There weren't nearly as many shoes in the window and it wasn't as brightly lit as it used to be. But the glass was sparkling clean, at least.

Nearby were some of the best shops in town, an elegant frock salon, a milliner's, a bookshop – places patronised by the more affluent citizens. She'd never even gone into such shops before she became an Aide, but was used to them now, especially book shops. Len had taught her to love reading.

The short winter's day was closing in fast and a bent old man hobbled along turning up the gas in the street lamps, moving slowly from one to the other with his pole. She'd watched him sometimes as a child and stood watching him again now. He didn't seem to have aged at all, had always been ancient in her eyes.

She carried on to the very end of the main street and then strolled back, meeting a couple of people she knew and stopping to chat. As she passed the station again, a train arrived and she was enveloped in a cloud of steam. Nothing was quite the same as the steam from a locomotive. It had a sweet, stale smell to it and seemed to cling to the buildings for a minute or two before dissipating slowly.

Then she realised she'd been standing there for a while and was thoroughly chilled, so turned and started walking slowly back.

She didn't want to return to the shop, but had no choice, for tonight at least.

She stopped at the chippie's to buy three portions of cod and chips. The owners greeted her cheerfully by name, as if they really were glad to see her, not just eager to take her money, and one of the customers asked her about London, which he had once visited.

When she got home, Vi saw that her father had found the money to buy some beer. The jug was half empty already and both he and Doris had glasses raised to their lips as she walked in. They looked at her bundle expectantly as she set the newspaper-wrapped packages on the table. The food smelled good. She was hungry now herself.

She went to fetch three plates since the others hadn't stirred. But before she could take the plates off the dresser, Arnie and Doris tore open their newspaper wrappings and fell on the food as if they hadn't eaten for days. She brought back one plate for herself, trying not to watch them as they stuffed the hot chips into their mouths and broke off bits of battered fish. Both of them gobbled the food so rapidly they made gulping noises, like dogs afraid someone would pinch the food from them.

That hadn't been unknown in her childhood because her father hadn't been averse to nipping a bit off his children's plates when their mother wasn't watching. Till Eric grew big enough to stop him, that was.

When someone came into the shop and needed serving, Doris cursed under her breath and rolled up her package, taking it with her. Vi hid a smile. The new Mrs Gill had already learned to protect her food.

Arnie didn't speak, just carried on chomping, and she couldn't think of anything to say either. Home! she thought bitterly. It was no home to her without her mum and she wasn't staying here for more than one night. Tomorrow she'd find herself some respectable lodgings then catch up with her sister and brother. Tonight she was too tired to go out again.

She would still look for work in Drayforth, though, because

she wanted to be near her sister's children. 'What's our Eric doing these days?'

'Still working for the rent man, doing a bit of this and that. It must pay well, because he's never short of a bob or two.' The scowl came back to her father's face. 'Though he doesn't share his good fortune with his family, the miserable sod.'

'Is Mungo Sully still Mr Kirby's rent man?'

'Yes, and he does other things for Mr Kirby too, leaves a lot of the collecting to our Eric. Done all right for hissen, Sully has, made a fortune out of the black market during the war. We was at school together, him an' me, but I got married young. *He* waited to get wed, an' he lives in a big house now down the eastern end of town. Wish I'd waited to marry.' He sighed.

It was an old complaint and she ignored it. 'Where's our Eric living?'

Doris, who had just returned from the shop, answered. 'Mayfield Place. Has his own house, four rooms, though what he needs that many for, a single man like him, I don't know.'

'And how's our Beryl?'

Her father shrugged. 'Haven't seen her for a while.'

'You haven't fallen out with her again?'

'Nothing to fall out with. She moved to Rochdale a few weeks before your mum died. Haven't seen her since. You'd think she'd have come back for the funeral and to visit sometimes, wouldn't you? But not bloody Beryl. Thinks she's better than me an' Doris, she does. She's turned into a right old tight-arse.'

Which meant Beryl had refused to lend him any money and didn't approve of his marriage. But why hadn't her sister let her know about the move? 'You said one of her children had died of the influenza?'

He nodded, mouth too full to speak.

'Which one.'

'Don't know.'

Beryl only had three children, you'd think he could remember something like losing one of them. 'Do you have her address?'

He shook his head.

'You must have.'

'Well, I bloody don't. She and that husband of hers are a right uppity pair. Never even said goodbye to me, they didn't, just moved away. I only heard about it at the pub, though I reckon your mother knew what was planned. I thought she'd have told you, but she must have died before she got round to it. It wasn't long after.'

Disappointment flooded through Vi, but she tried not to let it show. Perhaps Eric would know where Beryl lived. If not, someone else was bound to know. Her sister had a lot of friends.

It had been a long day and Vi was tired, so she cleared up then went to find the sacks and make up a bed. The other two began arguing about whether there was enough money for another jug of beer. To her credit, it was Doris who kept protesting at Arnie's desire to take more out of the drawer in the shop that they called 'the till'.

After a few minutes the discussion below erupted into a full-scale row, with things being thrown and much yelling. From the sounds of it, Doris had won and no more beer was bought.

It wasn't until the shop closed at ten-thirty that Vi was able to get to sleep, because the doorbell kept tinkling and the door banging shut.

What a homecoming!

As he walked from the station, Joss stopped for a moment opposite Bentley's Fine Footwear to study its familiar façade. His parents lived over the shop still, as they had done for most of their married life, as he had until he'd married. He'd be staying with them until he got his old home ready to live in again.

There was a housing shortage now, it seemed, so after Ada's death, Joss had continued to pay the rent on his old home. Most of his furniture was still there, but he'd have to get the children's beds back from his mother-in-law's before he could move them in with him. He was looking forward to seeing Roy and Iris again. He'd missed so much of their childhood.

In spite of the cold rain trickling down his neck, he stood for a little longer before going inside. It wasn't going to be easy, keeping his feelings about the baby from his mother.

The same old bell jangled on the end of its spring as he pushed the door open and his brother looked up from behind the counter, his polite smile changing to a beam of pleasure.

'Joss! Good to see you back, lad.' Wilf hurried across to shake hands with him and clap him on the back. 'You look tired.'

'Been a long day. Are Mum and Dad upstairs?'

'Yes. I'd better warn you, though: Dad's not very well still, but I'm managing all right without him.' He sighed. 'It's been hard to get stock and people are making do, so business isn't brisk. Let's hope that changes now the war's over.'

He seemed on the defensive and Joss suddenly realised why. Wilf had always been a delicate lad with a weedy physique and one leg shorter than the other. That was more or less corrected by one built-up shoe, but of course, he hadn't passed his medical. Wilf had stepped in to help their father in the shop after Joss volunteered but now his job was at risk. Their dad had always insisted the shop would go to Joss one day, as eldest, because it made no sense splitting up a business that could only support a limited number of people.

Joss didn't want to put his brother out of a job, but they might have to work out some sort of compromise if he couldn't find any other way of earning a living.

'I'll go up and see them.' He hefted his kitbag on to his shoulder again, picked up the suitcase and pushed through the familiar green plush curtains into the storeroom at the rear. The curtains had faded and were sagging at one side, but the room behind was arranged exactly as it had been when he left Drayforth, with the small wooden stepladder neatly tucked away on the right. Each time he'd come back there had been fewer shoe boxes on the ceiling-high shelves and now the stock only reached halfway up. Boxes would have been overflowing on to the floor before the war.

He looked to the left at the small workshop set up in an alcove, where his father did minor repairs, smiling wryly to see the tools laid out with a rigid precision which would have delighted Sarge, another stickler for keeping your belongings in order. The tools looked a bit dusty. How long was it since they'd been used?

Walking slowly up the stairs he called, 'It's me, Joss.'

There was an exclamation, running footsteps and his mother flung open the door so hard it bounced back against the wall. 'Oh, Joss love, you're back. You're really back.' She dissolved into tears.

He tried to give her a quick hug but she clung to him, murmuring his name over and over as she sobbed against his chest. 'What's all this?' he asked after a while, holding her at arm's length. 'You'll make me think you're sorry to see me if you don't stop crying.'

'I'm just so *glad* to have you back.' She patted his cheek. 'You look big and strong. Oh, I'm that happy!' She cried some more to prove her point.

A hacking cough from the nearby bedroom jerked her out of her weeping. 'Look at me, being silly like this. Your father's had the influenza, as I wrote and told you. It's left him with such a bad chest he can hardly breathe, and he gets dizzy if he walks around.' She lowered her voice as she added, 'He doesn't seem to be getting any better, though I've tried everything I know, and so has the doctor. Come and say hello to him, but you're not to go into the bedroom. I don't want you catching anything. That dreadful 'flu isn't over yet, you know. I heard about a new case in the Terraces only yesterday.'

So Joss stood in the doorway and exchanged a few words with his father, who could hardly speak without spluttering and wheezing.

'You'll stay here with us for a day or two, won't you, Joss love?' she asked as they left his father and went to sit in the living room. 'There's no food in your house and you'll have to make arrangements for the baby before you can move the children back in.'

He didn't want to think about the baby. 'How are Roy and Iris?'

'They're well. Staying with Ada's mother, as I wrote to tell you.

I had to ask Mrs Tomlinson if she could take them when your father fell ill – which she did, thank goodness.'

He hated to be obliged to his mother-in-law, who always tried to undermine his authority with the children, but he'd had no choice.

'You'll want to go and see the baby straight away, won't you, Joss? Eeh, to think you've never even seen your own daughter. She's such a bonny little thing, but Mrs Tomlinson said she was too old to look after a baby, so she wouldn't take her. She refuses even to touch poor Nora. Our Pam's got her hands full with her own family and anyway, she's due in a few weeks, so you'll *have* to make other arrangements for the baby quickly.'

She looked at him anxiously. 'Our Pam had her christened Nora – it was the name Ada chose – and it's too late to change it now, because that's how she was registered. I do hope you don't dislike that name, only my letter asking you about it must have gone astray because I never got a reply.'

The letter had arrived and Joss hadn't known how to reply, but he felt guilty now about leaving everything to his family.

'Listen to me, running on like this. Would you like a cup of tea first, Joss love, or do you want to go straight round to our Pam's?'

'Cup of tea, please. I'm parched.'

She looked sideways at him, a frown creasing her forehead. 'Nora's a lovely baby. You mustn't blame her for Ada's death like Mrs Tomlinson does. It was God's will.'

And was it God's will, he wondered, that he should be lumbered with someone else's offspring? If so, he knew what he thought of that sort of a god. 'Yes, I know. Now, are you going to put that kettle on or must I die of thirst?'

'Get on with you! Go and put your things in your old bedroom.' She gave him a mock slap on the arm and bustled through to the kitchen at the rear.

She'd already picked up on his reluctance to see the baby. He'd known she would, but he couldn't bear to reveal the truth to her – or to any of his family.

He went into the bedroom that had been his when he was a

lad. It hadn't changed at all and he would only just fit into the narrow bed now, but he'd slept in far worse places in France. He wondered if the two little attic rooms where his brother and sister had slept were still the same as well. They'd had a happy home here, in spite of having to keep quiet because of the shop beneath. This place was far more home to him still than the house he'd shared with Ada.

He'd made a serious mistake when he married her, the worst one of his whole life, and lived to regret it, by hell he had.

How he was to get himself out of the present mess, he didn't know.

# 8

Gerald Kirby drew in a deep breath to control his annoyance that his car wasn't waiting for him at the station. It was too far to walk home as well as being undignified, so he paced to and fro outside the entrance, glancing alternately at his pocket watch and the station clock with increasing impatience.

Just as he was wondering whether to see if there was a cab available, the car drew up before the station. His elderly chauffeur got out and hurried round to open the door for him. 'Sorry I couldn't get here on time, sir. The mistress was a bit late getting back from her tea party.'

Gerald nodded, biting back the sharp words he'd been about to utter. He might have known it was Maud's fault. Nothing would persuade her that the car was not for her use alone. The shortage of petrol because of the war had made him insist they could share a vehicle, so hers had been put into storage until the hostilities ended. A man like him, a Town Councillor who planned one day to become Mayor, needed to set an example to the citizens of Drayforth, so he hadn't got her car out of storage yet – but he would. In fact, he'd do it tomorrow. Hang appearances, he wanted his own car and chauffeur.

He leaned back against the tan leather upholstery as the shops gave way to terraced houses, each dwelling a step up from the one below on the steeper streets. Then they came to single dwellings with gardens and here the streets were wider, though still leading upwards. This end of town, the eastern side, was where the better sort of folk lived, and his residence was in the best part of it all, partway up the ridge.

As he looked up at the old mansion that stood sentinel on the very top of the ridge, well above his own, he felt a familiar twitch of irritation. No matter what inducements he'd offered, the Warburtons had refused to sell Fairview to him. They were as poor as church mice now, but clung to that house of theirs and would not be shaken loose, damn them. Well, it was no use forcing them out until the wartime shortages of building materials had eased and it was possible to build again.

When he got his hands on it, he'd knock the shabby old place down and build a large home – no, a *mansion* – that would astonish everyone with its luxury and modern amenities. He had no son, so he might as well enjoy the money he'd made.

There were signs of life returning to normal in the town. Why, only today he'd spotted Joss Bentley at the station in Manchester, no longer in uniform. Gerald never knew how to take Bentley, who had always been polite enough when serving in the shop, but with a faint hint of something behind that politeness that suggested the fellow didn't respect his betters as he should.

The new Mayor had the same faintly insolent edge to him these days. Palmer had been quiet before, not seeming the sort to make big changes or go against an important member of the Council's wishes. Gerald had been too busy making extra money out of the war to stand for mayor himself, so had supported the other man on the principle that it'd be easy to displace a nobody afterwards. He'd made a mistake there. It turned out Palmer had a passion for slum clearance, a passion he'd concealed before. At the Mayor's urging, the Council was about to appoint professional Health Visitors instead of the benevolent ladies they'd used before. Of all the stupid wastes of ratepayers' money!

The poor didn't want people poking about in their houses and lives and, more importantly, nor did their landlords. It was a waste of money to put better sewage systems into old properties that would eventually be knocked down, anyone with half an ounce of money sense knew that.

Well, Gerald would withdraw his support for Palmer at the next Council election and stand for Mayor himself. There were a lot of hidden powers in that position, and after all he'd done for this town, he deserved something in return.

The car drew up and he waited for the door to be opened before getting out, then made his way inside the house in a leisurely manner. It was, he felt, the mark of a gentleman not to seem in a hurry. He might not have been born a gentleman, but he'd made himself into one in every way that counted.

Maud was in the small sitting room at the rear, staring into space. She started as he rapped on the half-open door to gain her attention. 'Oh, Gerald, you're back. I didn't realise it was so late.'

'How did it go?'

'Not as you wanted. The Healeys would love to come to dinner, but her cousins have a prior engagement.'

'That's the third time Miss Warburton and her fool of a sister have refused to come here.'

'Yes. I'm sorry. If it's any consolation, they've not dined anywhere else, either. There's nothing else I can do, I'm afraid. It'd look bad to court another refusal. And now we're committed to entertaining the Healeys again.'

He bit back an angry comment. It wasn't Maud's fault that the Warburtons would have nothing to do with him socially, which might have been a way to *persuade* them to sell their house to him, but he'd hoped for more from her. He'd courted and married her because of her connections, such as the Healeys, who had never interacted with him socially before his marriage. But marrying Maud hadn't really got him into the top circles in this part of Lancashire. He summoned up a smile. 'Can't be helped. Fix it up with two other couples, will you? Let me know what Cook wants bought in and I'll arrange it.'

'All right.'

'I'll go and change for dinner.'

'I'll join you in a minute, just want to finish this letter.'

As he went upstairs he frowned. He wished he could tell what Maud was thinking. She didn't seem upset when he got angry with her, didn't seem to care whether he complimented her or not, and was cold and unresponsive in bed. He sometimes felt like slapping the arrogant look off her elegant, narrow face. Not that he would. He wasn't a wife beater, or a beater of any woman, come to that.

When she came up to their bedroom to change, he asked bluntly, 'Why did you marry me, Maud?'

'I was tired of being poor.' She laughed suddenly. 'You didn't think I believed all that talk about you loving me, did you? You're not the sort to fall in love. It was a marriage of convenience for both of us.'

'You seemed to believe it at the time.'

'It seemed to suit you better to pretend in public, but I didn't think you'd want to keep up that pretence in private.' As she went towards her dressing room to change, she turned. 'I do try to do what you want, Gerald, but your ownership of slum properties rather sticks in people's gullets. Can't you sell them and put your money into something more respectable? It'd make things a lot easier with my family and friends.'

'Why should I sell them? It's those slum properties which bring in the best profits.'

'How much money do you need, Gerald? You're the richest man in town already. I'd hoped we'd be able to travel after the war, go down to London occasionally, enjoy ourselves.'

'There's nothing that interests me in London and if, by travel, you mean go abroad, I've told you before, I'm not interested in that. I'm English and proud of it.'

He went into his own dressing room and began to change, muttering as he hurled his clothes into a corner. He would see if Sully had any ides about how to get the Warburtons to sell Fairview. Sully was very good at forcing people to do what he wanted.

Gerald felt a pang of guilt at that thought. Sully's ways were a bit rough sometimes and the two Warburton sisters were in their sixties. But he wanted that house. He'd tell Sully not to hurt them, just . . . find a way to persuade them.

* * *

The morning after her return to Drayforth, Vi got up early after a poor night's sleep. She'd found the floor uncomfortable, in spite of the pile of sacks. It was a good job she'd had her own blankets so at least she'd been warm enough. She'd brought up a bucket of water the previous evening and washed in it quickly, shivering. No heated water here. No proper lavatories, either, just a privy out at the end of the back yard.

Once her ablutions were finished she locked her suitcase carefully and went down to sort out something to eat. Because the kitchen was so dirty and cluttered, she automatically began to clear it up. She was a fool to do this and no one would thank her for it, but she simply couldn't bring herself to eat from dirty dishes.

When the table top and crockery were clean, she let herself out of the shop door, hoping the tinkle of the bell wouldn't wake the others, and went to the nearest baker's. It was still dark, but the shop was brightly lit and the air was full of the wonderful smell of new-baked bread. A woman came hurrying out with two loaves under her arm, so the first batch must be ready. Vi bought two loaves then was tempted by a currant teacake, biting into the flat round roll hungrily as she walked home. Nothing tasted as good as bread fresh from the oven

Her father's shop was still dark, showing the world that it wasn't yet open, but in the kitchen she found Doris sitting by the fire, yawning and scratching her head. Her stepmother's eyes brightened at the sight of the bread.

Vi put one loaf into the bread bin, which had been empty of all but mouldy crumbs before she'd cleaned it, and set the other on the bread board. 'Do we have any butter?'

'There's some in the shop. Help yourself.'

'Don't you pay for what you take from in there?'

Doris shrugged. 'Why should we? It's ours, isn't it?'

'No, it isn't. It's part of the business and if you don't pay for what you use, the stock will run down then you'll have no money left in the till to buy new stock.'

'*He* allus says to take what I want.'

'My mum used to stop him doing that. You pay yourself a wage from the profit the shop is making then you pay into the till for everything you use.'

Doris stared at her, a frown creasing her brow.

'If you want the business to fail, you're going the right way about it, leaving it in Dad's hands. He can never see beyond the end of his nose, so it's up to you to make a stand.'

There was a moment's silence, then the other woman smiled. 'No, it isn't. You're back now. You've run things before and you'll be able to do it again. But I will do as you say, I promise. I don't want the shop to fail.'

'I'm not working in it again. I'll be starting to look for a job and lodgings this very day.'

'Arnie's got his heart set on you working in the shop. He says you'll put some money in and it'll be like old times, all the shelves full. You don't look as if you're short of a bob or two, either. Them clothes of yours must have cost a fortune. Lovely coat, that is.'

'Well, my father won't get me back into the shop, whatever he does.' Vi went to get some butter and weigh it, then found a jar of jam, paying for them both before returning to the kitchen. 'We'd better eat while we can. They'll be coming into the shop soon, whether it's lit up or not.' She got on with her breakfast, eating the rest of the teacake properly off a plate. Shc noticed Doris hesitate, then get herself a plate. There was no sign of her father.

Vi nodded towards the bread. 'We used to have an arrangement to buy the broken bread and misshapes to sell in our shop. If you make an extra penny here and a penny there, it soon mounts up. You should dress more smartly and go and see if you can come to an agreement with the baker to take his leftovers again. But you'll have to pay cash for them. And it's no use sending Dad to make the arrangements. He only puts people's backs up.'

Doris chewed slowly, her forehead creased in thought. 'Why are you telling me all this? What's it to you if you're not staying?'

'I don't want the shop to fail. Mum was so proud of having built it up.'

'People speak well of her, still. She must have been a nice person.'

Vi's voice was thick with tears as she answered. 'She was. It was for her I stayed here so long, not for him.'

Doris looked at her sharply, but didn't comment.

At nine o'clock sharp Vi was ready to leave. Customers had been popping in for bits of this and that for 'the mester's breakfast' since seven o'clock, because the main breadwinner always got special treatment. Few of the women round here bought for more than the next meal, so it was always a slice of this and an ounce of that. She listened to Doris chatting to them and waited for a quiet moment to go out through the shop.

At the door she hesitated, wondering whether to interfere again, but she'd not feel right if she didn't do her best. She'd been surprised and pleased by how well her stepmother dealt with the customers, who clearly felt comfortable with her. 'You can't afford to give any more credit, Doris.'

'But they'll go to Denton's if we don't.'

'Let them. Let *him* run up bad debts. You can't afford to. Some of those women never pay up. My mum wouldn't give them even sixpence credit.' Vi looked round at the half-empty shelves. 'These should be full of goods for sale. And I bet you owe money to the suppliers.'

Doris nodded. 'Your Dad says it's your fault and you should have stayed with your family, not gone down to London.'

'If I had, he'd not have married you.' She let that sink in then said persuasively, 'This is your chance now, this shop, isn't it?' A nod proved her guess right. 'If you leave him to his old ways, Dad will lose it and then what will you live on? I'm surprised he's kept it so long.'

'I had a bit saved.' Doris was scowling now, so Vi left it at that. That explained the marriage, she thought, not only for the comfort in bed and the worker in the shop, but for the money. She wondered if her stepmother would take any of her advice or whether it was a waste of breath.

Well, she wanted to see her friend now. On the way there she bought another loaf and took it with her. Tess must be having a hard time managing without the job in the shop, especially if Joe was unable to work and there were children to feed. But perhaps he'd have a pension, if he'd been gassed.

Tess wasn't in her old house, but the new tenant was able to tell her where they were living now, so Vi went round to Lilybank Court, the most misnamed street in town, in her opinion. Things must be worse than she'd expected for the Donovans to have moved here. She looked in disgust at the stinking privy she had to pass to go through to the far end of the yard. You could tell it was one of Kirby's properties. He didn't care for anything but the money he could make from his rents.

There was a crying child inside the end house and she could hear Tess screaming, 'Be quiet! Be quiet!' in a voice shrill with desperation. The child continued to wail, but more softly now.

Vi knocked on the door and it was wrenched open.

'What do—? Oh, it's you, love. I'm – er – a bit busy just now.' Tess tried to bar the way.

'Let me come in and help you, then.' She watched her friend's shoulders slump and then Tess moved aside and she followed her inside.

'There's only the one room.'

Vi nodded. The place was clean, for Lilybank Court, but had hardly any furniture. There was a straw mattress on the floor in one corner and Joe was lying on it, his face white and bleached looking. He turned away towards the wall as she came in, but not before she'd seen the mortification on his face.

Tess looked at her for a minute, her lips trembling, then plumped down at the table and burst into tears. Two little girls were huddled in a corner, the bigger one with her arms round the smaller one.

As Vi put the loaf on the table the children stared at the food and she saw them lick their lips. No need to tell her they were hungry, they had the drawn, famine look on their faces. It wouldn't hurt them to wait a few minutes longer, though, so she went to put her arms round her friend, holding her till the tears stopped.

'Look what we've come to,' Tess hiccupped. 'I'm shamed for you to see us like this, Vi love, proper shamed I am.'

'I don't understand. Surely Joe gets a pension because of being gassed.'

Tess shook her head. 'The Pensions Board wouldn't give him one, on account of he had bronchitis and asthma before he signed up. They said he's no worse off now than if he hadn't been gassed, and it isn't true. And they s-said he could work if he wants to. He can't, he can hardly move a step without getting out of breath.'

Vi was stunned. She'd heard of cases where Pensions Boards had tried to cheat men out of their rights, but hadn't expected to find that here in Drayforth, especially with such an obvious case. 'Oh, Tess, love, I'm so sorry.'

'We've had to get help from the Panel and you know what they're like, won't give you anything until you've sold all you can. Joe could hardly walk but they still made him go before them. I had to nearly carry him into town but they treated him like he was just pretending to be ill. They sent him to the doctor but *he* said Joe would never work again, so then we had to go back before the Panel and answer more questions about what we owned. And then that Mrs Gilson come round to check that I was telling the truth, the old bitch. She even made me sell Mam's teapot. I pawned it instead, but I'll never be able to get it back, now.'

Tess dashed away more tears. 'And even then, they don't give you enough to live on. They said I could find charring work to help out. How can I? I've Joe to look after and the children too since my mam died. Spanish 'flu, it was, like your mother. I did what I could but she went that quickly. Eh, I miss her. It's not fair, is it?'

'No, it isn't. But maybe now I'm back, I can help.' Vi hugged her again.

Tess looked at her bleakly. 'How? My Joe can hardly catch his breath. *He* can't look after the childer an' I won't leave the little 'uns on their own. We'll all end up being sent to the poorhouse, at this rate. It's what Mrs Gilson said would happen if we didn't pull our socks up.'

Vi saw the two children still staring at the bread. 'I've brought you a loaf for today, so you can feed the children. Give me a few minutes and I'll fetch you something to put on it.'

'I can't take—'

'Of course you can. How many times did you help me when Mum was ill before the war? And then you helped in the shop so that I could go to London. I was so grateful for that.'

Tess swallowed hard. 'Well . . . just this once, then. And no need to waste your money on stuff to put on the bread. It's enough to have the loaf. It'll be a godsend because the food vouchers never last the week and the grocer I have to buy from with the vouchers allus gives short weight.'

Vi didn't comment. She knew how much the poor hated going asking for charity and how the grocer who was well in with the Panel, cheated those obliged to use his services with their vouchers. 'Look, you cut some slices of bread and I'll just nip out for a few bits and pieces. How's your Harry?'

Tess smiled proudly. 'He's eleven now and I don't know what I'd have done without him. He's out at the moment, trying to earn a penny or two.'

'Shouldn't he be at school?'

'He's not fit to be seen there. We've pawned or sold everything decent we had to wear. Mrs Gilson went through our things and wouldn't give us any money until we'd sold everything she told us to. Harry's new shoes, and mine too, that I was keeping for when these wore out.' A sob escaped her and she gulped for control.

'Oh, Tess.' Vi gave her another hug then went out, feeling furious. It was a crying shame the way the poor were treated by some people, as if they'd committed a crime by falling ill. Mrs Gilson was notorious for it. And Joe had lost his health in the service of his country, so surely he deserved better than this?

She hurried along the street, then changed her mind and went back to her father's shop. 'I'm buying some things for a friend,' she announced to Doris. 'So I might as well spend her money here, eh? I forgot to bring the shopping bag. Can you lend me one?'

Doris's face brightened. 'You can borrow mine.'

When Vi took the food to Tess, including some ham, her friend wept again. Joe was still pretending to be asleep, though Vi saw him watching her through half-closed eyes when he thought she wasn't looking. There was a bitter twist to his mouth that had never been there before and his breathing was a faint rasping sound in the background.

She was glad to get out of the court and into the street after the stale room which stank of that filthy, overflowing privy. Landlords who let things get this bad should be shot, she thought angrily. And so should the people on the Pensions Board and the Panel. Same people, really, Mrs Gilson and her cronies.

Vi's next stop was the library, where she intended to read the local newspaper, which was published twice a week. She could easily have afforded to buy one, but rain was threatening and if she read the paper in the library, she could avoid going back to her father's for a while. The first thing to do was to find lodgings, then she'd look for a job.

She could also glance through a few back copies to get some idea of what had been happening here. Yes, the *Chronicle* would be the best place to start, she was sure.

She only hoped she'd find herself a job quickly. Without that, she didn't know what she would do.

Joss had noticed how little food there was in the pantry, so ate sparingly at breakfast. 'I feel like a bit of fresh air,' he said, trying to sound casual. 'Do you want me to get you anything at the shops, Mum?'

His mother looked at him and blushed scarlet. 'I— let me find my purse.'

'I thought we had accounts for groceries.'

'I f-found it better to pay cash.'

She had never been able to lie easily. He put his arm round her shoulders and guided her back to sit at the kitchen table. 'Tell me what's wrong. Tell me everything.'

So she stumbled through a tale of difficulties in buying stocks of shoes, customers away at the war, others not buying new shoes unless they had to, and finally, in a low voice, with many glances over her shoulder, 'And your father hasn't been himself. He's been weak and ill for two months now. I'm so worried about him. The influenza nearly killed him and since then he just lies there, staring into space. It's as if he's lost heart, doesn't want to get better. And . . . we had to let Mrs Beale go, so I have to do the cleaning and washing myself. I'm sorry I couldn't take the children for you, but you see . . . I've as much as I can manage here.'

'I can see that. I'll go and visit Roy and Iris this morning and—'

'It's Tuesday. They'll be at school. You'll need to go and see them later this afternoon. You could walk home from school with them. It's such a long walk back at dinnertime it'd be no use going then. They've barely time to gobble down their food, but Mrs Tomlinson won't let them take sandwiches, I don't know why, or even let them come here for their dinners. I could manage that, at least. She doesn't like me to go and visit them very often, either. Says it unsettles them.'

'All right. I'll visit them later.'

'But you could go and see little Nora this morning, talk to Pam, make plans. You should have gone last night, really, but your father did enjoy your company. He brightened up quite a bit. I'm sure your sister will help you find someone to look after Nora while you're at work.'

He bit back a protest. He didn't want to see the baby, didn't want to at all, but it had to be done. 'All right. And on the way back, I'll do your shopping.'

'I'll get you some money.'

'I'll buy the things today. After all, I'm staying here for the present, so it's only fair that I pay for my keep.' He could see the relief on her face.

He stopped on the way out to talk to his brother about the shop. When he learned how little Wilf was taking as wages each week, he was horrified. 'You should get more than that.'

'There isn't any more. If Dad could still do the small repairs, it'd help a bit, but he can't.'

Joss hesitated. 'I don't want to come back here to work, Wilf. I'll look for a job and you can stay and—'

'There are a lot of men coming back from the Army, Joss. And there aren't a lot of jobs in Drayforth. Besides, what else are you trained for?'

'I'll find something, I'm sure.'

Wilf didn't argue but from his expression, Joss could see he wasn't optimistic.

This wasn't the homecoming he'd expected. He'd thought at least his parents and Wilf would be all right, whatever his own problems. Now that he could see how hard a time they were having, he didn't see how he could take Wilf's job away from him.

And then there was his promise to Captain Warburton to keep an eye on his sisters. Joss wasn't sure what he could do about that, but felt he had to try. You didn't break a promise to a dead comrade.

The library wasn't as warm as Vi had expected but she wrapped her scarf more tightly round her neck and went to find the latest copy of the *Chronicle*, sitting down to read it from cover to cover. In London she'd had time to learn how interesting newspapers could be, had relished the quiet hours of reading about the world she'd been cut off from for most of her life, stuck in that little shop, busy from early morning to late at night, serving an ounce of this, two ounces of that, a quarter pound of margarine – or butter for the ones who could afford it.

She pushed those memories aside and studied the advertisements, because she was determined to find some decent lodgings. Only three were on offer. She pulled out her little notebook, looking at it fondly because it brought back memories of her work with the Major. He'd teased her about it often, but it had been an invaluable tool to make sure she didn't forget anything, either the jobs he wanted her to do or questions she needed to ask him. So many questions in the early days, but he hadn't minded, said it was the sign of a conscientious worker.

She noted down the addresses quickly, using the propelling pencil they'd given her as a farewell present. It was an extravagance, really, a fancy pencil like this, but it was engraved with her name and she'd always keep it as a reminder of happier days. She shook her head over that thought. Happier days! What a way to think about the war.

Next she turned to the front page, which contained an interview with the Mayor, Mr Albert Palmer. She stared at the name in surprise. How had he got the mayor's job? She remembered him as a quiet-spoken man who owned a small workshop and employed a couple of other men and a group of women to make slippers. She knew from gossip in the shop that he'd helped others when they were in trouble, really helped them, not like Mrs Gilson's interference and bullying. People in the Backhill Terraces would run a mile to avoid her but they thought the world of Mr Palmer.

Surely he hadn't turned into the sort of man who stood for the Town Council and used it to further his own interests?

She'd intended to skim through the article but when the words 'Health Visitors' caught her eye, she settled down to read it carefully, then took out the notebook again. They wanted a Senior Health Visitor and two Health Visitors. Maybe here was a chance for her. Would Mrs Gilson be applying for the senior job? She didn't need the money, surely, but if she didn't get the job, she'd lose control of the charity work she'd been dominating for years.

And if Mrs Gilson got the job, would the woman who struck such fear into poor Tess and others like her even consider employing someone from Backhill Terraces? Vi stared at the article. Well, you didn't get jobs unless you applied. They could only say no, after all.

She'd not do anything until she'd gathered all the facts, though.

It never paid to rush in. She'd go to church on Sunday and see what information she could pick up there. She smiled at the thought. She'd been brought up a Methodist, her mother's choice not her father's because he never attended church. But she'd grown used to the Church of England in London, enjoying its rituals more than those at the little Methodist chapel in Drayforth. The Church of England had been Len's church, so she'd kept going there after he died. It had made her feel closer to him as she struggled to cope with her grief.

She glanced at the clock, put the notebook away and set off to look for lodgings. First things first, no use dwelling on sad things.

# 9

Joss walked slowly round to his sister's house, knocking on the door with a leaden feeling in his chest.

Pam was holding the baby against her shoulder as she opened the door. She gave him an awkward, one-armed hug then stepped back. Her faded print pinafore was stretched tightly across her belly and she looked tired.

'Come in, Joss love. You're looking well.' She led the way into the kitchen at the back and as the baby started grizzling, rocked her, murmuring 'Come on, Nora love, this is no way to greet your father.'

He held back, trying not to look at the baby. He didn't even want to touch it.

The door knocker sounded again. 'Just hold her a minute!' Pam thrust the baby into his arms and went to answer it.

There was no excuse now for not looking at the infant squirming against his chest. She smiled up at him, her eyes bright blue and guileless in a rosy face. Suddenly she had a look of Ada, not the woman he had lived with but the one he had courted, had fun with, thought he loved. Which just went to show how misleading appearances could be. He tried to ignore the smile, focusing on the fact that another man had fathered her.

But he couldn't, because not only was Nora continuing to smile, she was waving her arms wildly and panting in excitement, as if delighted to be in his arms.

'There, I knew she'd take to you,' Pam said from behind him. 'You always were good with children. It was only the woman next door wanting to borrow a cup of sugar. I told her I had none to spare, which is true. I shall be glad when we can buy as much as we want again. Sit down, love, and I'll make you a cup of tea.'

So he sat, feeling stiff, wanting to hand the baby back but not knowing what excuse to give for that. He concentrated on his sister, watching her boil the kettle and pour it into the pot – but he was still conscious of the infant in his arms. He saw Pam rub her back as she waited for the tea to brew.

'So, when's your own baby due?' he asked.

She looked down at herself with a smile. 'I've another month yet and it can't pass too quickly for me. I'm not having another and so I've told Michael. He can like that or lump it.' She lifted the teapot lid and stirred the liquid round then looked at him apologetically. 'That's why I had to get you home. I'm sorry to push you so hard, Joss, but I need you to take this young miss off my hands as soon as you can make arrangements. I can't cope with two babies, not the way I'm feeling. I'm tired all the time now.'

'Fair enough.'

'I've got the names of a couple of women who would look after Nora for you during the daytime and another who'll clean the house for you from time to time, only I don't know how you're going to afford them all. Unless business picks up at the shop, you won't be able to take anything like the wages you had before the war. Our Wilf's struggling to live on what's left after he gives something to Mum. Poor lad. I don't know where he's going to find another job when you take over again.'

He saw tears in her eyes. 'Don't worry about us, love. You've enough on your plate.'

'How can I help worrying? You're my brothers. You've lost your wife and Wilf's about to lose his job.' She rubbed the moisture from her eyes, then eased her back again.

'I'm going to try to find myself another sort of job, Pam. I don't want to go back into the shop, so maybe Wilf will still be able to go on working there.'

She looked at him in surprise. 'But Dad's always said the shop was to go to you because you're the eldest. You worked in it before the war.'

'Well, I knew no better then. Going away's changed a lot of things for me. I liked being in charge of things, organising people. I was good at it too.'

'But you lost your stripes.'

'Yes. Through my own stupidity. I learned a hard lesson from that. I'd not let anyone make me so angry another time.' He stared into the distance, putting his thoughts into words for the first time. 'I don't think I could bear to spend the rest of my life shut up with a pile of shoes, not after what I've seen.'

'You'll be careful how you tell Dad, won't you? He's very proud of what he's built up. But our Wilf loves working there, so maybe it'll work out all right.' Pam clicked her tongue in exasperation and reached out to right the baby. 'Watch how you're holding her. She's not a parcel of groceries.'

'Perhaps you should have her again now.' He held out the baby but Pam made no effort to take Nora off him, just looked at him, eyes narrowed, head slightly to one side. He sighed. He'd never been able to fool his sister.

'And perhaps I shouldn't. You'll have to learn to look after her, Joss. She's only got you now. Though Iris will help you when she comes back to live with you. She loves cuddling her little sister – when *that woman* will let her near us. I don't like to speak ill of anyone, but I think Mrs Tomlinson has been bullying those kids. They look proper cowed to me. She's certainly not spoiling them like she did Ada.'

He stared at her in shock. 'You can't mean that!'

'I do. And she's trying to set them against you. She seems to blame you for the death of her daughter – and she blames Nora too, won't have anything to do with the baby. The sooner you get Roy and Iris away from her, the better. You don't want them to grow up like Ada.' She patted his arm. 'I know what your wife was like, Joss love, what you had to put up with from her silly ways. And I didn't approve of her going to the pub. It's not the place a decent woman should be.'

He nearly told Pam then that it wasn't his baby, but he bit back the words just in time. Nora was his burden, his problem to sort out, and until he could see his way clearly, he'd keep his own counsel.

The baby began wriggling and her cries changed to a sharper note.

'She's got wind,' Pam said. 'Hold her against your shoulder and pat her back.'

He looked at her pleadingly, but she shook her head.

'You've done it before, with the others. And you'll be looking after this one on your own in the evenings once you've got your house set up again. I reckon if women could do men's jobs during the war, then men can do women's jobs too when the need arises.'

So he held the baby, jiggled her and had his first lesson on changing a nappy. He tried not to think how vulnerable a baby was, but couldn't avoid it when he saw how frail her little pink body was. Nora was a fine healthy child, but she couldn't even sit up on her own yet and would have rolled off the table edge if he hadn't caught her. And still she kept smiling and cooing at him. He wished she wouldn't. He wanted to hate her.

He felt deeply depressed as he walked back to the shop. Normally a man who'd lost a wife would have female relatives who'd care for such a young baby, but his mother and sister weren't in a position to help and there simply wasn't anyone else.

Whatever solution he found, he wasn't going to do anything that hurt a child who smiled out so innocently at the world, especially now he'd met her.

Vi knocked on the door of the first address given in the newspaper. It was answered by a sour-looking woman, who stared her up and down, making her feel uncomfortable. 'I'm looking for lodgings and saw your advert.'

'Where do you work?'

'I've only just returned to Drayforth after working in London. I've still to find a job.'

'Fine clothes for someone without a job. I don't take lodgers who aren't in *respectable* employment, and even then I insist on references.'

Vi was left staring at the closed door in shock. The woman hadn't even given her a chance to explain her situation!

As she turned and walked away, two others gossiping on a doorstep paused to study her, exchanging meaningful glances then resuming their low-voiced conversation.

Vi went to the second address, which wasn't far away. Again she knocked on the door and waited, pulling her coat collar up because the wind was rising and rain was threatening again.

This woman's expression was just as sour.

'I'm looking for lodgings.'

'Do you have a job?'

'Not yet, but I have excellent references and— Well!'

The door had been shut in her face again.

Taking a deep breath she set off for the third address.

This woman didn't even let her speak, just stared at her suspiciously and said, 'Aren't you Vi Gill?'

'I was before I married. I'm—'

Another door closed in her face. Why?

Vi moved slowly to the corner of the street where she paused, taking a minute to pull herself together before setting off for home. This was the last thing she'd expected. What on earth was she going to do if she wasn't able to find lodgings? Had her father upset people in town? She couldn't bear the thought of staying on at the shop.

Joss bought a copy of the *Chronicle* and his mother's groceries on the way back from his sister's. He had a brief chat with his brother as he went through the shop then a customer came in, so he made his way upstairs. He paused halfway up to listen and it was soon apparent that Wilf had a much better way with customers than he'd ever had, seeming genuinely interested in their foot problems.

His mother greeted him with a smile and took the string bag of groceries from him. 'Isn't she lovely?'

'Who?'

She looked at him in surprise. 'Nora, of course.'

'Oh. Um, yes, I suppose so.'

She came to lay one hand on his shoulder. 'Joss, dear, you mustn't blame her for Ada's death. She's only an innocent child. I've got that fond of her. I do wish I could look after her for you.'

'I don't *blame* her. It's not that . . . I . . .' He couldn't think what to say, only knew he couldn't take away his mother's pleasure in her latest grandchild by revealing the truth, not until he absolutely had to. 'Is there a cup of tea going?'

She looked at the clock. 'Half past twelve. Seems to me it's dinner time. Let me make you a ham sandwich. And I've got some scones and jam for afters.'

'Lovely.'

He watched her spread a piece of meat carefully across the bread. The ham was cut thinner than it used to be – she'd told him what slicer number to ask for at the grocer's – and was almost transparent. The food stuck in his throat and he had to force it down so as not to upset her. She didn't sit with him, said she'd eat later and took his father's plate in. He could hear her in the bedroom, coaxing his father to eat 'just a bit more, love'.

After the meal Joss read the newspaper from cover to cover, studying the job advertisements with care. There was nothing that seemed suitable. He only wished he knew what he wanted to do. All he was sure of was that he didn't want to be shut inside all day doing the same thing over and over again.

He felt so war-weary what he really longed for was to rest. But life didn't let you do that.

He became aware of his father coughing, heard Wilf moving about below and his mother came back, watching him while she ate her own dinner, the remains of his father's food and one scone. In the end, that clear gaze of hers drove him out again, even though it was raining. He stood in the shop doorway, looking down Halifax Road, wondering where to go, then shrugged and set off walking.

'Hoy, Joss!'

He turned round to see Wilf waving an umbrella at him, so

went back and took it with thanks. It was a miserable day out, but he couldn't face any more of his father's coughing or his mother's prattling about what a lovely baby Nora was.

When he found himself on Ridge Road, it seemed that fate had brought him here because he had no memory of taking this route. Grasping the umbrella shaft more firmly because the wind was stronger up here, he walked to the top end of the road. He wished it was summer and the leaves were out, instead of the bare dark branches whipping to and fro above him. At least these trees had branches, they hadn't all been blown off by shells. He stopped for a moment at the last house then turned into the driveway.

Fairview, the Warburtons' residence sat two hundred yards back from the street in its own grounds of several acres. He'd walked past it many a time and had always thought it a pretty house, old-fashioned but looking so right against the backdrop of trees, with the dull green slopes of moors stretching up to one side of it.

He started moving again. Since he was here, he might as well get this task over and done with. It'd be one less thing to dread.

Christina Warburton was dusting the drawing room when she saw a man turn into their drive. He was on foot, his face hidden at first by a large black umbrella. She tensed and called, 'Phyllis, a man's coming to the door.'

'Who is it?'

As he stopped in front of the house, the wind tossed the umbrella about and he struggled to close it, his face showing clearly now. 'A youngish man. No one I recognise.'

Her sister came to join her and they peered through the net curtains. 'He looks respectable enough. Not a gentleman, though.'

'No.'

The door knocker sounded and Christina moved away from the window. 'I'll go.' She opened the door. 'Can I help you?'

'Are you Miss Warburton?'

'I'm Christina Warburton. My elder sister is Miss Warburton.'

She gestured to her sister, who was standing at the rear of the hall.

'I need to see you both, really. You don't know me, but I served with your brother in France, Captain Peregrine Warburton.'

Her breath caught in her throat. 'You knew Perry?'

'Yes. He was my captain. I'm Joss Bentley. I wrote to you after he died and – and I promised him I'd come and see you when I got back to Drayforth.' More than just visit, the Captain had begged him to make sure his sisters were all right. 'I served under your brother for two years.'

'We got your letter.' Christina tried to blink away the tears, but felt one roll down her cheek and others blur her vision. She fumbled for her handkerchief. 'I'm sorry. We still miss Perry so much. Do come in, Mr Bentley. It's very kind of you to visit us. Would you care for a cup of tea? It's very cold and wet today.'

'Are you sure it's convenient?'

'We have very few engagements these days. Let me take your coat or you'll not feel the benefit when you go outside again. I'm afraid we lost our housemaid to the influenza and we haven't had time to replace her.' She had tried to find another maid, but young women these days wanted more money than she and her sister could afford. And even if they had been able to pay it, since the war maids turned up their noses at such an old-fashioned establishment, which didn't even have gas lighting upstairs. And of course, anyone working here would have to put up with Cook, who was very grumpy and really should have been retired – only she wouldn't leave because they couldn't do without her and she knew it. And if she did go, they couldn't afford to pay her the pension she deserved, either.

Christina hung the visitor's coat on the hall stand and let Phyllis lead the way into the sitting room and gesture to a chair.

He sat in a shabby leather armchair next to the brightly crackling wood fire, looking from one to the other, as if waiting for them to speak.

Christina let the warmth of the fire wash over her for a minute or two. She'd collected the wood herself, dragging fallen branches back to the house and paying a shabby man who came round looking for work a shilling to chop them up and stack them in an outhouse. She didn't know how they'd heat the place next winter, because there wasn't a lot of fallen wood left, probably by selling more of the family silver. She realised Mr Bentley was waiting for her to speak, pushed aside these worries and said, 'Please tell us about our brother – and how exactly he died.'

'He was my Captain and a finer officer you couldn't meet.' Joss hesitated, staring from one to the other, as if unsure how much to reveal.

Phyllis interrupted. 'How did he really die? The truth, if you please. We know they always pretend in the letters home that men get shot through the heart and die instantly because Perry mentioned once how hard those letters were to write.'

'Well – the Captain and I were both wounded in the same engagement and lay next to one another. He'd been shot in the stomach and I in the leg. We had to stay there in the mud until the stretcher bearers could get to us. So we talked. I was in pain, worried about losing my leg. Your brother wasn't really in pain, though. I think it's the shock that does that, thank goodness. I hoped they'd be able to save him, but he knew he was dying, wouldn't let me pretend. He died in my arms.'

Joss could see tears in both pairs of eyes, saw them reach for one another's hands, but their backs remained upright and they didn't ask him to stop. They were, he reckoned, as brave as their brother in their own way, real heroines, because if what the Captain had told him was right, they'd lost nearly all their money before the war and were hanging on here by the skin of their teeth, doing work servants used to do.

'He wanted me to tell you how much he'd appreciated your letters and how much he loved you both. He was sorry he'd been such a bad manager, said he'd never been good with money. Most of all, he was worried about how you'd cope but he begged you not to sell Fairview to Kirby. He loved this house, often spoke of it.'

'We love it too,' Miss Warburton murmured.

They asked him more questions, still demanding the truth, and he was led on to tell them more than he usually revealed to civilians about what life had been like over there.

When he fell silent, sighing wearily, Miss Christina looked at the clock and tutted gently. 'Here we are keeping you talking and not even giving you a cup of tea.'

'It doesn't m—' But she'd gone and he was left with the older sister, who must be at least twenty years older than her brother, in her sixties, he'd guess, and who looked very frail. 'I'm sorry if what I said upset you.'

She gave him a sad, gentle smile. 'It's better to know the truth, don't you think? Tell me about yourself, Mr Bentley. What are you going to do now the war is over? Go back into the family business? You *are* one of those Bentleys, are you not? I seem to remember you helping your father serve me when you were younger. You were tall even then. He was very good at adjusting shoes to suit my difficult foot. It made such a difference.'

He looked down, noticing that her shoes, while well polished, were worn and couldn't be giving her the support she needed for the bad leg. 'I don't want to go back to working in the shop, but I'm not trained for anything else except organising men, so I'm at a bit of a loss.' He shared something else with her. 'Your brother was talking about me going for an officer, only the war ended, so they didn't need any more officers.'

There was the sound of rattling crockery and Miss Christina came back, pushing a wheeled wooden tea trolley with a little embroidered cloth on the top. He got up to help her manoeuvre it across the soft, faded carpet which had little worn patches here and there.

'So useful, this trolley,' she said cheerfully.

Her lashes were damp and her eyes still over bright and he could tell she'd been crying.

There was a sudden hammering on the front door and Miss Warburton started, splashing tea into the saucer. 'Did you lock the door, Christina?'

Her sister put down the teacup and jumped to her feet. 'I don't know. I'll go and check.'

Joss watched in puzzlement as she fairly ran out of the room. 'Could you – go with her please, Mr Bentley?'

So he hurried out as well and was in time to see the door open before she got there and Mungo Sully appear in the entrance. Joss held back for a minute, wondering what this was about, why the ladies seemed afraid and why that fellow had dared come inside without being invited.

Christina stopped a few paces from the door. 'Please leave this house at once.'

'I will when I've had a word with you. Have you thought better about selling Mr Kirby this house?'

'We haven't changed our minds about that and we never shall. Please leave.'

When the man didn't move, Joss judged it time to step out into the hallway. 'The lady asked you to leave, Sully.'

The other man swung round, smiling confidently. He squinted for a moment, then mouthed the word 'Bentley', as he remembered who the other man was.

Joss studied him. A good fighter with a fearsome reputation but running to fat these days and clearly hadn't had a hard war. You didn't get a belly like that if you were suffering food shortages. 'I'll only ask you once more to do as the lady wishes.'

Sully set one hand flat against the wall, leaning on it. 'You'd be wise to watch your step, Bentley. Mr Kirby doesn't like people interfering in his affairs. I'm here to speak to the ladies, not you.'

Taking him by surprise, Joss leaped forward, knocked the hand away from the wall and while Sully was off balance, twisted his arm behind his back, a tactic he'd used many a time on drunken young soldiers. Sully strained for a moment, but Joss put pressure on the arm and after a couple of jerks his opponent stopped trying to break free. It was excruciatingly painful to resist this hold, Joss knew.

At the door, he shoved Sully out so that he ran down the outside steps, struggling to keep his balance. By the time the fellow turned round, Joss had slammed and locked the door, and was watching through the glass panel to one side of the entrance.

'I'll be back,' Sully roared, shaking a fist at the house.

Joss turned and saw Miss Christina standing halfway down the hall, one hand at her throat, her face chalk white. 'Are you all right?' As he hurried over to her, she took a deep, shuddering breath and nodded, but he could see she was upset, so without thinking he put his arm round her shoulders. 'Come and sit down.'

Joss didn't intend to leave until he understood what was going on. Clearly, they needed help, though he wasn't sure what he could do against Sully, especially if he was acting for Mr Kirby. Once Miss Christina had calmed down, he asked, 'Do you want to tell me what that was about?'

It was Miss Warburton who answered. 'Mr Kirby wishes to buy our house and land. Only we don't wish to sell, not at any price. We thought we'd convinced him of that, but that Sully creature has started coming to see us. We're – a bit isolated here, and there are men on the tramp who look a bit – rough. So we're always careful about answering the door. Luckily, we can see who it is from the drawing-room window.'

'Today's trouble was my own fault,' Miss Christina said. 'When I let you in today, I forgot to lock the door. I shan't make that mistake again.'

But Sully would come back again soon if his master was set on buying Fairview, Joss was sure. Look how he'd come walking right into the house today. 'Have you no man nearby to protect you?'

Miss Warburton shrugged. 'We can no longer afford to keep outdoor staff and our horses were taken for the war so the stable yard is empty. Our two grooms volunteered quite early on in the war.'

'How do you manage without a gig or something? It's quite a long way into town from here.'

Miss Christina smiled. 'I'm a good walker and I have a bicycle, so I can ride into town for fresh food on market day and bring it back on the bicycle rack. I leave our order with the grocer and he delivers it. He brings the meat as well, even though our orders are much smaller these days. People have been very kind.'

'I don't like to think of you on your own.'

'We shall be all right. I shan't leave the door unlocked again.'

When she escorted Joss out, something made him ask, 'May I come back again? I shall be worried about you and it's a nice walk out here. I could bring my children if it's fine at the weekend. They're old enough for a good walk now.'

'We should be happy to see you any time, Mr Bentley. And there's a swing in the stables that your children might enjoy, though you'd better check that the rope is still secure.'

But as he walked back into town, he worried about the two elderly ladies, one so frail and both so courageous. Only what could he do to help them if they were short of money? Joss wasn't flush with money and he had his own problems, not small ones, either.

The children should be home from school by now so he turned on to the road that led out to his mother-in-law's. He kept an eye open for Sully as he walked down from the Ridge. He wouldn't have put it past the brute to try to ambush him. But to his relief there was no sign of the man. Well, who'd want to hang around on a cold, rainy day like this?

But he was quite sure Sully would try to get back at him. He was known never to forgive an insult or forget a grievance.

Vi walked slowly back to her father's shop, taking shelter in a doorway as rain suddenly pelted down, running down the gutters and sending other pedestrains fleeing. As it eased off, she began walking again, lost in thought as she tried to work out what to do next.

When she bumped into someone, she muttered an apology. She'd taken a couple of steps before she realised who it was and swung round to call, 'Eric! Are you ignoring your own sister?'

He studied her. 'Our Vi? Dad said you were back but I'd not have recognised you in that fine get-up.'

'You're looking pretty fine yourself, better than I'd expected.'

'They say I've got a weak heart, but it doesn't stop me doing anything I want to. I allus find a way.' As he patted his chest, wind whistled around them and he shivered. 'Let's go into the tea shop. I'll treat you.'

'That'd be nice.'

They sat down in the cosy room full of small square tables. Gas lights were flaring, making faint hissing and popping sounds, and condensation had built up on the inside of the windows.

The waitress took their order and giggled when Eric winked at her and slipped her a shilling to make sure they got extra cakes.

'You're very generous with your money,' Vi said.

'Only when it suits me. You're probably as careful with yours as ever. Is Dad still on the cadge?'

'Yes.'

'And our dear stepmother? I bet she came as a pleasant surprise to you.'

'Doris doesn't seem too bad. She has more sense than Dad and she's a hard worker.'

'Everyone has more sense than that old fool. He was lucky he had you and Mum or he'd have lost the shop years ago.' Eric leaned back in his chair to study her. 'You dress better than you used to.'

'Lady Bingram provided our uniforms. They were always of the very best quality. This coat will last me for years.'

'Going back to work in the shop again?'

'No, definitely not. I'd like to find myself a more interesting job. If there's nothing round here, I'll go back to London. I may have to go anyway.' Indignation burned through her. 'Do you know, I was refused a room at two lodging houses today because I've not got a job yet! And the third woman wouldn't even talk to me. How can I find a job if I've nowhere to stay while I look? I'm not staying with Dad for more than a night or two, if I can help it. All he's got is a pile of sacks on the floor.'

He pursed his lips then said, 'You can stay with me if you like. I've got a spare bedroom.'

She stilled, staring at him. 'Why would you offer that?'

'You could take over the cooking. I've a woman who cleans for me a couple of times a week and I send my washing to the laundry, but I miss Mum's cooking. I used to pay her to cook for me and I'd find extra meat and eggs for her in return.'

'How much are you charging for the room?'

'Nothing if you'll do the cooking, though we'll share expenses.' He laughed. 'Don't look a gift horse in the mouth, our Vi.'

But she couldn't help wondering about his motives. When had Eric ever done anything out of kindness? There would be some sort of catch, there always was with him.

Only . . . she didn't want to sleep on the floor again. 'Show me the room, then.'

Joss hesitated outside the house where his mother-in-law lived, remembering Pam's words. Well, he didn't like Mrs Tomlinson, either, never had, not even when she was being nice to him as he courted Ada. Mr Tomlinson had been pleasant enough, a nonentity of a man, who'd made enough money to leave his wife comfortably circumstanced and had then died early, leaving her to enjoy her widowhood and the pressure she could bring on others because of her money.

He raised his hand and knocked on the door of the semi-detached residence, half expecting one of the children to come running to answer it. But it was an old woman's steps he heard coming along the hall and the door was opened only a crack.

She stared at him for a minute, then said, 'Would you mind going round to the back door, Joss? I don't want you treading in mud and leaving my carpets damp.' Without waiting for an answer she shut the door in his face.

'Welcome back,' he muttered as he walked round to the rear.

She opened the kitchen door with the greeting, 'Wipe your feet carefully.' His children were there. He'd expected them to rush at him for cuddles, begging to be lifted up as they used to do, but they simply sat and waited, looking at their grandmother as if for instructions.

Mrs Tomlinson turned to them. 'Say hello to your father, children.'

They chorused a greeting.

'Don't I get a hug now?' he asked.

Again they looked to their grandmother, who grimaced. 'I don't believe in people mauling one another around,' she said. 'Your children have learned a few manners with me, Joss, and I'd be grateful if you'd stick to my ways while you're visiting *my* house. I suppose you want a cup of tea.'

'I want a cuddle,' he said obstinately and pulled Iris, who was nearest, into his arms, loving the feel of her. 'I've missed you, pet,' he said into her hair, rocking her to and fro, ignoring his mother-in-law's sourly disapproving expression.

'You didn't come back,' Iris whispered. 'You stayed away after Mummy died.'

'You have to do as they tell you in the Army, love. But I'm back for good now and we'll soon be moving into our new home.'

'That's all the thanks I get for my care of them, is it?' Mrs Tomlinson said shrilly. 'Take them away without even discussing it with me first, without finding out if it's convenient or not.'

'I'm grateful to you for looking after them,' he said, choosing his words carefully. 'But they belong with me now.' He went to pull Roy into a hug, but his son drew back.

'Men don't hug one another,' he said. 'Only cissies do that.'

'Where did you hear that?' Joss demanded.

The boy's eyes flickered towards his grandmother, then he looked down and said gruffly, 'Everybody knows it.'

'Well, I don't. It's not cissie for a father to hug his children.'

'Don't want to, then.'

Joss surprised a smile of triumph on Mrs Tomlinson's thin features. Pam was right, he decided. What had the old devil been saying? The sooner he got his kids back, the better.

He made laborious conversation, but his mother-in-law hardly let the children speak, interrupting and answering for them the few times they tried to speak up.

After a while he brought up the subject nearest to his heart. 'I believe you have some of my furniture here? What exactly do you have apart from the children's beds? I must arrange to have it moved to our new house.'

'There's no rush, surely? It'd be better to wait for the Easter holidays and move the children then.'

'It's only natural that I'd want my family back, don't you think?'

Her mouth was still a tight, angry line and she shot words out like acid. 'You can't get Ada back and I don't see how you'll manage without her, but I don't suppose you care about how the children will suffer with only a man to look after them. And I'll thank you to remember that they're all I have left of her when you start trying to take them away from me. Fine thanks that is for all I've done for you.'

He could only repeat himself. 'I'm grateful for your help, you know I am. But I'm their father and they belong with me.'

She sniffed and looked away, scolding Iris about her table manners.

He bit his tongue. No use interfering in that small fuss over nothing or he'd bet she'd take it out on his children after he'd left. Even Ada hadn't liked leaving the children with her for long. And Mrs Tomlinson hadn't even mentioned Nora.

Tess waited until Joe was asleep to cry, though how she'd held the tears back for so long, she didn't know. She was at the end of her tether, wouldn't have been able to feed her children if Vi hadn't brought the food round, still couldn't see her way ahead.

The lady visitor turned up the next morning and as soon as he heard who was at the door, Joe turned over and pretended to be asleep. It was all he did lately: hide from the world.

'You shouldn't let your husband sleep in the daytime. That's no way for him to get better.'

'He had a bad night.'

Mrs Gilson turned to stare at the two little girls. 'It's been reported that you're not sending the older girl and boy to school, Mrs Donovan.'

'How can I do that when they don't have decent shoes to their feet and only ragged clothes to wear? You made me sell their other things.'

'You cannot receive support from the Panel if you have sellable goods in the house. And your son must have some sort of footwear because he doesn't appear to be at home and he's not at school today.' She pointed to the jar of jam on the table. 'Yet you have money for luxuries like that.'

'I didn't buy it. It was a present.'

'Who from? Not another man!'

Tess stared at her in shock. 'Of course not. My friend's just come back from London and she bought it for me.'

The lady visitor pulled out a little notebook and a silver pencil. 'What is her name?'

'That's none of your business. She's not asking you for help, I am.'

'You'll get nothing unless you can prove you need it – and unless you can prove you're not wasting the money we give you. Her name and address.'

'Violet Schofield. Mrs. She's a widow. Her husband was a soldier, killed in the war. She's staying at Gill's corner shop. He's her father.'

Mrs Gilson scribbled down the information. 'I shall check up on that.'

Tess lost her temper then and screamed at her, 'You can check all you like! I've sold everything I owned, there's nothing left. I don't know what else you expect me to do.'

'I've told you before that you could get a charring job to help out.'

'I daren't leave Jenny with Joe. He falls asleep. She's at an age where she's into everything.'

Mrs Gilson was unmoved. 'You're making excuses. You don't want to work.'

By that time the rage had passed and Tess had lost what little defiance she had. She could only stand there, head bowed and listen. On and on it went, a lecture about thrift and hard work. Only you had to have something to be thrifty *with* and she had nothing. And she couldn't work any harder without food. She felt so weak sometimes she could barely stay upright.

But every now and then she had to let it out. Like last night. Just a little weep when no one would know. It was seeing Vi that had done it. Her friend looked so smart and well.

At last Mrs Gilson left.

'Tess, love. Don't let her get to you.'

'I thought you were awake, Joe. Best thing you could do, stay out of it, or she'd have given you a lecture too. Do you want a drink of water?'

'What I want is to see you fed and happy, like you used to be. And I don't want women like her coming round scolding you when you don't deserve it.'

Then he was weeping too, great racking sobs, so she had to set aside her own worries to comfort him. But there wasn't really any comfort she could offer and much as she loved Vi, she hated her friend seeing them like this, hated it!

# 10

Mayfield Place was a row of ten houses that lay at the higher end of the Backhill Terraces. It was a short walk from the town centre.

'The rents are a bit higher here,' Eric said, 'because the houses are bigger, intended for a better class of people.'

But their red bricks were just as smoke-blackened as the rest of the town, Vi thought, because the outpourings from mills, manufactories and workshops were no respecters of social status. Only one end of Mayfield Place was open to the outside world, the other was closed off by the high walls of the laundry, above which a ragged banner of white steam drifted into the sky.

Eric went to the end house, next to the laundry wall, and unlocked the front door. 'Home sweet home.'

Vi started moving but had to jerk to a quick halt. In London she'd grown used to men standing back to let ladies go first, but such a courtesy would never have occurred to her brother, who walked inside without waiting for her. The hall was bare and the floorboards were in need of a good scrub, she noted. Could he not afford to furnish the house?

Eric clicked a switch on the wall. 'Electric lights upstairs and down. Mr Kirby likes modern conveniences. You should see his house. I went there with Sully once, and it's a marvel, that place.'

'People don't usually put electricity into terraced houses.'

'Mr Kirby owns part of the electric works. He'll get the extra profit from that, too.' He gestured to the front room, which was completely bare. 'I've not bought any furniture for this yet – or a carpet runner for the hall. It'd be a waste when there's only me.'

There was a small room behind the living room, also unfurnished, then the kitchen. It had a modern gas cooker, a table, two upright chairs and one big armchair. Eric pushed open a door at the far side to show a scullery with a gas boiler in one corner. He gestured to a door. 'That goes out to the yard.'

Vi could sense his pride in his home. 'It's a fine big house.'

'Come and see your room.' He strode out, again not waiting for her, simply assuming she'd follow. She noticed how slowly he climbed the stairs and that he was puffing by the time he reached the top, not just because he was plump.

Upstairs, the front bedroom was furnished comfortably enough, though none of the pieces of furniture matched. The other two bedrooms were bare. And there was a bathroom. Ah, she'd missed having the convenience of that.

'There's no furniture in the bedroom,' she said. 'It'd be as bad as Dad's.'

Eric scowled at her. 'I can get what's needed if we come to an agreement about the rest.'

She wondered what else they needed to agree about.

'We'll talk downstairs.'

He took the armchair and waved one hand. 'Bring the other chair across for yourself. Right, then. I'm prepared to let you live here for free if you'll cook the meals and . . .' The words trailed away and the scowl became more pronounced. 'If you tell this to anyone, I'll make sure you regret the day you were born.'

She blinked in surprise. 'I can keep a secret. We *are* family, after all.'

He considered this, then the scowl lessened a little and he nodded. 'Yes, family. Mum used to say that. What I really want is for you to show me how to live nicely, like the nobs do. What knives and forks to use, what clothes to wear, how to deal with fancy folk. I watch them sometimes and they treat each other differently. And I don't know where to start. Plus I want you to help me get furniture for the front room so that it looks . . .' Again the words trailed off and he waved one hand in frustration. 'I want it to look *tasteful*, so people will *see* I've come up in the world.'

She was thoroughly confused now. Was this her brother speaking? When had Eric ever cared about the finer things in life? 'Why?'

'The war's been my big chance. I've got a bit of money behind me, a steady job and – I want to get wed.'

'Do I know her?'

'I've not started looking yet. I don't want a woman like Doris, though. I want a better sort, only I don't know how to meet them, or how to talk to them. You do. So it'll be worth letting you have the room free for a few months if you help me – as long as you don't tell anyone what I'm trying to do. I'm not having folk laughing at me.'

'I see. Well, I can certainly help you with some of that, but I won't be home in time to cook every evening if I get a job. And I do want to find one, Eric. I'm not going back to that shop, whatever Dad says. I can do simple things during the week and cook proper meals at weekends, though. I enjoy cooking. And I can also make sure your house gets cleaned properly, as well as helping with the other things.'

'I pay someone to clean it now.'

'Well, your hall floor needs a thorough scrubbing down the edges and the windows are dull.' She was suddenly worried by a vicious look that came into his eyes. 'You may not be giving the woman enough time to do the job properly, though. I'll know how to check that for you.'

'Mmm.' He stared into the fire, which was blazing up now, chewing the inside of his mouth as he thought things through.

She waited. No good ever came of trying to hurry Eric.

He slapped one hand down suddenly on the arm of his chair. 'All right. We'll give it a try. I'll get you some furniture for the back bedroom. I cleared out a house last week for Mr Kirby.'

'I'm not having a dirty old mattress full of bed bugs, and if you want your house to be a bit better than others, you'll think twice about what you get, not for me but for your own pride. Your own bedroom is a right old mess. Nothing matches. Later, once I've settled into a job, I want to rent my own house. Perhaps you can help me with getting one, since you seem to be working as a rent man?'

A sly smile crept over his face. 'Rent man and general assistant to Sully. I'll take over from him one day working for Mr Kirby. You'll see. He's showing his age, Sully is.'

Sully had been a prominent figure in the poorer streets for as long as she could remember. She couldn't see him handing over his power to anyone as long as there was breath in his body, but her brother seemed sure of what he was saying, so perhaps he knew more than she did.

'That's settled then.' Eric stuck out one hand and solemnly shook hers.

'Do you know our Beryl's new address?'

'No, but I can ask around. Why?'

'I want to see her, of course.'

'You're not to tell her about our agreement.'

'I'll only tell her that I'm living with you, I promise. Stop worrying. If you can't trust your family, who can you trust?'

'I don't trust anyone.'

That was obvious. 'Well, you can trust me. Now, how soon can you get some furniture? I want to move in as quickly as I can.'

'Tomorrow. Mr Kirby's got a second-hand shop now where we sell stuff we've had to take in lieu of rent. Good stuff, some of it, too. I'll come for you at Dad's at ten o'clock tomorrow and you can help me choose.'

'All right.'

'Good. Now, I'm hungry and want my tea. Shut the door as you go out.'

She walked slowly back to the shop. She'd have to get fish and chips again tonight, or some pies, and she had no doubt she'd be the one who paid for them. Or she might buy herself a roll from the baker's and have it with a bit of cheese, leaving her father and Doris to get their own tea. No, better make it pies all round. No use making an enemy of her father if she didn't need to.

But as the corner shop came into view, she experienced a sudden desperate longing to be back at Lady Bingram's in London. She felt as if she had taken ten steps backwards by coming here.

And her sister wasn't even living in the town any more. She had to wonder about staying in Drayforth now, she really did.

The following morning, early, Joss went to inspect his house. Most of the furniture was still there, but some of the smaller items were missing and the back bedroom, which Roy and Iris had occupied, was empty. The whole place felt damp.

He was in the kitchen when the door knocker sounded.

A man stood on the doorstep, puffy and unhealthy looking with thinning hair. His hand was raised to wield the knocker a second time. 'I thought I saw you go in. I'm Eric Gill. I work for Mr Kirby. Here you are. Saves me a journey.' He thrust an envelope into Joss's hand.

'What's this?'

'Notice to quit.'

*'What?'*

'Mr Kirby needs the house for someone else and you've not even been occupying it. He's offering very generous terms. You can leave today and save a week's rent, no notice needed, or you can pay for another week if you need time to find somewhere else.' He smiled, a bland, insincere smile, as if he hadn't just delivered a severe blow.

Joss realised with a sick feeling of helplessness what had caused this sudden eviction: his encounter with Sully at the Warburtons'. He bit back an angry protest. He wasn't going to give the fellow the satisfaction of begging. 'I'll leave at once.'

'Need to get your stuff out by four o'clock today, then.'

'I'll arrange that.'

'Right. I'll be here for the handover. Two keys, you were given. We'll want them both back or I'll have to charge you for a replacement.'

He walked off down the street whistling cheerfully.

Only then did Joss allow himself to sag against the wall of the narrow hallway. What next? It seemed to be one thing after another lately.

He pulled out his watch and jerked upright. Hell, he only had six hours to get his things moved out! He'd have to put them in storage until he found another house. Well, he'd rather pay money for that than pay an extra week's rent to Kirby. Locking the door, he hurried round to Meldon's, the storage and removals firm where he'd played as a lad. It was still there, but his childhood friend Peter Meldon was dead now, more's the pity, had copped it on the Somme in 1916.

Sam Meldon was sitting slumped in his office, looking much older and haggard. He looked up as Joss tapped on the door. 'Yes? Oh, it's you, Joss lad. They said you were back.'

'Yes. Look, I need some furniture storing for a week or two, Mr Meldon, and it'll need moving today because I have to be out of the house by four o'clock.'

'I'm sorry. We've no space free.' Sam hesitated then beckoned Joss closer to whisper, 'I don't know what you did to upset Mungo Sully, but it means I can't help you, I'm afraid. I rent this place from Mr Kirby, you see.'

Joss stood speechless with shock for a moment or two at this further blow, then asked in a low voice, 'Do you know anyone who can store the stuff for me?'

'I doubt anyone will dare. Word's gone round.'

'Hell and damnation!'

Sam leaned even closer. 'You could get one of the farmers to move it for you, perhaps. I'd try Don Welling at Green Heys. He's got no love for Sully. But you'll have to find somewhere else to store the stuff because Don won't have room. His youngest son and family have moved into his barn. The poor sod has just lost his job.' He put one finger to his lips, glanced sideways and said in a louder voice, 'I'm very busy so I must ask you to leave now, Mr Bentley.'

By this, Joss understood that someone here was not to be trusted. He walked out, noticing a man walking away from the office window. He felt as if he'd been kicked in the guts – and by Sam Meldon, of all people!

Where the hell could he store furniture at such short notice? And how was he to get it away from the house?

He walked slowly along the street, looking up as a sudden gust of wind nearly blew his bowler hat off. In the distance he saw the chimneys of Fairview and stopped walking, struck by a sudden idea. The two ladies who lived at Fairview were clearly short of money. Why not ask them if he could store his things in their stables? He could pay them the same as he'd have paid Meldon. What had he to lose? Only his time and that was precious today, so he strode off towards the ridge, praying they'd agree.

As he walked, his thoughts circled round and round. What upset him most of all about this mess was that he'd have to ask his mother-in-law to look after his children for a bit longer. No, not ask, *beg*. She'd certainly make him do that, the spiteful bitch.

That morning, after another poor night's sleep on the hard floor, Vi waited impatiently for Eric to come and fetch her.

During a lull in the shop, Doris came to join her by the fire, rubbing her hands together. 'Cold, isn't it?' She looked nervously at her stepdaughter. 'I stopped Arnie taking money out of the till yesterday.'

'I heard you. Well done.'

'I had to stop him again this morning and he went off in a huff. I've got most of the money in a pouch under my apron now. Well, it's usually me who serves these days.' She began drawing patterns on the table with one fingertip, avoiding Vi's eyes as she asked, 'Will you come with me to the baker's? I shan't know what to say to them.'

Vi was surprised by this request and by the confidences that had preceded it.

When she didn't get an immediate answer, Doris rushed on, 'You were right. It's my chance, you see, this shop is. To provide for my old age, I mean. Only chance I've got now your dad's spent my money. I was a fool to give it all to him, only I was desperate to get wed. Arnie didn't want to marry me until he found out I had some money saved. He was drunk for a week after we married, the sod. On my money.'

Vi hadn't expected to feel sorry for Doris, but she did. 'I'm happy to help you in any way I can. And here's another suggestion: if you really want to improve things, you should clear out the rubbish from the window and make the glass shine, so that it looks clean and attractive. Mum used to keep piles of tins there, nicely arranged, the sort of things people are always needing. The window looks a mess now. And Mum used to buy food that was going off and put it outside the door as a special bargain in a sort of box on legs. I used to write the signs for her.'

'I've seen them signs.' Doris hurried across to the dresser and fumbled in the drawers. 'Here, look. I've kept 'em.' She pulled out some pieces of yellowing card.

She was so humbly eager that Vi's heart was touched, in spite of her resentment that her father should marry someone like this so soon after her mother's death. 'I'll come with you to the baker's after I get back today. Have you got some nicer clothes than those?'

'Yes. But I have to keep 'em locked in my trunk or he'd have pawned them. He'd do owt for drinking money, that one would. If I'd known how bad he was . . .'

Vi didn't comment on the fact that it definitely wasn't a love match. The two of them didn't even seem to like one another. 'Another thing: it'd look better if you wore a clean apron every day. Mum had a few. They might still be around. They'll be a bit small for you, but better than nothing.'

'I've not wore her things. I didn't like to. They're in a box in the attic. I hid 'em from him.'

'We'll get them down later and see how they fit.' To Vi's amazement, Doris burst into tears, thanking her over and over again.

The shop bell went just then and Doris pulled back, wiping her tears on her sleeve. 'Thanks,' she repeated gruffly and went out to serve a customer.

Vi's father came back a couple of minutes later and flung

himself into a chair, scowling at her. 'You had to poke your nose in, didn't you?'

'What do you mean?'

'Get Doris cheating me like you and your Ma used to do.'

From the smell that wafted around him, she realised he'd been drinking, early as it was. 'Go and sleep it off,' she said scornfully. 'No one's been cheating you. We're trying to make the shop profitable, that's all.'

He raised one meaty fist. 'Don't you cheek me. I can still give you a thump.'

'Better not, Dad,' a voice said behind him.

Arnie swung round and let his fist drop. 'Here's another ungrateful sod.'

Eric smiled at him, not a nice smile. 'I don't want to hear that you've been thumping our Vi,' he said slowly and emphatically. 'I'd be really, really upset if she got hurt.'

Arnie glared at them both and went upstairs without another word.

'What's got into him?' Eric asked.

'Doris has stopped him pinching money from the till.'

'That whore! She's probably taking it herself.'

'No, she isn't. She's trying to do the right thing to make the business profitable.' Vi saw no softening of her brother's expression and added quickly, 'She's the best chance we've got of keeping Dad under control. If you intend to move up in the world, you'll not want him making a drunken spectacle of himself, will you?'

Eric looked at her then towards the shop and grimaced. 'She isn't fit to kiss Mum's shoes.'

That was one thing they shared, at least, a fondness for their mother. 'No one could replace Mum, I agree. But Doris isn't afraid of Dad and she's desperate for some security. She'll make a useful ally to prevent him from embarrassing us.'

'I'd better keep my eye on them, then, see how she does. I'm not helping her if she throws money away.'

'She isn't stupid, listens to advice and works hard. He's hardly lifting a finger these days.'

Eric nodded. 'All right. As I said, I'll keep an eye on them. Now, are you ready? I have to be somewhere at four o'clock and we've a lot to do before then.'

'Yes, I'm ready.' She pulled on her leather gloves.

He looked at her approvingly as they walked down the street. 'You always did look trim and tidy, just like Mum, but now you look like quality.'

She stole a glance sideways, not used to receiving compliments from her brother. His clothes might not be ragged, but they were cheap and ill-fitting. That could be improved. She couldn't imagine who would want to marry him, only there was a shortage of men thanks to the war, so perhaps he'd achieve his ambition.

She didn't envy the woman who got him, though. He could be a mean devil if he considered himself badly done to, Eric could.

Phyllis was sitting mending near the window when she saw a man turn off the street and hurry down the drive. 'Christina, come quickly!' she called and waited, motionless, to see who it was. Then she recognised the man and sighed in relief. 'It's all right. It's that nice Mr Bentley again.'

Christina went to open the door and found their visitor gasping for breath. She gestured him inside. 'Is something wrong.'

'Yes. Sorry to be – like this.'

'Come into the drawing room and sit down. You need to catch your breath.'

He followed her and managed to control his breathing enough to explain his dilemma.

'That man Sully again!' Miss Warburton said in tones of loathing. She looked at her sister, received a nod and smiled at their visitor. 'We have plenty of space here. Take him out to look at the stables, Christina, and I'll get Cook to make him a cup of tea.'

'Thanks but I've no time for tea, Miss Warburton. I need to find someone to move my things, someone who's not afraid of Sully. I doubt this is Mr Kirby's doing. Why would a man as rich as him take an interest in me? Eh, I'd give my right arm for a motor car today.'

'You could take my bicycle,' Christina offered as they walked out to the stables.

'You don't need it?'

'Not for a day or two.'

'You're both being so kind. I will take it, thank you very much. I don't mind admitting that I'm desperate.'

The stables were dusty and neglected but dry and with no signs of leaks. There was plenty of room for his furniture. He rode off on the cycle to call on the owner of Green Heys farm. Mr Welling scowled at the mere mention of Sully.

'We can help you move your stuff. My son can go with you and help you clear the house, if you slip him a bob or two. He's out of work at the moment.'

Joss had to swallow hard to hold back his relief, which was so great it'd brought tears to his eyes.

By dint of hard work, he and Tim Welling had the house cleared well before four o'clock and he was even able to sweep it out. He nipped back to the shop to find out where the second key was and returned with them both clinking in his pocket.

He found Tim standing protectively in front of the loaded cart, facing Gill and a surly fellow who was in need of a shave.

'The house is dirty. I'll have to charge you for having it cleaned,' Gill said at once.

'It's not dirty and I'm not paying you a penny more,' Joss retorted. 'Mr Kirby is lucky to have had it rented out for a few months without any wear and tear. You should be paying me a rebate.' As the other man eyed him up and down, he folded his arms and stared straight back at him.

After a moment or two Gill shrugged. 'I'll let you off, seeing you're a returned soldier.'

'Here are the keys then.'

As he slapped them hard into the rent agent's hand, the fellow standing next to him moved a step forward, but Gill shook his head and the man took a step backwards again.

Tim swung up on the cart and Joss got up beside him, keeping an eye on the two men. When they were out of earshot, he let out a long sigh of relief. 'I thought we were in for a fight then.'

'Gill doesn't fight,' Tim said. 'He's got a dicky heart, or so people say. Fred goes around with him in case there's trouble, but there isn't usually. Gill's not as bad as Sully. He does what he has to the easiest way he can.'

'Kirby wasn't this powerful when I left Drayforth.'

'There wasn't anyone to stop him during the war, Dad says, because the policemen went off to fight. There were a couple of special constables here who were in his pay, so no official ever questioned his black market activities.'

'I hate bloody war profiteers.'

'So do I. Where did you serve?'

They fell into a discussion about their wartime experiences, which ended only as they arrived at Fairview and began unloading the furniture into the stables.

Joss insisted on paying the ladies a week's money in advance, then went off to speak to his mother-in-law, grateful for the bicycle.

Christina watched from behind the net curtains as Mr Bentley rode off down the drive. He looked exhausted. And the poor man didn't have a home for his three children now. Life was so unfair. She looked round. They, on the other hand, had too much space. It was impossible to heat it or even keep it dusted and clean. If only Mr Bentley had a wife, they might have invited them to make a temporary home here, in return for some help around the house and garden.

She went back to work on the account books, which were hard to balance properly. She had never been good at figures. There was very little money left in the cash box and even Mr Bentley's few shillings would be a help.

It was getting time to sell another piece of silver or a painting, maybe. Only, prices were so low because of the war and she hated bargaining with pawnbrokers and jewellers, absolutely hated it. And she was nervous of going into Manchester on her own, even though Perry had said she should sell there.

She wondered suddenly if a man selling things would get more for them than she did. Perry had, the one time he'd helped her. Such a pity he'd never married. He'd been the last male Warburton. But he'd never shown an interest in women. The name would die with herself and her sister.

If anything happened to Phyllis, who wasn't in the best of health, Christina didn't know what she'd do. She was ten years older than Perry but ten years younger than her sister, and in a lot better health, so it was bound to happen one day.

Life was not – very promising. She blinked away a tear. You just had to soldier on, maintaining your dignity. That was all you could do sometimes.

Jean Tomlinson watched the children carefully as they wiped their feet first on the mat outside the door, then on the mat inside. They hung up their damp coats and changed into their slippers near the door, then looked at her for permission to go to the table. She'd set out the glass of milk and two biscuits which she gave them when they got home from school and she sat with them as they ate.

She didn't encourage speaking with the mouth full, so waited until they'd finished to question them about school, then sent Iris to do her piano practice. She set Roy some arithmetic problems until Iris had finished. After that he could do his half hour on the piano. She ignored the look of misery on his face. He hated arithmetic and wasn't very fond of learning the piano either, but she knew what was good for the children and made sure they buckled down to it. She'd been too soft with Ada and look what had come of it. She wasn't going to be too soft with these two.

When she heard footsteps coming round the side of the house, she stiffened. It sounded like . . . A tall form appeared behind the frosted glass of the upper part of the back door but not until he had knocked twice did she get up to answer it. 'Joss.'

'Mrs Tomlinson. May I come in?'

'Of course. Wipe your feet carefully.'

When he'd done that, he smiled at his son, then the smile faded as he turned to her. 'Could I speak to you in private?'

'Go and sit in your bedroom, Roy.'

The boy stood up.

'Take your exercise book with you and continue with your work.'

With a loud sigh he did so. She turned to Joss, looking at him in disapproval. You'd think he'd have made more effort with his appearance when coming to visit a lady.

'I'm afraid I've been told to leave the house I've been renting since Ada died, so I can't have the children till I find somewhere else for us all to live. Can you keep them till then?'

'Why did you have to leave it?'

'I upset Sully.'

'That was foolish. The man controls half the houses in town on behalf of Mr Kirby. You'll have trouble finding anywhere to live now.' But she was glad of that, because it meant she could keep the children and see that they were brought up properly.

'In the meantime . . .?'

'Yes, of course I'll have the children. Not the baby, though. I'm too old for babies.'

'I realise that. I'll have to find somewhere else for her. My mother's got her hands full looking after my father and my sister's near her time. I'll just have a word with the children before I go, if I may?'

She waited till he'd got to his feet to state her terms. 'If I keep the children, I shall have to set some rules, I'm afraid. This is the time of day for their piano lessons and homework. Indeed, it's not convenient to have you coming here every day. It upsets my routine. Wednesdays and Sundays for visiting, I think.'

'I'd like to see them more often than that.'

'It doesn't suit me, I'm afraid.'

He stared at her, then nodded reluctantly. 'Very well. Can I see the children before I leave now, please?'

She enjoyed refusing his request, hated to see him looking alive and well when her Ada was dead. 'They're busy. It's Wednesday tomorrow. Not long to wait.'

After he'd left she let herself smile. But a moment later she winced at the sounds coming from the front room and went in to supervise Iris's scales, making her do them again and again till she got them perfect, rapping her knuckles with a ruler every time she made a mistake. Then she called Roy down to do his practice.

'Where's Dad?' he asked.

'He had to leave.'

'Did he say when we're going to live with him?'

'It's not convenient for him just now, so he's leaving you with me. That'll be lovely, won't it?'

There was silence, then Roy nudged Iris and both children bowed their heads and muttered a yes.

She picked up the ruler again. 'Come along, Roy. Piano practice now. Iris, you may sit here and read your story book.'

# 11

Vi unpacked her suitcase and took some things out of her trunk, locking them again, because she wouldn't put it past Eric to go snooping through her things. She looked round the bedroom with relief. It was sparsely furnished, but the bed was comfortable and there was adequate clean bedding, even if it was second-hand stuff. She now had a wardrobe and dressing table. More than enough for her needs at the moment.

'What's in the trunk you sent up to the attic?'

She jumped in shock as Eric spoke from just behind her. It was none of his business but she didn't want to upset him. 'Some of Len's stuff and things we bought for the home we hoped to have one day.' She'd started collecting linen and smaller items soon after they married, ready for peacetime. Len had loved going through them with her, making plans for after the war, talking about what colour they'd distemper the walls, what furniture they'd buy. 'This trunk contains my clothes and a few books, so I'll leave it here.'

Eric looked round the room. 'Not got a photo of your husband?'

'I do have some but I don't need a photo to remember him. He was a good man.' And anyway, looking at photos of Len made her sad.

'Did you like being married?'

She'd forgotten Eric's habit of asking question after question when something interested him. 'Very much indeed.'

'And did you like being an Aide?'

'I loved it. The work was interesting and the other Aides were fun to be with. They were all hard workers, too, chosen specially by her ladyship.'

'I suppose you've seen the last of Lady Bingram now.'

'I shouldn't think so. I'll let her have my address here, if you don't mind. She'll be coming up north to visit her estate and if I know her, she'll pop in unexpectedly for a quick visit. If I ever find myself in trouble, I know I can turn to her. She's a wonderful woman, Eric.'

He was frowning. 'Why would she come and see you if she doesn't employ you any more?'

'Because she considers us her friends. The Aides did more than just work for her, we all lived together like a big, happy family. Why, we even used to call her Daphne in private.'

His mouth fell open in shock. 'You called a ladyship by her first name!'

Vi nodded. She watched him drumming his fingertips on the nearest surface, which happened to be the door frame. It was a habit he'd had even as a lad when he was digesting some piece of information.

'I think you'll be even more useful to me than I'd expected,' he said at last. 'Now, what's for tea?'

'I'll nip out and get something I can cook quickly. How about a couple of chops and some mashed potatoes?'

'Get an apple pie from the baker's while you're at it, the big baker's on Halifax Road, not the one in Backhill. I like apple pies.'

'You always did. What about the money for all this food?' Knowing Eric's way of getting the better of people if they let him, she was starting off as she meant to continue.

Another thoughtful silence, then, 'We'll put money in a jar on the kitchen mantelpiece. We'll both put some in every week.'

'I don't eat half what you do so I'm not putting in as much. Two-thirds from you and one third from me would be fair, don't you think?'

Another assessing gaze, then a nod. 'All right. You never ate enough to keep a flea going in the old days an' you've not put on an ounce of weight since that I can see. Mum was scrawny too. I take after Dad in looks, but I'm not a fool like him.'

Everyone in London had always teased her about how little she ate. So had Len. But she always felt well and had plenty of energy, so she didn't care what they thought.

'I'll want accounts keeping, our Vi. I like to know where every penny goes.'

She was intrigued by how much he'd changed and knew he wouldn't have learned to do anything if he didn't see a use for it. 'All right. Do you—?'

But she was talking to thin air. He'd gone downstairs again, his curiosity satisfied for the moment. He didn't chat for the pleasure of it, their Eric, only if he was interested in something. He hadn't changed all that much, though he had a harder look to his face these days.

She put on her hat and coat. There was just time to go with Doris to see the baker, then she'd buy the food for tea.

The baker listened to Vi's request, then looked at Doris, who had smartened herself up considerably, even if the clothes were rather brightly coloured.

'Could be useful,' he allowed after a moment's thought. 'It'll bring us in more for the broken bits than if we tried to sell 'em cheap at the end of the day. We don't always get rid of them all.' Another stare, then, 'Your ma allus paid cash. Your dad wouldn't do that, so I stopped dealing with him.'

'I can pay cash,' Doris said quickly.

He looked at Vi. 'You working back at the shop again?'

'No, but I'm helping Doris settle in. You know what Dad's like.'

'I won't do business with *him* again, no matter what.'

'Doris will be handling that side of things from now on.'

They left the shop with two big bags of broken pieces. When they got back, Vi showed Doris how to divide them into amounts that would fit into paper bags and how to calculate a small profit on each, even a farthing helped, but still allow the customers a bargain.

Her father came in while they were working and reached out

to grab a piece of bread. Doris slapped his hand out of the way. 'If you want any of this, you pay – and not from the till, neither.'

'You'll be sorry you ganged up on me,' he growled.

Doris grabbed a tin of sardines and thumped it on the counter for emphasis. 'And *you* will be sorry you wasted all my savings if you don't let me start earning them back, Arnie Gill!'

'I'm bigger 'n' you. I can just *take* what I want.'

'And you're usually drunk, so you don't know what you're doing half the time.'

His voice became aggrieved. 'You like a drink too.'

'A drink, not the amount of beer you swill down. I've seen enough drunken fools to make sure I'll never get drunk again. And if you thump me, I'll wait till you're asleep and thump you with whatever's to hand. You'll never feel safe for a minute. I mean that. Cross my heart and hope to die.' She suited the action to the words.

'Bitch!' He swung round and opened the till, yelping in shock. 'Where's the money? Haven't you took owt today?'

'I've got it safe. I don't want no one pinching it. Asking for trouble it was, leaving it in the drawer.' Doris folded her arms.

Vi hoped her father hadn't noticed how his wife's hands were shaking.

'How are we to live if we don't take money out of the till?'

Vi took over, trying to help Doris hammer the point home. 'You take out a week's money at a time, and how much you take depends on how much you've sold during the week. Ten per cent would be a fair amount. You know that as well as I do, Dad. It's what Mum always did.'

'*She* knew how to run a shop. This one doesn't, so I'm in charge now.'

'You're hardly ever here these days, and I'm showing Doris what to do, so she'll be fine from now on.'

He brightened up. 'You're coming back to work here?'

'No. I told you: I'll never do that again.'

'Too good for us now, are you?'

'I came here to stay with you, didn't I? And I'm living with our Eric now. That doesn't sound as if I look down on my family.' Vi turned to her stepmother. 'Do you need anything else?'

'Not now, love. You get off. You've Eric's tea to cook. You want to keep on the right side of him.'

Vi smiled at her father. 'Eric says he'll keep an eye on the shop from now on, for Mum's sake. We don't want you going out of business, do we?'

He scowled at her. '*You* brought him into things again.'

'Of course I did. He can be a big help, can Eric.' She winked at Doris, then walked briskly back to Mayfield Place, stopping on the way to buy the food for tea. She felt sorry for Doris, who'd got a poor bargain in her father . . . just as her mother had. Vi's husband had been a good man, but he'd been killed, while her father was still going strong. It didn't seem fair.

On the way home she met Mr Bentley and when he smiled and stopped, she did too. He was another good man. She'd taken to him straight away.

'How are things?' he asked.

'I'm starting to get settled. I need to find a job now. And you?'

'Things aren't going as well as I'd expected, but I'll sort something out.'

'Are you working back in the shop?'

'No. My brother took over from me and there's not enough work for two.' He sighed. 'I have to find a house to rent. I crossed Sully, who got his assistant to throw me out of my house. It won't be easy to find another, because Sully's put the word round.'

'I'm sorry. He's a horrible man.' *Assistant?* Could that be Eric? She hoped not.

'I need someone to look after my baby for me as well.' He sighed.

'I hope you find someone soon.' The town hall clock chimed the hour and she stepped back. 'I didn't realise it was so late. I must be going. I've my brother's tea to cook.'

When she reached the corner she stopped and stole a quick glance back at him. To her surprise, he was still standing where she'd left him, watching her.

He raised one hand in a wave then walked away.

Why had he been staring like that?

And why had she betrayed her interest by stopping to look back? He was a fine figure of a man, must have lots of women showing an interest. She didn't want him to think she was . . . Anyway, he'd not fancy a scrawny female like her and . . . She blushed at the thoughts that were going through her mind as she hurried up the hill to Eric's house.

What on earth had got into her?

The following day Sully turned up at Fairview again. The sisters watched from their window as he tried the front door then hammered on it. When they didn't answer, he stood back a bit, studying the house, and yelled, 'I know you're there. You're foolish to ignore Mr Kirby's offer. If you go on at this rate, you'll get nothing for this old ruin. It's a wonder it hasn't burnt down before now. It'd burn up really easily, this place would.'

Laughing, he ambled off down the drive, stopping to kick a rosebush as he went, breaking off the central stem.

Shuddering, the two sisters looked at one another.

'Burn down!' Phyllis clutched Christina's arm. 'Kirby wouldn't mind if Fairview burned down. He wants to knock it down anyway. He wouldn't . . . Surely he wouldn't? He doesn't seem *that* bad.'

'No, but Sully is. And there'd be no one to help us if he did set the place on fire.' She hesitated. 'I wonder . . . Come and sit down, dearest. I have an idea . . .'

When Joss brought back the bicycle, she went outside to help him put it away. 'Have you found anywhere to live yet, Mr Bentley?'

'No. I hope you didn't mind me keeping the bicycle till this afternoon. It was a big help. I went everywhere looking for a house, but no one has any available for rent – or they say they don't, even though I saw a couple of empty ones with a "To Rent" sign in the window. Still, that's not your problem.'

'I may be able to help. Could you spare me a few minutes? We'll just put the bicycle away first.'

She led the way towards the rear and he followed. She let him put the bicycle away for her in a storeroom at the end of the stable block and padlocked it carefully. She'd be lost without it. She turned and pointed. 'That cottage was for the head gardener. It's empty now and I haven't been inside it for a while. Let's see if it's still habitable.'

He looked at her, mouth half-open as if he'd guessed what she was going to suggest, then followed her across the back yard. The hope in his eyes touched her.

He followed her around the cottage, which had three bedrooms upstairs, living room, kitchen and scullery downstairs. 'It's a bit old-fashioned, but there is a gas cooker and sink.' She looked round at the cobwebs which draped the corners, the dust which lay thick on surfaces and grimaced. 'It needs a good clean.' When she tried the tap in the kitchen it wouldn't turn.

He turned it on for her easily and some brownish water gushed out, turning clear after the first minute or so.

'It's not in very good condition, but we wondered, my sister and I, if you'd like to live here. You'd have to clean it out yourself, though. We couldn't do that. There's plenty of room for you and your children, and we wouldn't mind them playing in the garden. We like children.'

Joss swallowed hard, afraid to speak in case his voice broke. He'd been feeling utterly downhearted at leaving Roy and Iris with Mrs Tomlinson and now, out of the blue, here was an offer of help . . . of hope. It seemed too good to be true, a cottage with lovely big rooms like these. 'Are you sure?'

'Very sure. And – please don't be offended, but we'd be happy for you to stay here rent-free if you'd – help us out now and then.'

'Rent-free!' He watched her bite her lip, looking down, then looking back at him anxiously.

'It's a bit of a poisoned chalice we're offering you, I'm afraid. That Sully person has been here again today. He didn't get in, but he shouted at us, said how quickly the house would burn down.'

*'He threatened to burn it down?'*

'Not exactly. He just said it'd burn quickly. But that frightened us. So we thought . . . maybe we should have other people around. There's only my sister and Cook living here now. The woman who comes in to clean for us is a daily.'

Joss had to let out a long, shuddering breath before he could speak, so relieved was he. 'I'd love to live here, Miss Christina, but it's a bit complicated with the children. My wife died in childbirth and my sister can't look after the baby any longer because she's expecting one of her own soon. So I'll need to find someone to care for the child and do some housework for me. And I have to find a job, too. The shoe shop can only support my brother and parents, and anyway, I don't want to go back to that. I do have some money saved, though.'

'Well, it'd be a start to move in, wouldn't it?'

'You're sure? Then I thank you from the bottom of my heart. I'll do all I can to help you about the place in return. I'm pretty handy with repairs and such.'

'That would be wonderful. And there are certain – um – commissions you could undertake for us as well, for which we'd pay you.'

Joss saw colour stain her cheeks as she explained that they were having to sell their valuables one by one to survive. He hadn't realised things were so bad. She made no complaint, just told him the unvarnished truth.

'I'd be happy to help you.'

'You would?'

'Yes. And I'm sure I can get more money because I'll try several places in Manchester so that I can compare prices.'

'We thought it'd be fair to give you ten per cent of what you get for each item. Would that be acceptable?'

'Very acceptable. If I didn't have to support my family, I'd do it for you without pay, for the Captain's sake. But as it is, I promise you I'll do my very best for you, get as much as I can.'

'I know you will. And of course, we'll meet your expenses for going into Manchester.'

'Just the train fare, that's all.' As he took her hand, to shake on the bargain, he felt how frail and delicate hers was. An elderly lady's hand, with carefully cared for nails, but with reddened skin as if she'd had her hands in water. Her blouse was faded, but he was pretty sure it was silk. Like her sister's, her shoes were worn out, but highly polished. Perhaps he could get enough for the things she was selling for them to buy some new shoes. He could never bear to see people in broken-down footwear.

'What do you want me to sell for you?'

'It's a piece of silver. It's been in the family for over a hundred years and I hate to part with it, but I must. Come and see.'

She took him in via the rear of the house this time, and showed him a storeroom with a locked door. Inside were cupboards, each of which was again locked. 'The silver store,' she said, opening a cupboard and taking out an epergne, a lovely piece. 'We had another one, slightly smaller. I thought it'd be quite valuable but I only got fifty pounds for it. I won't let this one go for less than that and it ought to bring more.'

He picked it up, studying the fine workmanship with appreciation. 'It's beautiful. And surely it's worth more than fifty pounds?'

She nodded. 'It ought to be.'

'Well, if you'll wrap it up for me, I'll take it into Manchester as soon as I can. It'll be quite safe at my parents' because there's someone in the house all the time. Oh, and you'd better give me a letter authorising me to sell it on your behalf. I'm going to visit reputable jewellers, not pawnbrokers.'

She produced a fancy padded leather case and he stopped her putting the epergne into it. 'That shows I've got something valuable. Find me an old shopping bag and a ragged cloth to wrap the silver in so that no one will suspect what's inside.'

She stared at him for a moment or two, then smiled. 'How clever!'

Worried that he might be waylaid by Sully and terrified of losing the silver, Joss went and reconnoitred before he left the grounds. He saw a man crouching in some bushes just outside the front gates, Ted Fitch, a nasty type who worked for Sully.

Grateful for his military training, he climbed over the rear wall of the property, slipped quietly down the steep rough ground to the next street, which meant climbing over someone's garden wall. At one point a woman came out of the house and he ducked hastily behind a shed, waiting till she'd shaken the crumbs from a tablecloth. When she went back inside without giving any sign that she'd noticed him, he let out his breath in a whoosh, waited a moment or two, then moved down the side of the house, thankful that gardens here were quite big, so that he didn't have to pass close to the kitchen window.

He kept a careful watch for anyone following him as he made his way quickly into town, feeling safer when he was on the main street with lots of people around.

After he'd left the shopping bag at home in his bedroom, he went round to the police station and reported a suspicious character lurking near Fairview. 'I'm worried about Miss Warburton and her sister. Perhaps he's planning to rob them. The ladies are on their own out there.'

The Constable, who was sloppily dressed and older than the usual policeman, took down the details, but didn't really seem interested.

Joss slapped his hand down on the counter and raised his voice. 'If I hear that those ladies have been attacked, I'll report you to the officer in charge of this area for negligence.' He looked up to see another man in uniform standing in the doorway of an office to one side, watching him. He was pleased to see a sergeant's insignia on the man's arm.

'Is there a problem?' the stranger asked.

'I'm reporting a suspicious character lurking near Fairview, where two elderly ladies are living on their own. Your constable here doesn't seem interested.'

The man came forward, holding out one hand. 'Rob Piper, just returned from the war. I'm the new sergeant in charge and I *am* interested.'

'Joss Bentley, also just back from the war, except that I've yet to find myself a job.'

'Come into my office.' Piper indicated a chair and added in a low voice, 'I'll just leave the door open, if you don't mind, and keep an eye on that fellow. I've never seen such sloppy policing in my life.'

Joss explained the situation again, also telling him about Sully's visits and the way he'd walked into the house without being invited, the threat implied in what he'd said. When he'd finished, Piper looked thoughtful.

'I'll definitely tell my men to keep their eyes open when they're patrolling and if you see the old ladies, tell them to report any further problems to me. Better give me your address, too.'

'I'm one of the Bentleys who own the shoe shop on Halifax Road, so you'll not find me hard to contact. I'm staying there temporarily till I can get a home together for my children.'

'And your interest in the Misses Warburton?'

'I'm going to be living in a cottage in their grounds and I'm doing a little business for them.' He hesitated, then said, 'In confidence, I'm selling a piece of silver for them because they're temporarily embarrassed for money. Their brother was killed in the war, you see.' For some reason, he was sure Piper wouldn't repeat that to anyone.

'They're not the only ones to lose their menfolk and find themselves in financial trouble. The war's changed a lot of things for everyone, people of their class included.'

Joss went on his way feeling a little better about the situation, but his satisfaction faded as he arrived at his sister's house. He didn't want to spend time with that baby.

Pam was holding Nora again as she opened the front door. 'Ah, there you are, Joss.'

He explained what had happened, then asked the name of the woman who might look after Nora for him, explaining about the offer of a house.

Pam frowned. 'It's a long way into town. You'll have to start early in the morning once you've found yourself a job.'

'I know. But I don't have any choice, thanks to Sully. I'll go and see this Mrs Lowe then.'

That same morning Vi read Eric's newspaper after he'd gone to work. It was only because she was studying the Jobs Vacant Section carefully looking for another advert for The Health Visitor positions, that she saw a small notice at the bottom of a column. You'd think they'd have taken out a bigger advert for that.

Those interested in the three positions were to obtain details from the Town Clerk. She took in a deep breath as hope flooded through her. She was sure she could do a job like that after her experience in the Major's unit.

She went down to the Town Hall and spoke to the clerk on the front counter. She'd been at school with Donny, a pleasant lad he'd been but not ambitious. You could still see that in his face. She wondered how he'd avoided being called up.

'You'll need to write a letter and provide supporting details.' Leaning forward as he handed her some roneoed papers, he added in a low voice, 'Waste of your time, Vi love. Mrs Gilson only ever appoints her friends.'

'I thought she'd have been too old for this job. And anyway, she's a lady, why would she need it?'

'She likes bossing people round. She's already talking about what she's going to do and who's going to be working with her.'

Disappointed, Vi walked away, wondering if it was even worth bothering to apply. It'd be hard to work with Mrs Gilson and . . . She stopped and told herself not to listen to Donny. He didn't know everything. She'd write an application so good they'd be *forced* to consider her seriously. There weren't many suitable jobs in Drayforth. This might be the only one to interest her.

She spent the rest of the day composing her application, doing it properly, as she had seen other people do in the unit in London. She made copies of her testimonials in her best handwriting, wrote out her final letter and then took it along to the Town Hall late that afternoon.

Donny wasn't there and after she'd waited for a while, with no one answering the bell on the counter, a man peered out of an office. He looked round with a frown, then turned back to her.

'Can I help you, madam?'

'I wanted to hand in my application for a Health Visitor job. But there's no one here.'

He came out of the office. 'You can give it to me.'

'Certainly. But I'd like a receipt for it.' That was another thing she'd learned to do. 'Could I ask who you are?'

He smiled. 'I'm the Mayor, actually. Albert Palmer at your service.' He held out his hand.

'Pleased to meet you,' she said as she shook his hand. 'I'm Mrs Schofield.'

'Ah. I'm afraid we have a rule about not employing married women. We prefer to keep our jobs for the breadwinner of the family.'

'I'm a widow. My husband was killed in France.'

'That would be all right, then.' He looked down at her application. 'The applications are all to come to me, so I'll write you out a receipt and then I'll be in touch later. We're allowing until tomorrow evening for people to apply, then we'll interview the best candidates.' He didn't say that this was the first one he'd received, even though it was the second week the advertisement had been in the paper. He still didn't understand why Donny had put in such a small advertisement after he'd been told to pay for a box round it.

Vi waited for the receipt and walked back, feeling she'd spent a useful day. She'd only just got back to Drayforth in time, though. What if she'd gone looking for work a week later?

Surely she'd get one of these jobs?

When Mrs Schofield had left, Albert walked back into his office and opened the envelope, letting out a whistle as he saw the glowing testimonials and the names of her referees.

He heard movement outside and went to speak to the clerk about leaving the desk unattended for so long.

'I wasn't gone long, Mr Palmer. I had to take another application round to Mrs Gilson. She likes them taking to her straight away and she doesn't live far.'

'I beg your pardon?'

The man looked at him in surprise at the sharp tone. 'That's what we always do when she needs help.'

'How many applications have you received?'

'Four, Mr Palmer.'

'Then you'd better go round and get them all back again. They're to come to me first this time, as I've already told you.'

'Councillor Kirby said that had been a mistake, you being new to the job, and told me to do things the usual way.'

'Then I shall remind you that I'm the one in charge here, Donny, and suggest that in future you ask me before changing any of my instructions.' He didn't intend to be a mere figure-head as Mayor, and fortunately he had a private income now, so could spend as much time as he wanted here at the Town Hall. It was a good thing, too, because the Chief Clerk was clearly in Kirby's pocket. In fact, it was a mass of corruption here. But he knew better than to tackle that head on.

'Yes, Mr Palmer. Sorry, sir.'

'You'd better go and bring me back the applications, then. I'll keep the Town Hall open until you return.'

There was fear on the man's face, but Albert didn't relent. Mrs Gilson was an old dragon and the sooner they got rid of her and people like her, the better as far as he was concerned. He'd clipped her wings a little and later he'd find a way to replace her because she had no sympathy with those she was supposed to be helping. But he was treading carefully with the reforms he wished to introduce, because if he rocked the boat too much, he'd not get re-elected.

He locked the application in his personal filing cabinet, one he'd brought from home, to which only he had the key. He wasn't leaving anything to chance.

He was very impressed by Mrs Schofield and if she was telling the truth in her application, she would be perfect for one of the jobs. But he'd write to Lady Bingram and Major Warren to check the details first. He knew Kirby was waiting for him to slip up.

No time like the present. Whistling, Albert pulled out some official, headed notepaper and wrote two letters.

When the clerk returned empty-handed, Albert was amazed.

'I did try, sir, honest, but she refused to give them to me.'

'Very well. You can go home now.'

'Do you want me to put those letters in the post for you? The office boy's taken the mail for today.'

'No, I'll do it myself.' He glanced at the clock. 'I can just catch the final post.' He left the caretaker, who was hovering in the entrance hall, to lock up, then took the letters to the post himself before walking round to Mrs Gilson's.

The maid who opened the door looked at him unhappily. 'My mistress isn't at home, Mr Palmer.'

'Oh, I think you'll find she's at home to me.' He walked past her into the hall and stood waiting.

There was a whispered conversation in the room to his right, then the maid came out looking upset. 'If you'll go in, sir.'

In the parlour Freda Gilson was standing in front of the fire waiting for him, red patches flaring in each cheek. 'I do not appreciate being disturbed like this, Mr Palmer. I've had a very busy day. Surely, whatever it is can wait until tomorrow?'

'No. A mistake has been made and it needs rectifying immediately. The applications for the positions of health visitor have come to you instead of me, as I instructed.' He watched with interest as her bosom swelled visibly and the colour in her cheeks deepened till her whole face was puce.

'I have *always* dealt with such matters in the past, Mayor, and no one had ever found fault with what I've done.'

He was willing to spare a few conciliatory words, not willing to back down. 'You've given a lot to this town, Mrs Gilson, and it's greatly appreciated. However, the system has changed and the Health Visitors we appoint from now on will be paid professionals, not lady volunteers.' He paused and looked at her questioningly. 'And I'm surprised that I've not received an application from you for the Senior Health Visitor position. Do you intend to retire?'

If only the old harridan would. It'd save him a lot of trouble.

'Mr Kirby said it wouldn't be necessary for me to apply for my *own job*.'

'Mr Kirby is not Mayor. And you've been working in a voluntary capacity, not coming in every day, or being paid, apart from expenses. So it isn't quite the same job. You'll therefore need to apply and work to the rules, if you obtain the position.'

The silence was deafening. He waited her out.

'I'll have my application ready tomorrow, then,' she said at last. 'But I take leave to tell you, I feel insulted at having to do it.' She reached for the bell. 'Now, I really must get on. My maid will show you out.'

'You haven't yet given me the other applications.'

Their eyes met and hers were the first to drop. She muttered something and left the room without a word, returning with three envelopes, which she thrust into his hands. 'There!'

They'd been opened, he saw. 'Thank you. And in future, kindly don't open letters that are not your concern.'

'It *is* my concern who works with me.'

'*If* you get the job, dear lady, if you get the job. I should hate to have someone in such an important role who can't adapt to modern ways.'

She looked at him in shock.

He studied the envelopes. 'These are all? I was sure the clerk said there had been four.'

'The other one was ridiculous. I threw it away.'

'I hope you didn't. That is an official, public document and the law states quite clearly that it is an offence to tamper with or destroy it.'

'It may still be in my waste paper basket.' She walked out and he followed her into the hall, watching through the open door of a small room as she fumbled through some pieces of screwed up paper. Eventually she sorted out three, smoothed them on her desk and then brought them to him.

'I'll show myself out,' he said. 'Good evening, Mrs Gilson.'

She didn't say a word as she walked to the door with him and she slammed it hard behind him.

He whistled cheerfully as he walked back to the Town Hall, which was closed now. Letting himself in by the side entrance, he switched on the electric lights that had caused such a furore in town a few months ago when he'd had them installed, and went into his office.

Two of the applications were very brief, and came from Mrs Gilson's lady friends.

One was indeed ridiculous, but it wasn't the one Mrs Gilson had screwed up. It was another one that was crumpled, from a Miss Twineham, clearly a woman of experience in this area. She was a relative of the Healeys and said they could give character references. She had job references from her war work, good ones too.

He smiled as he locked all the applications away. He now had two women who seemed suitable. He'd have to give the senior job to Mrs Gilson, though, no getting away from that. And she would undoubtedly take the matter of her subordinates to Kirby, but the fact that a relation of the Healeys was one of the favoured applicants should make a difference. Kirby wouldn't want to offend one of the few families to accept him socially.

Albert was looking forward very much to changing how this town was run, even if he did have to take it slowly.

# 12

Christina cycled into town the following morning to buy some meat and bread. She quite enjoyed cycling and it made the trips much quicker. She didn't like leaving Phyllis alone for too long.

She wheeled the bicycle along the main street, seeing a big car pull up and Maud Kirby get out. When the younger woman waved and came across to say hello, Christina tried to summon up a smile, but today she couldn't.

'How are you, Miss Christina? I've not seen you for ages and thought you must be unwell. You and your sister don't attend Lily Dearby's luncheons any more.'

Maud looked so well fed and immaculately dressed, Christina suddenly became aware that her own face was flushed from cycling and there were very visible darns in her gloves. Anger rose, was held back for a moment, then boiled over.

'My sister and I don't attend such functions any longer because we can't afford to return people's hospitality.' To her surprise, Maud looked upset.

'I didn't realise things were so bad.'

'Well, they are. Please excuse me. I've the shopping to do and then I have to push it all back up that hill.'

'Look – come and have a cup of tea first. There's a cold wind today. Afterwards, I'll drive you back. We can put your bicycle in the boot.'

Christina hesitated.

'Do come.' Maud gave her a wry smile. 'I know you don't want to meet my husband, but I'd still like to keep in touch. Your sister was very kind to my mother when they were both young and Mother always spoke well of her.'

Christina hesitated and was lost. It was cold and she'd love a cup of tea. Leaning the bicycle against the wall next to the tea shop, she allowed herself to be shepherded inside. It was so long since she'd been able to afford this that she'd forgotten how pleasant it was to sit down and be fussed over by a waitress, not to mention how delicious the pastries were at Rose's Tea Rooms.

Maud waited till they were on their second cups of tea. 'Excuse me, but did your brother leave things in a mess financially?'

Christina stiffened.

'Please don't be angry, but my first husband went through all our money and I know what it's like to be left penniless. Why do you think I remarried?'

Christina looked down at the hand on her arm and blinked furiously. 'Poor Perry did his best, but he wasn't brought up to be a businessman and he made some unwise investments, I'm afraid.'

Maud's voice was low, wouldn't carry past their table. 'If I can help in any way?'

It came out before Christina could stop it. 'You could tell your husband to stop hounding us to sell Fairview to him, because we won't. It's our *home*! It's all we have left.'

'*Hounding?* Gerald is hounding you?'

'Yes. Well, his man Sully is. He walks into the house uninvited if we don't lock the door. And yesterday –' she found it hard to continue, but was determined to bring this out in the open – 'Sully shouted out before he left that the house would burn down easily.' Shaking, she fumbled for her handkerchief and dabbed at her eyes, beyond caring who saw her.

Maud took hold of her hand, clasping it in both hers. 'I didn't know. I promise you, Miss Christina, I didn't know. I'll have a word with Gerald this very evening. I doubt he knows what Sully's doing, either. That's quite outrageous and I promise you, it'll stop.'

After that, she walked round the market with Christina, chatting of pleasanter things, then insisted on driving her home, with the bicycle sticking out of the boot of the car.

'Is it hard to drive a motor car?' Christina asked wistfully.

'No. I'll teach you if you like.'

'I couldn't ask you to—'

'I've all too much time on my hands, because Gerald doesn't like me lifting a finger around the house.' She got out and helped unload the bicycle and shopping, before walking her companion to the front door where she repeated, 'I promise you, the trouble will stop.'

Christina didn't say anything, but she didn't think anyone would be able to stop Gerald Kirby going after something he wanted. And if he couldn't get to them one way, he'd try another.

Maud hadn't questioned what she'd said, had instantly accepted that her husband was behaving so badly. What sort of a marriage did they have?

That night Maud watched her husband eat his meal as if he hadn't a care in the world. She'd thought very carefully about how to approach this, was learning how to manage him – well, sometimes she could manage him.

'You're going to make a lot of enemies among the county folk,' she said casually as he poured himself a glass of brandy after the meal.

He paused, decanter in mid-air. 'I beg your pardon?'

'I said: you're going to make yourself a lot of enemies among the people you're trying to woo.'

He finished pouring and put the stopper into the decanter, setting it down carefully and picking the glass up to take a sip. 'You're no doubt going to explain yourself?'

'Of course. But I wanted to make that point first. It's the Warburtons. The way you're treating them is despicable and it's bound to come out.'

Silence. He waited, one eyebrow raised.

'I met Miss Christina in town today. The poor dear has to cycle in to go shopping. I insisted on taking her for tea at Rose's. All part of wooing certain people.'

'I doubt the Warburtons will be wooed, whatever you do.'

'Well, you're wrong there. Miss Christina has agreed to let me take her shopping every market day in my car – thank you for getting it out of storage, by the way. If that's not a start on wooing her, I don't know what is. And I've offered to teach her to drive, though she hasn't agreed to that yet. I think she will.'

'Yes. I see. Well done.'

'But she was very upset, nearly in tears in Rose's. That Sully of yours is apparently making a dreadful nuisance of himself. He threatened to burn down Fairview today.'

Gerald gaped at her. There was no other word for it, he couldn't conceal his shock. She was pleased to think this wasn't by his orders. 'I thought you'd not have told him to go so far.'

'You're sure he really did this?'

'He said their house would burn easily, which amounts to a threat, don't you think? If she's been telling other people about that and it does burn down, you'll never convince the county set you didn't have a hand in it.'

'I'd *like* it to burn down, but I did *not* tell Sully to threaten her with arson. I would never—'

'Never put yourself at such risk,' she finished for him. 'I know. What did you intend to do to make them sell?'

He was silent. 'I'm still considering that.'

'You're wasting your time, you know.'

'I always get what I want.'

'They won't move. It's their *home*.'

'They've no money. They'll have to leave it one day. And I intend to be the person who buys it.'

'I don't know why you have this fixation about Fairview.' She gestured round. 'We have a perfectly good house here. I like it.'

'I have a fancy to live on the top of the Ridge. I've wanted that since I was a small boy with a patch on the seat of my breeches, and I shan't change – whatever you say and do.'

'Well, at least call Sully off them. People have long memories for harm done to one of their own.'

'One of their own!' he spat at her. 'What the hell does it take to join the county set? I could buy and sell most of them.'

'Money won't do it. You've found that out already.' She frowned, trying to find an answer that would get through to him. 'It takes time and patience, plus behaviour that is considered gentlemanly. You're trying to push things along too quickly.' She took a sip of coffee, even though it was cold now, avoiding his eyes.

'Very well.'

She breathed a sigh of relief. 'Shall I play to you?' She saw him smile, not his usual tight smile but a genuine one. It was incongruous that a man as ruthless and money-loving as Gerald should also be fond of classical music. She had a modest talent, she knew, but he loved to hear her play the piano.

She went to sit at the piano and began with his favourite tune 'Liebestraum'. It wasn't one of her favourites, too flowery, but it always put him in a good mood.

She'd said enough for tonight, but she knew he'd still be trying to find a way to get hold of Fairview. Well, she'd find way to stop him, if anyone could. She'd no intention of letting him throw the poor old Warburton sisters out of their home.

Eric, told curtly to wait in the entrance area of Kirby's place of business while Sully had a quiet word with their employer, winked at the lass sitting at the front counter and put one finger to his lips. He moved quietly towards the door through which Sully had disappeared, knowing that for a shilling she'd keep quiet about him eavesdropping. Well, she couldn't reveal it now without betraying the fact that she'd allowed this to happen several times before.

He was finding out quite a lot about what was going on, building up a picture that even Mr Kirby didn't know all the details of.

He grinned as he listened to the conversation. Sully was getting a right earful today. Serve the bugger right. Eric couldn't stand Sully, who thought he admired him. Admired! If he couldn't do the job better than Sully without half the trouble caused by Sully's confrontations, he didn't know how to breathe.

'You'll stay away from Fairview from now on,' Kirby finished, 'and when I give you instructions, you'll follow them to the letter without adding threats of your own. *To the letter!*'

'Yes, sir. I was just trying to help, sir, move things along, like.'

'Then help by doing as I say, and doing only that in future. The war's over now and we have to become law-abiding citizens.'

Eric smiled. Kirby might turn law-abiding, but Sully never would. The man was a bully. However, although he was ruthless and cunning, he wasn't quick-witted and he knew only one way to achieve what he wanted: brute force.

As the interview started to wind down, Eric ambled back to his chair, leaving a shilling on the counter as he passed. By the time he sat down, the coin had vanished. When he looked towards the girl, she was busy typing, clacking away on that machine as if butter wouldn't melt in her mouth.

Sully was in a foul mood for the rest of the day, which Eric accepted philosophically.

As the afternoon drew on, he began to feel peckish and wondered what Vi would be making for tea tonight. She was a good little cook. And she didn't natter on at you in the evenings, but sat reading one of those books of hers, or writing letters. He couldn't abide women whose tongues never stopped flapping.

His sister knew a lot too, the sorts of things he wanted to know. She hadn't wasted her chances in London.

Vi looked up as Eric came into the kitchen. He sniffed the air and smiled, but didn't say anything, just nodded approvingly.

'Ten minutes,' she said.

Another nod.

'Go and wash your hands.'

He looked at them in mild surprise. 'They're not dirty.'

'You wanted to learn the ways of the nobs. They always wash their hands before they eat.'

'I wouldn't have thought they ever got their hands dirty.'

'They don't. But they're very clean with their food and they don't get upset stomachs nearly as often as folk in the Backhill Terraces.'

He went into the scullery, washed his hands then came and sat at the table. He didn't say anything, or even look at her as he waited for his food.

Vi sighed. She missed a bit of a chat in the evenings. 'I went to the Town Hall today with my application.' Ah, she had his attention now.

'The Mayor took it himself. But Donny Gibbs was on the front counter and he whispered that Mrs Gilson would be making the appointments and she only gave the jobs to her friends. Pity. I'd have loved one of those jobs.'

'You'll find something else.'

She began serving up. 'If we were nobs, we'd have the food in dishes and then we'd help ourselves.'

'Waste of clean dishes, that.'

'I know. But you said to tell you things, so I am.'

'We could try it, I suppose.'

'No, thank you. I've enough washing up to do as it is.' She brought the plates to the table, his piled high with food, hers with a much more modest portion, and sat down.

He glanced at her plate. 'No wonder you're so small.'

She watched him put a huge forkful of food into his mouth, chew and close his eyes blissfully. She'd never seen a man enjoy his food as Eric did.

'I could pay you to be my housekeeper instead,' he said suddenly.

'No, thank you.'

He frowned. 'It'd be a cushy job.'

'It'd be boring. I'd never meet new people, never do anything that gave me real satisfaction. I'm not fond of housework, Eric. I do it because I have to and because I want things to be clean, but I don't enjoy it. I'm like you. I've got a brain and I'm not happy unless I'm using it.'

Tess came home from doing the shopping to find Joe missing. She couldn't imagine where he was, because he could hardly walk and never went out willingly.

Then a neighbour came flying through the door without knocking. 'Come quick!'

'What is it?'

The neighbour looked at the girls and jerked her head, so Tess followed her outside.

'I'm sorry, love, but your Joe's hanged himself. They're cutting him down now. He did it down the back of the laundry, in that old shed.'

Tess stared at her in shock, pressing her breast with one hand as the enormity of this sank in. For a moment she could only stand there, while the world seemed to spin around her. 'Look after – the girls for me. I – don't want them to . . .'

The neighbour patted her arm. 'I'll take them home with me.'

Tears streaming down her cheeks, Tess set off running, repeating his name to herself under her breath, 'Joe, Joe, Joe.' It couldn't be true. It couldn't.

But when she got there, she saw that it was. They'd cut him down and the manager of the laundry was in the middle of the group looking down at the still figure.

She paused on the edge of the crowd.

Someone said, 'It's his wife.' The crowd parted to let her through and she had to move forward, didn't want to, wished it was all a nightmare.

She stopped next to the body. Joe looked so small and thin. He didn't look as bad as she'd expected, though he looked bad enough. She buried her face in her hands for a minute, not wanting to show them how intense her grief was. War hadn't killed him, but Mrs Gilson had. Her hatred for that woman almost scalded her throat.

'If it's any comfort, he did it properly,' someone said from next to her. 'He made sure the knot was tied right and his neck broke, so he didn't suffer.'

Could you hang yourself properly? she wondered, feeling sick. She looked down at Joe again, saw that everyone else was doing the same, so pulled off her pinafore and threw it over his face. She couldn't stand to see them all gawping at him like that, not her Joe.

'They've sent for the police,' the same voice murmured, then the man spoke more loudly, 'Find his wife a chair, someone. Have you no pity?'

She was sitting down on a rough bench someone had brought in from outside when the policeman arrived, and it was the new fellow, the stranger who'd just started in the town. She pulled her arms more tightly across herself to hold in the dark tide of grief that was threatening to wash her away.

The Sergeant spoke to her gently, but she couldn't seem to concentrate on the words. He left her sitting there and cleared the area of everyone but herself, the manager and the man who'd found Joe. She was vaguely grateful for that, but everything still seemed to be happening at a great distance.

He examined the body, asked the men some questions quietly before coming across to sit beside her. 'Mrs Donovan, I'm sorry to intrude on your grief, but if I can just ask you: was there any reason that you know of for your husband to take his own life?'

She bowed her head, wondering what to say, then looked up at him, finding his gaze so sympathetic that it gave her courage to tell the truth. 'He'd been gassed, but they wouldn't give him a pension because it wasn't as badly as some. He'd had asthma all his life, you see, bronchitis as well, and hid it so that he could join up like the other men. What with the asthma and the gassing, he could hardly move without gasping for breath. But the Pensions Board wouldn't give him any money because that Mrs Gilson said it was the asthma that was making him unable to work, not the gassing. So we didn't get our twenty-five shillings a week.'

She had to pause for a minute. 'I hate her, you know. It's because of her that Joe lost hope. I heard how she *made* the Pensions Board refuse him. I had a job then, so we scraped along for a bit, but when Mam died I'd no one to look after the children, look after Joe too, come to that. He couldn't seem to concentrate and our youngest scalded herself one day when he was watching them. So I had to give up my job or who knew what would happen to the children.

'The Panel made us sell everything we owned. Everything! Even the kids' decent school shoes and clothes. Joe kept saying

I'd be better off without him, but I'm not. *I'm not!*' Then the grief overcame her and she couldn't say another word for sobbing.

When she managed to stop, she found that the new sergeant had his arm round her, letting her weep against his chest. Embarrassed, she pulled away.

He asked in a very gentle voice, 'Can you manage now, Mrs Donovan?'

'I'll have to, won't I?'

He fished in his pocket and pulled out a clean handkerchief, but someone had folded her pinafore and put it next to her so she used that to mop her face. They'd found a blanket to cover Joe with, thank goodness. One of his boots was poking out, showing the hole in its sole. More tears began leaking out of her eyes at the sight of that hole, but she felt too drained to sob: old and drained and hopeless.

Then someone pushed through the crowd and Vi appeared. The sergeant jumped up to stop her, but after talking to Vi for a moment, he stood aside. It was heaven to have Vi's arm round her, to hear her friend's voice, to know someone would look after her, just till she got used to it all.

'Let's get you home now, Tess love. There's nothing else you can do here. They have to get a doctor to look at Joe before you can have the body back and bury him.'

Then Tess realised something else and let out a wail. 'He'll only have a pauper's funeral. Oh, Vi, I can't *bear* that for him! The war killed him as surely as it killed the men who were shot. He deserves a proper burial, at least.'

There was a movement just outside the door and she saw that a crowd of people had gathered. After her outburst they started looking at one another and suddenly they were pulling coins out of their pockets and putting them in a cap one man whipped off his head.

'I can't take their money,' she whispered to Vi, agonised at the thought of having to accept yet more charity.

'Why not? They're only giving a few pennies each. You'd do the same in their place.'

'But I—' She broke off. Yes, she would have given in their place. It wasn't the meagre charity the Panel offered so grudgingly, but was given out of the goodness of their hearts. She nodded, beyond words.

By the time the two women left, Tess's pinafore was full of coins and she clutched it to her breast as they walked through the streets.

'If it's not enough to pay for a funeral, I'll make up the difference,' Vi said.

'I can't let you do that.'

'You can't stop me.'

But when they got back to the house, Tess looked at her friend. 'Will you look after the money for me? If that Mrs Gilson knows I've got it, she'll take it off me.'

'Surely not!'

'She will. She's a terrible woman. If she dropped dead tomorrow there's a lot of people in this town who'd cheer, and I'd be one of them.'

So of course Vi took charge of the money. Could Mrs Gilson really be that bad? Well, she'd never find out, because it didn't sound as if she had any chance of getting that job.

When Eric came home, Vi told him what had happened, still indignant. 'Will you help me organise a funeral? Just a simple one.'

'How much money have you got?'

She told him.

'That isn't enough, even for the cheapest funeral.'

'I'll make up the difference myself.'

'Why? He's not even a relative.'

'He's Tess's husband and she's a close friend of mine. And she was good to our mother.' She saw that had made him think.

'But still, it's a lot of money.'

'I've got some savings.'

There was a knock on the door. An old man stood there, nodded to them and said hurriedly, 'We took another collection in the laundry after work. I think you'll have enough money for the funeral now. Mrs Donovan said you were arranging it.' He held out his cap, which was heavy with coins.

Vi took it from him. 'That's very kind of them.'

'Joe Donovan fought for our country. That bloody Pensions Board ought to be shot for not looking after him, and the Panel too. Pardon my swearing, but it gets me proper mad, the way some folk act.'

'Me too. Please tell everyone thank you. Give me a minute to find something to put this in.'

When he'd gone, Eric looked at her, still with a faint air of puzzlement. 'I can never understand why they do that sort of thing.'

'Wouldn't you help a friend out?'

'I haven't got any friends. They stop you getting on, friends do, and ask you to do things for them. I've not got time for that. I helped Mam and I'd help you if you needed it, our Beryl too, perhaps, but I'd not help anyone else.'

'If you want to mix with the nobs, Eric, you have to show that you care for people who're worse off than you.'

'Mr Kirby doesn't.'

'And the other nobs hate him. You should have seen the expression on Lady Bingram's face when his name came up one day and she usually thinks the best of people. I think it's good business sense to treat people fairly and gain their respect. They work harder for employers they respect.'

'You can't be too soft with folk or they'll do nowt.'

'I agree. You mustn't be too soft, but you mustn't be too hard, either. Like Kirby and that Mungo Sully. I don't know how you can bear working with *him*.'

'I'm learning a lot from him.'

'A lot of wrong things.'

'I'm making money.'

'But not looking ahead far enough to how you're going to enjoy that money, find a wife, bring up children. If people hate you, your family will have a bad time.'

Eric shook his head in bafflement. 'Eh, you came back from London with some funny ideas, our Vi.'

'I went to London with these same ideas. They're what Mum tried to teach us.'

'Well, she was too soft as well. Look at how our dad walked all over her.'

Vi stopped trying to reason with him. She'd never been able to figure out what went on inside Eric's head. She hated to think of him working with Sully, though, getting the same sort of reputation. That man was feared in the Backhill area for good reasons. It was whispered that he'd even committed murder.

People were starting to fear Eric as well. She'd heard the whispers. But he didn't have a name for brutality – not yet, anyway. She prayed he never would. Her mother would turn in her grave if he did.

# 13

Albert Palmer studied the two best applications for the Health Visitor jobs. He was going to have trouble with Mrs Gilson about them. And as for her own application – he flicked it with one finger so that it lifted in the air and wafted further along his desk – all she seemed to care about was saving money for the Pensions Board and the Panel, and stopping 'the improvident' from obtaining relief. She didn't once mention the welfare of those she was supposed to be helping, the need to see that children were properly fed, got an education.

His own grandfather had died in the poorhouse and his father had spent some time in it as a lad, so Albert had heard what it was like to be so helpless. He was very much against treating decent people like criminals. Not that he held any brief for drunks who wasted their wages and let their families go hungry – no, of course he didn't – but drunkenness had decreased since the beginning of the war, what with pubs closing down, opening hours being limited and the strength of beer falling markedly. Not a bad thing, that, though the damned temperance campaigners went too far, in his opinion. A couple of pints of beer never hurt anyone.

He went back to the applications. He had to find some allies or he'd never get these two women appointed. He leaned back, chewing one thumb, wondering whom he dared approach. Kirby's wife? He'd met her a few times and rather liked her. But Kirby was sure to be on Mrs Gilson's side. On the other hand, maybe the fellow could be kept from interfering if his wife was one of those helping appoint the new Health Visitors. Only Albert wasn't sure whether she'd support the Gilson woman or use her common sense and appoint the best people for the job.

How about asking Miss Warburton to help? She'd been good to him as a lad, he'd never forgotten her kindness. And Warburton was still a name to be reckoned with in the district.

He racked his brain but couldn't come up with anyone else he'd even half trust. So he went back to Maud Kirby. At least asking her help would keep Gilson out of the interviewing.

He reread the glowing references Mrs Schofield had given him in support of her application, then Lady Bingram's reply to his letter, which had come by return of post, and Major Warren's, which had come the following day, on official notepaper. They both spoke very highly of Mrs Schofield and the Major said she was a heroine, had actually saved his life during an air raid, at some risk to her own.

Yesterday's heroine, Albert thought wryly. He'd read that phrase in the newspaper and it fitted not only Mrs Schofield, but a cousin of his, who'd been praised for her war work on the railways. Then, almost as soon as the war ended, people had started jeering at her in the street and yelling at her to get back into the kitchen and leave the jobs for the men. She'd been so upset by that after all she'd done. He'd been disgusted.

That afternoon he drove himself up to Fairview. To his surprise Miss Christina Warburton opened the door to him herself.

'Albert Palmer. Mayor Palmer, I should say. How nice to see you!'

'I was always Albert to you and your sister when I was a lad. I wonder, may I have a word with you both?'

He declined an offer of tea and explained why he'd come.

Miss Warburton looked surprised, then shook her head. 'Sadly, my health isn't very good, Mr Palmer, or I'd be happy to help you. I don't get out much at all, only into the garden.'

'I'm sorry to hear that.' He looked at her sister. 'Perhaps you'd help me out, then, Miss Christina?'

'I don't think I'd know how to choose someone for a job.'

'There's nothing to it. You read the applications and talk to the candidates without frightening them. Afterwards the three of us work out who'd be the best person.'

'Do it, Christina!' Miss Warburton said. 'You ought to get out and about more, and people in our position have a duty to the community, you know Papa always told us that.'

'Well . . . all right.'

'I'll send a car for you at half-past ten on Monday and drive you back afterwards. No, it's no trouble at all, Miss Christina.'

He felt sad as he drove back at the thought of how neglected the beautiful house and gardens were. And the small sitting room had been shabby too. They must be as short of money as gossip said, poor things. Perry Warburton had been a charming fellow, but not noted for his practicality or money sense.

When their visitor had gone, Phyllis smiled at her sister. 'It makes me happy to see you taking your proper place in town life again.'

'That's all very well, but what am I going to wear? Everything I own is old-fashioned or worn, and as for my shoes . . . they're a disgrace. Oh, I do hope Mr Bentley will get us enough money for the epergne to buy some new ones. I wonder what's taking him so long?'

'I'm sure he'll get us as much as he can, more than we would ourselves. He seems a very dependable sort of man and Perry wrote highly of him in that last letter. Don't be impatient. Mr Bentley said he'd ask around, not take the first offer.' But her sister wasn't really listening.

'I think I'll wear my navy blue dress,' Christina said. 'And I'll take up the hem. That'd make it look more modern, don't you think? Women are wearing skirts much shorter these days. I see them in town with hems halfway up their calves.'

Phyllis pulled a face. 'I always think it's indecent to show your legs in public.'

Christina stood up and raised her skirt a little, staring down at her ankles. 'Well, I'm going to do it. My ankles are quite neat, still. Will you help me with the hem? You're so much better at sewing than I am.'

'I suppose so. But I don't approve.'

A little later, once they'd pinned up the hem and started work, Phyllis said suddenly, 'I could lend you my navy hat, if you like.'

'It's a bit old-fashioned.'

'I've seen drawings in those magazines the Healeys gave us. Hats are much simpler these days. Mine is the right shape and if we take most of the trimming off it and just leave one spray of feathers, we could use a new piece of ribbon to trim it. There are still a few rolls of ribbon in the sewing room.'

'Oh, would you do that for me? You have such a good eye for style.' Christina smiled. 'It's fun to fuss about what to wear, just like old times, isn't it?'

But that remark made her sister look sad again. 'Not really. In those days you'd have had a new dress to wear and good shoes.'

'I'll give these a really good polish.'

'Someone would have polished them for you in the old days.'

Joss went to the major pawnbroker in Drayforth, who offered him only fifty pounds for the epergne.

When Joss protested, the man shrugged. 'Take it or leave it'.

So he left it.

Next he went to the jewellery shop in the town centre, the one the richer folk patronised.

'Too old-fashioned,' the owner said. 'We don't deal in things like that these days. There's no call. It's mainly wedding rings and brooches.'

'How much do you think it's worth?'

'Hard to say. A thing's only worth what it'll fetch. A hundred or two, I suppose, but it's not my speciality really. Go into Manchester and try Dobson and Hawke.'

So on the Saturday Joss went into Manchester. The trouble was, the man at Dobson and Hawke didn't believe he was entitled to sell the epergne and threatened to call the police.

The second jeweller Joss visited took him into the office and seemed interested in buying the epergne, but suddenly a policeman came in.

'Is this the man, sir?'

Joss's heart sank.

The manager nodded.

The policeman turned to Joss. 'I shall have to ask you to accompany us to the police station and answer some questions about that.' He pointed to the epergne.

Joss was so embarrassed he couldn't wait to get out of the shop. At the police station he produced the letter from Miss Warburton, authorising him to sell the epergne for her, but the man interviewing him only shrugged.

'Anyone could have written that. It's not even on headed notepaper.'

Joss stood racking his brain, horrified to find himself in this situation. What was he going to do? How could he prove he hadn't taken the epergne?

Eric arranged Joe's funeral for late on Saturday afternoon, after the doctor had certified that no foul play had been involved and the magistrate had authorised the release of the body. 'I've got it done for you as cheap as you can without it being a pauper's funeral,' he told his sister.

'Thank you, Eric. That's very kind of you.'

He stared at her, affronted. 'Not *kind*. I'm trying to save money for you. This way, you won't have to shell out your savings, which I still think is a daft idea.'

'Well, thank you anyway. I'd better go and tell Tess.'

He nodded, losing interest now that he'd sorted things out.

The funeral was a hurried affair, with a cheap wooden coffin taken to the cemetery by cart, not hearse. But the cart had a piece of black material covering it and there was a black plume on the tired old horse. This small display seemed to comfort Tess and most important of all, her Joe wasn't being buried in the mass paupers' graves at the back of the cemetery, but had his own plot.

After it was all over, Vi walked slowly back with her friend and the three children followed, subdued today. 'What are you going to do now?'

Tess shook her head. 'I don't know. If my mother was alive, I could manage, but I don't want to leave Jenny and Cora with someone who won't care for them properly. I'll have to see if I can find someone to look after them, then try to find a job.'

They both knew it'd be hard for a woman to find any job that paid enough to support her family, pay the rent, even on one room in Lilybank Court, and pay for a child minder. Women's wages were only about half of men's.

As the seconds ticked away slowly on the police station clock, Joss suddenly remembered Rob Piper. 'The new police sergeant in Drayforth knows me. You could telephone him and check up.'

But the sergeant was out and the constable said it'd be an hour before he returned and approved of this, so Joss had to wait in the station, shut in a chilly little room which contained only a table and four chairs.

An hour later the older policeman came to fetch him and gestured to the telephone. 'Sergeant Piper wants to speak to you to confirm it really is you.'

Joss picked up the earpiece and after a short conversation, passed it back to the man next to him.

After a few more questions and answers, the conversation ended and the sergeant turned to him. 'That's all right, then. I hope you can see our side of things, Mr Bentley. You're not the sort of man to own that epergne and we have to protect homes and property.'

'I do see your point of view. No offence taken. I wonder if you can help me, though. In case anyone else doubts me, could they telephone you for confirmation? You see, there are two elderly ladies depending on the money I get for this. Their brother died in the service of our country and they're penniless.' He waited.

The police officer nodded, his attitude completely different now. 'Yes, sir. We could give you a letter stating that we know your situation and confirming that you're selling this epergne honestly. The jeweller can telephone us if that's not enough.'

'Thank you.'

So he had to wait around for another half-hour while a letter was composed, typed up by the female typewriter, the only female Joss had seen in the station, and signed by the sergeant.

Outside the station, Joss paused for a moment to draw in a deep breath and let the residue of his anger slip away. Once, he would have fired up at this treatment, got angry, done something silly. Not now. He had two – no, three – children depending on him, and he couldn't afford to give in to his emotions.

He went back to the same jeweller's shop, just to rub it in their face. This time he was greeted with courtesy, assured that they had only been doing their duty and then offered a price that made him blink. *Three hundred pounds!* Those poor ladies had been grossly cheated on the smaller epergne.

He stared at the plump, elderly gentleman, who was looking smug and pleased, as if he felt it a good bargain. Maybe he could push the price even higher. He shook his head and sighed. 'I'd hoped for a little more than that.' He explained again about the ladies' brother having been killed in France. 'Perhaps I'll try other jewellers.'

The man pursed his lips and stared at the ceiling for a moment or two, then looked back at the epergne. 'Very well. I'll give you another twenty pounds, but that's my final word.'

Joss pretended to consider this, then nodded. 'All right. And if the need arises again, I hope I can come to you on their behalf?'

'We shall be happy to oblige, now that we know everything is quite above board. This is a very high quality piece. I'll just go and fetch the money.'

Joss looked at the wad of five-pound notes and began to worry about being robbed. 'I wonder if you have somewhere I could go to put this inside my clothing? I don't want to risk pick-pockets.'

'Very sensible of you, sir. Actually, I happen to have an old money belt, which I shall be pleased to give you.' He pulled the item out of a drawer. 'Let me show you into the back room. You can put it on in private there.'

Joss went home with the money not only inside the belt but

underneath his long-sleeved woollen vest, which was securely tucked into his knee-length under-drawers. Even so, he was conscious of it the whole time, worrying about keeping it safe. He'd never carried so much money on him in his whole life before.

It was only on the train that he realised he'd be entitled to thirty-two pounds of that money, having agreed to take a ten per cent commission. He fought a battle with himself all the way home as to whether he'd accept this sum. It would give him and his family security for months. But he didn't like to take so much from the old ladies.

At dinner Maud waited until her husband had eaten the soup, then said brightly, 'I had a visit from the Mayor today. He wants me to help him appoint the two new Health Visitors.'

Gerald frowned at her. 'I hope you said no. He's upsetting Freda Gilson with his reforms and it's she who should be making the appointments. She does a good job of doling out charity only to those who deserve it, and even then our rates are too high.'

'He can't appoint her to the new position on his own, dear. It wouldn't be right. He needs two ladies to help him with the interviews.'

'Why you?'

'Why not? And anyway, it's a good opportunity for us.'

'It sounds more like a waste of your valuable time to me.'

She smiled. 'Ah, but guess who the other lady is who's been asked to assist him.'

Gerald sighed and waited, clearly more interested in his dinner.

'Miss Christina Warburton!'

He twitched to instant attention. 'Ah.'

'You did want me to get on better terms with her, did you not? When I found out, I was sure you'd approve, so I accepted.'

'You're right. But make sure you appoint the women Mrs Gilson wants, not the ones Palmer wants.'

'I shall do neither. I intend to appoint the ones who are most suitable for the positions.'

'And how the hell would you know that?'

'I shall ask them questions about their experience and read their references.'

'Look here, Maud, I don't want you upsetting Mrs Gilson. She's been very helpful to me. It's women like her who keep the rates down and men like Palmer who put them up, with his expensive ideas about pampering the poor.'

'I shall do my best not to upset the apple cart, dear.'

Maud rang the bell for the maid to serve the main course. She would do exactly as she'd planned, favouring neither side. Gerald wouldn't be there. She would. She was quite looking forward to it, actually. It wasn't much fun living with Gerald. He might be rich, but he worked long hours and didn't really enjoy social life, only seeing it as something that could bring him useful acquaintances. So she had a lot of spare time on her hands and so far hadn't made a really close friend in Drayforth.

And she didn't enjoy sharing a bed with Gerald, either. He had little consideration for his wife and sought only his own satisfaction.

She left him to consume a huge meal in silence and concentrated on her own plate and her own thoughts.

Life never brought you what you'd expected. But now that she had her car back, she'd have more freedom. She intended to drive it herself. She didn't need a chauffeur to tell her husband where she'd been. She was sure Gerald wouldn't approve of her being so independent, but that was too bad. She'd make up some tale to prove it was better that way if she was giving Christina Warburton lifts. He was surprisingly persuadable about social matters.

Since Palmer had taken the applications from her, he'd seen Mrs Gilson slip into a side street to avoid him, which suited him because he couldn't stand the woman. She had always dealt mainly with the Town Clerk, because Meedon was a meek little fellow whom she could bully. But Albert made sure the Town Clerk understood that from now on, the Mayor's wishes were to be respected, so she'd not managed to get her hands on the other application.

He'd asked Meedon exactly what Mrs Gilson did and the man had said in a shocked tone, 'Whatever needs doing, and all voluntarily without taking a penny. She's very experienced, so I leave it to her. She's a wonderful woman, Mrs Gilson, she is indeed. Our rates would be much higher if it weren't for her work, not only visiting the poor, but sitting on the Panel and the Pensions Board. I pass on problems or messages from the various committees and she takes care of them.'

Which wasn't much use in explaining how she dealt with people needing help, what resources she drew on to help them through bad patches, how successful she was in helping them.

However he needed to talk to her about the interview, so sent the clerk to ask her to pop in and see him on the Saturday morning, if she didn't mind.

When she was shown into his office, she looked at Albert warily.

He smiled at her. 'Would you kindly tell me what you've been doing this past week, to give me an idea of your duties before we start interviewing the applicants for the Health Visitor positions? Of course, the work will change when there are more staff to deal with problems, but it will help to know what you've been doing.' He noted her relax just a little and listened to her rambling talk with his official smile on his face.

'That's very helpful, thank you.' He felt angry at the scornful way in which she spoke about people in trouble but hid his feelings under what he thought of as his mayoral smile, which he'd perfected in front of the mirror before running for office and which he could summon up at will.

'When are we going to go through the applications, Mr Palmer?'

'Well, I'm in a bit of an anomalous position. You haven't been officially appointed to the Senior Health Visitor position yet, so I can hardly share them with you.' He watched her eyes narrow. 'I've therefore invited Mrs Kirby and Miss Christina Warburton to help me select the candidates – which of course includes the senior position. I think those ladies are a good choice, don't you?'

'I'm not sure Miss Christina Warburton will know much about it.'

'Oh? I've always found her a very sensible woman. I used to know them both when I was a youth and did odd jobs for the family. Now, if you could be here on Monday morning at eleven o'clock, we'll have the interviews for the senior position first.'

'*Interviews?* There are other people being interviewed for my—?' she broke off, glaring at him.

'Just one other.' No wonder the people she helped were afraid of her. If looks could kill he'd be lying under his desk dead.

'May I ask who the other person is?'

'I'm afraid that's confidential, my dear lady.'

She breathed deeply, then stood up. 'I see. I'll take my leave, then.'

He watched her go, wondering if she'd go running straight to Kirby or wait to see what happened at the interview. Sadly, she'd have to be appointed, because there'd be an uproar if she wasn't – from the wealthier citizens at least, the ones whose votes had put Albert in this position. But he didn't intend to let Mrs Gilson take this for granted.

Whistling under his breath he locked his filing cabinet carefully and made his way home.

When he got back to Drayforth, Joss called in at the police station and thanked Rob for helping him.

The other man grinned. 'Bit of a quandary for you, eh? I hope you got a good sum for the silver?'

'Yes.' Joss patted his midriff. 'I wonder . . . You couldn't walk up to Fairview with me, could you? Someone was following me the other day and I'd hate to lose the ladies' money.' He was amazed at the sudden change in his companion.

'You're sure about being followed?'

'Yes. And given that Mungo Sully has been pestering the ladies, well . . .'

Rob looked up at the clock then at the constable standing outside at the desk. 'I will come with you. I'd like a word with them anyway, and you can introduce me. I can't abide people taking advantage of old ladies and cheating them.'

'You'd better see the local pawn shop, then. They only gave her fifty pounds for an epergne like the one I sold today. I asked the jeweller I dealt with and he said if it was the same quality, it'd be worth at least two hundred. They're apparently rather special pieces made by a famous silversmith.'

'The pawn shop, eh? I'll put it on my list of things to be attended to. Not that I can do anything about their prices, but I can make sure they stick to the law. Proper little nest of vipers we've got here in town, don't you think?'

'Yes. A few folk took the opportunity to feather their own nests while we were away risking our lives. It makes me angry even to think of it, think of the lads who died.' It was a common complaint among men coming back, but it didn't make it any less valid. Some folk had had a hard time on the home front, while others had lined their pockets and boasted of having had 'a good war'.

The two men walked up the hill, chatting easily, enjoying each other's company.

'Ever thought of joining the police?' Rob asked as they turned into Ridge Road. 'We need some decent fellows, lost too many.'

Joss shook his head. 'No. I've had enough of being regimented and ordered round.'

'What are you going to do, then?'

'Damned if I know. But I've some money put by, so it's not desperate.'

As they walked along the drive, Rob stopped to stare at the house. 'Sad to see beautiful old places like this going to pot.'

'As long as it lasts the ladies out, that's the main thing.'

'Kirby has a point, though. They don't need all this land. You could build quite a few houses here and still leave them a good big garden. There's a shortage of good houses.'

'*He* doesn't want to build houses. He wants to build one for himself, even bigger than theirs, if rumours are true. That'll benefit no one.' Joss knocked at the door.

Miss Christina opened it. 'Mr Bentley.' Her eyes went to his companion.

'This is Sergeant Piper. He's new to the town. I thought you should meet him in case there's any more trouble.'

She inclined her head. 'I'm pleased to make your acquaintance, sergeant. Do come in.'

When they were in the hall, Joss said, 'I've completed your little errand. And did quite well for you.'

She stared at him, hope in her eyes.

'I got three hundred and twenty pounds.'

'Oh, my!' She collapsed on to a chair in the hall, one hand to her mouth for a moment, then began fanning her face.

'Are you all right?'

She nodded. 'Yes. It was just the shock. I'm all right. I can't believe you got so much for it.'

'You were cheated on the smaller piece, Miss Christina, and you'd have got more money if you'd sold them as a matched pair, apparently.'

'I would? Oh dear, I wish I'd known that. I feel so ignorant sometimes.' She pulled herself together with a visible effort. 'Fancy keeping you standing in the hall like this. Do come into the sitting room. It's the only place where we've got a fire and it's such a cold day.' She led the way and made the introductions, then sat down beside her sister. 'Phyllis, dear, Mr Bentley has done better than we could ever have expected. Three hundred and twenty pounds. We can live for months on that.'

The two women looked at one another, clearly close to tears.

Joss felt so sorry for them, he couldn't speak either for a moment or two. Then he suddenly had an idea. 'Why don't I try to buy back the other epergne and then take it into Manchester to sell? You'd have to give me the money for it, though.'

Miss Christina stared at him. 'Could we do that?'

'We could try.'

It was Rob who brought the discussion back to practicalities. 'Where are you going to keep the money – or shall you put it into the bank? That would be safer.'

'Into the bank, of course. Well, most of it. We'll need some to buy back the other epergne. And we owe you some, Mr Bentley. Ten per cent, we said, and you've certainly earned it.'

'I can't take that much. It wouldn't be fair.'

She drew herself up and gave him a suddenly frosty look. 'We agreed on ten per cent and you will accept no less.'

No argument would move her from that stance.

When Joss gave in, Rob took over again. 'I'd like to send a constable to escort you into town with the money on Monday, if that's all right? I believe you've been having a bit of trouble out here lately?'

It was Miss Warburton who spoke. 'That would be very kind of you, sergeant.'

Christina laughed. 'I shan't need an escort, thank you. I'm helping the Mayor to interview women for the new Health Visitor positions and he's promised to send a car for me.'

'That's all right, but what about until then?' Rob insisted. 'I really don't like to think of the two of you here with no man within call.'

'How about I come and stay here?' Joss suggested. 'I shan't consider I've earned my share until I've seen that money safely into the bank. And anyway, I need to clean out that cottage.' He turned to explain to Rob about coming to live here.

'We accept,' Phyllis said.

Joss suddenly remembered where the money was. 'I need to be private to get the money for you. It's in a money belt under my clothes, for safety.'

'Good idea,' Rob said. 'And where are you going to keep it, Miss Warburton?'

'In Father's safe.'

'Let me check it out.'

When the money had been retrieved and put into the safe, the men took their leave.

'I'll come back after tea. I need to get my clothes and my mother will have my meal ready.' Joss guessed there wouldn't be much food in the house and didn't want to take theirs.

The two men strode into town.

'I don't like taking that much money off them,' Joss worried. 'It doesn't seem fair.'

'You'll not get them to accept what they see as charity, lad. But you can help them in other ways, like staying there to keep an eye on the money.'

Joss walked back to Fairview an hour later, carrying a cake his mother had baked and his kitbag with his nightclothes in it. As if he didn't have enough responsibilities! Now there were two elderly ladies relying on him.

But they had a cottage where he could live, if only he could work out how to have the baby cared for, it might be the very thing.

After he'd settled the immediate problems, he'd try to find out who the father was, though that wasn't going to be easy to do without giving away his reasons for asking. He didn't want to blacken Ada's name, but better do that than be saddled with someone else's child for the next twenty years.

Even as that thought crossed his mind, an image of the rosy baby smiling up at him made him falter in his steps, but he pushed it away, focusing on the practical aspects of what to do on Monday after he'd seen the money safely off to the bank. He mustn't weaken where the baby was concerned, or it'd be another mouth to feed.

The first thing would be to put his share of the money into his own bank account. He'd feel a lot more secure with that behind him. Then he'd see about someone to look after the baby.

# 14

On the Sunday Joss woke up and couldn't for a moment think where he was. Then he realised he was at Fairview and allowed himself to lie for a few minutes in the comfort of a double bed. He'd been prepared to sleep rough in the cottage, but the sisters had insisted he sleep in the house. After a while, he fumbled for the matches to light the candle. Picking up his pocket watch, he looked at the time. Eight o'clock. Just getting light. They'd said breakfast was at nine.

He lay back again, but couldn't settle, so in the end he got up and washed in the cold water he'd brought up the night before. He'd have to fetch up some hot water from the kitchen to shave with, though.

Downstairs he found Miss Christina trying to light the fire in the old-fashioned stove.

'Let me do that.' He riddled the grate and looked at the pile of wood in surprise.

She sat by the table watching him. 'Coal is so expensive,' she said as if she could read his mind, 'and we had plenty of wood lying around in the grounds.'

'Very sensible to use it, then.' He lit the fire and waited for it to burn up, enjoying the crackling sound and the bright dancing flames. 'Now, do you want me to boil you a kettle?'

'I'll do that.'

'Let me. I'm very handy in the kitchen.' You had to be when you had a wife as silly as Ada.

She took a cup of tea up to her sister, then came back to join him.

'The wood is getting low. Shall I bring some more in for you before I shave?'

'Yes, please. It's in the stables to keep it dry.'

He went out and found a pile of wood chunks but no kindling, so chopped up some small pieces and filled an old basket with them, wondering if this was yet another task Miss Christina had to do herself. There was hoar frost on the grass outside but the activity warmed him up nicely.

In the kitchen he found her cutting the bread.

'I'm afraid we can only offer you toast and boiled eggs for breakfast. Cook is quite elderly and we give her Sunday off, so she has a lie-in.'

'One egg and toast would be fine, thank you. But I'll just nip up and shave first.'

When he came down the table was set in the kitchen and she indicated a place with a smile.

'We buy the eggs from the farmer whose son helped you move your things. They're much fresher than the ones we used to get from town.'

It was cosy eating together. The silences didn't feel awkward and Miss Christina showed a lively interest in the world.

After he'd eaten, he wondered whether to start on the cottage or pay the ladies back for their generosity. 'Are there any jobs you want doing, things that need mending, perhaps? And I want to go and see my children this afternoon if that's all right with you.'

She looked at him and her eyes were suddenly too bright. 'There are so many things that I hardly know where to start, Mr Bentley, but if you could put an extra bolt on the front door and this kitchen door, we'll feel a lot safer. The old ones are a bit loose. There are some tools and things like bolts and screws in the storeroom at the end of the stables. One of the gardeners was quite a handyman in the old days and Papa believed in keeping a stock of everyday items. I'll get you the key. And you might like to check your cottage, too, see if the locks are all right there.'

Joss went off whistling happily, glad to have something useful to do for them.

She was a brave lady, Miss Christina, as brave as her brother in her own way. And had a sense of humour under that aristocratic face.

When he turned up at his mother-in-law's in the early afternoon, he found the children dressed for Sunday school.

'We said you would visit on Saturdays, I believe.' Mrs Tomlinson made no attempt to invite him in.

'Something urgent cropped up.'

'Then I'll have to ask you to wait until Tuesday, the arranged day.' She started to close the door in his face.

His anger boiled up and he shoved it backwards so hard it banged against the wall.

She let out a yelp of shock.

'If you don't let me see my children, I'll take them away at once, even if they have to sleep on the floor at my mother's. I'm their father and don't you *ever* forget that.' He reined himself in and waited.

'They have to go to Sunday School.'

'It won't hurt them to miss a week. I'm taking them out visiting someone this afternoon.'

'Your mother can see them at any time.'

'It's not her, though I'll take them to see her another day. They're going to meet the Warburton ladies. I used to serve under their brother and he asked me to help them out, which I'm doing. They want to meet the children.'

She stared at him like a gaping goldfish. 'Oh.'

He remembered suddenly how snobbish she was. 'Well? I don't want to keep the ladies waiting.'

'The children haven't changed into their best clothes yet. Er – come in. They won't be long.'

'They don't need their best clothes.'

'*To visit the Warburtons!* Of course they do.'

'They'll be tramping round the garden, helping me collect wood for the ladies.'

'I don't call that visiting. They'll be acting as unpaid servants. I'm surprised you'll allow it.'

'As their father I can allow them to do what I choose.'

He didn't start relaxing until he was walking up Ridge Road, holding six-year-old Iris by the hand, with nine-year-old Roy – who professed himself too old to hold hands – skipping and sometimes running beside him.

At Fairview he told the children to wait and went into the house by the kitchen door. Quickly he explained to Miss Christina what he'd had to do to get the children away from their grandmother.

He hadn't mistaken the twinkle in her eye. Indeed, it turned into a broad smile now.

'You'd better bring them in, then, Mr Bentley, so that they really have met us. And if you'll fetch some more milk and eggs from the farm later on, I think we can find them a glass of milk to drink and two boiled eggs for their tea.

'Miss Christina, you're a trooper!' He saw a slight flush stain her cheeks.

'My sister and I both like children.'

After their introduction to the ladies, he and the children went to visit the cottage where they'd be living.

'Grandmother says we can't come to live here with you,' Roy said. 'She says a man on his own won't be able to manage and even if we come, we'll soon be going back to her.'

'Well, she's wrong, but we won't tell her that yet.'

'No, it'll make her angry and then she'll hit us,' Iris said.

He stilled. 'Does she hit you often?'

His daughter nodded. 'Every day when we do our piano practice, she hits us with a ruler and smacks our legs at other times if we're naughty. See.' She held out her hands and he realised that the faint markings on them were bruises.

Joss had trouble holding back his fury. That's when he decided.

One week. He'd have them out and living with him within the week, whatever it cost him to do it. He'd do it sooner if the cottage didn't need so much work.

They had a simple tea of eggs and toast for the children, with bread and cheese for him. They followed that with pieces of his mother's cake, then Miss Warburton played the piano for them and the children were encouraged to sing to their kind hostesses.

Halfway home Iris stopped walking and began to sob. 'I don't want to go back.'

Joss's throat felt full of tears. 'I know, love. But it'll only be for a short time, I promise you.'

On the way back he picked up the milk pail which he'd left just inside the gates of Fairview and carried on past it to the farm, buying milk, more eggs and cheese. He did like a piece of crumbly Lancashire cheese with a nice nip to it. Best of all, he arranged for his furniture to be delivered to the cottage the very next day.

But nothing seemed to appease the anger that was simmering inside him at the thought of *that woman* hurting his children. How could she?

When he carried the things into the kitchen Miss Christina looked at him. 'Pardon me, Mr Bentley, but what's happened to upset you?'

And he couldn't hold back, telling her what the children had let slip.

She shook her head sadly. 'You must bring them here as soon as possible.'

'I have to find someone to care for the baby first, and someone to do my housework as well.'

On Monday morning Maud drove herself to town, parked her car and began to walk towards the Town Hall just as Christina Warburton was being helped out of a smaller car by the Mayor, who tipped his hat to her and hurried inside. Another man got out of the car and walked away.

Maud greeted Christina, noting with approval the shortened skirt and the smarter appearance. Actually, she was by far the more attractive of the two Warburton sisters, with a sweet smile, large grey-blue eyes and soft brown hair which had only two wings of grey at the temples.

'How are you this morning, Miss Christina?' She didn't wait to be asked but linked her arm in the other woman's with a smile.

Christina didn't protest at the familiarity but clutched her companion's arm. 'A bit nervous, I'm afraid. I've never done this sort of thing before. And do, please, call me Christina.'

'I've not interviewed anyone before, either. But I'm determined to choose the women who'll be best for Drayforth. Men can have rather fixed views.' She saw a twinkle of amusement in her companion's eyes. Well, everyone in town must realise how bossy Gerald was.

They walked through the entrance and were greeted with a flattering amount of fuss by the counter clerk, who ushered them straight to the Mayor's office.

Albert waited until the door had closed behind the clerk and the ladies were seated, then said quietly, 'Sorry I couldn't wait to escort you inside. I had to set things out. I didn't like to leave the papers lying around while I was away. Now, before people start coming in and out, I must tell you that I've had to be very firm with Mrs Gilson, who'd not expected to apply for her own job and had assumed she'd be the one who selected her two subordinates without reference to anyone else. So she's angry before we even start.'

'The woman has a lot of support in the town,' Maud said.

'Among the upper classes, perhaps. The poorer folk hate her. How does your husband feel about her?'

'He feels she's done a good job.' Maud hesitated, then admitted, 'I'm not so sure about that, though. I'm not surprised the poorer people hate her. She can be very harsh with people who're in distress. I saw her reduce a woman to tears in the street once, and that upset me, because the woman looked so ragged and pale. And I hear that a man killed himself last week because of not getting an Army disability pension. She must have been involved in that.'

'Yes, poor fellow. If I'd known, I'd have done something about his case, but Mrs Gilson keeps things to herself. *That* is going to change, I promise you. Proper records will be kept under the new system. There's another candidate for the senior position who has excellent references and experience of working in a *professional* capacity, which makes it even harder.' He pushed some papers across the table. 'Perhaps you'd like to look at the two applications?'

Both ladies read them carefully, then exchanged the papers.

When she'd read the second set Christina frowned at him. 'Mrs Gilson seems more concerned to save money than help people.'

He nodded, then there was a knock on the door and he put one finger to his lips before calling, 'Yes?'

A woman poked her head round the door. 'Tea, Mr Palmer?' She pushed a tea trolley inside and looked at them questioningly.

'Thank you, Jean. We'll serve ourselves.'

'I'll pour, shall I?' Maud did this while studying the Mayor covertly. Albert and her husband didn't get on, but they'd still invited him to dinner once or twice. He'd refused. He was an attractive man, in spite of his steel-grey hair and horn-rimmed spectacles. Unlike her husband, whose waist was definitely thickening, he was slim and upright still.

'The other lady sounds so much more caring,' Christina said with a sigh. 'Mrs Gilson seems to believe the poor fall ill or lose their jobs on purpose.'

Albert leaned forward. 'Luckily, this Miss Twineham has applied for one of the two health visitor positions as well. And an equally strong candidate has also applied. I think, if they are as suitable as they sound, we might appoint the two ladies who are most fitted to *those* positions – if you agree – not Mrs Gilson's friends. Here. Read their applications. They're dreadful.'

Once again the ladies bent over letters and papers.

'Who is this Violet Schofield?' Maud asked. 'Do we know her?

Her maiden name sounds familiar. Gill. Now where have I seen the word Gill?'

'Her father owns a corner shop. She's not a *lady*. But she'll know first-hand what it's like to live in the Backhill Terraces and her war experiences make her perfect for this job.'

Christina waved the papers she'd been studying. 'Major Warren says Mrs Schofield is quite a heroine. How I'd like to have done something like joining Daphne Bingram's Aides!'

'You did what you could for the war effort,' Maud said gently.

'Knitting! Raising money. Not even that during the past two years as my sister's health declined and our financial situation became – difficult. I felt so *inadequate*! Which is why I was glad to help out today. My sister and I were brought up to *serve* those less fortunate than ourselves, not merely take our money and position for granted.'

Albert waited a moment then said gently. 'So, are wc all agreed? If we like the looks of Miss Twineham, we'll offer her one of the other two jobs. Then after lunch, which will be served in a private room at the Charnley Arms Hotel, we'll see if Mrs Schofield is as good as she sounds.'

He rang a little hand bell and the clerk came to the door.

'Show Mrs Gilson in, please.'

Joss stood back once he'd helped Miss Christina into the Mayor's car, but the driver's door opened again and Mr Palmer called out, 'Do you want a lift into town?'

He was grateful for that, as it felt safer. After he'd said goodbye, he went straight to the bank to deposit most of his money. It was the easiest money he'd ever earned in his life, even if it had cost him an hour or two at a police station under suspicion. Afterwards he went to see the woman Pam had suggested might look after the baby for him.

He didn't take to Mrs Oates, though there was no reason for it that he could put his finger on. Her house was immaculately clean, there was a baby of about nine months in a high chair and a toddler in a playpen. The baby looked unhappy, as if it'd been crying. She looked rather old to have such young children, but these things happened.

'Your own two seem very well behaved.'

'Mine are grown up. These are the other two children I'm looking after.'

'Oh. I see.'

'I'm a widow, Mr Bentley. I couldn't make enough money to live on from looking after one child, and after all, it's only what most mothers do, caring for several children, isn't it? Tell me what exactly you need.'

He explained about Nora and where he'd be living. 'I was hoping you could keep Nora all the time, just for the next month or two.'

'I'm afraid not. I do value my sleep. And I can't have her on Sundays, when I go to church.'

'I see. How about her washing? Would you be able to do that?'

'I'll rinse out what she dirties here, but washing it properly will be your responsibility. What time would you be bringing her in the mornings?'

'I don't know yet. I still have to find a job.' He saw the way she frowned at that. 'I have my gratuity and money saved, if you're worried about getting paid.'

Her frown lifted slightly. The world suddenly seemed to be full of women who had to make their own way in life, he thought. Things had changed a lot in the past few years.

He agreed to let her know, because somehow, he couldn't commit himself to giving Nora into her care. She had such a grim expression and unless he was mistaken, the toddler had flinched away from Mrs Oates when she went near the playpen.

He sighed as he walked back to his mother's. How the hell was he going to manage to run a house, look after children, take Nora backwards and forwards every day, and earn a living?

When he went into the shop he heard a baby crying, angry roars not wails. Pam must be here with Nora. There was no one in the shop, so he went quickly through it and up the stairs. It was unusual not to see Wilf on duty there.

He found his mother trying to pacify Nora, who was squirming in her arms, red-faced. 'Oh, thank goodness you're back! Our Pam's gone into labour early and they've had to bring the baby round here. And then that Eric Gill came to see Wilf and told him he has to get out of his house straight away.'

'*What?* But why?'

'He doesn't know. If he gets out by tomorrow, they'll refund the week's rent, as long as the house is left clean. Our Wilf was that upset.'

Joss suddenly guessed why, but didn't say. It must be because of him, another way of Sully getting back at him. 'Where's Wilf going to live?'

'Here. And I'm really sorry, but if you can move out today or tomorrow, it'll make it all so much easier. You did say Miss Warburton would let you have that cottage, didn't you?'

'Yes. It'll take me a day or two to move in, though.'

'Have you found anyone to look after Nora yet?'

'There's a woman Pam told me about, Mrs Oates, but I don't need her until I find a job.' He'd look for someone else in the meantime, someone kinder. Just because he didn't want the baby didn't mean he was going to let anyone make Nora unhappy.

'What a relief! I'm too old to look after a little baby. Here, you can give her the bottle. I've got to get your father's dinner, as well as keeping an eye on the shop.' She turned to go then swung round and came to give him a quick hug. 'I'm sorry to throw you out, Joss love, but it's probably for the best. The shop isn't making enough to support two households and your father and I've had to dip into our savings. That can't go on. We shall all have to muck in together, see if we can economise. And on top of it all, Wilf's wife is expecting again. Poor Libby. She's never well when she's in the family way. If business gets any worse, I don't know how we'll all survive, what with the doctor's bills and all . . .' Her words trailed off as she went into the kitchen.

Joss sat down with the child. He'd bottle fed his own sometimes when they were babies, because Ada hadn't been able to feed them herself for long. He enjoyed making Nora chuckle afterwards, didn't enjoy changing her nappy, but he could hardly leave that to his mother and anyway, he didn't like to see a child in a dirty nappy. Their soft skin chafed so easily.

It wasn't Nora's fault her mother had cheated on him, after all.

He'd take her for a walk in the pram later. For the moment he had to work out how he was going to move into the cottage and look after three children. He'd have to keep an eye on the jobs vacant as well as everything else.

It was going to be – difficult.

Then the shop's doorbell rang and his mother peered out of the kitchen. 'Oh, you've finished. Thank goodness. Can you go and serve in the shop, love? The prices are on the boxes. Give her to me. I'll prop her in a corner of the couch.'

So he went back into the shop and managed to sell a pair of shoes, making the customer laugh and giving non-committal answers to her questions about what he was going to do with himself.

Just as the customer was leaving, Wilf came back. 'Oh, good. You were able to serve in the shop. Mum's too old for climbing up and down the ladder.'

'I sold a pair of shoes, too. Haven't lost my touch. Do you want me to take over for the day? You must have a million things to do.'

'That'd be a big help. Sure you don't mind?'

'Of course not.' He'd take Nora for a walk another time. 'Why has Sully thrown you out?'

'I don't know. Gill said *he* didn't know, either, and was just obeying orders. He was quite polite actually. I'd rather deal with him than Sully any day.'

Joss wondered what Sully would do once he moved into the cottage. The man was noted for paying back those who upset him. That added another layer of worry to the mountain Joss seemed to be struggling under.

The other applicant for the senior position was shown into the waiting room while Freda Gilson was sitting there. It was already ten minutes after the time she'd been given for the interview and she considered such unpunctuality extremely bad manners.

When the other woman smiled at her, Freda ignored it and kept her distance. Far too young and pretty for such a job. No, not pretty . . . elegant. When you looked closely the creature was too thin and had a rather large nose.

Then Freda was called to the Mayor's office. She answered the questions put to her, but had to set her interviewers straight on several points, because it was quite clear they knew nothing about such work. Well, how could a Warburton have any experience of life in the Backhill Terraces?

At the end of the interview, the Mayor stood up and escorted Freda out to the waiting room, gesturing to the stranger to come back with him. 'If you'll sit here, my dear Mrs Gilson, I'll get someone to bring you a cup of tea.'

She inclined her head, still simmering with indignation that she had to go through this. It wasn't as if she needed the money they were offering, but she had made this job her life and what would she do with her time otherwise? Her husband was dead and her daughters had married and moved away. She'd suggested living with one of them to help with the children, but they'd turned her down. Ungrateful, that's what they were.

Her thoughts returned to this job. It would be unthinkable to lose out to a stranger who was so much younger than her. Humiliating! Whatever it took, whoever she had to go to for support, she wasn't having that.

Surely they wouldn't dare appoint anyone else?

Elizabeth Twineham followed the Mayor across the hall and took a seat, studying the other two women as she made herself comfortable.

'We were very impressed with your application, Miss Twineham. You seem to have had a great deal of experience in welfare work.'

She'd planned what to say and was pleased when they let her say it without interruptions. 'I have, first as a clergyman's daughter, then during the war working in Manchester. I find it very satisfying to help those less fortunate than myself. In Manchester there were a lot of soldiers' wives, who'd moved away from their homes, and had no one to turn to, poor things.'

'What about those who are improvident?'

'The whole family isn't usually improvident. One does what one can if the husband is a drunkard or the wife a poor manager, but one can't work miracles. I really hate to see children going hungry, though.'

She answered questions from both women, then the Mayor began to fiddle with the papers on his desk. When he looked up, his expression was regretful, so she braced herself for a rejection.

'I wonder if I can be frank with you, Miss Twineham? What I say mustn't go beyond these walls, however, and I'll deny I ever said it, if necessary.'

She looked at him in surprise.

'Mrs Gilson has been doing similar work in this town for the past twenty years, though in a voluntary and – um – ad hoc capacity. She's well respected here, so—'

The woman next to him leaned forward and smiled at Elizabeth. 'What the Mayor is trying to say tactfully is that we find ourselves in a quandary. All three of us are agreed that you are the most suitable candidate, but . . .' she spread her hands, 'it would cause an uproar in Drayforth if Mrs Gilson didn't get the job.'

'She's over sixty, though,' Miss Warburton said. 'She shouldn't really be applying for a job like this at her age.'

Elizabeth saw the surprise on the other two's faces.

'Are you sure of that?' the Mayor asked. 'Mrs Gilson said she was fifty-five on her application.'

Miss Warburton laughed. 'Did she really? I must have missed that. She and my sister were born in the same year and used to play together as girls. I don't remember exactly when Mrs Gilson's birthday is – some time in the autumn I think – but my sister turns sixty-three this coming May.'

Elizabeth watched in surprise as the Mayor looked first surprised then pleased by this information and Mrs Kirby tried but failed to hold back a snort of laughter.

He turned to Elizabeth. 'You applied for a Health Visitor job as well as the senior position. Would you accept the junior post *for the time being*? No promises made about the future, but we'll bear you in mind if an opportunity arises.'

She thought about this. She hadn't liked the looks of the woman who would be her superior and who hadn't even had the courtesy to reply to her greeting in the waiting room, but still, a job was a job and after her years of independence during the war, she would hate to rely on her father's support again, hate to go back and live under his thumb as well. 'Yes, I suppose so.'

Both women beamed at her.

'Congratulations, the job is yours,' Mrs Kirby said at once. 'You may count on my help at any time. Could we ask you to say nothing about your new job until this afternoon, though? We have another position to fill and three more women to interview. If you return here at about four o'clock, we'll make it official then and introduce you to the other successful applicant.'

'Yes, of course.'

Miss Warburton leaned forward with a smile. 'There's a very nice tea room where you could buy luncheon. And there's a reading room in the library. You may enjoy reading our town's twice-weekly newspaper.'

Elizabeth stood up, grateful for this information, liking this woman with her gentle voice and warm smile. 'Thank you. I can look at the advertisements for lodgings while I'm there.'

Mindful of the Mayor's warning, she didn't allow herself to smile as she walked out, but inside she was jubilant. Since the war had ended, most jobs seemed to be going back to the men – or were being abolished, as hers had been. When you had no husband to support you and your father was a clergyman of restricted means and autocratic temperament, having a job and income of your own made such a difference – even though the money offered for the lower-level position was barely enough to live on. Well, she had a little saved, knew how to live frugally.

* * *

'I think we did the best we could,' Albert said, once Miss Twineham had left. 'I suppose we'd better bring back Mrs Gilson and offer her the job.'

Maud pulled a face. 'Pity she's so well-connected in the town. 'Can we at least tell her the job is going to change?'

'We can tell her, but I doubt she'll listen.'

'We could put it in writing.'

He sighed. 'But will she heed it?'

'I'll do it, if you like, and make sure she heeds it. With Miss Warburton's help, of course.'

'I'm not sure I know enough,' Christina said.

'Two heads are better than one, surely? I can drive over to your house, if that's not imposing, and we'll discuss it where no one can overhear. How about the day after tomorrow in the afternoon?'

'Well, all right. If you really think I'll be of use.'

'I'm sure you will.'

'Ready?' Albert went to the door and beckoned to the clerk. 'Ask Mrs Gilson to step inside, will you please?'

He went back to his place, but stood up again as Mrs Gilson entered. 'Do sit down. I'm pleased to tell you that we've decided to appoint you to the new position of Senior Health Visitor.'

She inclined her head.

'It's a *new* position. There will be some changes in the way the job is to be done,' Maud put in. 'We'll give you a list of what's expected of you in writing next week.'

Mrs Gilson drew herself up. 'Surely I should be involved in drawing up the list of requirements? No one in this town knows as much about this sort of work as I do.'

'Your experience is with the old system, which used volunteers,' Maud said firmly. 'From now on, there will be rules and regulations about how the work is done.'

'And the new system will be kinder to those in need,' Christina put in. 'It isn't always their fault that they've no money.'

Maud gave her a wink and an approving nod.

Mrs Gilson stared at her through narrowed eyes, lips pursed, but said nothing.

'Any questions?' Albert asked.

'Yes. Now that I've been appointed, I will naturally expect to be involved in selecting my assistants.'

'I'm afraid not. We shall be choosing people to fit in with the new ways we've decided upon, not the old, and you're not yet familiar with those.'

She opened her mouth to protest, then snapped it shut again. 'I warn you: I can't work with unsuitable people.'

'We'll take great care whom we appoint,' Maud said.

When Freda Gilson had left, Albert looked at his two companions. 'There's going to be trouble.'

'I know. But we can make sure the people appointed are aware that she doesn't have the power to dismiss them.'

He looked at her in surprise. 'I didn't expect to find you so completely on my side about the reforms, I must admit, Mrs Kirby.'

'I didn't expect to find it all so interesting.' Maud laughed. 'I sometimes find myself without useful employment and time can hang heavily. If I can help you in other ways, Mr Palmer, I'd be glad to do so.'

'So would I,' Christina said. 'If you want me, that is.'

'That's very kind of you both. I can definitely use the help of such modern-thinking ladies.' He looked at the wall clock and said in a lighter tone, 'Well, I don't know about you two, but I'm feeling quite sharp-set. I've ordered lunch for us in a private room at the Charnley Arms. Perhaps you'd like to – um – powder your noses first?'

In the ladies' room Maud smiled at their joint reflections in the mirror. 'We make a good team, don't we?'

'You think – I did all right, Maud?'

'Oh, yes. And you know so much about the town. As a relative newcomer, even though I have cousins here, I'm still learning.' She saw the relief on her companion's face. 'This Mayor has some good ideas, don't you think?'

'Yes. And I do so agree with him about the slums. It must be dreadful to live in such places. We used to own some of the Backhill Terraces, but we never let the houses get so dilapidated. I cycle into town sometimes, you see, and there's a short cut that avoids the main road, so I see how things are deteriorating.' She looked sideways. 'I hope you don't mind me speaking frankly, but what about your husband? Will he approve of what you're doing?'

'No, he won't. But that won't stop me.' She tried to laugh, but it came out as a rather sharp sound. 'It wasn't a love match, you know, but a marriage of convenience. I needed his money and he needed my connections. You see, I can be equally frank.'

'Does that make you happy?'

Maud shrugged. 'What's happiness? I fell in love with my first husband, but he was a hopeless manager and wasted his family money. At least Gerald has the sense to hold on to his money. I was wondering where to find the money for the rent when he appeared on the horizon.' She grimaced. She hadn't expected to confide in Christina.

A hand touched her shoulder gently. 'Life never gives us quite what we want or expect, does it?'

They were both silent for a moment or two, then Maud pulled herself together. 'Mr Palmer will be wondering what's happened to us.'

As they walked outside, Christina looked at the bank, which was opposite the town's oldest hostelry. 'I have to go to the bank first, I'm afraid, because it might be closed by the time we finish this afternoon. If you'd like to go ahead, I'll join you shortly.'

She went into the bank and was greeted by name. 'I wish to deposit this money in our account.' She took the envelope containing the notes out of her handbag and pushed it across the counter, waiting as the elderly clerk counted it and confirmed the amount with her.

It was a relief not to be carrying such a large sum any longer. She was happy to think of the remaining money in her handbag, some of which she intended to spend on new shoes this very day, if there was time.

She'd never entered a public house on her own before, because neither her father nor her brother had approved of ladies going into them. She hesitated just inside the doorway of the Charnley Arms, feeling nervous, but a woman came towards her, smiling.

'Miss Christina, the Mayor is waiting for you upstairs. Let me show you the way.'

'Thank you.' Then she realised why the woman had seemed familiar. 'Why, it's Hilda Doyle! How nice to see you again, my dear.'

'It's nice to see you too, Miss Warburton. But I'm Hilda Wray now. My husband's the landlord here.'

'It must be a very interesting life. You look well.'

'I am, thank you. And how is Miss Warburton?'

'Rather frail these days, I'm afraid.'

Christina followed their former senior housemaid up the stairs and into a private dining room, where she thoroughly enjoyed the rare luxury of eating a three-course luncheon that was well presented and served, and after which she wouldn't have to wash the dishes.

She was pleased to have a day out and to be doing something useful, happiest of all to have so much money in the bank. Why, it'd last them for a year at least, with care.

And since there were lots of other pieces of silver which they could sell, she was going to have a new dress made as well as buying shoes. Just one new dress to lift the spirits.

# 15

Gerald Kirby, who'd been standing to one side in the bank, didn't greet Miss Warburton in case she snubbed him publicly. He watched covertly as she deposited quite a large sum of money. Where the hell had she got that from? He'd been hoping the Warburtons would be driven by sheer poverty to accept his offer, but if there was money coming in, he'd have to find some other way of convincing them to sell.

He waited till she'd left before stepping forward to conduct his own business, then strolled thoughtfully back to his office.

How was he going to get hold of that house?

Unfortunately Maud was right. It wouldn't look good if he was seen to hound two elderly ladies, last survivors of what had been the town's leading family. But he'd never have asked Sully to set fire to the shabby old place, even though it would be no loss to anyone. That would be too dangerous, both to himself and to them. He didn't want to risk imprisonment for himself – or risk killing them. Why, one of them was house-bound and might not get out quickly enough. He wasn't going to let the matter drop, though, whatever Maud said.

Vi was feeling a little nervous as she walked into the Town Hall for her interview. She was shown into a waiting room with hard wooden chairs set neatly round the walls. Two fashionably dressed ladies had their heads close together in the far corner. They stopped talking to look her up and down in a way she thought ill-mannered, then began whispering again, making it quite clear they found her an object for scornful amusement.

The clerk opened the door and beckoned to one of the ladies, who followed him out, patting her hair and touching her hat as if to make sure it was straight.

The other took out a compact and studied her face in its little mirror, then put it away and leaned back, tapping her fingers on the arm of her chair.

Vi had more sense than to try to chat to her.

Ten minutes later, the first lady returned and began to whisper to her friend again, keeping an eye on the door, stopping as soon as footsteps approached.

The other lady left the room.

'You don't stand a chance, you know.'

Vi blinked in shock. 'I beg your pardon?'

'You don't stand a chance. If you have any sense you'll withdraw your application and stop wasting everyone's time. Mrs Gilson won't employ someone like *you*, someone who comes from the Backhill Terraces. It'd be like setting a thief to catch a thief.'

'You don't know anything about me.'

'We have our ways of finding out and we know enough to be sure you're not at all suitable for this job, whatever you got up to during the war.'

Vi felt angry but realised it was a blatant attempt to upset her. It had the opposite effect, however, stiffening her backbone instead. She didn't attempt to reply, simply stared at the woman. She kept her gaze fixed just above the woman's right eyebrow, a trick Daphne had taught her, and saw the other begin to fidget. In the end the woman pulled out her compact again, studied her face and glared at Vi. 'What are you staring at?'

'You.' Vi continued to focus on the eyebrow, which had been plucked to a thin line and looked, to her mind, ridiculous.

The other lady returned from her interview just then, scowling across at the stranger as she went to sit down. Vi abandoned the eyebrow to focus on the floor, which would have been better for a good scrubbing. To her relief, the clerk soon came back for her.

She was shown into the Mayor's office and found herself facing him, Mrs Kirby and the younger Miss Warburton. She'd expected Mrs Gilson to be here and was glad not to have to face her yet.

They asked questions about her experience and seemed genuinely interested in what she'd seen and done in London, not trying to trick her or cast doubt on her responses.

When the questions stopped, the Mayor looked at his two companions and raised one eyebrow. They both nodded and he turned back to Vi. 'Mrs Schofield, we'd like to offer you the job of Health Visitor.'

For a moment or two she couldn't form a single word, she was so taken aback. Then she beamed at them. 'I accept. And thank you.'

'I wonder if you'd mind waiting here while I go and tell the other candidates they've not been successful,' the Mayor said.

'Congratulations!' Miss Warburton said as soon as he'd left. 'I'm sure you'll do very well after all you've seen and done during the war. I was most impressed by your references, Mrs Schofield.'

'I too am pleased you're able to take the job. When can you start?'

This remark made Vi stare at Mrs Kirby, who was the last person she'd expected to support her. 'As soon as you like.'

'Good. There's a lot needs doing. Mrs Gilson has, of course, been given the senior post, but we'll introduce you to the lady who's got the other position like yours in a few minutes.'

'May I ask who she is?'

'Her name's Elizabeth Twineham and she too has been employed on war work. I think the two of you will get on well.'

Funny, Mrs Kirby being involved in this, Vi thought as she walked home, when it was Mr Kirby's ill-maintained properties that were causing some of the health problems in the town.

She wondered what would happen when they tried to get him to clean up his slums, which the Mayor had said was one of the aims in appointing Health Visitors. It wouldn't be easy, she was sure. But it was about time something was done. People shouldn't have to live in places like Lilybank Court.

This reminded her that she needed to go and check that Tess

was all right. She'd do that first thing tomorrow morning. She hated to see children going hungry, but of course you couldn't help the whole world.

In the middle of the afternoon, the cart bringing Wilf's household goods arrived at the rear of the shop and his two friends who owned the cart began to carry the pieces of furniture upstairs.

Wilf went to watch them start, then came back into the shop. 'I can take over here if you've got things to do, Joss lad. Libby and Mum will be the ones to say where everything goes and I'm no good at carrying heavy stuff.'

'Thanks. I think the best thing I can do is get the baby out of the way, so I'll take her for an outing.' Joss put Nora into the shabby old pram his sister had bought for him from a neighbour and set off to walk to Fairview and make arrangements to move into the cottage as soon as possible.

He had to knock twice on the door before anyone answered, then it was Miss Warburton herself.

'I'm sorry to keep you waiting, Mr Bentley, but I can't walk very fast these days and I had to make sure it wasn't that man.'

'I'm sorry if I sounded impatient. I'll remember next time. I came to ask you if I can move into the cottage tomorrow. Sully's thrown my brother out of his house, so Wilf and his family are moving in with my parents over the shop and they need my bedroom.'

'Of course you can move in. It's because you helped us, isn't it? That man's trying to hurt your family as well.'

Joss didn't attempt to deny this. Miss Warburton wasn't stupid. Neither of the sisters was.

'Is that your new baby? Let me see her.' She moved slowly and painfully down the steps and bent over the pram, touching Nora's rosy cheek with one fingertip, her expression tender. 'She's lovely. Have you found someone to look after her?'

He kept his eyes away from the baby, who was indeed pretty, but he didn't intend to get too fond of her because he still intended to give the child into her real father's care. 'I found someone but

I didn't take to her, I must admit. I'll look after her myself till I find a job. Thanks to your generosity, I can take my time. Well, since it's all right to move in, I'd better go and see the farmer about bringing over my furniture.'

Miss Warburton stepped back, hesitated, then looked at the baby. 'I could look after her for a while, if you like, and you could use Christina's bicycle. It shouldn't take you more than half an hour to get to Green Heys and back, then. If you carry the baby inside, she can lie on the couch near me. I'll be very careful with her, I promise you.'

'Are you sure?'

Her voice softened. 'Very sure. I love babies.'

He settled Nora down and hurried round to the stables for the bicycle, hoping they could bring his furniture across first thing in the morning.

Some people were so kind, it warmed your heart, made you realise there was hope in the world. He really liked the two old ladies.

Wilf turned round as the shop door opened. 'Miss Christina. How nice to see you. And Mrs Kirby. How can I help you, ladies?'

Christina moved forward. 'I need a new pair of shoes, Mr Bentley, something sturdy that will last well and be comfortable to walk in.'

'Come and sit down and I'll fetch you something to try. I think I have just the thing. Mrs Kirby, would you like to take a seat as well?'

'I'll have a look at your stock first.'

'I'm afraid we haven't much in that would suit you at the moment.' He could tell by her sympathetic expression and quick nod that she understood perfectly well why.

Even with their limited stocks, he found Miss Christina exactly what she needed. People might not be buying many fancy shoes these days, but they still needed good shoes for walking and working in.

When she'd paid, he turned to show the ladies to the door,

but Mrs Kirby said, 'I need a pair of walking shoes, too. Not for walking in the countryside, but round the town.'

To his delight he sold a second pair, explaining to her exactly why one style was better than another for her purpose and the shape of her narrow, elegant feet.

He watched them go outside and get into the big black car, wondering why Mrs Kirby needed shoes like that. She usually went everywhere by car and had never bought such unfashionable shoes from them before. Well, she bought most of her footwear in London, flimsy, fashionable things that weren't designed to last, or even to support the feet properly. He couldn't help noticing what people wore on their feet. He loved his work.

He wished every day had as good sales as this: two pairs of their most expensive shoes, as well as two pairs of cheaper shoes and three pairs of cheap slippers. They'd not have counted as a good day's sales before the war, but they did now. Before the war, they'd not have stocked such shoddy slippers, but he'd found they sold steadily, so his father had had to give in on that point and lower his standards. Every penny counted these days.

Wilf looked at the little clock on the shelf behind the counter. Only five o'clock. He was tempted to close early, but shook his head on the thought. No. You had to provide the best service you possibly could, especially in times like these, so he'd stay open till six, as always. Some shops stayed open longer, but people didn't seem to buy shoes later in the evenings, for some strange reason, so it wasn't worth staying open.

He sighed as he listened to things being moved around above him and heavy footsteps going up and down the back stairs. His wife was very upset at losing their home and so was he, still couldn't understand why they'd been thrown out.

When the noises stopped, Libby popped her head through the curtains at the back of the shop. 'I'll just go back home – I mean to the old house for a final clear-up.'

He knew her too well. She was nervous, her voice quivering a little, her face pale.

That did it. He wasn't letting her go on her own. Sully might turn up and bully her.

'Wait for me. I'll shut the shop early today.'

It was a pity Joss hadn't come back, but Wilf had to look after Libby.

It was dark now, but the street lamps were lit and they linked arms as they walked. It was such a comfort having a wife like Libby. He was a lucky man.

Gerald went home early but Maud didn't return until well after five o'clock. He couldn't settle to reading the rest of the newspaper, so paced up and down, stopping occasionally to stare sourly out of the window. A person as wealthy as him ought to have a view. Instead, he had to look out at the tall stone walls that encircled his garden. That never failed to irritate him.

When he heard the sound of the car and his wife's footsteps, he stuck his head out of their private parlour. 'Like a G and T?'

'Love one. Just have to visit the cloakroom first.'

He made two gin and tonics, waiting with hers in his hand until he heard the faint sound of water running and the door of the small convenience room at the back of the hall open and close again.

Maud came in and flung herself into a chair, taking the glass from him and gulping down a mouthful with a murmur of pleasure. 'Wonderful. I'm exhausted.'

'What happened?'

She explained, watching his frown darken.

'I thought you were going to support Mrs Gilson, Maud.'

'I did. We appointed her, even though she wasn't the best candidate by a long way.'

'But you said you'd appointed two strangers to the other positions. You know Mrs Gilson already has a group of women who help her and she told me herself that two of them have applied for those jobs and are very capable. I assured her she'd have our support and now you're making a liar of me.'

'Well, the two women we appointed are outstanding, far better than her cronies.'

'Tell me about them.'

He listened, sipping absently. 'The Twineham woman is from a good family?'

'Yes, a distant connection of mine, actually, though I don't really know her side of the family, just that we're related somehow.'

'Well, *she* should get on all right with Gilson, but the other female doesn't sound to be at all the right sort of person. Fancy appointing someone from the Backhill Terraces!'

'Mrs Schofield has superb references and a great deal of experience in welfare work. Major Warren said she was a heroine during the war.'

'She probably earned his goodwill on her back.'

'She's not that sort. She saved his life, actually, at some risk to her own.' Maud scowled at him. 'You know, you have a very nasty view of the world, Gerald.'

'I prefer to call it realistic. And the woman won't do. You must find some way to get rid of her. I don't want you getting involved in such matters again, if you're not going to do as I tell you.'

'How will you stop me from being involved? Lock me in my room?'

'If I have to.'

She sat up very straight and looked him squarely in the eye. 'If you do, the minute the door is opened, I'll leave you and this house for good.'

'And give up the comfortable life my money provides? I think not.'

'I still have family who would take me in, and who would be interested in my tale of how cruel you'd been to me.'

'I haven't been cruel, dammit!'

'No, and you'd better not be, because I won't put up with it.' Suddenly her grievances boiled over and she could no more have held them back than she could have stopped breathing. 'I pay a high price for my comforts, Gerald. I live with a man who doesn't know how to be affectionate, is very poor company both in bed and out of it, and who only married me for my connections.'

She saw fury etch deep lines across his face and wondered for a moment if she'd gone too far. But he said nothing, only breathed out very slowly then picked up his glass and took a sip. As he gazed down into the clear liquid afterwards, though, his knuckles were white against the glass.

Silence sat heavily between them and she was annoyed with herself as well as him. She usually managed him better than this, prided herself on that. In the end she couldn't stand it any longer. 'Would you really keep me a prisoner?'

'Of course I wouldn't. I spoke in anger. I apologise.'

'I accept your apology.' She got up and went to refill her glass. 'Another?'

He drained the last mouthful and nodded, holding it out.

Maud tried to smooth things over a little as she poured their drinks. 'If you'd let me finish explaining . . . Christina Warburton is in full agreement with the appointments we made today. In fact, she and I are planning to do a few things together to help the Mayor set up the new system. I'm going over to her house to discuss that the day after tomorrow.'

He sat up eagerly, his frown vanishing completely. 'She's invited you to visit her house?'

'I invited myself and she agreed without hesitation. You did say you wanted to get to know the leading families, did you not? But for the moment, it's just her and me. Not you. That's how relationships are built. The Warburtons won't come round to dinner here until they know they can trust me. And they won't come at all if you and your pet thug continue to upset them.'

But she could see that her final words had gone over his head. She'd have to try again to make him see how he was harming his standing in the town by his ownership of slums and his employment of a man like Sully. She hid a smile. Well, she'd struck another small blow today, buying a pair of shoes she'd never use, as a sort of recompense for the way he'd treated Joss Bentley.

Gerald had no idea about relationships. She hadn't realised quite how unfeeling he was when she married him or she might have thought twice about it. But there again, she'd hated being poor.

She was tied to him now, however, and had to make the best of things. She didn't really want to leave him and live in genteel poverty.

As Joss was pushing the pram down the street, he met Vi coming the other way. He couldn't think of her as Mrs Schofield, somehow. She appeared radiantly happy and on impulse, he stopped. 'You look as if something really good has happened.'

'It has. I've just been appointed to one of the new Health Visitor positions.'

'Congratulations.'

'Thank you.' She looked into the pram. 'Isn't she lovely? You must be very proud of her.'

He tried to smile but couldn't.

'What's wrong?'

For a moment he was tempted to tell her the full truth about Nora, which surprised him. He hardly knew this woman, yet always felt comfortable with her. But he wasn't rushing into anything, would take his time and get to know her, see if he stayed interested. Wanting to talk to her a little longer, he shared his immediate worries.

'Sully threw me out of my home, and now he's thrown my brother out of his house as well, just to get back at me because I stopped him bullying the Warburtons. The only place I can find for my family to live is a cottage in the grounds of Fairview, which means a long walk into town.' He bit back further words. 'Sorry, I shouldn't complain, should I? Those lads who died would be glad to have my problems. And at least I have a home.'

'Maybe I could help? It's what I did during the war, find solutions to problems for the wives of lads who'd been killed while attached to our unit, or for the lads themselves if they were badly injured.'

He looked down at the sleeping baby, her little pink fingers curled up next to her cheek. He couldn't seem to hate her, however hard he tried. 'Any advice you care to offer would be gratefully received, Mrs Schofield. I have to move into the cottage quickly and when I find a job, I have to find someone to look after Nora here. But I need to have the cottage cleaned out first.'

'Have you got someone to do the cleaning?'

'Not yet. I was going to ask my sister if she knew anyone, only she's just had a baby.'

'Well, I know someone. She's desperate to earn some money.'

'You do? I'll be happy to pay her.'

'It's my friend Tess. She lost her husband recently. He'd been gassed and took his own life.'

'Joe Donovan,' he said quietly. 'I heard about it. I used to play with him sometimes when we were lads, though my mother didn't like me associating with the Irish. I'd be happy to help his widow.'

'She'd have to bring her two little girls with her, but I'm sure she wouldn't let that slow her down. She's a good worker, used to work in our shop.'

His face brightened. 'Could you ask her at once? I need her to come tomorrow, if possible.'

'We could go and see her now. She's not far away, in Lilybank Court.'

He pulled a face.

'I know. It's a terrible place, but she does her best to keep it clean. And anyway, she has no choice. It's all she can afford.'

'You're sure she'll do a good job?'

'Very sure. But if you like, I'll come up to check what needs doing tomorrow morning and then I'll come up again in the evening to make sure everything is to your satisfaction.'

'I couldn't impose on you like that.'

She shrugged. 'I'm not starting work till next week and to tell you the truth, time is hanging rather heavily after my busy life in London. I'm living with my brother in Mayfield Place and he has a woman who does the main cleaning.'

They stopped walking as they came to Lilybank Court.

'I'll go in first and check that everything is all right, then I'll wave and you can join me, Mr Bentley. She won't mind you bringing the pram inside, I'm sure.'

He stood at the entrance to the filthy courtyard and wondered what he was getting into. How dreadful it must be to live here.

Vi knocked on the door and when a voice called to come in, she opened it. Tess was sitting at the table and had clearly been crying. She went to put an arm round her friend.

'What's wrong, love?'

'Mrs Gilson. She couldn't come herself today but she sent someone else and the woman searched the whole room in case I'd hidden anything that could be sold, or had any food that I couldn't explain.'

'Gilson's a dreadful woman. I got the job and I'm going to be working for her, but she won't find it easy to bully me and I shan't let her get me down.'

'She will do.'

'No. I'm different when I'm working, Tess. I had to deal with all sorts of people during the war and I learned to stick up for what was right. Anyway, never mind that. Do you want a temporary job cleaning?'

Tess brightened. 'Yes. Who is it for?'

'Joss Bentley, of the shoe-shop family. He's moving into a cottage the Warburtons have in the grounds of Fairview and it's not been used for a while. Trouble is, he has to move in tomorrow. Can you get up there first thing to scrub it out? I told him you'd have to take the girls with you and he doesn't mind about that.'

Tess nodded. 'Of course I can go. How much is he paying?'

'I've not discussed that. How about five shillings for the day's work?'

'That'd be wonderful. I'd have to tell the Panel, though. I have to report any money I can earn. They'll knock it off the money they give me, but I'd rather earn it than be given charity, far rather.'

'Tell them four shillings and keep the other to yourself. Now, Mr Bentley's waiting outside.'

Tess jumped to her feet. 'You're not going to bring him in here?'

'Yes, I am. He'll be pleased when he sees how clean you keep this place. I don't know how you manage when you can't afford soap. It's a real credit to you.'

'You just have to scrub harder.'

Vi went to the door and waved . . .

Half an hour later when she and Joss parted company, she smiled to think she'd helped two people today. Then she thought about the motherless baby and felt sad. Joss didn't really care about the baby, she could tell that. And she, who'd longed for one, hadn't managed to get one. If she had, she'd love it with all that was in her.

She didn't let herself dwell on that. What can't be cured, must be endured, she always said, and be thankful for what you have got.

# 16

Eric went round to Wilf Bentley's house to check that everything had been left clean. Daft, this was, chucking out good tenants who'd never been late with the rent and all out of spite! But Sully was like that, could hold a grudge for years, everyone knew it, and was vicious in his paybacks for imagined insults. Mr Kirby wouldn't like it if he knew this was happening. He was very particular about who rented his better properties and preferred to keep good tenants.

Through the front door Eric saw the Bentleys standing at the far end of the hall. The woman was sobbing against her husband, who was trying to comfort her. Eric could see at a glance that the place was immaculate. Well, he'd expected nothing less. Best get this over with. He cleared his throat and they jerked round.

Bentley moved to stand protectively in front of his wife. 'It's ready for you to inspect.'

'I can see it's all right.'

'Don't you want to go upstairs?'

'No. I know you've always looked after it.'

'Then why throw us out?' the woman cried.

Eric made his voice as soft and reasonable as he could. 'Sometimes I just have to do as I'm ordered, Mrs Bentley, as I told you earlier.'

'What if *he* ordered you to kill someone? I suppose you'd do that too,' she said bitterly.

'Shh, love.'

Eric watched with interest as Bentley put his arm lovingly round his wife. She was a plain little thing and he was pale and weedy, but they seemed very fond of one another. He'd never understood how people fell in love. He never had.

He fumbled in his pocket and pulled out the week's rent he'd offered them to get out easily. Sully would complain about that, but let him. It was worth something not to have to clean a place out or face malicious damage.

Bentley took the money, then they gathered up their cleaning materials in silence and left.

'*What if he ordered you to kill someone? I suppose you'd do that too,*' she'd said. The idea intrigued Eric and he stood thinking it over. Would he? No, definitely not. He didn't enjoy violence. And even Sully wouldn't order a murder.

But if Sully ordered him to do something else nasty and he refused, Eric would be out of a job quick as a wink and he didn't fancy that, either. It meant a lot to him, this job did, and there was no other available in Drayforth that would bring in anything like the money, besides which he couldn't do physical labour, not with his heart. It went tickety-tick if anything upset him, though he didn't let on about that to anyone.

He sighed. What he really wanted was Sully's job. He'd do it better, he knew, and without need for the nasty tricks Sully played on those who displeased him. Eric wasn't a do-gooder, or anything like that, but he took satisfaction in making things happen smoothly and efficiently.

Mrs Bentley's words lingered in his mind all the way home, and with them the thought that he too was at Sully's mercy. That didn't please him at all.

Vi wasn't in when he got home, so he made himself a cup of tea and sat down to read the newspaper.

When she came in, she looked at him as if she didn't like him and demanded, 'Why did you have to throw Wilf Bentley out of his house?'

'Sully wanted him out. He's Joss Bentley's brother and Sully's taken against *him*, so anyone connected to him is in trouble as well.'

'Why has he taken against Joss?'

Eric shrugged. 'Bentley stopped him pestering the Warburtons, bested him in a fight too. Sully'd been trying to frighten them out of Fairview.'

'How long is Sully going to go on trying to hurt Joss?'

Eric caught a tone in her voice. 'You're on first names with him? Bentley?'

She nodded. 'We shared a compartment on the train and I've spoken to him a few times since. I like him.'

'You'd be wise to stay away from him. If Sully's holding a grudge, he won't stop till he finds a way to destroy Bentley or drive him out of Drayforth.'

'He'd better not. Joss is working for the Warburton sisters and *they* have a lot of connections, too.'

Another thing to think about. Eric knew how much Kirby wanted to get in with folk from the better families. He'd have to keep his eyes and ears open. It never did any good to act without considering everything first, especially when something was important. He'd been gathering some interesting information about Sully for a while now, but wasn't sure how to use it.

Vi put her pinafore on and began to tidy the kitchen. 'Well, I'm going up to Fairview to help Joss tomorrow, wise or not. Tess is going to scrub his new place out and I'm going to help him organise things.'

'Why the hell should you do that? Is Bentley paying you?'

'No. I'm doing it out of kindness. He has children, one of them a baby. I don't like to see little ones suffer.'

'Mind your own business, Vi.'

'It *is* my business to help people.' She looked at him, head on one side, beaming smile on her face. 'You didn't ask me about the interview.'

'You got the job?'

'Yes. I'm to start next Monday. Mrs Gilson got the senior job, worse luck, but the woman working with me is a relative of Mrs Kirby. She's lovely.'

'Mrs Kirby is?' He frowned. His employer's wife didn't seem the sort to win Vi's approval.

'No, Elizabeth Twineham, the other Health Visitor.'

'How much are they paying you?'

'Thirty shillings a week.'

'Good money for a woman.'

'That sort of remark always makes me angry. It ought not to make any difference whether you're a woman or not. It's whether you can do the job that counts.'

'You came back from London with some daft ideas, our Vi. Of course men need to be paid more. They've got families to support.'

'You haven't. Yet you still get paid more.'

'Well, I will have a family to support one day.'

'You'll have to get married first. And what about widows? Shouldn't they be paid more? They've got families to support too. Like Tess has.'

'I don't know where you get these stupid ideas from.'

As she opened her mouth to protest, he held up one hand.

'Don't go on about it, our Vi. I'm hungry. What are we having for tea?'

'Oh. Sorry. I was so happy I forgot to buy anything. I'll nip round to the shop and buy some ham.'

He was always ravenous by this time of day and this idea didn't please him. 'I never buy ham from Dad's shop. It's not good stuff or well kept. Tell you what. I'll buy you tea at the Charnley Arms to celebrate your new job. The food's good there. I'll go and get changed into my best suit.' He went upstairs whistling, pleased with himself for giving her a treat. His offer had surprised her. Well, he enjoyed surprising people. And he enjoyed spending a bit of money on himself, just every now and then. He worked hard for it so he deserved to have some pleasure from it.

As he buttoned his clean shirt and put in his cuff links, he wished Vi wouldn't interfere in people's lives. He could understand her helping Tess. Women who were friends did help one another. But why was she helping Bentley?

A dreadful thought stopped him in his tracks and he went to

the landing to shout down, 'You don't fancy that Bentley fellow for a husband, do you? That's not why you're helping him?'

She came out of the kitchen and stared up at him, her mouth open in shock. 'I hardly know him. Honestly, Eric, it's you who gets the daft ideas.'

Reassured, he went back into his bedroom and knotted his best tie carefully, looking round in satisfaction at the new matching furniture Vi had helped him choose. She was good at things like that.

To his surprise, he enjoyed her company that evening. She took the Charnley Arms in her stride and chatted about places she'd dined out at while she was in the Aides. She'd seen and done a lot in London, while he'd never even visited the capital, and she'd mixed with some rich people, called a titled lady by her first name. She'd gone up in the world and so would he.

'Now I've got the job, we'll need extra help in the house,' she said as they walked home, her arm resting lightly in his. 'Eric? Did you hear what I said?'

'Yes.' He unlocked the front door and led the way inside.

'We'll need extra help.'

'Can you arrange that? I'll pay.'

'Yes, of course.'

'Good.' He sat down with his newspaper, wondering why he'd offered to pay for the help. It wasn't like him. Still, Vi was his sister, so it didn't matter. He'd not show such weakness to others. People took advantage if you seemed at all soft.

But he did wish Vi wasn't involved with Bentley. That could only lead to trouble. He'd have to watch out for her from now on. And keep an eye on her and Bentley.

Tess was up before it was light, waking even before the knocker-up went down the road, rattling his long pole with its wires at the end against the window panes of those who paid him to wake them up. She had the sleepy, protesting children washed and dressed quickly, Harry too, even though he wouldn't have to leave for school for quite some time.

There wasn't enough bread left for them all, so she did without. She was used to that, lately, and didn't even feel hungry most of the time. She'd have some money by the end of the day and would be able to buy something for their tea. She'd eat then. 'Now, don't be late for school,' she warned her son. He shrugged and began playing with the dominoes he'd made himself from bits of wood. Eh, he was that clever with his hands!

She ushered the two little girls out of the door into the dark, frosty morning and held the hand of each one. It wouldn't be light for a while yet, but there were plenty of people around, going to work in the mill, or to some of the small workshops a few streets away from the town centre.

It took them twenty minutes to get to Fairview, because Jenny couldn't walk as fast as her older sister and mother. In the end, afraid of being late, Tess picked Jenny up and carried her up the last part of Ridge Hill. Cora plodded along happily beside her, chatting and commenting on the big, fancy houses with so many lighted windows, even at this hour of the morning.

'The maids will be doing the cleaning,' Tess said. 'They do a lot before the masters and mistresses get up.' Her stomach rumbled as they walked the last hundred yards. *You'll get fed later*, she told it.

When she got to the gates of Fairview, she put Jenny down, stopping for a moment to catch her breath. She heard footsteps crunching on gravel and saw Mr Bentley coming round from the back of the house holding up a lantern. She hurried over to him. 'I'm not late, am I?'

'No, you're nice and early. I've got the fire lit and some water heating. I had to bring the baby with me, though. Mum's busy helping Wilf and Libby settle in.'

The kitchen in the cottage felt warm after the chilly air outside and she held out her hands to the fire grate for a minute or two.

'I've just brewed a pot of tea. Let me pour you a cup.' He lifted the teapot with a smile.

'That'd be lovely.' Tea was a rare treat for her these days.

'And there's milk for the girls if they want it.'

Tess hesitated, not wanting to give too much away, then said,

'Could we keep it till dinnertime for them, please? I didn't have time to pack sandwiches.'

After a moment's silence, during which he studied her face as if he'd never seen her before, he said, 'You didn't have any food to pack, did you?'

She could feel herself flushing with shame, but couldn't lie to him. 'No.'

'Did you have any breakfast?'

'I'm never hungry in the mornings.'

'Well, maybe the walk has given you an appetite. There's a loaf there and a pat of butter. I'll cut you a slice.'

Her mouth watered as she watched him do that. He spread the butter so thickly she could almost taste it even before she took a bite. She closed her eyes blissfully as she chewed, then had a drink of tea, and felt energy flooding into her.

He bent to the children, who were standing shyly behind her. 'Would you like a buttie too?'

She couldn't stop them nodding and he cut more slices of bread, spreading the butter just as thickly for them. She caught his eye for a moment, swallowing hard, almost overwhelmed by this small act of kindness.

'I can't bear to see children going short,' he said quietly, his gaze steady on hers.

'Thank you, Mr Bentley.' She swallowed the last of her bread and drained her cup.

'There's another cup of tea in the pot,' he said. 'No sense letting it go to waste.'

She watched him share out the hot liquid equally. Two cups of tea. What a treat! He was a lovely man, Mr Bentley, as kind as her friend Vi.

The baby began to cry and his expression changed, growing cooler. Poor man. Tending the little one must remind him of how his wife had died.

'I'll see to her, if you want,' she offered. 'I like babies.'

'Thanks. She's been fed so she probably needs changing. My mother sent some stuff.' He pointed to the bag.

Tess had to change the baby on the floor, but there was a clean sack there, as if he'd prepared a place in advance. She blew bubbles on the baby's bare belly and soon had her laughing, the fat chuckles backed up by some wild waving of arms and legs.

But Mr Bentley didn't stay to watch. Poor man. Poor baby, too. She'd seen other men take against children who'd cost them their wives' lives.

Tess wrapped Nora up warmly and put her outside in the pram with the hood up to protect her from the wind. It was still dark, but there was plenty of light streaming out of the windows of the cottage because there were no curtains yet. She told Cora to stay by the window and watch both the baby and Jenny. Young as she was, Cora was very sensible. 'It'll soon be light and you can play out for a bit, but you're not to go beyond the cottage garden,' she warned and gave them each a quick hug as they nodded. They were such good children. She was lucky to have them. How could Joe have borne to leave them? She was angry with him for that, sad too.

'Here.' Mr Bentley appeared beside her. 'I found this in a corner of the stables.' He held out a ball to Cora. 'You can play catches with it when it gets light.'

Tess nudged her daughter and hissed, 'What do you say?'

'Thank you, Mr Bentley.' The child moved off, her little sister following her.

He turned to Tess. 'Now, I'm going to work you hard. Can you start by cleaning the bedrooms? I'll light a fire in each so that they'll dry out quickly. The men can't bring my furniture over till after milking, so they'll be a while yet.'

After that Tess was too busy to dwell on her own problems. She kept an eye on the baby and her own children as she worked, keeping an ear cocked when she couldn't see them.

When the baby began to cry for her bottle, she again offered to look after the child and Mr Bentley nodded, explaining about the powdered milk and how to mix it. Tess had never used the stuff. You couldn't beat mother's milk for strong babies, and it was cheaper. She'd been eating better then, so had had no trouble feeding her own babies.

Mr Bentley worked steadily alongside her, coming and going, clearing away cobwebs, sweeping out the rooms she still had to scrub.

By the time the cart arrived with his furniture, the bedrooms were dry, thanks to the fires. She stopped work to watch the first furniture brought in, then went back to washing down the windows in the next room.

Later in the morning, the lady from the big house came across. Miss Christina smiled at the baby and jiggled the pram around, then came inside, chatting with Mr Bentley as if he was an old friend, even coming across to speak to Tess.

If only everyone was like these two, the world would be an easier place, it would that, Tess thought.

'Shall I take the baby up to the house for a while?' Miss Christina asked Joss. 'My sister loved playing with her yesterday.'

'Are you sure?'

'Oh, yes. Very sure. It cheered Phyllis up enormously. And at midday we'll send across a pan of soup. Cook had some ham bones and made more than we need.' She smiled at Tess. 'We'll send enough for you all.'

'Thank you. You're very kind.'

'You've helped us more than I can say, Mr Bentley. And you've incurred that horrible man's wrath because of it.'

Tess couldn't believe a grand lady would be so kind in a practical way. As soon as the cart went away, Miss Christina beckoned from the kitchen door and Mr Bentley went across to fetch the pan of soup.

'Could you get the table ready?' he asked Tess. 'Bowls for all of us.'

When he brought back the pan, he ladled out such generous portions she knew she'd need no tea. She made sure the girls ate neatly, her eyes filling with tears of pleasure as she watched them eat so much good food.

'Get on with your own meal,' a quiet voice said beside her.

'I get more pleasure from seeing them eat.'

'And I'll get pleasure from seeing you eat, Tess.'

After their dinner, she washed the dishes, fed the baby and went to work again.

Vi spent the day doing the washing and drying it on the wooden clothes horse near the fire. She also supervised Eric's cleaner, watching Millie work. The woman was doing a good job, but kept glancing anxiously at the clock. As she'd guessed, there wasn't enough time allowed to do the job properly.

'We need things doing better than this,' she began.

'I never stop,' Millie said anxiously. 'Honest, Mrs Schofield. But men don't understand how much time it takes.'

'That's all right. I wasn't saying you're not a good worker. I meant, you need more time working here. I told my brother and he's happy to pay you for some extra hours if you can spare them.'

Millie's face lit up.

'How much more can you work?'

'As much as you like. To tell the truth, we're allus short of money, because my Bert drinks a lot since he come back from the war.'

'We could pay you daily if that'd help, then you could buy food with the money on your way home.'

'Bert won't like that.'

'I'll get my brother to have a word with him if he gives you any trouble.'

Millie looked at her in amazement. 'Mr Gill won't want to bother with that.'

'He will if I tell him. He wouldn't notice on his own, but I'll make sure he understands your problem.'

Upon that, Millie shed a few tears, then went back to her work.

Eric was equally surprised when he came home for his dinner and Vi told him what she wanted him to do.

'I can't interfere between a man and wife,' he protested.

'Of course you can. You're paying her to clean for you. If she doesn't get enough to eat, she won't be able to work as hard.'

He clamped his mouth shut and frowned down at his plate. She'd learned not to interrupt him when he was thinking.

'All right,' he said at last, picking up his knife and fork. 'I'm not a do-gooder, but I can see she needs to eat. She's as thin as a lath, that one. And the house looks cleaner today.'

'She worked longer hours. And she's coming back this afternoon.'

He nodded and ate a mouthful, then smiled at the plate of corned beef hash she'd made for him. 'I like your cooking, Vi. I hear soldiers complain about bully beef stew, but this is good.' He grinned. 'I bet you didn't get the corned beef from Dad's shop.'

'No. I buy it from the butcher's and he makes his own. Though you can get good tinned meat nowadays. Now the war's over, the shortages will end and we'll be able to keep a tin or two in the pantry in case we need a sudden meal. I'm afraid you've got the same for your tea. I've no time to cook something different. You can only have one bowlful for lunch, and you'll have to fill up on bread and jam, or an apple.'

'That's all right. I like bread and jam.'

In the middle of the afternoon Vi set out, calling in at the shop to see if Doris was all right. The window was clean and had piles of tins neatly stacked in it. That pleased her, but also surprised her. She hadn't expected Doris to do everything she told her.

When the customer had left they had a quick chat.

'Dad leaving the till alone?'

'Oh, yes.' Doris smirked. 'I threatened to cut his rations off if he didn't, and what with that and your brother, he's kept his hands off the money. But he's still drinking and I don't know how he's managing that or where he's getting the money from.'

'I'll ask Eric to keep an eye out. The window looks nice now.'

Doris was so touchingly pleased at this praise that some of Vi's resentment of her stepmother lessened. It just went to show, she thought as she walked up the hill. You could never be sure what people would do. They often surprised you when you gave them a chance to make good. She'd seen it time and again in her work in London. Mind you, she'd been disappointed a few times as well.

She met Mungo Sully's bully coming down it. Ted raised his cap to her with mocking courtesy and walked past, whistling. She stopped to watch him. What was he doing up here on the Ridge? Kirby didn't have any rental properties in this area. A shiver of apprehension ran up her spine. He was up to no good, she was sure.

She watched him till he vanished from sight then turned and walked on again, quickening her pace, worrying that something might have happened at Fairview.

Joss greeted her with a smile. 'Tess is a treasure,' he said. 'I'm grateful to you for finding her.'

They walked round the house and Vi was amazed at how much they'd got done today. 'You must have worked so hard.'

'We did. And talking of work, I'd better go back and pay Tess. You have time to stay for a cup of tea afterwards, don't you?'

In the kitchen he took the damp cloth out of Tess's hands. 'That's enough for today. Time for you to go home and rest.' He held out two half-crown coins. 'Here's your money. Can you come again tomorrow? Same price, five shillings.'

Tess's face lit up. 'Oh, yes. I'd be glad to.'

Vi watched her go, wishing she could find her friend a permanent way of making a living, but there were few employers who'd allow the children to come along as this one had.

'They're a well-behaved pair of kids,' Joss said abruptly, as if he'd read her mind. 'Need feeding up a bit, though.'

He gestured to her to sit down at the wooden kitchen table and busied himself making the tea, setting out two cups that didn't match the saucers with a grimace. 'I've not unpacked the rest yet. I hope you don't mind these.'

'Tea tastes the same, whatever the cup's like.'

When it was ready, they sat and sipped. Good quality tea, she noticed, the sort she preferred. 'When are you going to fetch your children here, Mr Bentley?'

'Tomorrow. Eh, I've missed them.' He gestured to the sleeping baby. 'I'll leave this one with Tess and fetch Roy and Iris up here after school. I'll nip across in the morning to ask their grandmother to pack their things. I've already arranged to borrow a cart so that I can bring their beds and toys and stuff.'

She saw his expression soften when he spoke of his older children. He didn't always look like that when he spoke of the baby, though. Sometimes when he picked Nora up, his expression became grim, a man doing his duty, not acting from love of a child. Other times he smiled fondly at her.

She wondered why that was. Nora was such a lovely child.

She looked at the clock. 'I'd better get back now. I have to cook tea for my brother.'

She'd rather have stayed, though. She enjoyed chatting to Joss, enjoyed it too much. What had got into her lately?

# 17

Eric went into the office to deposit some receipts after paying tradesmen for repairs to some of the better properties. 'All done,' he said to Sully. 'And they made a good job of it too. I checked that carefully before I handed over the money.'

'Have you let that house in Deery Lane yet?'

'No. The Bentleys have only just moved out. I paid them a week's rent and they left it perfect, but I want to find some good tenants.'

Sully scowled at him. 'I told you not to pay them.'

'What's the difference? It'd have cost the same to get someone else in to clean it.'

'The difference is that them Bentleys get the money an' I'd rather they didn't. I'd pay anyone rather than them, pay them double if necessary.'

Eric saw movement from Mr Kirby's office and raised his voice slightly, knowing that Sully was a bit deaf and would never notice. 'There's another difference you forget. If you will chuck good tenants out for spite, they can do a lot of damage to a property. Those are nice, sound houses and we have to look after them for Mr Kirby.'

Footsteps moved closer, not making enough noise for Sully to notice, but there was nothing wrong with Eric's hearing. He held his breath, waiting to see if their employer spoke. About time Kirby realised what was going on.

'Who've you thrown out, Sully?' Mr Kirby asked.

The older man swung round quickly. 'Didn't know you were back, sir.'

'I've been back a while. Who have you thrown out?'

'The Bentleys, younger son of the shoe shop fellow.'

'Why?'

'They weren't good tenants, were damaging the property.' His glance dared his assistant to contradict him, so Eric bit his tongue.

Later, when Sully had gone out, Mr Kirby came out of his office again. 'A word with you, Gill.' He closed the office door and asked in a low voice, 'Were the Bentleys good tenants?'

Eric bit his lip, not certain whether to tell him the truth or not.

'I'll find out one way or the other, so you may as well tell me. Your first loyalty is to me, not Sully, because I'm the one who pays you.'

'Excuse me, sir, but I'm afraid of losing my job.'

Kirby gave him an assessing stare. 'Very sensible of you, but I've no intention of sacking you. I've noticed how much more smoothly things have been going since you took over some of the properties.'

'Yes, sir.' Eric took a deep breath and risked his all. 'And since you ask, the Bentleys were excellent tenants, sir.'

'So why throw them out?'

'Joss Bentley stopped Sully when he was trying to frighten the old ladies at Fairview. Sully never forgives an insult, so he went after the brother as well. If past dealings are anything to go by, Sully won't rest till he chases Bentley out of the town.' Because he was watching carefully, he saw the thin lips tighten to a bloodless line and because his hearing was excellent, he heard the little growl of anger beneath that breath.

'I see. I think I must keep a more careful eye on Sully from now on. He's getting on a bit, stuck in the old ways, perhaps. Is there anything else I ought to know?'

Eric hesitated.

'If you tell me the truth, Gill, I'll not let Sully sack you. At the moment, I want no more trouble causing for the Warburtons. *None whatsoever*. If there is a potential problem in that regard, you are to disobey Sully if necessary and come straight to me. If you can't find me, you are to stop it happening, whatever the cost.'

Eric let out a long slow breath, trying to hide his surprise. 'Yes, sir.'

'I hope you mean that.'

'I hope *you* mean you won't let me be sacked, sir.'

Kirby let out a sound that might have been a laugh, then jerked his head in dismissal.

Eric wasn't fool enough to feel safe at that reassurance, but he was caught between the devil and the deep blue sea here. Damn! He'd rather have chosen his own time to move against Sully – and his own way.

He didn't trust Kirby, whatever assurances his employer gave him. And he most certainly didn't trust Sully, never had. The two of them had worked together for as long as he'd been alive. That weighted the scales against a newcomer like himself, he was quite sure.

Tess walked slowly down the hill, thinking of Vi and Mr Bentley. If ever two people looked comfortable together they did. She hoped something would come of it. He was a lovely man.

And if anyone deserved something good to happen to her, Vi did, because she was always helping other people, and she hadn't had much luck in life herself.

Tess hadn't had much luck, either, but maybe her luck was turning. She hoped so. She did want to give her children a good start in life.

As she turned into the street that led to Lilybank Court, she stopped in horror. Her possessions were strewn all over the pavement. Her sacking beds were exposed for everyone to see. Even as she watched, two men carried out her table and tossed it on top of the other stuff so carelessly that it fell over. She let go of the children's hands to run forward. 'Stop! What are you doing? Stop that!'

One of the men turned towards her, smiling. 'Ah, Mrs Donovan. Just in time. Mr Sully wants you and your things out of the area before morning.' He gestured towards her pitiful heap of possessions. 'We gave you a helping hand to move your things out of your room.'

'But why? I'm not behind with the rent.'

Another man came and threw a chair on to the heap, threw it hard, breaking one of its legs on purpose.

Her temper rose then. It had been one thing after another lately and she couldn't take any more. With a cry of protest she darted in front of the man who had turned to go back for something else. He tried to put her out of the way and she struggled, screeching at him, calling out to her neighbours to help her.

But no one did.

With another laugh the man threw her to the ground and she lay there sobbing. Now they really would put her in the workhouse, take her children from her. She had nowhere to go, nowhere.

Eric was walking home, still worrying about his job, when he heard screams and shouts. A woman. A man's voice laughing at her. The voice rose higher, screaming for help. He was going to walk past, but the shouting was coming from Lilybank Court, which was one of Mr Kirby's properties, so with a sigh he turned into it.

He saw Tess Donovan struggling with Ted Fitch, one of the men Sully used on difficult evictions, and his heart sank. With Mr Kirby's orders still echoing in his mind, he didn't dare walk away though. When the man threw Tess to the ground and drew back his foot to kick her, Eric stepped between them. 'What the hell's going on?'

'Mr Sully wants her out tonight, Mr Gill.'

'Why? I usually deal with these properties. He said nothing to me.'

Ted grinned. 'She's been cleaning for Bentley. Saw her myself up at Fairview and tipped him the word.'

'You didn't – cause a fuss up there?'

'No, course not. I never mess with the nobs. It don't pay. I come back an' told Mr Sully, an' he said to throw her straight out.' He kicked the pile of things, sending some ragged pieces of clothing into a muddy puddle.

'Stop that!' Eric said sharply. 'No need to damage her stuff.'

Ted shrugged but stopped.

The other man came out with a rickety chair. He was about to toss it onto the pile when Ted caught one of the legs.

'Mr Gill doesn't want her things damaging. Is that everything? Right, I'll go and lock up.' He pulled a padlock out of his pocket.

The neighbours who'd been peering out of doors and windows had vanished when Eric appeared, but Tess's three children were standing weeping a little distance away. The lad had his arms round the little lasses and was scowling at Eric.

The two men came back out, whistling.

'Give me the padlock key then,' Eric said. 'I'll be the one as has to let the room again tomorrow.' He accepted the small brass key, stared at it for a minute then said, 'All right. You've done what you came for. You can get off home now.'

After they'd gone, he turned to Tess. His first instinct was to walk away and leave her, but he knew Vi was fond of her and he never forgot how Tess had helped his mother in the shop. She'd been a good worker and you didn't forget things like that. 'Come on, Tess.' He held out one hand to pull her to her feet, but she shrank away and got up without his help.

But the sight of her things piled on the pavement was too much for her and she began to weep again, turning her face to the wall, one arm across her eyes, her whole body shaking with her anguish.

'Stop that!' he said sharply. 'We have to find you somewhere to sleep.'

'There isn't anywhere but the workhouse and I'll kill myself before I go into that place.'

Vi would kick up a big fuss if he let that happen, he knew. He stood silently for a minute, chewing his lip.

The little girls were crying, so Tess turned towards them and held out her arms. They rushed to her, cuddling against her, the boy beside them, glowering at Eric.

He suddenly remembered what Vi had told him about Fairview, the cottage Bentley was moving into, the empty stables. 'You'll have to go back to Fairview,' he said abruptly. 'I heard the stables are empty and I reckon the old ladies will let you shelter there till you find somewhere else to live.' It was the only place she'd be able to find once Sully put the word round, but he wasn't going to tell her that now. He wanted her off his patch of ground, didn't want to risk his job.

'What's happening here?'

Eric swung round to see the new Police Sergeant. That was all he needed. But he didn't intend to take the blame for this. 'Mr Sully had her evicted. I've only just found out.'

The Sergeant gave him a look of disgust and went to put an arm round Tess, who was still sobbing her heart out. 'Do you have friends you could stay with, love?'

She shook her head. 'If I go to anyone I know, Sully will chuck them out as well.'

'I'd heard he was spiteful.'

'She'd be best going to ask for help at Fairview,' Eric said. 'That's where Bentley's staying – she's been cleaning for him, that's what upset Sully.' But Sully wouldn't meddle with the folk there, Mr Kirby would see to that. 'My sister says they've got some stables that are empty, with living space over them.'

All he got in return was a suspicious glance and 'Why are you telling us this?'

'Because Tess used to help my mother and I don't forget things like that. And she's my sister's friend.'

Sergeant Piper turned back to Tess. 'Is that true? Do you trust him?'

She hesitated, then shook her head helplessly. 'I don't know. But his sister *is* my friend. Besides, what choice do I have?' She tried to wipe away the tears but more followed and the Sergeant pulled out his pocket handkerchief.

Eric seized the opportunity to slip away.

This was the last thing he needed. Now *he* would be in Sully's bad books, because that bugger was bound to find out he'd helped Tess.

Damn!

* * *

Vi was on her way home when she met the sad little procession coming up the hill. The new policeman and a lad she didn't recognise were pushing a heavily laden handcart and Tess was stumbling behind them, holding Jenny's hand. Cora was walking behind them with Harry.

Vi ran forward to them. 'What's happened?'

Tess tried to speak but her words were muffled by another burst of weeping.

The Sergeant stopped to wipe his brow. 'Sully's thrown her out of her home. She reckons it's because she's been working for Bentley.'

Vi couldn't move for a moment or two, unable to believe that this could have happened. 'I thought it was my brother who looked after Lilybank Court, not Sully.'

'Your Eric came along as it was happening,' Tess said. 'He didn't know about it. He stopped Ted Fitch from destroying my furniture and he said—'

As Tess gulped and struggled to continue speaking, Vi felt a leaden feeling settle in her belly. 'Our Eric was part of this?'

'No. He was just passing by. But he couldn't let me go back, could he? He has to do as Mr Sully tells him. But your Eric told me to come and ask for shelter at Fairview. Do you think they'll help me? There's no one else could take me in and even if I did have any family, I couldn't ask them for help, because then Sully would throw them out as well. You know what he's like.'

'I'll come with you to ask them.'

'Oh, Vi, would you? I'd be that grateful. I don't know where to turn next.'

The Sergeant gave Vi a little nod, as if to say he was glad of her help. 'Shall we move on again, then, ladies?'

She tried to keep her expression cheerful but she wasn't at all sure the Warburtons would help Tess. Why should they? The woman was nothing to them. But they might at least allow her to stay for a few days. Surely they would?

Eric walked slowly home. There were no lights so Vi mustn't be back yet. Thank goodness for electricity, he thought as he went inside. Not many houses had it, but he could just snap on a switch and the rooms were filled with light. But he was worried about what had just happened. He didn't want to lose his job and home because he'd upset Sully.

In the kitchen he got the fire blazing and put the kettle on to boil. While he was waiting for it, he sat down to have a think.

Fancy Sully taking out his anger about Bentley on a poor creature like Tess Donovan! It was stupid, a waste of time and energy, didn't bring in more money, either, because she'd always paid her rent as best she could, better than most in Lilybank Court, that was certain.

If the Warburtons didn't take Tess in, he didn't know what he'd do. But he'd have to do something because Vi wouldn't let her friend down. She might even bring Tess and the kids back here. And what would Sully think about *that*? Or Mr Kirby?

Eric pressed one hand against his chest as his heart fluttered wildly for a moment or two. '*Quiet now,*' he murmured to it and gradually it settled down, as it always did.

The kettle whistled and he poured the boiling water into the teapot, rinsed it and threw the hot water into the bowl he used for washing his hands, then spooned in two heaped teaspoons of best tea and poured in the boiling water.

As he sat waiting the four minutes it took to brew it to his satisfaction, he continued thinking. Life was getting a bit complicated for a rent man, what with returned servicemen who deserved a bit of respect, whatever Sully said, and the pressure for extra living accommodation.

If he hadn't taken Vi to live with him, he'd not have needed to get involved. But he'd found that life was more interesting when you lived with someone you liked. It had surprised him how much he enjoyed his sister's company and her cooking too.

He sighed and got up to pour himself a cup, spooning in two heaped teaspoons of sugar and stirring the black liquid gently. He didn't like milk in his tea, didn't like milk and cream at all. They made him feel sick.

If he'd been a praying sort of man, he'd have been on his knees praying that the Warburtons would let Tess stay in their stables. As it was he sipped and thought, thought and sipped. But he didn't get any clever ideas. Not one. Well, it was a ticklish situation and they usually took some sorting out.

# 18

When they got closer to Fairview, Vi said, 'I'll go ahead and let them know we're coming.' She hammered on Joss's door, seeing a faint light in the hallway and hoping he hadn't left yet. She sagged against the wall in relief as she heard footsteps coming towards her.

The door was flung open and he stood there with his overcoat on. They were only just in time.

'What's wrong?'

'It's Tess. Oh, Joss, Sully's thrown her out of her home because she helped you today.'

He blinked and said nothing, then shook his head in bafflement. 'I can never understand folk who act like that. Where is she?'

'Coming up the hill with all her possessions in a handcart, hoping they'll let her stay somewhere for a few days. She keeps crying. I've never seen her in such a state. Oh, Joss, she has hardly anything left at all now, it's all rags and worn-out stuff. And she's terrified of being put in the workhouse. She says she daren't ask anyone else to take her in or Sully will throw them out too.'

He muttered something under his breath and she looked at him anxiously. 'It was my brother who suggested bringing her here. Eric said it was her only chance of finding somewhere to live in Drayforth. You told me there were unused rooms over the stables. Do you think Miss Warburton would let her and the children stay there, for a while at least? Tess hasn't any money, not a penny to her name, but she'd do some cleaning for them in return.'

'We can only ask.' Then, at the sound of wheels on gravel and footsteps, he looked beyond his companion to the group of people who'd just arrived at the gate. He hurried over to them. 'Come inside and get warm, Tess. I'm sorry working here has got you in trouble.'

She didn't move until Sergeant Piper put his arm round her and guided her towards the house.

'You'd better all wait inside,' Joss said. 'I'll go across and talk to the old ladies. Vi, will you come with me?'

'Of course.'

It was dark outside and she stumbled.

'Here, take my hand. We'll go to the kitchen door.'

He took her hand in his big warm one before she could speak and kept hold of it till they were standing outside the brightly lit kitchen, whose light streamed out into the darkness. Then he looked down at their clasped hands and gave her a quick smile before letting go. 'It felt nice in mine.'

She didn't try to pretend, couldn't. 'Yes, it did.'

When he knocked, there were exclamations inside and someone peered through the window.

'It's Mr Bentley,' a voice said and there was the sound of a bolt being slid along its track before the door opened.

'Is something wrong?' Miss Christina asked, looking anxiously from one to the other.

'I'm sorry to trouble you but we need your help,' Joss said.

'Come in.'

Vi looked round curiously. It reminded her of the kitchen at Lady Bingram's house, only this one was shabby and old-fashioned. No gas cooker, just a big, blackleaded kitchen range. No gas lights, either, just oil lamps.

A thin old woman in a white apron that was too big for her turned from the pan she'd been stirring to stare openly at them. Miss Warburton was gazing at them from a wooden rocking chair in one corner.

Once the door was shut, Joss gave a quick summary of what had happened to Tess.

The two sisters exchanged glances and quick nods.

'The poor woman. Bring her across to meet my sister, will you, Mr Bentley? Mrs Schofield, can we offer you a chair?'

Vi sat down and looked at the table, which had three places neatly set for tea. 'I'm sorry to disturb you at meal time.'

'It doesn't matter. This young woman is a friend of yours, I gather?' Miss Christina asked.

'Yes. I've known her for years. She used to help my mother in the shop.'

'She's – respectable?'

'Very. Her husband died recently. Well, he killed himself actually.' Vi explained about poor Joe.

Footsteps outside heralded the return of Joss with Tess and her three children, accompanied by Sergeant Piper. They stood close together near the door, all looking pale and tired. The two little girls were as tear-stained as their mother, and Harry, who was holding his smaller sister's hand, was scowling.

'You look frozen,' Phyllis exclaimed. 'Do come nearer the fire, children.'

Christina studied Tess for a minute, then smiled. 'My dear, the rooms above the stables haven't been used for years, but if you can make yourself comfortable there, you're welcome to use them.'

'Just one will do us.'

'Take as many as you need. They're not very big.'

Tess's voice was burred with tears. 'We only have the furniture for one room now. Mrs Gilson made me sell the rest.'

'If I remember rightly, there are beds there already and some wooden chairs, plus a table in the day room. Mr Bentley, Sergeant Piper, could you and Mrs Schofield go and find the best place for Tess to stay and unload her things? In the meantime we'll give them a bite to eat . . . Oh, my dear, my dear!'

Tess had collapsed on the floor, sobbing wildly, this kindness more than she could take.

'She's in no fit state to do anything,' Phyllis said. 'They can sleep in the servants' quarters in the attic tonight, then we can move them into the stables tomorrow when it's light.'

'Good idea!' Christina turned to the men. 'Mr Bentley, could you help Mrs Donovan up to bed? And perhaps you'd help her to undress, Mrs Schofield? Leave the children here and we'll feed them, then you can take a tray up to the mother. I think she should eat before she goes to sleep. She's very thin.'

'She's been stinting herself to feed the children.'

'I'll go and unload her things from the cart,' the Sergeant said.

'Take this lamp. You can put them in the biggest room. We'll sort them out tomorrow.'

When the Police Sergeant had left, Christina smiled at the children. 'Sit down at the table, my dears, and we'll get you something to eat, then you can go and sleep near your mother.'

Harry swallowed hard and spoke in a suspiciously thickened voice. 'We shall need to have a wash first, miss. We're all mucky. They threw our things into the puddles, you see, an' we had to pull them out.'

Cook shook her head and tutted. 'To treat folk like that! There's water and a towel in the scullery, Miss Christina. You can show them where.'

When the children had followed Christina out of the room, Cook looked across at Phyllis and smiled. 'It's what you needed, miss. An interest.'

'Strange sort of interest.'

'It's the Lord's work, helping the poor, and little children especially.'

Phyllis smiled. Cook always became biblical when something moved her. But she was right. It did feel good to help someone. And life had been rather tedious since she had been confined to the house by her twisted joints.

When Vi got home, two hours after teatime, Eric thought there must have been trouble up at Fairview, she glared at him so fiercely.

'Couldn't you have stopped them?'

He set his cup down carefully, not pretending he didn't understand what she was referring to. 'Not if I wanted to keep my job. I told Tess where to go, didn't I? Even that might land me in trouble. Did the old ladies take them in?'

'Yes. They're sleeping in the attics tonight, the old servants' quarters. Then they're to move out to the rooms above the stables and make a home there.'

'Well, that's all right then.'

'No, it's *not* all right! What does Sully think he's *doing*?'

'Getting back at anyone who's helped Bentley. I told you to stay away from the man. I don't want you to be next on Sully's list.'

'I'll do no such thing. Joss is a friend and I don't desert friends when they need me.'

Eric opened his mouth and closed it again, she looked so furious.

She went to take off her things, then got him something to eat, slamming the plates and cutlery down in front of him. It was only fried eggs on toast. She didn't eat much herself, even less than usual, and she didn't chat to him, spent most of her time frowning down at her plate and stirring the food around.

Eh, Vi reminded him so much of their mother when she went all fierce like that. He didn't understand women, never had, but if they believed in something they could fight harder than men.

What would it be like to marry a decent woman? Living with Vi was showing him a bit, but he had to find out how to deal with the bedroom stuff and he couldn't ask her about that. And he'd better not wait much longer to get wed, either. He wanted kids of his own, to see his name carried on.

But first he had to sort out this business with Sully.

After tea, he put on his hat and coat. 'I'm going out for a bit.'

'Fine.'

'Don't wait up for me.'

'I won't.'

He rolled his eyes as he went out. How long was she going to stay mad at him? It wasn't his fault Sully had thrown Tess out.

Gerald studied his wife across the dinner table. 'When are you going to see Christina Warburton again?'

'Tomorrow afternoon. Look, I've been thinking. If I get involved in charity work, it'll be a good way to win friends of the right sort for us.'

'Bit of a bore for you.'

'No. Actually, what is boring is having so many servants I don't have to lift a finger. I need something to occupy my time.'

'I thought ladies went shopping and took tea with one another to do that.'

'I don't enjoy the company of certain ladies all that much. Freda Gilson may not have much money, but she's got all the right connections and she sits at the centre of local society like a spider in its web. I can't stand the woman!'

He looked at her in surprise. 'You never said this before.' As she grinned, he remembered suddenly one of the reasons he'd decided to marry her: she was intelligent and although she did the right thing socially, she was rather irreverent about it all in private, which amused him.

'I was settling in before, feeling my way in Drayforth. And there was the war. That gave me things to do, made me feel useful. Now it's over—' She gave one of her graceful shrugs and smiled. 'If I don't find something useful to do, I'll go mad.'

He didn't know what to say to that. His first wife had been a peaceful creature, happy with her home and embroidery, though deeply sad at her inability to give him a child. His second wife was a puzzle in many ways, and he wasn't always sure he understood her, which alternately intrigued and infuriated him.

There was a knock on the door and the maid poked her head round it. 'Sorry to interrupt you, sir, but there's a man at the back door, a Mr Gill. Says he's something to tell you and it can't wait.'

'Ah.' Gerald stood up. 'Please excuse me, my dear.' He followed the maid out, stopping in the hall to say, 'You were right to interrupt me, Jane. If Gill ever comes round again, you're to fetch me straight away, whatever I'm doing. But don't say his name when others are with me, just tell me there's a man to see me.'

'Yes, sir.'

'Show him into my office.'

From behind his desk, he watched Gill walk slowly along the corridor. The man's eyes flickered everywhere, his expression alert and assessing rather than overawed. Not for the first time, Gerald realised there was considerable intelligence behind that unprepossessing, puffy face. He didn't offer a seat. 'What is it?'

'You said to tell you if anything happened that affected the Warburton ladies, sir.'

'I certainly did. Go on.'

'Sully threw a woman out of her room in Lilybank Court this afternoon because she'd been cleaning for Joss Bentley.'

Gerald stared at him, trying to make sense of this and not succeeding. 'I fail to see a connection.'

'Sully's making sure no one will have anything to do with Bentley, frightening them off. He's done it before. Doesn't stop till the person who's upset him leaves town.'

'Has he run mad?'

Eric shrugged. He certainly thought so.

'Well, go on. There must be more to it if you've come to see me at home. How are the Warburtons involved?'

'Well, sir, Bentley's moved into a cottage in their grounds and now the woman Sully threw out has taken refuge at Fairview. The old ladies have taken her in, so they'll know that she was a tenant of yours. I thought it best to let you know straight away, not wait till tomorrow. And I'd rather Sully doesn't find out about me telling you, if you don't mind.'

Kirby paused, thinking through what he'd been told. 'How did you find out about this?'

'I was passing Lilybank Court when they threw Tess out – she's a decent woman, just lost her husband, who was gassed in the war. People won't like it, her being treated like that. So I stepped in and stopped the men from breaking up her furniture then sent them away.'

'Breaking up her furniture!'

'Yes. She's only got a few bits and pieces left. The Panel made her sell everything before they'd give her any money when her husband couldn't work. I felt sorry for her.'

'Sully *has* run mad!' He looked at Gill. 'Is there anything more?'

'Well . . . my sister is involved, too. She's just come back from doing war work in London as one of Lady Bingram's Aides and she's one of the new health visitors. Tess is a friend of hers and our Vi's not one to pass by when someone's in trouble. So I'm a bit worried that Sully will try to get back at my sister as well – or even at me.'

'I can assure you he won't. Is that all? Right, then.' Gerald stood up. 'Keep me informed if anything else happens. And well done for coming straight here tonight.' He pulled the bell and when the maid arrived, said, 'Show this man out – and remember what I said about names. No bandying them around.'

When he went back to the dining room, Gerald found it empty and followed the trail of lights into the sitting room. His wife looked up from where she was reading a book.

'Trouble?'

He hesitated, then sat down and told her.

'You need to get rid of that Sully. If he goes on doing things like this, no one will speak to you.'

'Not an easy thing to do, get rid of him. We go back a long way, Sully and I.'

She shrugged. 'Either you want to be accepted socially or you don't.'

He didn't intend to explain to her why it wasn't as easy as it sounded to dismiss Sully, who enjoyed what he did and had said several times that he never wanted to retire.

After he left Kirby's house, Eric went down to the pub. Someone was bound to have seen him in the street tonight and the pub was as good an excuse as any for being out on such a cold evening.

He ordered a pint of ale, nodded a greeting to a few men and sat down in the lounge area. He didn't enjoy standing up to drink in the public bar, especially since he usually drank alone. A man came and slipped into the chair next to Eric and he turned sideways in surprise. 'Sergeant Piper. What are you drinking?'

'I'll buy my own, thank you. No offence, but it's better in my position not to be obliged to anyone.'

Eric said nothing, but as Piper didn't move away, he assumed the policeman wanted to speak to him.

'It's one thing to throw a family out of their house if they can't pay the rent,' the Sergeant said in a low voice. 'But if there's any damage to their property while that's happening, I'll personally charge the person concerned with malicious damage, whether the owner presses charges or not.'

'If it'd been me throwing them out, there'd have been no damage,' Eric said quietly.

'I've heard that you're not as – rough with people. But I'm warning everyone who works with Sully.'

'Mmm.'

The Sergeant moved off without another word.

Through the mirror Eric saw Piper walk into the public room, lean on Fitch's table and say something to him that made Fitch scowl, then Piper left by the side door.

Eric didn't allow the smile to reach his lips as he picked up his half-empty glass. Useful, that, for his purpose. He'd make sure Sully and Mr Kirby both knew that he and Fitch had been warned.

He didn't go back home after he left the pub. He used his key and slipped into the office the back way, drawing the blinds before using his electric torch to get out the papers he wanted. He was systematically familiarising himself with the contents of the locked drawers, and making notes.

Knowledge of any sort could be very useful indeed. Especially now.

And Sully had been up to a few little tricks here.

The following morning Tess woke with a start, horrified to see that it was already light. There were no knockers-up round here to let you know it was time to get up, because rich people could sleep as long as they liked. Ashamed to have slept in, she went to find the children and shook them awake, then returned to her bedroom to pour out some of the cold water from the big jug standing in a fancy bowl on a little table in her room. Eh, the luxury of being able to wash in private. She couldn't resist washing all over with the beautiful white soap, holding the towel to her cheek and marvelling at how soft it was.

When they were all dressed, she took the yawning children downstairs and found the kitchen already warm and Miss Christina setting the breakfast things out.

'Sorry I'm late getting up, miss. I never usually sleep in. What do you want me to do first?'

'Eat your breakfast, of course. Are you and the children hungry?'

Tess stared at her, then felt tears well in her eyes again at this unexpected kindness. She had to stop crying. It got you nowhere, crying didn't.

Christina pointed to the table. 'Sit down, all of you. I put a pot of porridge on the top of the cooker last night before I came up to bed. It's best cooked slowly like that. We have sugar and cream to put on it.'

'I don't know how to thank you – for being so kind to us, miss,' Tess said, her voice breaking in the middle of this speech. 'I thought— I was frightened we'd wind up in the poorhouse yesterday.'

'I think we can do better than that for you. Here.' She thrust a cup of tea into Tess's hands. 'Get that down you, eat your porridge and then we'll talk. I don't know about you, but I'm hungry. My sister isn't strong, so she doesn't get up till later and Cook is quite old now, so I always get the breakfasts.'

It did Tess's heart good to see her children tucking into big bowls of porridge with cream poured over the top and sugar lavishly sprinkled over that. She had to be reminded twice to eat her own food, then drifted off into a daydream again till she suddenly realised Miss Christina was speaking to her.

'The girls stayed with you yesterday while you worked, didn't they?'

'They're not old enough to go to school yet. They won't be any trouble, though, I promise you.'

'So it's just the boy going to school, then. I'll put some food up for him because it's too far to come back here at dinner time.'

Which kindness to her son made tears well up again in Tess's eyes, but she winked them away.

When they'd all finished eating, she gathered the plates together and took them into the scullery while Miss Christina made some sandwiches for Harry. Cheese, they were, and such generous slices of it, too.

After Harry had left, Tess looked at her benefactor and waited to be told what to do.

'My sister and I had a chat last night. We thought that if the stable quarters are suitable as a home for you and your children, you could stay there rent free and all of you eat with us, if you'll help in the house as much as you can. We don't have a lot of money to pay you, but we can give you a shilling or two. What do you think?'

Tess couldn't help it. She bowed her head and wept again, then found Miss Christina's arms round her and a voice in her ears murmuring, 'Oh, my dear girl, you've had such a bad time lately, haven't you?'

# 19

Nora woke Joss in the middle of the night, crying on and on till he had to light a candle and find out what was wrong. She was writhing about, her little face screwed up in pain. He picked her up and found her soaking wet, so changed her nappy. To his horror, he'd not fastened one of the safety pins properly and it had dug into her and made her bleed – not a lot, but enough to make him feel physically sick at his own carelessness when she was so helpless. He took her back to bed with him, cuddling her close and making soothing noises until she fell asleep.

The next thing he knew he was awake and it was fully light. The baby was lying next to him on the bed, her eyes wide open and a smile on her face. She made some soft cooing noises and he couldn't resist touching the rosy skin of her cheek. Then he picked up his pocket watch from the washstand, horrified to find it was past eight o'clock. He pulled his clothes on anyhow and carried Nora down to the kitchen.

He'd have to buy an alarm clock so that he didn't sleep in again once the children were here. He didn't want Roy and Iris to be late for school.

Christina carried up a tray to her sister's room and found Phyllis already dressed. 'I didn't know you were awake. Couldn't you sleep?'

'I slept far better than usual, but this morning I wanted to get up and help where I can.' She smiled. 'It's wrong to be glad something so terrible has happened, but I think these people's misfortunes are good for us. Our lives were very – tedious before, weren't they? I tried not to complain, but I was so bored. And now we'll not only be helping that family and Mr Bentley too, but you won't have to do so much cleaning, either.'

'Shall I pour you a cup of tea?'

'No, we'll take it down with us, I think. I want to come to the stables with you and Tess.'

Half an hour later the three women walked across the back yard. Joss came out of his house to greet them and joined the exploration group.

Phyllis pulled herself painfully up the stairs and found the others waiting for her at the top. Joss offered his arm and with a smile, she took it. 'Lead the way, Christina.'

There was a larger room with two tables and bench seats, which was in quite good condition. There were several small bedrooms, each with a single bed, and two larger ones, each with three single beds in it.

'Goodness, it's years since I've been out here,' Phyllis said, sitting on the edge of a bed and trying it out. 'Father didn't allow us to come up here when the men were living here, of course, and after they'd all left, we closed it up.'

'There are no washing facilities,' Christina said.

'There's a tap in the stables and another in the yard,' Joss said. 'I'm sure Tess will manage just fine with that.'

'You can use the day room for your living room,' Christina said. 'It's got a fireplace and a bar to hang pans on, rather old-fashioned, I'm afraid. But there's plenty of wood for heating.'

Phyllis moved towards the door. 'We'll leave you to look round in peace, Tess. Take your time. Then perhaps Joss will help you bring your own things up.'

Downstairs, she whispered to Joss, 'Do you have time to help her settle in? She'll feel better when she has a home again.'

To her surprise he suddenly gave her a big hug, turning to do the same to Christina. Then he stepped back, still smiling. 'You're wonderful, ladies. I'll fill up your coal scuttles with wood now, shall I? And when Tess is settled in, I need to go and see my mother-in-law and make arrangements for my own children to come here.'

'I'd be happy to look after Nora for you,' Phyllis said quickly.

In the kitchen they found Cook making preparations for luncheon, eager to hear how things had gone.

It was a long time, Phyllis thought, since time had passed so pleasantly, with so much to think about and do.

After he'd helped Tess, Joss left the baby with Miss Warburton, whose eyes lit up at the sight of Nora. Then, he made sure he was looking smart and set off to walk to his mother-in-law's. He felt so happy at the thought of having Roy and Iris back to live with him, kept making plans for doing things with them.

Mrs Tomlinson opened the door with her usual sour expression and his happy mood evaporated immediately.

'I don't know why you've come round at this hour, Joss. I said you could see the children after school. They're not even here now.'

'I need to talk to you.' To his annoyance there was a distinct hesitation before she opened the door and let him in, reminding him unnecessarily to wipe his feet.

When they were seated, he began the little speech he'd prepared. 'I want to thank you for taking in the children after their mother died. I'll always be grateful for that. However, I've now got a home to offer them, so I'll be having them back to live with me again.' He watched spots of red burn in her cheeks and her expression grow vicious, all in the blink of an eye, which reminded him of Ada. Just so had his wife's sunny moods changed if she was thwarted. Even the children had learned to tread carefully with their mother when she got a certain expression on her face. They must have had to do the same here, poor things.

Mrs Tomlinson's words were thrown at him like daggers. 'I can't possibly allow that. A man on his own can't take care of two children as well as earn a living. And girls need a woman's care. I owe it to Ada – the only thing I can do for her now – to look after Iris and Roy properly.'

He held back his anger with some effort. 'I'm sorry, but they're my children and I want them living with me. Besides, there *is* a woman who'll be helping me in the house, so you've no need to worry.'

'Oh? And who is she? Some slut you've taken up with?'

Her words took his breath away and it was a minute before he could speak. 'I've not taken up with anyone in that way and don't you dare suggest it. This is a decent widow who needs to earn money by cleaning.' He sought for other arguments to persuade her. 'And what's more, one of the new Health Visitors is also helping me.'

'I don't believe you.'

'Why would I lie about it?'

'Who is she, this Health Visitor?'

'Mrs Schofield.'

'I know no one of that name, and I've lived in Drayforth all my life. It's Mrs Gilson who does the visiting to poor families and you're not so poor that you need the Panel's help, surely?'

'Of course not. But things are changing. There are two other ladies involved in the health visiting now, or there will be from next week. This one is a widow. Schofield is her married name. She's been working in London during the war, but she's come back to live in Drayforth now with her brother. He's—'

She cut him off without really listening, in that annoying way she had. 'That's beside the point. The children are best left with me. *I* am a relative, these women aren't.'

He stood up. 'I don't wish to get into an argument with you, but as their father, I have every right to do as I please with my children. Roy and Iris are coming to live with me and that's that. I'll be back this afternoon to collect them after they come home from school, so I'd be obliged if you'd have their things packed. I've a cart coming for their beds and other bits and pieces as well, and—'

'Well, they're not coming with you.'

'They're coming if I have to break the door down to get them.' He regretted his words the moment he'd uttered them, but she was such an infuriating woman. She'd drive a teetotaller to drink, that one would.

'Don't you dare threaten me in my own house! Get out this minute and don't come back!' She stood up and marched to the door, flinging it open and slamming it behind him the minute he was outside.

He didn't look back or try to argue, but strode away, stopping at the end of the street to calm down and think what to do. He'd better go and buy some food for tonight and tomorrow morning.

That woman wasn't going to stop him having his children back. He knew how unhappy they were with her and he'd tell the truth about that if he had to. He was trying not to upset her any more than he had to. She'd lost her daughter and the one thing he was sure about was that she'd loved Ada deeply in her own way, and sincerely mourned her.

He wondered why Mrs Tomlinson hadn't mentioned Nora, though, when talking about his children? She didn't seem to have had anything to do with the new baby.

When Joss had gone, Mrs Tomlinson went into the kitchen and pulled a bottle out of the back of the top shelf of the cupboard, pouring herself a glass of gin – just one, never more than one, she wasn't a drunkard. But a little drink did wonders if you were upset. Restorative, that was the word. Medicinal. Sitting down, she sipped the neat spirit slowly until she had calmed down.

When the glass was empty, she washed it, put the bottle away then chewed a strong peppermint.

Ada's children were not going to be dragged up any old how by *that man*. She'd seen how unhappy he'd made her daughter, how rough he was with the children, tossing them around, not teaching them proper manners. And he'd rarely taken them to church, as a decent father should. Decent! Ha! She knew how short of money he'd always kept her Ada and he didn't even have a job at the moment, so how could he possibly support a family? His gratuity money would soon run out and Bentley's shoe shop wasn't thriving, anyone could see that, apart from the fact that his brother was working there now, not him.

No, it was her duty to keep the children with her and she'd

never shrunk from doing her duty. She'd spoiled Ada, she knew that now, but she wasn't going to spoil Ada's children. Their behaviour was already improving and would get better still.

She wasn't having the baby, though. Not with what she knew about that child. The baby was *his* fault, though, not her daughter's. He'd *driven* Ada to it. Desperate, she'd been. It said in the Book of Common Prayer *Ye that do truly and earnestly repent you of your sins*. And Ada had been truly repentant, had wept on her mother's bosom then begged for forgiveness on her knees.

Putting on her best hat and coat, Mrs Tomlinson set off for town. There was a lady from church who would help her, she was sure. She smiled grimly. Her son-in-law would get a shock when he returned. Take the children away from her, indeed. Over her dead body!

Vi had intended to go up to Fairview early to see if Tess was all right, but fate conspired against her. The scullery tap had always been wobbly, but this morning when she turned it on, the whole thing fell off and water poured out of the pipe into the sink. She tried to jam the tap on again, but it wouldn't stay there, so she had to go running for help. A plumber came back with her, shut off the water at the stop cock and went away again for a new tap. By the time he'd finished, the morning was gone.

Even modern houses, it seemed, could have problems. Faulty tap, the man said as he finished the repairs. Shoddily made. The thread had sheared right off. Why they'd used taps like this when building the better sort of houses, he couldn't understand.

Vi couldn't help suspecting that Sully had got a bribe from the builder. It was common knowledge that tradesmen who wanted to work on Kirby's properties had to pay Sully a percentage of the money they earned. Probably it had been the same with the builder.

It was nearly noon by the time the house was set to rights, so Vi had a quick sandwich then set off, stopping at her father's shop for a few supplies for Tess.

For once Arnie was there, but he stepped back when he saw

his daughter and made a sweeping gesture towards Doris. 'It's no use me trying to serve you, Vi'let. I'm not even allowed to touch the money in my own till now, am I? She'll be all humble and grateful that you condescended to shop here, though, I'm sure.' With that he shuffled away into the back room.

Doris rolled her eyes then quickly and efficiently got what Vi needed.

'How's it going?'

'It'd be all right if your father would pull his weight, the lazy sod.'

'The shop looks better.'

Doris looked round with a proprietorial eye. 'I'm sorting things out gradually. Can't do everything at once, but I'm doing my best.'

'You're doing well.'

Vi walked away hoping her father wouldn't do anything to spoil Doris's obvious pleasure in her new job. She felt sorry for the poor woman in the same way she'd felt sorry for her mother. He was a rotten husband.

She found Tess at the rear of Fairview, shaking a rug energetically in the yard. No need to ask how her friend was: Tess was humming happily as she worked.

She turned, saw Vi and broke off to beam at her. 'Me and the kids have found ourselves a home again, and a better one than before. I've got a job as well, all thanks to you. I'm ever so grateful.' She lowered her voice. 'And Miss Warburton is teaching my Cora to sew right this minute, and Jenny's watching them. Can you imagine that? The girls have really taken to her and when I worried to Miss Christina about them troubling her, she said her sister had always loved children and it was doing them both good to have some company around the place.'

Then Tess's smile faded and she glanced towards the cottage. 'I think something's upset poor Mr Bentley, though. He came home looking that angry and upset. But when I asked what was wrong, he stared at me like I'd grown two heads and said I should finish at his place for the day and come back another time. And when I left, he slammed the door so hard it made all the windows rattle.'

'I'd better go and see him then.'

'He'll talk to you if he'll talk to anyone,' Tess said with a nudge. 'I know it's early days yet and I won't say anything to upset the applecart, but I think you two are perfect for one another. You're both that kind. I can't thank you enough for helping me an' the kids. And I'm happy to keep an eye on the baby for him. She's no trouble, bless her, loves a cuddle she does.'

Vi walked away across the yard, shocked by her friend's assumptions about Joss. Was it so obvious that she was attracted to him? What if he thought she was setting her cap at him? He might not like that. But what if he did want her too? That thought made her shiver.

She knocked on the front door, and had to knock again before it was flung open and he stood glaring at her as if she was his enemy. 'I know something's wrong, Joss. Can I help in any way?'

He closed his eyes for a moment and the anger burning in them had vanished by the time he opened them again. He gazed into her eyes for a heart-stopping moment, then with an inarticulate murmur, pulled her into his arms and held her close. She could feel the tension emanating from him, so put her arms round his waist and leaned against his chest, hugging him right back.

A glorious eternity later, when he still hadn't moved, she pulled away a little and laughed shakily, her main worries answered. 'Let's go into the house, shall we? It looks bad, us standing pressed together like this.'

Without a word, he laced his arm round her waist and they walked slowly along the corridor to the kitchen.

She didn't try to pull away, didn't want to. 'What's happened to upset you, Joss love?'

'I went to see my mother-in-law, to arrange about bringing Roy and Iris here to live with me. She didn't even give me time to explain properly, jumped to conclusions about you and Tess, and then . . .'

Vi listened without comment as he explained what had happened, growing angry herself. How dare Mrs Tomlinson judge people like that, without ever having met them? She must have a nasty mind. 'What are you going to do?'

'Go round with the cart as arranged and take the children away from her, by force if necessary.'

When Vi didn't respond, he waited a minute and asked, 'What are you thinking?'

'That could be a bit difficult. You can't go breaking into her house, can you?'

'But they're *my* children. And they're unhappy living with her.' He ran one hand through his hair, leaving it standing on end. 'I'm too angry to think straight. Eh, I'm so glad you came, Vi.' His smile was warm with affection and trust. 'I needed you.'

She reached out to caress his cheek before she even considered what she was doing, how she was betraying herself. When he pulled her closer and bent his head to kiss her, she offered her lips willingly. But the wild feelings that ran through her at his slightest touch stunned her. She'd never felt anything like this with Len.

'What is it?' Joss asked, looking down at her anxiously as she jerked away.

'I was just – surprised at how I felt when you kissed me. With Len it was more – gentle.'

'I'm a bit like a hungry man staring at a feast,' he said ruefully. 'And this isn't the time to deal with you and me. But we will make time later, after I've sorted the children out . . . won't we, Vi? Get to know one another, see how we go?'

She told him the simple truth. 'Yes, I'd like that.' Then she gave him a little push. 'Go and sit down on the other side of the table now, Joss, where you won't – um, distract me.'

She waited till he'd done that, still worrying about what he'd threatened to do. 'We have to plan this carefully. You can't go rushing in like a bull at a gate. You simply can't afford to get into trouble with the police. That'll do no one any good, least of all your children.'

* * *

Mrs Tomlinson jammed a second hatpin into her best hat, nodded at her reflection in the mirror and picked up her handbag. She didn't like asking favours, or making her private business public, but it had to be done. *That man* had to be stopped. He'd ruined Ada's life and he wasn't going to ruin the children's.

At the Town Hall, she asked to see Mrs Gilson.

'She's not in today, love,' the man at the desk told her. 'You'll have to come again tomorrow. Morning would be best.'

She drew herself up. 'I'll thank you not to address me so familiarly, young man. It's madam to you, if you don't know my name.'

Swinging round, she marched out. She knew where Mrs Gilson lived and this matter was too urgent to be left until tomorrow. If Joss did indeed try to break her door down to get those children, she intended to be ready for him.

At Mrs Gilson's house she stopped, put one hand up to press it against her chest, trying to still her beating heart, then gathered her courage together and marched down the garden path to the front door.

A maid answered it.

'I'd like to see Mrs Gilson please. My name's Mrs Tomlinson and I'm a member of her church. It's very urgent or I'd not disturb her at home.'

The maid left her standing on the doorstep and disappeared into a room to the right, then re-appeared and gestured to the room. 'Please go in, Mrs Tomlinson.'

Mrs Gilson looked across the room at her, as if assessing every stitch she wore. 'I recognise you from church. Please sit down, Mrs Tomlinson. How can I help you?'

She tried to speak calmly, but the anger took over and words tumbled out of her mouth, so many that she couldn't remember afterwards exactly what she'd said.

'You say this man, the father of your grandchildren, is living in an immoral relationship?'

'I don't know about *living* with anyone. But I don't like the idea of this woman who'll be coming and going. Who knows what they'll get up to? He hasn't got a job, you know, so he'll be there all the time while she's supposed to be cleaning. And he always was one for the women. Never went to church, either. Doesn't believe in God, he told me once.'

Mrs Gilson sucked in her breath at this. 'Shocking.'

'And it's not only the woman who cleans for him. There's some other woman helping him as well. I've seen them out walking together. You can tell there's something going on between them by the way they look at one another. He says she's a Health Visitor, but I can't believe that. Surely a lady like you wouldn't employ a woman who comes from the Backhill Terraces?' She ran out of words and sat waiting for guidance.

'Would this woman be called Schofield?' Freda asked, almost purring as fate handed her this weapon.

'Yes, that's her name. He said she'd been working in London during the war.'

'And we all know what young women get up to in a big city without anyone to keep an eye on them.' Freda didn't believe that a titled person like Lady Bingram would have kept those women in order. Everyone knew the aristocracy had slacker morals than ordinary people.

'You were quite right to come to me, my dear Mrs Tomlinson. And right to worry about the children, too. Far better to leave them with a woman like yourself, a churchgoer, someone with a proper sense of what's right and wrong. Now this is what I suggest you do first . . .'

Vi walked into town with Joss, having again left little Nora in Tess's and Miss Warburton's capable hands.

They met Elizabeth Twineham walking along the main street, looking upset. Even though they were in a hurry, Vi felt she had to stop for a moment. After all, Elizabeth was a stranger in the town. 'Is something wrong?'

'I'm trying to find lodgings and no one will even give me a chance, although the people I visited were advertising rooms to rent in the newspaper. And the last one said, "I'm not taking a woman like you" as if she knew something bad about me. How could she? I've never seen her before in her life. Do I look like an immoral woman?'

'No, of course you don't. I had the same reaction myself. I wonder . . . No, surely she wouldn't . . .' Vi broke off, hesitating to put her thoughts into words.

'Who wouldn't do what?' Elizabeth asked.

'Mrs Gilson. Surely she'd not tell people to refuse you lodgings?'

Elizabeth blinked in shock. '*Tell them to refuse me?* But why would she do that?'

'She didn't want either of us appointed as Health Visitors. She intended those jobs to go to her own friends. And she has a lot of power in this town, always seems to get her own way.'

'But if I don't find lodgings, how can I start work here next week? You don't know anywhere else I could try, do you?'

Vi considered this, then looked at Joss. 'You don't suppose the Warburtons would rent Elizabeth a room, do you, just for the time being? Or would that be asking too much?' He'd said several times how both ladies were looking brighter for having more company.

He shrugged impatiently and glanced across at the station clock. 'They might.'

Elizabeth stepped back. 'I shouldn't trouble you. You've obviously got something else on your mind at the moment.'

Vi was torn between the two of them. But it wouldn't hurt to have another witness today, she was sure. 'Why don't you come with us? After we've finished our business we're going back to Fairview and we can ask about a room for you then. Miss Christina Warburton was one of those who interviewed us. She's a lovely lady.'

'But I can't ask her to—'

'Of course you can. Even if it's only temporary, I'm sure she'll help. And you do have to find somewhere quite quickly.' And if the Warburtons didn't take Elizabeth in, she'd ask Eric if she could share her bedroom with Elizabeth until something did turn up. There was usually a way to get things done, she'd found. You just had to keep trying new approaches until one worked.

They walked briskly along the road to the elementary school that served the eastern half of the town, the school the children of the better-off families attended. Joss led the way inside, knowing where the headmaster's room was because he'd been educated here himself.

Mr Dunbar was working at his desk with the door open so that he could listen to what was going on in the rest of the school. That door rarely closed. Joss smiled as the headmaster looked up. Nothing escaped that man's notice. Joss remembered being hauled up before him for some misdemeanour when he was a lad and shivering in his shoes as he waited to see whether he'd get the cane. Not that Mr Dunbar used the cane very often. He didn't even raise his voice most of the time, didn't need to.

The headmaster got up from his desk and came round it, hand outstretched. 'Bentley! I'd heard you were back, and about time too.'

Joss shook hands quickly, impatient to see Iris and Roy, then realised what the other had said. 'Why "about time too"?'

'Because those children of yours need you. They've grown very quiet since they've been living with their grandmother. I don't like to see youngsters looking so cowed. It's one thing to be well-behaved, I insist on that in my school, but they're definitely cowed, jump if a teacher so much as looks at them.'

'Well, I'm taking them back to live with me now. Only Mrs Tomlinson is making a fuss and says she won't let them come to me. So I thought if I took them from school – if you would let them out a little early, that is – I could leave them with friends while I get back their clothes and beds from her. I don't want them involved in a fuss. Especially after what you've said.'

Mr Dunbar pursed his lips. 'Hmm.' He skewered Vi with a very sharp glance. 'And who might your companion be?'

'Mrs Schofield is one of the new Health Visitors. She's been helping me sort a few things out for the children.'

'I'm glad to make your acquaintance, Mrs Schofield. We shall no doubt be meeting again. The eastern side of town is not immune from troubles, though not as many as my colleague Mr

Minton faces in the Backhill Elementary School.' He picked up a little bell and rang it.

A lad came running.

'Fetch Roy and Iris Bentley to me, if you please.'

'They aren't here, sir. Their grandmother came to collect them at afternoon playtime.'

'No one asked my permission to let them go.'

'I heard her tell Miss Ware she had your permission, sir. She wouldn't even wait for them to get their schoolbags, just left straight away. Shall I fetch Miss Ware?'

'No, I'm sure she thought she was doing the right thing. Thank you, lad. Go and fetch Roy and Iris's things.' He turned back to Joss. 'What shall you do now?'

'I don't know.'

'Well, if I can help in any way, let me know. Ah, here are your children's satchels.'

A young woman brought them in. 'I've just heard. I'm so sorry, Mr Dunbar. It never occurred to me that she was telling lies. She's always seemed to *respectable*.'

'Yes. People often surprise us. You'll be more wary in future, no doubt.'

'Yes, sir.'

He turned back to Joss. 'I don't envy you.'

# 20

Joss and Vi went outside to where Elizabeth was waiting for them.

'Their grandmother has already taken them from school without permission,' Vi explained quickly, then turned to Joss. 'What do you want to do?'

'Go straight round to her house and demand my children.'

'And if she doesn't let them come to you?' She watched him rub his forehead and leave the brim of his bowler hat crooked, feeling an urge to straighten it for him. But she didn't let herself make such an intimate gesture in public.

'I don't know. See a magistrate, I suppose. You were right. It'd not look good to try to break into her house.'

'Let's go round to see her, then. We ought at least to give her the opportunity to do the right thing. Elizabeth, if I give you directions to Fairview, could you go there and tell the old ladies I sent you, explain that you're looking for a room? I think they'll accommodate you, even if it's only temporary. And . . . tell them what's happening about Joss's children, too, will you?'

'Yes.'

They parted company, Joss striding along until he realised Vi was having difficulty keeping up.

'Sorry.' He slowed down.

When they got to Mrs Tomlinson's house, Vi laid one hand on his arm. 'Remember, whatever she does, stay polite. Don't lose your temper.'

'It won't be easy. She's a dreadful, spiteful woman, says such things—'

'Whatever she says or does, you mustn't let her goad you into doing anything foolish. That'd give her ammunition against you.'

He nodded. 'You might as well stay here. There's no point in you facing her rudeness.'

'All right.'

Joss braced himself, walked up to the front door and knocked. He waited, then knocked again. There was no answer, no sign of movement inside the house, not even a twitch of the net curtains.

He turned and called to Vi, 'I'm going round the back.'

'Be careful.'

The house was semi-detached, set in neat gardens. Joss walked round the side, moving as quietly as he could. Through the kitchen window he saw Mrs Tomlinson standing looking down the hall towards the front door. There was no sign of his children. When he rapped on the window pane, he saw her jump in shock and spin round.

'Go away!' Her voice was shrill.

'I want my children back.'

'Well, you can't have them.'

'I'm their father, for heaven's sake.'

'But you're not a good father. I've been to see Mrs Gilson and she agrees it's better if they stay with me. If you don't go away, my neighbour will fetch the magistrate and Mrs Gilson will tell him how things stand and he'll make an order against you. He'll trust her judgement. And will you please tell *that woman* to get away from the front of my house. I don't want her sort round here.'

'I'm not giving up. And I'll thank you to be polite to Mrs Schofield. You know nothing about her.' He remembered suddenly that his children's bedrooms were at the rear of the house. They might be up there. Ada had said her mother often punished her by locking her in her bedroom for hours on end when she was a child. Looking up and praying they could hear him, he shouted, 'Iris, Roy, I want you to come and live with me, and I'm going to find a way to do it. I'm your father and I love you.'

'You don't know what love is, or my Ada wouldn't have—'

Mrs Tomlinson broke off and listened for a moment before running out of the kitchen.

He glanced up and saw his children's faces pressed against the window. 'I love you,' he yelled again.

The faces vanished abruptly and there was the sound of a slap. He heard it quite distinctly because the window was open at the top. Then Iris started crying.

He nearly lost control then, jerking forward, fist raised to hammer on the door. But he remembered Vi's stern warnings and after a moment let his fist fall. With one last glance upwards, he went back to the front of the house to tell her what had happened. It tore him apart to leave his six-year-old daughter weeping and at the mercy of that woman's anger.

'It might be a good idea to go and see the magistrate now and get in first, Joss.'

'I can't think of anything else to do.' But he turned towards the house and yelled, 'I'll be back!'

They set off for town again but before they'd gone more than a few streets they met Sergeant Piper riding a bicycle towards them.

He braked and called, 'Just a minute, Mr Bentley. I was coming to find you.'

They exchanged startled glances and Vi slid her hand into Joss's for comfort.

Elizabeth followed Vi's directions and easily found Fairview. The house looked shabby but in spite of its size, it had a homelike, welcoming air. That gave her the courage to knock on the front door.

She waited and was just raising her hand to knock again when the door opened and a young woman in a huge pinafore far too big for her stood there, jiggling a crying baby in her arms.

'Could I see Miss Warburton, please, or her sister, Miss Christina? Mrs Schofield sent me.'

The woman gave her a warm smile. 'Better come in quickly. You're letting all the warm air out, not that it's all that warm in the hall, but it's better than outside.' She broke off to shush the baby and rock it about. 'If you wait here, miss, I'll go and find someone.'

A voice spoke from the rear of the hall. 'I'll see the lady, Tess. Miss Christina has a visitor.' She looked across at Elizabeth. 'I'm Miss Warburton. What can I do for you?'

'I'm Elizabeth Twineham. Mrs Schofield sent me to see you, to ask if . . .' She faltered to a halt. It seemed such a cheeky thing to do, ask a stranger to take you in.

'Come and sit down. The hall is very draughty.'

She followed her hostess into a small sitting room at the rear and took the seat opposite her near a cheerful fire where chunks of wood were crackling, shifting and sending sparks spinning up the chimney. Taking a deep breath, she explained why Mrs Schofield had sent her here.

Her companion looked at her, and a very searching gaze it was too. 'You say Mrs Schofield thinks Freda Gilson might have told people not to give you lodgings?'

'Yes. They didn't only refuse me, they said things about my morals – things which weren't true, but how would they know anyway?'

'Hmm. I'm sorry to say, Mrs Schofield could be right. Freda always was spiteful, even as a girl, and would stoop to any trick to get her own way. Let me see . . .' She sat frowning at the fire, then stood up. 'I think we need to discuss this with my sister and Mrs Kirby too.'

'Mrs Kirby!'

'Yes. They both interviewed you for the job, after all. It's most opportune that Mrs Kirby is visiting us at the moment. She definitely ought to be made aware of the situation.'

Elizabeth felt more worried than ever. It didn't seem opportune to her that Mrs Kirby was here, more like a nasty twist of fate. Perhaps she shouldn't have come to Fairview, only it was too late to do anything about that, and she was desperate. After Miss Warburton had limped out of the room, time really did seem to stand still. The clock on the mantelpiece ticked away the seconds – surely more slowly than any clock ever had before? – and the big hand reluctantly jerked forward three times.

Footsteps came back across the hall, moving more quickly this time, and Miss Christina Warburton appeared. 'Miss Twineham, I'm so sorry to hear about your problems. Would you come and join us in the drawing room? I'm sure we'll find a way to help you.'

'I'm sorry to give you any trouble.'

'My dear, don't look so worried. Mrs Schofield was quite right to send you to us. She's such a sensible, practical woman!' She paused in the doorway. 'I think we'll have a tea tray while we're at it. It's a very chilly day. You go and sit down while I ask Tess to make us some.'

When they were all seated, Mrs Kirby asked, 'Would you explain exactly what happened when you tried to find lodgings?'

As the recital came to an end, the elegantly dressed woman frowned. 'There seems little doubt to me that Freda has spread the word not to take Miss Twineham in, though I doubt we'd be able to prove it. This doesn't augur well for our new service, does it, Christina?'

'No. Not with Freda in charge still.'

'We'll have to keep a close eye on her. Maybe if we give her enough rope, she'll hang herself. In the meantime, we'll find somewhere for you to stay, Miss Twineham. You can come to me temporarily. You are a distant relative of some sort, after all.'

'Very distant.'

'No need. She can take a room here,' Phyllis said. 'We'd appreciate the extra money from rent and enjoy her company too, I'm sure.'

'I couldn't impose.'

She smiled at Elizabeth. 'My dear, we've got eight unused bedrooms upstairs, so it's no trouble. The only thing is, you'd have to do your own cleaning and washing.'

Elizabeth stared at them, then closed her eyes for a moment in sheer relief, swallowing hard and hoping the tears that had welled in her eyes wouldn't leak out. 'I'd be very happy to do that and I c-can't thank you enough.' She had to pause for a moment to compose herself. 'I'm eager to take up this job, you see, because it sounds interesting and worthwhile. And to tell the truth, I'm not enjoying living with my father again after moving away during the war. He's very set in his ways and he thinks I'm a giddy young thing who needs a firm hand. I've quarrelled with him and don't want to go back and beg to be taken in again. I brought all my things with me and left them at the station.'

'Our father was just the same,' Miss Warburton said sympathetically. 'I was forty-six when he died and he was still treating me as a child.'

'That's settled, then.' Mrs Kirby stood up. 'Christina, do you want to come to my house tomorrow to carry on with what we were doing? I can easily send our chauffeur to fetch you. We still have quite a few things to work out, don't we? Or I could come here again. Whichever you prefer.'

There was silence and Elizabeth realised that there were undertones to what seemed a simple enough suggestion. Christina looked at her sister, who pursed her lips, then gave a slight nod.

'I'll come to you if you can send the car for me, Maud.'

On the way into town Mrs Kirby said very little but she looked pleased about something. She waited outside the station till Elizabeth had retrieved her luggage, then drove her back to Fairview.

Miss Christina showed her up to the bedroom, then she and Tess helped Elizabeth carry the luggage up. She lingered at the door afterwards. 'We have quite a community here now. Mr Bentley is living in a cottage behind the house, and Tess is living above the old stables with her children.'

'You haven't said how much you want to charge me.'

'How much would you usually pay for lodgings?'

Elizabeth told her how much she'd been paying during the war for breakfast and an evening meal during the week, and all meals at weekends.

'That would be fine with us.'

'Are you sure? The bedroom is beautifully spacious.'

'And beautifully shabby, too. Have you had luncheon?'

'No. But it's all right.'

'Nonsense. We can easily make you a sandwich.'

After she'd eaten, Elizabeth climbed the stairs and stood by her bedroom window for a moment or two. There was a lovely view over the town from the rear of the house, which also looked down on to the yard. She wandered round the room, touching pieces of furniture, bouncing on the double bed, sitting for a moment at the little writing table near the window and drawing a pattern in the dust on top of the waist-high bookcase.

She felt at home already.

Sergeant Piper seemed ill at ease, Vi thought as the three of them stood there with a chill wind blowing round them. He got off the bicycle, leaned it against a lamppost but seemed uncertain what to say. 'Look, I had a report that you were causing trouble at a Mrs Tomlinson's house. And Bentley, I was told that your woman friend was also involved in the disturbance.'

*'What?'*

Vi stepped in hastily before Joss could say something he'd regret. 'Nonsense. Mr Bentley knocked on the front door – is that causing trouble? I simply stood in the street and waited for him.'

'Who sent the message?' Joss asked in a sharp voice. 'My mother-in-law couldn't have done it, because she didn't leave the house. When I went round the back she was in the kitchen and all that happened was she told me to leave. I called up to my children telling them that I loved them, then came away.'

The Sergeant was frowning now. 'I had a visit from Mrs Gilson earlier this afternoon. She was worried that you might cause trouble, even hurt her friend Mrs Tomlinson. I was – surprised, I must admit. You don't seem the sort to cause a disturbance of the peace. Anyway, I said I'd be ready if anything happened, thinking I'd hear no more about it. But a lad came dashing round a short time ago with a scribbled note to say you were at the house *and* causing trouble, that Mrs Tomlinson was afraid you might break in and hurt her. So I had to come and investigate.'

Vi squeezed Joss's arm tightly, giving him a warning look.

He patted her hand quickly then turned back to Piper. 'You can see for yourself that we're not even at Mrs Tomlinson's house and as my friend Mrs Schofield said, all I did was knock on the door – twice. When my mother-in-law refused to answer it, I went round to the back to speak to her, since I was sure she was at home. I rapped on the kitchen window once.'

'And that's all you did? You didn't – break any windows?'

'Of course I didn't. Oh, I did yell out that I'd be back as we were leaving. I thought I'd find a magistrate and ask for help in getting my children back.' He sighed. 'I heard her slap someone and Iris start to cry. My daughter is only six, Sergeant. That upset me. If anyone's disturbing the peace, it's my mother-in-law.'

The Sergeant turned to Vi. 'That's all that happened?'

'Yes, and I'd be prepared to swear to it in court,' she said quietly.

'You two are – friends? Mrs Gilson implied—' Piper broke off in embarrassment.

Vi gave Joss's arm another squeeze and stepped into the breach. 'We're courting, actually. That's not against the law, is it? I'm one of the new Health Visitors who've just been appointed. Joss and I met before we both came back to Drayforth.'

The look on Piper's face said he immediately understood the ramifications of that statement. Vi could guess that Mrs Gilson was making her displeasure at the new appointments known.

The look on Joss's face at her words was first surprise, then he gave her a quick, wry grin. It was always easy to understand what he was thinking, even though Vi hadn't known him for long. She smiled back.

'Would it be best if we went to see the magistrate ourselves?' Joss said. 'Or a lawyer, perhaps? Can my mother-in-law really keep my children from me? Surely as their father, it's for me to decide what happens to them?'

'I don't know for certain. I shouldn't think she could keep them from you for no reason. But the chief magistrate is – um – a close friend of Mrs Gilson's, so perhaps you'd be better finding a lawyer and letting him handle matters. I know it'll cost you more but that's what I'd do in your place.' He avoided their eyes as he added in a whisper, 'Graves could handle it for you. He's of an independent turn of mind and seems very skilful at dealing with the situation in this town.'

There was a pregnant silence, then Joss said, 'I'll do that. Thank you for the advice.'

'I'll walk back into town with you.'

'No need to trouble yourself.'

Vi tugged his arm. 'Joss, I think it'd be better if the Sergeant comes with us. That way we shall have a witness who can prove we didn't do anything questionable.' She was getting more than a little worried about Mrs Gilson's power. She'd never clashed with the woman before, because their paths had never crossed. Well, she'd been working all hours in the shop before the war. But she knew about her. Who didn't? Would she really be able to work with her? Would she be allowed to? The woman was clearly trying to find a way to discredit her.

'All right.' Joss pulled Vi's arm through his again and started walking, mouth set in a thin line. He didn't speak all the way into town.

Sergeant Piper stopped outside Mr Graves' rooms and waited there till they'd gone inside.

Vi led the way with a heavy heart. She couldn't believe this was happening in Drayforth. It had always been such a quiet little town. And she couldn't believe she'd told the sergeant she and Joss were courting, when that was by no means clear. But Joss hadn't seemed upset about it. On the contrary.

She watched him as he told Mr Graves' clerk how urgent their need was. A fine figure of a man, her Joss. Yes, he was definitely her Joss now. Len would have liked him, would have approved of her finding someone else.

Mrs Tomlinson unlocked the bedroom door and burst inside, smacking the children good and hard, several times, till they were cowering away from her, sobbing. 'Don't you *ever* – disobey me – again,' she panted, unable to resist the temptation of kicking each of them as they lay huddled on the floor. 'I told you not to go near the window, but I know you did so because I heard the floorboards creak.' She left them then, locking them in again, hearing Iris sobbing and glad of it.

That'd teach them!

Downstairs she drew the kitchen curtains, went to the cupboard and poured herself a glass of gin. Blood was pounding in her temples and she felt a little distant and dizzy, but the drink didn't perform its usual magic and hardly calmed her down at all.

Thinking she heard a sound outside, she put the bottle hurriedly away, but it was only the neighbour going out into his back yard.

She was surprised the police hadn't arrived, but it didn't matter. Some of the neighbours must have heard *him* shouting outside her house. The cheek of it! In a superior neighbourhood like this.

She began pacing up and down the hall. What was her son-in-law doing? If only she knew. And why hadn't the police arrived?

Something must have gone wrong with Mrs Gilson's plan. But *he* wouldn't get permission to take the children away from her, not with Mrs Gilson on her side. And they were still young enough to be carefully moulded. They wouldn't leave her, let alone go astray, as Ada had.

Mr Kirby called Eric into his office while Sully was out. 'How are things going today?'

'As usual. I don't think he knows I came to see you last night.'

But even as he was speaking the outer door slammed open and Sully came striding back in, his henchman Ted behind him, grinning.

'You're fired!' he roared, pointing one finger at Eric. 'And I want you out of that house by the end of the day, as well.'

Kirby stood up. 'Now look here, Sully—'

Eric held his breath. Would Kirby stand by him?

Sully swung round, looked at Ted and said curtly, 'Wait outside.'

When the outer door had closed he moved right up to the desk and said bluntly, 'I know more about you, Kirby, than you realise. I have *evidence* about what you got up to during the war and I'll not hesitate to send it to the police if you interfere in this particular matter.'

'If you reveal anything, it'll land you in trouble as well,' Kirby said quietly.

'It'd be worth it.' Sully gave a nasty smile. 'But I don't think you'd do that. You're too intent on social climbing these days.'

The two men stared at one another and it was Kirby who looked away first.

Sully's smile broadened and he thumped on the desk with one fist, making both other men jump in shock. 'I'm not letting anyone take what I have away from me . . . *not even you . . . sir.*'

After that silence seemed to echo round the office and Eric could feel his heart pounding.

'Do as he says, Gill,' Kirby said at last. 'I'll find you another job somewhere else.'

'Do I have to get out of my house too, Mr Kirby?' Eric asked.

'Yes!' Sully's voice rang with triumph.

'But there aren't any other houses in town to rent.'

Sully turned round and gave Eric a push, opened the door and sent him staggering backwards through it into Ted's arms. 'You'll have to leave town then, won't you, and find a house and job somewhere else?'

Behind Sully's back, Eric saw Kirby give a quick shake of his head and put one finger to his lips.

He hesitated, wondering if he dared trust the man, then Sully shoved him again and Ted pulled him away. He turned and walked into his own office, closely followed by Ted.

'I have to get my coat and things,' he said as the other barred his way for a moment.

'Don't try to take any of Mr Sully's papers.'

'Why should I?' He didn't need to anyway. He had copies of what he needed at home.

It only hit Eric as he stood outside that he hadn't the faintest idea where he'd go, what he'd do. His whole world had suddenly crashed around him and though Kirby's silent signal seemed to promise that this matter wasn't over, Eric didn't know if he could rely on his employer – *former* employer.

# 21

As Vi and Joss left the lawyer's office, they ran into Eric, walking slowly along the street. He looked so white and ill, Vi hurried across the road to him. 'Eric? What's wrong?'

He stared at her for a moment as if he didn't recognise her, then blinked and focused on her properly. 'You'd better come home and I'll tell you.' He stared at Joss in an unfriendly way. 'Summat's cropped up an' it's urgent. She'll see you another time.'

She hesitated, looking at Joss.

'Dammit, Vi,' Eric shouted. 'I've just lost my job an' been thrown out of my house, which means you've not got a home after today, neither.'

*'What?'*

'It were Sully's doing. I'll sort it all out, sort him out too, but I need time. You'll have to go back to Dad's an' I suppose I'll have to cram in there too, though what I'll do with my furniture, I don't know. Well? Don't just stand there. Say goodbye to your fellow an' let's get started.'

She couldn't seem to make her brain work and when she felt Joss's arm go round her, she leaned against him for a moment, glad of his strength. 'I don't want to go back to Dad's. I couldn't bear it.'

'You won't need to,' Joss said. 'The Warburtons will take you in. And I bet they'd store the furniture in the old stables, too.'

Eric looked at Joss with less hostility. 'I'd pay them for that. I'm not short of a bob or two. I bought some new stuff last week an' I'd hate to see it dumped on the street.'

'Let's go back to the house. We can't talk here. You never know who'll be listening.'

So Vi found herself walking to Mayfield Place between the two men, her arm once again securely tucked into Joss's. 'I'm sorry to involve you,' she told him. 'You've got troubles enough of your own at the moment.' She explained to Eric quickly about the children.

Joss smiled down at her, such a warm smile it took her breath away, then he turned to her brother. 'Vi and I are courting.'

Eric stopped walking for a moment. 'What next?' he muttered and set off again, hands thrust deep into his pockets.

At the house he led the way inside. 'I've to be out of here by the end of the day, and if I'm not, that bugger will send his men to throw my furniture out and no doubt they'll help themselves to some of my stuff while they're at it.' He looked round with anguish on his face. 'I've worked *that hard* to get here . . . an' now I've lost everything.'

'Show me how much stuff you have, then I'll go and see the Warburtons. After that we have to find someone to cart your stuff,' Joss said. 'Melton won't cart it. He's too afraid of Sully. I wish I had a motorcycle. I'm going to waste so much time walking everywhere.'

'I know a fellow who has one,' Eric said. 'He'll lend it to you for five bob as long as you don't tell him about me losing my job. I'll pay.' He took the coins out of his pocket.

Joss left the others packing and headed for Fairview then Green's farm.

Vi sent Eric out for straw and tea chests, and grimly began to pull stuff out of the kitchen cupboards. It was a good thing Eric had only sparsely furnished the house.

She kept remembering how she'd told Sergeant Piper she was courting. And then Joss had told her brother the same thing. He must have meant it, then. Warmth spread through her. Goodness, her feelings for Joss were so different from her feelings for Len, much stronger, much more . . . disturbing. She blushed hotly at that thought.

Shaking her head, she tried to concentrate on what she was doing, but knew she wasn't her usual efficient self.

She wanted things to come right with Joss, wanted it so much!

* * *

Joss rode the motorcycle carefully up the hill, getting used to the feel of it. He parked behind Fairview and knocked on the kitchen door.

Tess opened it. 'Hello, Joss. Do you—'

'I'm in a hurry, love. Where are the ladies?'

'In the sitting room. But—'

He pushed past her and went to knock on the door, poking his head round it as he heard a voice call something.

'Sorry to disturb you, ladies, but I need your help, or rather, Mrs Schofield does.' He explained what had happened and then looked from one to the other, trying to gauge their feelings.

'What next?' Christina exclaimed.

'That man Sully is causing a lot of trouble in this town,' Miss Warburton said severely. 'But of course Mrs Schofield can have one of our bedrooms. What about her brother?'

Joss looked at her in puzzlement.

'We'd be happy to store his furniture, but where is he going to stay?'

'I suppose he'll go to his father's shop.'

'Didn't you say that Sully picks on the relatives of people who've upset him? Who owns the shop?'

'Kirby owns that whole street.'

'So if Gill goes there, Sully might throw the father out as well?'

'I suppose so.'

'What sort of man is he, her brother?'

Joss had a quick think, then shook his head in bafflement. 'I don't really know. He's hard in one sense, well, you have to be when you're collecting rents. But he's not like Sully. He threw my brother out of his house, but there was no rough treatment. In fact, my brother said Gill is known for not doing things roughly if he can help it. But I don't know him personally.' He had another think. 'I don't dislike him either.'

'He's your Mrs Schofield's brother. That's in his favour.'

Joss felt his cheeks go warm at the sound of *your Mrs Schofield*. 'I'd better tell you that Vi and I – we're officially courting.'

Miss Christina clapped her hands together. 'I knew it! You look so right together.'

'Do we?' It seemed everyone had guessed how he felt, before he was even sure of it himself. Was he sure now? Oh, yes! It might only have been a couple of weeks – well, not even that. But Vi was special. It hadn't taken him long to fall in love with her. He smiled involuntarily, then realised Miss Christina was speaking again.

'Gill had better stay above the stables. There are plenty of rooms there. Though if he misbehaves in any way, we'll throw him out at once. But I do believe everyone should be given a chance to mend their ways. And someone has to collect rents, after all, and they can't be too soft. Our father was always grumbling about poor payers in the days when we owned houses in town.'

'That's a very kind offer.'

'What about your children?' Miss Warburton asked. 'You didn't bring them back with you.'

His happiness vanished and he explained quickly about Mrs Tomlinson, then glanced at the clock.

'I'm sorry to hear that. You must be upset.'

He had to swallow hard before he could speak and even then his voice came out husky. 'Yes. I am. Because I think she's ill-treating them. I'm pinning my faith on the lawyer, Mr Graves. He was sure he could help, but said it'd take time.'

Once Gill had left the office, Sully turned to Kirby. 'We're better off without that one. He was too soft with tenants.'

'On the contrary, he was a very efficient worker and got the rents without too much trouble.'

'Well, it was him or me.' He didn't repeat his earlier threat, didn't need to.

Kirby shrugged. 'Gill is not to be hurt in any way. I can't afford to be linked to any more violence. It doesn't look good for a man in my position.'

Their glances locked for a moment then Sully grunted. 'If you insist. But you'd better make sure he leaves town. He's bound to have picked up some bits of information about us an' we don't want him to—'

'I said *no violence*, and I meant it! If he chooses to stay in Drayforth, that's his business. I don't want trouble with anyone from now on.' Gerald waited, saw that Sully wasn't going to agree to this, then added, 'Now the war is over, things have changed and we have to change with them.'

'Well, new times or not, I'd better be getting on with my *old* work. You still want your rents collecting an' your properties repairing, I s'pose?'

When he'd left, Gerald sat thinking hard. He didn't dare upset Sully, not with things going so well with the Warburtons. Maud was doing him proud there.

It was a pity, though. He didn't feel right about sacking Gill, not only sacking but turning him out of his home. The man had only been doing as Gerald told him.

But life was hard and you had to protect yourself first and foremost. Sully knew too much about a lot of things, including Gerald's black market dealings, which had been on quite a large scale.

Eric listened to Joss in astonishment. 'Them ladies are offering *me* somewhere to live as well as our Vi? Why would they do that?'

'Because your sister and I have been helping them.'

'But – people don't like me. They don't usually want owt to do with me.'

Joss was only too well aware of that. 'The Warburtons believe in giving everyone a chance to make something of their lives.' He glanced apologetically at Vi, but couldn't help adding, 'I was annoyed when you turned first me, then my brother and his family out of our homes.'

'I had to do as I was ordered. And I made it as easy for your brother and his wife as I could,' Eric said in an aggrieved tone, 'and if anyone says owt else, they're lying. It's partly because of you Bentleys that I've lost my job.'

'Well, just remember. If you do anything to upset those ladies, I'll throw you out of Fairview myself. Oh, and the Greens will move your furniture.'

'Thanks. I don't forget people as have done me favours.' Eric grinned. 'Even when they're as grumpy about it as you are.' What counted was that he'd found a temporary home, somewhere his things would be safe. If Sully knew about the information hidden in the attic at Mayfield Terrace, he'd throw a blue fit and then come after it – and after Eric, too.

Vi nudged him. 'Come on. We've got to get everything packed. What time is your friend coming, Joss?'

'As soon as he can. It'll take two or three loads to move everything, because he's only got a farm cart, so he can start with the big stuff while you're packing up the smaller things. He's bringing a labourer he knows. It'll cost more, but it'll mean your things will be safer while they're being taken up to Fairview.'

'You could have gone with them.'

'I prefer to stay near Vi. I don't trust Sully an inch.'

Eric nodded. 'All right. Look, I've got to get some stuff out of the attic. There's not much, so I might as well clear that first. I'll be down to help you here as soon as I've finished.'

He turned to leave then realised something else had to be said, so stopped at the door. 'I – er – I'm grateful for your help, Bentley. Whether you agree with me coming to live at Fairview or not.'

As the final load was carried out to the cart, Sully's man Ted slouched up to the door, smirking. 'Mr Sully sent me to do a final check, to make sure you've left everything clean. If not, you'll be charged extra. We all know how sloppy men are about looking after a house. And you don't want no trouble, do you?'

Vi pushed forward, angry at this blatant blackmail. 'You'll not find a thing out of place here because I've been in charge of the housekeeping.' She gestured to Joss and Eric to stay back, then beckoned to the man on the cart. 'Would you come inside with us, please, Mr Green? You'll be able to bear witness that everything is in order.'

In glacial silence she escorted Ted round the house. 'Any complaints?' she asked as the tour finished. When he didn't at first respond, she said firmly, 'Because if there are, I'm sending Mr Bentley to fetch our lawyer before I stir another inch.'

He hesitated, then shook his head.

'You heard that, Mr Green?'

'I did.'

She moved to the door. 'Eric, give him the house keys and let's be going.'

'You're a terror, Vi Schofield,' Joss said, grinning. 'I'd not like to cross you.'

'I only stood up for myself.'

'Thanks, Sis.' Also smiling, Eric turned to Green. 'Can I ride on the cart? I'm not good at walking up hills at the best of times, and I'm exhausted now.'

'Yes, why not? Here, let me help you up.'

Vi looked at him in concern. He looked a greasy white, not at all well. She was a bit worried at how puffed he got when he tried to do anything physical.

Since Joss had returned the motorcycle, she took the arm he offered and they walked along behind the slow-moving cart. By now it was dusk and the town's lamplighters were moving along the streets lower down the hill, having already lit up the better parts of town.

'I never thought I'd be moving house today,' Vi said as they trudged upwards. 'I'm a bit worried about Eric. He doesn't look well.'

'I'm more worried about you. You look tired.'

'I am. It's been a long day.' She glanced back over her shoulder. 'I'm sorry to leave that house. It was very comfortable. Having electricity makes life so much easier, doesn't it?'

'My parents have it in the shop, but they didn't install it in the living areas, I've never understood why.'

'They probably didn't see it as part of everyday life in those days. I got used to it at Lady Bingram's.'

At Fairview, they split up, Joss to sort out Eric's accommodation and the storage of the last load, Vi to go into the house and make sure everything was all right there.

As Green and his friend began to unload the rest of Eric and Vi's things, Joss took a lamp and led the way upstairs. 'They call this the day room, it's a sort of sitting room.'

Tess's children were there. When the youngsters saw Eric, they stared at him apprehensively, and even Harry was struck dumb. They were only too well aware who he was.

It was Harry who recovered first. 'Miss Warburton says you're to go and get a meal at the house when you've finished here. They're keeping something for you in the kitchen.'

'We had a lovely tea,' the older girl confided to Joss. 'We had to sit at the table and eat it fancy, though. Miss Warburton showed me how to hold my knife. I had a lovely plate with flowers on.'

Joss was touched by these confidences. All three children still had the gaunt, famine look, that said they'd been going short for a while. His two were much sturdier and rosier, so their grandmother must have been feeding them properly, at least.

As the men went along the corridor, Eric whispered, 'Do they mean for me to go to the house for a meal as well?'

'Of course they do.'

'That's nice of them. They're taking in a lot of people. Why do they do it?'

'Out of the goodness of their hearts. They're the kindest people you'll ever meet and if you do anything to upset them, you'll have me to answer to.'

'Why would I want to upset them? I don't like to upset anyone, let alone someone who's doing me a favour. I can pay them for the food and room, so they'll not be out of pocket.'

'They'd be offended if you tried to do that tonight. The meal is their way of making you welcome. You might offer to pay for your keep from tomorrow, though.' He saw Eric's brow wrinkle as if this puzzled him, but didn't want to linger and talk. If this man hadn't been Vi's brother, he'd not have wanted anything to do with him. He flung open the door at the end. 'Will this room be all right?'

Eric peered inside. 'It's a bit small.'

'You can take the room next to it as well, if you like. The ones at this end of the corridor are all empty. Come on. I'll help you carry up the bed, then we'll sort out the rest of the furniture tomorrow. I'm famished.'

'I'm not so good at carrying stuff up stairs.' Eric patted his chest. 'Dicky heart. I'll pay the men extra to carry my things up now. I know which of 'em I want kept safe.'

They were just in time to get the men to do this before they left, then Joss led the way to the kitchen door.

Inside, Eric hovered behind him, trying to take it all in at once. He'd never seen a kitchen as large and grand as this one. Vi was sitting at a table, looking tired but relaxed, an empty plate in front of her. A scrawny old woman in a big white pinafore was sitting at the other end of the table drinking a cup of tea.

Vi looked up. 'There you are. Did you get settled in, Eric? This is Cook. Cook, this is my brother.'

Tess appeared in the scullery doorway, her arms and hands wet so that she had to hold them up not to drip on the floor. 'The baby's with Miss Warburton, Mr Bentley. Nora's been fed an' changed and she's ready to go down.'

'I'll get their food,' Vi said quickly as Cook started to heave herself up. 'You've been on your feet enough today.'

'Thank you, dear. I'm not as young as I was.'

'You're still a wonderful cook, though. Eric, Joss, you can wash your hands in the scullery, the room where Tess is.'

Once the men had finished eating, Vi nudged her brother. 'You'll want to thank Miss Warburton and her sister Miss Christina for letting you stay here, won't you? And they want to meet you.'

He nodded and she led the way to the small sitting room.

Phyllis studied him as openly as he was studying the room. 'I hope you'll be comfortable here, Mr Gill.'

'Yes. And thank you very much for letting me stay. Took me by surprise, it did, Sully sacking me and throwing me out, but I've money saved and can pay you rent.'

'We'll discuss that when we find out how long you're staying.

For the first few days, given that you're in trouble, we wouldn't dream of charging you rent.'

He stared at her again. She really meant it. 'That's very handsome of you.'

'Shall you be able to find another job?'

'I'll be looking into that tomorrow. I've got an idea or two.'

'We'll leave you now,' Vi said, nudging him. 'Do you want me to carry Nora back to her father, Miss Warburton?'

'I suppose so.' She laughed self-consciously. 'I must admit, I'm loving having her. If Mr Bentley wants me to keep an eye on her for an hour or two tomorrow, I'm happy to oblige. I do love babies. Oh, and Mr Gill, porridge will be provided for breakfast tomorrow. Just come to the kitchen when you're ready.'

'I can't understand them two,' he said in a low voice to his sister as they went back to the kitchen. 'Never met anyone like 'em in my life.'

'Lady Bingram's just the same.' Vi stopped for a moment, trying to explain to him. 'They feel that they've been so fortunate in their families having a lot of money, it's their duty to help others less fortunate.'

'But them old ladies haven't got money now. Everyone knows that.'

'They still have a large house and they still want to help others.'

He shook his head in bafflement.

When Gerald went home from his place of business, he found Maud in a foul mood and she threw words at him before he'd even sat down.

'What's the point of me trying to make you socially acceptable if you will keep doing stupid and unkind things?' she demanded.

He stopped in the doorway. 'What am I supposed to have done now?'

'Not *supposed*, you have done it.'

'What?'

'Not only sacked Eric Gill, but thrown him and his sister out of their home.'

'I wasn't aware that you cared about Eric Gill, or even knew of his existence.'

'Oh, I know him. A plump man who collects your rents. I don't care about him, but his sister is another matter. She's one of the women Christina Warburton and I appointed as Health Visitors, and she's an admirable young woman. She was a heroine during the war, saved lives, Daphne Bingram said, when the Mayor took up her references. And *you* have to throw a woman like her out of her home! What will people say? More important, what will the Warburtons say? *Why* did you do it?'

'Gill upset Sully.'

Maud's eyes narrowed. 'And you're afraid of Sully because he knows too much about your wartime activities.'

He didn't say anything. What was there to say? You could never fool Maud.

'You'd better find a way to get rid of Sully, then. He's like a bomb waiting to explode.'

He was startled. 'Kill him, you mean?'

'Of course I don't! Dear Lord, you haven't been killing people, have you, Gerald?'

'Certainly not.'

'Thank goodness for that. But there must be some way to get rid of Sully. Wouldn't he like to retire in luxury to the seaside?'

'I've tried that. He refused. He enjoys his work and his power among the lower classes in town.'

'Does he have a wife?'

'No. He usually finds some poor woman to bully into sleeping with him.'

'Has he *no* weaknesses? Surely there's something you can use to force him out?'

'I'm looking into it.'

'You'd better do more than that. You'd better find a way. Christina told me this afternoon that she was very upset when she heard about Mrs Schofield losing her home.'

'I'll find Mrs Schofield some other house to live in, then. But not her brother.'

Maud let out a sniff of amusement. 'She's already found somewhere else. She's renting a room from the Warburtons. And they've given her brother a room too.'

Gerald closed his eyes for a minute, then said curtly, 'Do you want a G and T?'

'Yes, please.'

He didn't continue the discussion and Maud didn't push him about what he was going to do, thank goodness. Because he didn't know. And she probably realised that. But she'd put him on warning that he had to think of something. So he would. He was at his best when pushed into a corner, had been even as a child.

But what? Sully was a wily old devil.

# 22

After they'd eaten, Joss and Eric walked back to the stables together in a state of temporary truce. Both were exhausted and thinking of nothing but their beds. Eric was carrying two lighted candle lanterns, old-fashioned but still needed here. Joss was pushing the squeaky old pram. In it Nora lay warmly wrapped in a faded but soft baby blanket that Miss Warburton had found in the linen closet.

At the cottage Eric went inside, set one lantern down on the hall stand and stood back so that Joss could heave the pram into the hall.

'What are you going to do now?' Joss asked. 'I doubt Sully will be content till he's chased you out of town.'

Eric smiled grimly, the flickering of the lantern lighting his face from below and making it seem like an evil mask. 'He's in for a few surprises, that one, and so is Mr Kirby. I'm not that easy to get rid of. Look, about our Vi . . .'

'Yes?'

'She's a good lass. Make sure you don't hurt her.' Without waiting for an answer, he went back out and disappeared in the direction of the stables.

Surprised by this, because Eric was a man commonly supposed to have no warm feelings about anyone or anything, Joss locked the front door carefully. Leaving the pram at the foot of the stairs, he went to light an oil lamp and take it up to the bedroom, then came back down for the baby. He was desperately tired and hoped she wouldn't wake in the night.

His footsteps echoed on the uncarpeted stairs and landing, a mournful sound. He'd expected to have his children with him tonight and it felt lonely in the cottage. Nora snuffled in her sleep and cuddled closer to him and he was glad to touch another living creature. He laid her carefully in the cot and looked down at her little face, so bonny and rosy, eyelashes resting on her cheeks. When awake she was a gurgling, happy creature. She'd captivated Miss Warburton and Tess too, it seemed.

But it wouldn't do to get fond of her, because he definitely didn't intend to keep her, however much scandal that might cause. She wasn't his, dammit. She wasn't his!

Roy sat upright in bed so that he wouldn't fall asleep. It was hard to stay awake, though. He kept yawning and nodding off, then waking with a start.

The lights began to go out in the nearby houses. Across the back gardens he could see squares of light suddenly vanish from the rear of the row behind theirs. But he didn't dare move until his grandmother had fallen asleep. She never went to bed till really late, but she made them go to bed early, which wasn't fair.

At last he heard her come up the stairs then gave her plenty of time to settle to sleep, before sliding out of the bed and getting dressed. He woke Iris, putting one hand across her mouth and hissing, 'Shh!'

'What's the matter?' She looked round in fear. 'Grandma isn't coming, is she?'

'No. I've been lying here thinking ever since we came to bed. She's been telling us lies about Dad.' He ignored Iris's gasp at this criticism of the woman who terrified them both. 'He *does* want to have us with him. He shouted it out to us as loudly as he could when he came here. He can't get into the house to fetch us, though, without breaking down the door and I think the police might get angry with him if he did that, so . . . we're going to escape and go to him instead.'

Iris's eyes grew wide and fearful in the moonlight. 'How can we escape? She's locked us in.'

'We'll have to climb out of the window.'

'But it's a long way down. We might fall and hurt ourselves.'

'I read how to do it in my friend Ben's comic. You have to make a rope from sheets and climb down it.'

'I can't climb ropes.'

'It's easy. Me and Ben had a try at it once last year. His mam got mad about the sheets, though.' Roy had fallen off the first time he'd tried to go down the makeshift rope. He didn't tell Iris that.

She went to look out of the window and then gazed pleadingly at him. 'I daren't.'

'You'll be all right. Mum always used to say how nimble you were. Anyway, you *have to* do it, because if you don't, you'll be here on your own. With *her*! I'm not staying here any more, I'm going to Dad.'

Iris was looking so terrified he wondered if she could manage the climb. But he'd thought and thought, and it was the only way they could escape. His Dad was living at Fairview and Roy knew where that was. Even at night he was sure he could find his way there. 'I know. I'll throw the pillows down first, so if we fall we'll have a soft landing.'

Iris frowned as he picked up the pillows, still not looking convinced. But his body was covered in bruises from where their grandma had hit them after his father's visit and so was Iris's. He hated to see her hurt. She was so little. It had to be stopped.

Throwing caution to the wind, he dropped the pillows out of the window, managing to land them into a rough pile. 'Get dressed quickly. Put some warm clothes on, but not your best ones. And Iris – even if you fall, you mustn't cry out or you'll waken *her*.'

She nodded and began to get dressed.

He took the sheets off their beds and tied them together, using the knots he and his friend had learned from a boys' annual. He'd practised them on bits of string, hoping they'd come in useful one day and now they had. It just went to show.

He smiled at his sister as he tied the sheet rope to the nearest bed leg. 'It'll be all right. Don't be frightened. The pillows are there at the bottom and they'll make a soft landing if you fall. Now, I'll go first and you watch how easy it is.'

She didn't protest, but when he climbed on to the window sill, he saw how dark it was outside and how far down they had to climb. An icy wind tugged at his clothes and he shivered. But they had no choice, especially now he'd thrown the pillows out. His grandmother would murder him if she found them lying on the lawn.

He took hold of the rope, the end of which was swaying to and fro. Holding it tightly, he levered himself gradually over the windowsill. 'See,' he whispered, 'you go feet first and keep tight hold of the rope.' The bed shifted a little, jerking him and making his heart pound, but it stopped moving and the knots held firm. He began to ease himself down the rope.

When he got to the lawn, he let go and sighed in relief, then waved to Iris to join him.

But she didn't move.

He made urgent beckoning gestures with one hand and she turned round on the windowsill, her feet sticking out. Then she stopped moving again.

He didn't dare shout up to her, could only watch and pray, *Please don't give up! Please.* She edged off the windowsill a little at a time, sliding her body downwards till she had her feet on the first knot.

Another pause, which seemed to go on for ever, then she started downwards. He relaxed a little, thinking it was going to be all right, but then she froze again as a gust of wind made the rope sway to and fro. When she set off, she suddenly lost her grasp and slipped, letting out a loud cry of fear as she fell to the ground.

He darted forward, terrified of finding her dead, but she'd landed on the pillows. She looked up at him and smiled, a wobbly little smile. He pulled her up into his arms, crushing her to his chest, trying to hold back tears of relief because boys didn't cry, especially when they were leading people to safety.

Then he remembered that she'd cried out and looked anxiously up at the house. A light had come on inside, showing clearly through the landing window. His grandmother must have heard Iris's yell, even from her bedroom at the front!

* * *

Vi went to bed feeling so tired she almost didn't bother to get undressed. But that was sloppy behaviour, so she took her clothes off and slipped into her high-necked, long-sleeved flannel nightdress, laying her things neatly on a chair.

When she lay down, the double bed felt so big and strange she stayed fully awake. She had a sudden memory of what it had been like to lie and cuddle Len on nights like this, how the warmth of his body had soon lulled her into sleep, how wonderful it was to have another person with you, loving you.

Well, there was no one to cuddle up to now and she was being silly. Those days were gone.

Only – if Joss did care about her, then maybe there would be another man to share a bed with soon. That thought sent a thrill running through her body, ending up in the pit of her belly. But he was so big and strong, so good-looking, and she was just a scrawny little creature. How could someone like him, who could have his pick of much prettier women, want someone like her?

Doubts hovered and though she tried to banish them, she couldn't. Had she pushed herself at him? Was he too kind to tell her he wasn't really interested? Or was he just courting her because he needed a mother for his children and thought she was a capable person?

Heaven help her, but even if that was the case, she'd still marry him. She might not be able to have children of her own, but there were three motherless youngsters who needed loving and she could do it, she knew she could. She had longed for children for so many years.

She was just dozing off when something crashed through the window and glass showered that side of the room. She sat bolt upright. Why would someone do that? This wasn't a street in town where a passing drunk might lob something through a window. The person would have had to come out here specially.

There was a knock on the door and a wavering line of candlelight showed underneath it. She slipped out of bed on the side away from the window, grateful for her habit of leaving her slippers handy. Grabbing her dressing gown from the chair, she opened the door and saw Elizabeth standing there holding up a candle. She didn't like the thought of the candle lighting up the interior of the room in case it made them better targets, so blew it out without even asking, whispering, 'We don't want to show them where we are.'

'Who do you think it is? Lads out to cause mischief or . . .' Elizabeth's voice trailed away.

The moon was bright enough to show Vi the other woman's expression, which showed determination rather than fear.

'Or Sully trying to make me get out of town,' Vi finished for her.

'Could it be Mrs Gilson up to more tricks?'

'I don't think she'd damage the Warburtons' house. No, it must be Sully, trying to frighten me.'

Another candle wavered towards them along the corridor and she turned to see Christina approaching. 'Best blow your candle out, or it'll show them where we are.'

At that moment another window smashed somewhere nearby.

'We have to keep calm and not panic,' Vi said firmly.

Christina's voice was just as firm. 'I'm not panicking, I'm getting very angry. This must be that man Sully's work. I shall complain to Mr Kirby. I'm sure *he* doesn't know about this. Why, his wife is a friend of mine and he keeps inviting us to his house.'

'I think it'd be a very good idea to complain to him.'

There were sounds outside, yells and the grunts of men struggling. Because of the glass in her room, Vi dashed into Elizabeth's bedroom and looked out of the window. Two men were fighting in the back yard, one of them Joss. Another was standing in the shadows and even as she looked, he moved forward, clearly looking for a way to join the fight.

Joss was holding his own against one assailant, but he couldn't fight two at once.

'Mr Bentley needs help!' She pushed past the others and ran out of the room without waiting for an answer.

* * *

For a moment Roy couldn't think what to do, just stared up at the light in the landing window in horror. Then he picked up the pillows and shoved Iris towards the garden shed, getting out of sight behind it. There was nothing he could do about the sheet, which was swinging to and fro gently. If the wind got up again, it'd flap and draw attention to itself, so he prayed that it would stay calm.

The light moved into the kitchen and his grandmother peered out of the window.

Suddenly inspired, he meowed like a cat, just a couple of times.

The light went away almost immediately. Its faint glow appeared in the landing window, then vanished.

'We have to stay here and wait for her to go to sleep again,' he whispered to Iris, putting his arm round her shoulders, 'because we have to walk right below her bedroom to get out of the garden.'

She nodded and snuggled against him.

He decided to count up to five hundred. Surely by then their grandma would be asleep? It was cold out here but he tried not to shiver as he stood where he could protect Iris from the wind.

Vi rushed down the stairs and into the kitchen. She glanced round for a weapon and picked up the steel used for sharpening knives, which hung on the wall. She flung the door open and saw that the third man had now joined the two struggling in the yard. They had Joss down on the ground. She paused briefly to assess the situation, then slipped round to one side of the heaving mass without a noise and waited her opportunity to bring the heavy steel bar down on the second man's shoulder.

He let out a yell and turned to fend her off, trying to snatch the weapon from her. But by then Elizabeth had joined her, brandishing a rolling pin.

He took a quick step backwards and put two fingers to his mouth, whistling loudly then running away.

The other attacker tried to get up and follow him, but Joss grabbed the man's ankle and dragged him down again.

Seizing her chance to help, Vi grabbed the man's other leg,

holding on to it in spite of his attempts to kick her away. Joss let go of the other leg and grabbed the man's arm. By then Elizabeth was with them, helping hold the fellow down.

Joss twisted the man's arm back so far he yelled in pain and stopped struggling. 'OK. I've got him. He'll dislocate his shoulder if he tries to pull away. Someone fetch me a rope.'

Another voice spoke. 'I've fetched one already.' Eric knelt down and it took only a minute for the two of them to truss up the intruder and roll him over.

'I'm sorry Ted got away, but you'll do instead,' Eric said. 'You're a fool to come here. Do you think Mr Kirby will want his posh friends hurting?'

The man glared at him. 'It's not the old biddies we was after, but that fancy piece of Bentley's.'

Joss slapped him hard across the side of the head. 'Don't you *ever* speak of Mrs Schofield in that way again!'

Eric smiled grimly. 'You should have hit him harder. I would have. I don't like anyone talking about my sister like that.' He heaved himself to his feet and looked round. 'Is there somewhere we can lock him up till morning? Somewhere safe, where his friend can't set him free. We can't drag him into town at this hour of the night.'

Christina called from the kitchen doorway. 'We could lock him in the coal cellar. He'll get dirty, but it serves him right. It's through the kitchen. I'll fetch you the key.'

'Seems it was ladies to the rescue tonight,' Joss joked, ignoring his prisoner's glare.

'We had to learn to defend ourselves at night in the war,' Elizabeth said. 'I always took a rounders bat with me when I went out after dark. If this is going to happen regularly in Drayforth, I'd better buy myself another one.'

A baby began to wail from inside Joss's cottage, rapidly building up to a loud, indignant protest about something.

'I'll see to Nora,' Vi said. 'You get this one locked away safely.'

'I left a lantern burning low on the landing,' Joss called out.

She went into the cottage and up the stairs, turning up the

lantern and holding it up as she followed the loud howling noises. She set it down on the mantelpiece and lifted the baby out of her cot, cuddling Nora close, not caring about the child's soaking nightdress. She couldn't help thinking how much she'd like to be a mother to this child.

As if to prove how delightful she was, the baby stopped crying and made a cooing noise instead. Then she smiled up at Vi. 'Eh, you're a lovely little thing, aren't you?'

Nora gurgled agreement and waved her arms vigorously.

'You're a little love, you are,' Vi said, wondering yet again why Joss didn't seem to show any affection for his youngest, when he spoke so fondly of the other two. Was it because Nora had caused his wife's death? Had he been that devoted to Ada? She didn't think so from what he'd said. It was all very puzzling.

Sighing, she pressed a kiss to the baby's forehead and carried her downstairs to change the soaking nappy.

*Four hundred and ninety-nine . . . five hundred,* Roy counted inside his head. At last! He nudged Iris and they crept round the side of the house. No need to tell her to be quiet. Her hand was trembling in his.

The front garden gate was another problem, being close to his grandmother's bedroom. Roy opened it very slowly, only enough to let them both out, terrified of it squeaking. But it made no noise and he closed it with a sigh of relief, holding the catch and slipping it quietly back into place. He didn't want the gate to bang and wake *her* up. Then he took his sister's hand again and they set off.

Everything seemed different in the dark. He kept looking round, half expecting to see eyes staring at him, figures in the shadows. But it was after midnight and they met no one as they started the long walk to Fairview. The houses they passed looked deserted, with no lights showing, but he was more relieved than he'd have admitted to find the street lamps still lit.

Iris plodded doggedly along beside him, her breath misting the air around her neat little head, her brown curls tucked into a knitted woollen bonnet with a pixie point on the top.

After a while he could tell she was tiring because she was walking more slowly, stumbling more often. 'How about we sit down for a minute or two?' he whispered.

'It's too cold.'

She was right, really, but he kept worrying about her. 'You're sure you didn't hurt yourself when you fell?'

'No. It's where she kicked me that hurts. How much further is it?'

'We're more than halfway.' They weren't but he hoped it would cheer her up to think so.

She nodded and continued walking, but her steps got slower and slower. At last she stopped, panting as she sagged against him.

'How about I give you a piggy back?' he asked.

Her voice was a faint whisper. 'Please.'

She was heavier than he'd expected but he was older and he was a boy, so he had to do it. It seemed a long way to go still. He wasn't sure he could manage to carry her so far.

When a figure really did step out of the shadows in front of them, he couldn't help himself, but yelled out in fright. Then he realised it was Sergeant Piper, the new policeman. Had Grandma sent him after them? Roy took a quick step backwards, letting Iris slide down to the ground and grabbing her hand.

'I'm not going back to my grandma's. I'm not! I won't let her hurt Iris any more.'

The man hurrying down the hill from Fairview didn't see the small group until he was nearly on them as he rounded a corner. He stopped dead then turned and fled.

Rob Piper ran to the corner, but didn't pursue him. No need. Even after only a few weeks in town, he recognised that big, shambling figure: Sully's pet thug, Ted something or other. What was the fellow doing out at this time of night? He must have been up to something if he'd turn and flee at the mere sight of a policeman.

But there were more important things to deal with at the moment, so Rob returned to the children. They hadn't tried to run away, were obviously exhausted. The boy was standing protectively in front of his sister. 'What are you two doing out at this hour of the night?'

The little girl began to cry and Rob could see that the boy's eyes were bright with unshed tears.

# 23

Joss went back to the cottage after they'd locked Fred up in the cellar. He closed the front door quietly and walked along the shadowed hallway to find Vi sitting by the kitchen table, cradling Nora in her arms and rocking her slightly. She was singing a lullaby and didn't hear him come in, so continued to croon softly. The simple beauty of this scene, the tender way Vi was smiling down at the baby, made his breath catch in his throat.

She looked up and turned that same tender smile on him, whispering, 'I'll just go and put her down. She needed changing.'

'Would you like a cup of cocoa?' He didn't want Vi to leave yet.

'That'd be nice, Joss. I won't be a minute.'

Humming the same tune Vi had been singing, he lit the gas and put some milk on to boil, then got out two cups and the cocoa powder.

By the time Vi rejoined him, he was stirring the cocoa powder to a paste with water and was ready to pour in the hot milk. 'Sugar?'

'Just one, please.'

She took the cup from him, cradling it in her hands and trying to hide a shiver. She was wearing her night things, a cream flannel nightdress, the edge and high neck showing under a blue woollen dressing gown, and plain cloth slippers. These simple garments were far more attractive to him than Ada's shoddy, frilled nighties and mules with bedraggled fluff on them. He'd hated the sound of her slopping around in her worn-out slippers, cheap and tawdry stuff his family would never stock.

Vi looked so wholesome and neat he wanted quite desperately

to touch her. Instead, he shut the door leading into the hall, paused for a minute to compose himself and relit a burner on the gas cooker, using it as a heater. 'That'll take the chill off.'

He joined her at the table and they both took sips of the hot, sweet liquid, sighing in pleasure at exactly the same time and smiling at one another.

'You need those cuts washing,' she said, staring at his face. 'And you're going to have a bruise on one cheek. Shall I—'

As she started to get up he put out one hand to stop her. 'In a minute. Drink your cocoa while it's hot.' He should have taken his hand off her arm, but he couldn't. He put his cup down any old how and took hers from her hand. Watching her eyes to make sure she wanted this, he pulled her into his arms. Her welcoming smile made his heart beat faster.

At first he simply held her close. 'You smell of lavender,' he murmured, inhaling deeply.

'I always put dried lavender flowers in my clothes drawers.'

He tipped up her chin and kissed her gently, then more urgently. Her lips were soft and willing, felt so right against his. When he drew away, he stared into her eyes. 'I love you, Vi.'

'I love you too, Joss.'

'When did you realise? I was attracted to you on the train, right from the start. I was so angry when those soldiers came into our compartment.'

'So was I.'

He realised they were sitting smiling foolishly at one another and took another mouthful of cocoa.

After they'd finished he pulled her to her feet and kissed her again. When he stopped this time, they were both breathing deeply and he let out a long, shuddering sigh, cuddling her against his chest, willing himself to go no further. 'You'd better get back to the big house before I drag you upstairs to my bed.'

She leaned back a little and clicked her tongue in exasperation. 'What am I thinking of! I need to bathe your poor face. It must hurt.'

'You kissed it better. I'd rather you did that again.'

She chuckled and went to get some warm water from the kettle, then pulled a clean handkerchief out of her pocket. Only Vi would emerge from a fight with a clean handkerchief, he thought fondly.

When she'd finished, she hesitated. 'I suppose I'd better go.'

'Yes. Pity.'

She gave him one of those clear bright smiles as he walked with her to the door. And before she left she put up one hand to caress his unbruised cheek, such a brief gesture, but it nearly undid his careful self-control. He'd made love to Ada many times before they married. With Vi, he wanted to do things properly, waiting till afterwards, showing respect for her in every way.

He stood watching as she began to cross the yard towards the kitchen, his happiness quickly replaced by worries. What was Vi going to say when she found out the baby wasn't his, that he didn't intend to raise Nora?

Suddenly he heard a noise at the front of the big house, someone starting to walk up the gravelled drive. Vi must have heard it too because she swung round and came running back to his side.

'What was that? Have they come back, Joss?'

'I don't know. Shh.' He moved forward as quietly as he could, then realised she was following him. 'Stay there,' he whispered. 'If it's them, go into the house and lock the door.'

She shook her head.

He had to protect her, so before he moved on, he picked up a spade that was leaning against a wall. Vi selected a hoe. Eh, she was a gallant creature, his dear love, ready to fight by his side again.

When he got round to the front of the house, however, he stopped, straining to see clearly who it was. The street lamp at the end of the drive gave enough light to show the Police Sergeant walking towards them, easily recognisable by his high helmet, and next to him were two smaller figures who were surely—

'*Dad!*' Roy's cry made Joss throw aside the spade and run forward to scoop his son up into his arms and swing him round, then do the same to his daughter. After that he knelt down, trying to cuddle them both at once.

It was a minute or two before he realised Rob was looking down at him with a sympathetic smile. He stood up, keeping his arms round the children's shoulders, wondering what the hell was going on.

'I found these two on their way up here, only Miss Iris was too tired to walk any further and was shivering. So, as your house was much nearer than their grandmother's, I brought them here.'

He winked as he said that and Joss thanked providence for giving him an unexpected ally. 'Let's get them into the warmth, then. Will you come with us, Vi?'

'Of course.'

He picked Iris up and led the way across the yard, with Roy walking very close to him. Inside the cottage he said gently, 'We'll get you two warm first, eh? Then you can tell us what happened.'

'I'll go and find some blankets to wrap round them,' Vi said.

'Take them off my bed in the front room.'

When she'd gone Rob looked at him in the bright light of the oil lamp. 'What's happened to you? You look like you've been in a fight.'

'I have. Some bug—, rascals threw stones through the bedroom windows of the big house an hour or so ago and woke everyone up. There were two of them. One got away but we caught the other and locked him in the coal cellar.'

'Ah! I nearly bumped into a fellow on the way up here, but he ran off. I recognised him though, Ted, big chap, hunches his shoulders.'

'I know him. And the one in the cellar is another of Sully's men.'

As Vi came back down with the blankets and wrapped one round each child, Joss saw Rob's eyes widen as he took in the fact that she was in her nightclothes, and said hastily, 'Vi came back after the fight to help me with the baby. She was just on her way home when you arrived.'

There was a knock at the door and he opened it to find Miss Christina standing there, with Elizabeth beside her.

'We saw you from the kitchen and were wondering if everything was all right?'

'It certainly is. My children have come to join me. Come in and hear the tale.'

He nearly had a fit when he heard about the risks his children had taken to escape. 'Roy, that was dangerous. Your sister's only little. She might have been badly hurt.'

His son stared at him reproachfully. 'She *is* badly hurt. Grandma kicked us as well as hitting us this time.'

*'What?'*

'See for yourself if you don't believe me!' Roy dropped the blanket, yanked his shirt out of his trousers and showed them a back covered with bruises, some old, some new, a recent one much larger than the others. Then he held out his hands. The knuckles were badly bruised too. 'Iris is the same.'

'That old harridan!' Joss exclaimed. 'I'll be round to see her in the morning and—'

Rob laid one hand on his shoulder. 'Let's do this the proper way or you'll be landing yourself in trouble and that won't help your children.' He turned to the ladies. 'Mrs Schofield, could you and Miss Christina help Iris undress and put her to bed? See that she's – all right.'

Vi nodded. She knew what he was asking, for them to check the little girl for signs of being beaten.

'I'll fill you both a hot water bottle,' Joss said. 'You'd better go up as well, Roy. It's the middle of the night and we all need to get some sleep.'

'You won't send me back to *her*?'

'No.'

'Promise.'

'I promise. Cross my heart and hope to die.' Solemnly he made the required signs across his chest and this seemed to reassure his son.

Once the children were in bed, the adults gathered in the kitchen, all of them solemn-faced now.

'How was the little lass?' Rob asked.

'As badly beaten as her brother,' Vi said quietly.

'How can anyone do that to children?' Christina looked at the policeman. 'If you need me to bear witness in court to what I've just seen, I'll be very happy to do so. There's no doubt it comes from beating, not an accident. I think my word counts for something in this town still.'

'Thank you. It was why I asked you to help put her to bed, I must confess.'

'I'll go and see Mr Graves about this first thing in the morning,' Joss promised.

'Good. That's the best way.' Rob looked across at Miss Christina. 'Could I come and check that your villain is secure before I go? If he is, I'd like to leave him in your cellar until morning and send the prisoners' van up for him then. Is that all right? I don't fancy walking him back through the streets on my own.'

'Certainly. I'm sure he'll be quite secure, though. My grandfather used to lock up poachers in that part of the cellars. Come and see for yourself.'

Rob stood up, waiting till the three ladies had gone out then saying quietly to Joss, 'Good thing I decided to do a patrol myself tonight, eh? I like to keep on top of everything my men do.'

'A very good thing. Thanks for bringing the children to me not *her*.'

'I did wonder about it, given that Mrs Tomlinson is making such a fuss and has the ear of Mrs Gilson and the magistrate. But I knew I'd done the right thing, even before I saw their bruises. They were terrified of being taken back. That's a brave lad you've got there, Bentley.'

'A bit too brave for my liking. When I think of them climbing down a sheet ladder . . .' He shuddered.

After he'd locked the front door again, hoping this would be the last interruption of the night, Joss went upstairs and peered into the bedroom his children were sharing.

Roy jerked upright in bed, then sagged back. 'Dad?'

'Yes.'

'I thought for a minute you were *her*.'

'I told you: I won't let her take you back again, son.' He saw the boy's shoulders heaving and went across the room to take Roy in his arms and hold him till he'd wept himself out.

Eventually Roy pulled away, wiping his eyes on the sheet and muttering, 'Boys shouldn't cry.'

'They should for important things like this.'

'You won't tell anyone, though, will you?'

'Of course not. Now, we'd both better try to get an hour or two's sleep. It's nearly morning.'

'Night, Dad. And . . . you've locked all the doors, haven't you?'

'Oh, yes. And the windows downstairs.'

Joss shook his head sadly as he got into bed. He felt he'd let his children down. His mother-in-law had a lot to answer for.

Just before ten the next morning someone hammered on the cottage door and woke Joss. When he looked out of his bedroom window, his heart sank. Mrs Tomlinson stood there, flanked by Mrs Gilson and the magistrate's clerk.

He dashed into his children's bedroom and woke them. 'Get your clothes together. There isn't time to get dressed. Your grandmother's at the front door. Before I answer it, I want you to slip out the back way. Wait till you hear me let them inside, then run to the kitchen door of the big house. See Mrs Schofield and ask her if she can keep you there for me.'

Tears filled Iris's eyes, but he said sharply, 'No time to cry. Let's get you out of here.'

He shepherded them downstairs as the doorknocker was applied for the fourth time and Mrs Gilson called loudly, 'We know you're in there, Bentley. If you don't answer, I'll send for the police and keep watch here till they come.'

He shoved the children out of the back door and went to answer the front one.

Mrs Tomlinson pushed past him, taking him by surprise. 'Where are they? They must have come to you because there's nowhere else they can go.'

Mrs Gilson glared at him from the other side. 'You should be ashamed of yourself, Bentley, after all this kind woman has done for you.'

'This kind woman beats my children regularly.'

'Spare the rod and spoil the child!' snapped his mother-in-law, who had been to look into the downstairs rooms one after the other. 'Where are they?'

'They're not here.'

Mrs Gilson nudged the clerk. 'Go and search upstairs. I'll keep an eye on him.' She turned to Joss again. 'We have legal authority to take the children back to safety, so you'd better not try to stop us.'

He leaned against the wall and waved one hand. 'Go ahead. Search. They're not here.'

The clerk went upstairs and was soon down again. 'They're not up there.'

'They must be. Did you search the attics?'

'Yes, Mrs Gilson.'

'They'll be hiding. You can't have looked properly.' Mrs Tomlinson marched up the stairs. Her voice floated down a minute later. 'They might not be here, but it's clear they slept in the back bedroom.'

She clattered down the stairs again and planted herself in front of Joss. *'Where are they?'*

When he didn't answer, Mrs Gilson came closer. 'Answer her, Bentley, or we'll make sure you're arrested for flouting the law.'

As she passed the kitchen window, Tess saw the three people at the cottage and rushed to find Vi. It was Cook who watched the children come round the rear of the house and run across the yard, looking back over their shoulders as if terrified of something. She hobbled across to open the door and locked it quickly after them.

As she turned round, Vi came hurrying into the kitchen, followed by Elizabeth.

Iris was crying silently and Roy was looking white and terrified.

'Before you tell us what's wrong,' Vi went to pick up the little girl, 'we'll go into another room where you can't be seen from the yard.'

Iris began sobbing more loudly but when her brother said, 'Shh!' she gulped and buried her face in Vi's shoulder.

The two women took the children into the small sitting room, where the Warburtons were enjoying a cup of tea.

'What on earth's happened now?' Christina exclaimed.

'I don't know. But I think we were wrong to let Joss and his children sleep on,' Vi said. 'Tess says Mrs Gilson and Mrs Tomlinson went into the cottage, together with the magistrate's clerk. A minute later the children came running across here.'

'Dad said to ask Mrs Schofield to look after us,' Roy volunteered.

It was Phyllis who took the lead. 'We'll all look after you, and I promise you'll be quite safe here, young man. Did you bring some clothes? Good. Go up with Miss Twineham and get dressed. Christina, would you go across and ask Mrs Gilson to come and speak to me. I do not wish to see the grandmother. Mrs Schofield, please ask Tess to take the children up some breakfast, then kindly join me in the drawing room.'

Even though she had to lean heavily on her walking stick, Phyllis Warburton looked as majestic as Queen Mary herself as she walked slowly into the icy cold drawing room and took a seat. Since her arthritis made it difficult for her to bend, she waited until Vi came back and asked her to light the fire.

'What shall you do?' Vi struck a match and touched the edges of the crumpled newspaper underneath the pile of kindling.

'Tell her the truth about those children and how badly they'd been treated.'

'You sound very confident.'

'The day I can't best Freda Gilson will be the day they lay me in my coffin. Besides, she's not all bad. She really does want to help people, even if she treats them too harshly. If we can prove the grandmother is ill-treating the children, Freda will soon change her tune.'

'And if she doesn't?'

That question remained unanswered because footsteps approached the room.

Christina hurried across to the cottage and since no one answered her knock, ventured inside and followed the sound of voices to the kitchen. There she found Joss standing facing the hall with his arms folded across his chest, his expression that of a man goaded but holding back his temper. The clerk was to one side and Mrs Gilson and Mrs Tomlinson were standing shoulder to shoulder with their backs to the front door.

The latter's shrill voice echoed down the hall, '. . . don't deserve to be their father and—'

'Excuse me.'

Mrs Tomlinson was speaking too loudly to hear, but Joss saw Christina and raised one eyebrow in a silent question. She gave him a quick nod, waited a minute, then said much more loudly, 'Excuse me, please.'

Mrs Gilson swung round. 'Ah. Just the person I wanted to see. Did this man bring his children to you, Christina? He's acting quite illegally in keeping them from their grandmother's care, you know.'

'Phyllis would like to speak to you about it. No, not you, Mrs Tomlinson. Just Mrs Gilson. Perhaps the rest of you could wait here in the cottage for a few minutes?'

She didn't wait but walked out with Freda at her side, annoyed when the other woman trailed behind them.

'I must protest at being left out. They're *my* grandchildren.'

'It would be best to bring Mrs Tomlinson,' Freda said. 'She has vital information to give us. I'm afraid you've been sadly misled by this Schofield woman, which proves what I said all along: she's not at all suitable for employment as a Health Visitor. We'll have to find someone else and luckily—'

Christina cut her short. 'Time enough to deal with the Health Visitor situation when this matter is sorted out. At the moment my sister doesn't want to see Mrs Tomlinson, and knowing what I know, I certainly don't want her even entering our house.'

'But the Schofield woman is acting against the law, which says a great deal about her character!'

Christina stopped walking and said very loudly and emphatically, 'I'm quite satisfied with Lady Bingram's assurances about Mrs Schofield's character and I believe she'll make an excellent Health Visitor.'

'Anyone can be misled by those who are cunning enough.'

'Are you accusing me of being a fool? Look in your own mirror if you want to see someone who's been misled.' They'd reached the front door and Christina didn't wait for an answer but opened it, allowing Mrs Gilson inside. She barred the way to Mrs Tomlinson, who was still close behind them. The woman hesitated then moved back down the outside steps, but the look she threw at Christina would have curdled milk.

In the drawing room, Phyllis was sitting in state, with Vi standing behind her armchair.

Freda Gilson cast a look of loathing at Vi and let Christina seat her in the chair opposite.

Phyllis took over. 'Thank you, Vi dear. I think, after all, I'll speak to Mrs Gilson alone. I'll ring when I need you.' She waited until the door had closed, then said without preamble, 'You always did use any trick you could to get your own way, Freda. But this time I'm not having it. Your eagerness to discredit Mrs Schofield means you've neglected to check whether the children really are being properly cared for.'

'On the contrary, as I was explaining to your sister on the way here, it's you who have been grossly misled, both by Mr Bentley and by that female.'

'About what?'

'Why, about the children, of course. Their grandmother is the obvious person to care for them. Their father hasn't even got a job, and anyway, a man can't possibly look after two young children and a baby.'

'He has got a job.'

'Since when? He's lying if he told you so, believe me. I know his sort.'

'Since I'm his employer, I don't see how I can be mistaken.' Phyllis watched with great inner glee as Freda's mouth dropped open in shock.

'Well, he still can't look after them properly, not a man on his own.'

'Of course not, which is why my sister and I will be helping him. Surely you're not suggesting we're incapable?'

There was dead silence in the room, then, 'It's very kind of you, but there is no need to trouble yourselves. Their grandmother has a prior right. They are her only daughter's children, after all.'

'The woman's beating them quite severely.'

'They're exaggerating, my dear Phyllis, if they've told you that. Children do need a firm hand at times and a slap or two never does them any harm.'

'I can easily prove my point. In the meantime, I'm sending for my own doctor to tend to them. I'm particularly worried about the little girl. Christina, my dear, will you kindly ring for Vi then the two of you can escort Mrs Gilson up to the children's bedroom and show her the proof?'

Christina stood up. 'Certainly.' She tugged the bell pull, then turned to their visitor. 'If you upset those children in any way, Freda, I shall remove you from their presence by force if necessary.'

*'Well!'*

In grim silence, Freda accompanied the two of them upstairs.

When she followed them into the bedroom, Iris cried out in fear and tried to hide under the bedclothes. Vi went to sit on the bed and comfort her, explaining that the lady only wanted to see her bruises and would be gone in a minute or two.

She pulled up Iris's nightdress, exposing a back that was a mass of bruises, one particularly large.

Freda sucked in her breath and looked from one woman to the other, her expression horrified. There was a long, pregnant silence, then she turned to Iris and asked in a much gentler tone of voice, 'How did you get those bruises, dear?'

The little girl looked up at her, then at Vi, who nodded encouragingly and said, 'Just tell the lady the truth, dear.'

'Grandma hit me.'

'And that big bruise at the side?'

'She kicked me when she was mad at Dad. She kicked Roy, too.'

Freda drew in a long breath, let it out slowly then looked at the two women. 'I don't know what to say. I'm shocked.' After a moment's thought, she added, 'And you and your sister will be helping to care for them here, Christina? Is that right?'

'Yes. Phyllis has brightened considerably in the past few days and you know how she's always loved children. We were both in rather low spirits, actually, but with Mr Bentley's help, we're improving our financial circumstances, and the extra company means we no longer have a dull moment.'

Mrs Gilson glanced across at Roy, who looked pleadingly at Vi.

'The lady needs to see your back, dear, if you're not to return to your grandmother.'

With a sigh he let her lift up the top of his pyjamas.

Mrs Gilson left the room and went downstairs, all the fight gone out of her.

'I hadn't realised,' she said to Phyllis once the door was closed behind them. 'Mrs Tomlinson is a pillar of the church, she seems so . . . but to hurt children like that. It doesn't bear thinking of.' She drew in a deep breath, her expression angry. 'She is a whited sepulchre and I shall never speak to her again.'

'Mrs Schofield, on the other hand, has been very helpful in saving those children,' Christina pointed out.

'Very – um, laudable.' But the glance Freda cast Vi was one of pure loathing.

Christina hid a smile. Clearly nothing had changed Freda's mind about who she wanted to work with her. 'I intend to take a personal interest in our new Health Visitors scheme from now on,' she said brightly, 'as does my friend Mrs Kirby. Working together, we shall be able to do so much more good.'

Phyllis said quietly, 'I'd like to speak to Mrs Tomlinson now. I intend to tell her myself that her misdeeds have been revealed and advise her to withdraw all her objections to the children returning to their father's care. I think she'll listen to me. Let me do the talking, if you please, Freda.'

When Mrs Gilson had left, she frowned and looked at her two companions. 'What I don't understand is why the grandmother has made no attempt to look after the baby.'

'Nor do I,' Vi said with a puzzled frown. 'You'd think she'd want them all.'

'Well, will you ask Mrs Tomlinson to come and see me, please, my dear? Then we can get rid of her for good and those poor little children can stop being afraid. Afterwards, I'd like to discuss something else with you.'

Christina was delighted to see her sister acting like her old, lively self again and wondered what she wanted to discuss. In the meantime, there was luncheon to be considered, then she had to get ready to visit Maud.

She hoped Maud would agree with what they'd done and continue to support dear Vi and Elizabeth. Why, oh why had they appointed Freda Gilson? Whatever the Mayor said, she wasn't a suitable person in this modern age.

# 24

Eric woke to instant awareness of where he was and what he had to do. He squinted at his watch, propped next to the bed. Gone half past eight, later than his usual waking time. He got dressed quickly, took a drink of water from the stable tap and then, puffing laboriously, carried a chair upstairs, before going back for a small table.

Putting these in the cubicle next to his bedroom, he began to sort through some important papers which contained the figures he'd acquired secretly from Kirby's office. He'd brought them here in a drawer, hidden under some clothes. The rest of his things he'd tumbled into sheets, bundling them up anyhow.

Ignoring his stomach's rumblings, he worked until he'd put together the summary he wanted, muttering to himself from time to time and once stopping to gaze into space for a while, ticking the points off on his fingers.

When loud voices outside disturbed him, he went to peep into the yard through the window of the living area in which Tess's two little girls were playing with a rag doll. Their brother came across to stand beside him and together they watched the various comings and goings. As good as a picture show, this was, Eric thought.

'What are they doing?' the lad asked.

'That old woman in black is Iris and Roy's grandmother and she wants to keep them from their father, Mr Bentley. They escaped from her house last night and came here.'

'I'd like to see anyone try to keep me from my mam. I'd get a big stick and hit them.'

'Good lad,' Eric murmured absent-mindedly.

Not until all seemed peaceful again did he go across to the kitchen of the big house and ask if he could buy some food. By then he was ravenous. He'd usually have had his breakfast and be ready for a piece of cake by this time of the morning. But some things were more important than food.

Tess opened the door.

'The lady said something about porridge for breakfast. I hope I'm not too late. I can pay for it.'

Tess turned to look at Cook for orders.

The old woman stared at him as if he was a worm. 'If I had my way, *you* wouldn't be at Fairview at all.'

Tess gave him a wink. 'Since Miss Warburton invited him, I think she'd want us to feed him, don't you, Cook? But there's no reason he can't pay for the food.'

'I'm quite happy to do that,' Eric said quickly.

'The porridge all got eaten. My Harry's got hollow legs. I could make a few sandwiches, though. What do you think, Cook? Won't take me a minute and it'll get Mr Gill out from under our feet.'

'Yes. And it'll be three shillings a day for your food, young man, payable to me each morning.'

'Thank you.' He fumbled in his pocket, selected a florin and a shilling coin and put them on the table. 'Um – do you think your Harry could run an errand for me later, Tess? It's really important.'

'Where do you want him to go?'

'I need to get a message to Mr Kirby, but I don't want it to fall into Sully's hands.'

'No need to send my Harry, and I'd rather he didn't go near Sully, anyway. Miss Christina is going to visit Mrs Kirby this afternoon. She's ever such a nice lady and I'm sure she'll take your letter. Do you want me to ask her?'

'I'd be much obliged, Tess. Thanks.'

She'd been working as they chatted and now loaded a tray with a pile of cheese sandwiches and a piece of cake, as well as a big beaker of tea. 'There you are. Could you bring the tray back when you've finished?'

'Thanks. I will. And you won't forget to ask Miss Christina for me?'

She nodded.

He carried the food back and settled down to enjoy it. Plain but filling. He could have done with more cake, though.

After he'd eaten he made sure to carry the tray straight back and praise the cake. He also slipped some papers to Tess when Cook had gone out, the first rough copies of the accounts he'd been compiling, which he'd now made fair copies of. 'Could you keep these safe for me somewhere in the house, love? You never know who's coming in and out of them stables and if I'm to get my job back, I can't have anyone finding them.'

'All right. I can hide these in the broom cupboard – that's it there. See this shelf at the side? If I can shove the papers behind those packets, no one will ever guess where they are.'

'Good. I'll make it worth your while once I get my job back,' he promised.

'If we can't help one another, it's a poor lookout,' she said. 'I was very fond of your mother. Now, I've got to get on with my work.'

He hesitated, then added, 'If anything happens to me, give them papers to that new police sergeant.' That made her gape at him.

Smiling grimly, he walked back. He'd fallen lucky being allowed to come here, but he didn't intend to stay here for long. He was going to settle Sully's hash good and proper, *and* get both his home and job back – no, not his own job, Sully's.

He wasn't pleased with Kirby, though. Letting a chap get the sack was no way to repay someone who'd helped you. If this didn't work out, he'd tell the police what was going on and to hell with them all. Eric had done nothing against the law, after all.

After she'd cleared up the broken glass in the two bedrooms, Vi spent the latter part of the morning keeping an eye on the Bentley children. Joss had gone into town and would be sending back the glazier to sort out the two windows. He'd brought the baby across to her, as well, but Miss Phyllis had commandeered Nora.

Vi needed to talk to Joss about the baby. Yet again, she'd seen him hand Nora over with every sign of relief, not even bending to kiss the rosy little cheek. It was as if he was glad to get rid of the child. This couldn't go on. Children noticed such things, and even if the baby was too young to realise how he felt, the other two weren't.

Vi was determined to find out what was wrong.

Christina got out of the car that had been sent for her and studied Kirby's house. It was a nice old place and she'd known the family who used to live here quite well when she was young. The previous owner, a widow her own age, was living in comfort by the seaside at St Anne's now and hadn't been back to Drayforth since she sold the place. Kirby had refurbished it so lavishly the whole town had talked about it for months, but Christina had never actually seen the inside.

'Are you going to come in or shall we hold our meeting out here?'

She turned to smile at Maud. 'The garden's looking very well cared for.'

'But?'

'It's a bit too neat for my taste.'

'For mine, too, but Gerald prefers it this way.'

Inside, the house was greatly changed. Christina tried not to stare at the electric light fitting in the hallway, a huge upside down bowl suspended from three chains. Now, that was extravagance. Even wealthy people were usually content to have electricity only in their living rooms and dining rooms, not seeing the need for it in the rest of the house. She sighed enviously. She'd have it installed at Fairview if they could afford it, that and the telephone.

Maud's voice pulled her out of this brief daydream. 'Let me take your coat and hat, then come through to my sitting room.'

The letter in her pocket crackled as she slipped her arms out and folded the coat, reminding her of her promise. She took it out. 'I'll explain about this in a minute.'

To Christina's relief, the room they went into was cosy and full of comfortable clutter. But it had both an electric light in the ceiling and an electric standard lamp behind one chair. How clearly one must be able to see to read or embroider in the evenings, and just by turning the lights on! No lighting oil lamps or moving candles around.

She allowed herself to be settled, then held out the letter. 'I've been asked to give you this. It's for your husband.'

Maud took it and stared at the neatly printed name on the envelope. 'Who is it from?'

'An employee who was sacked recently, unjustly he tells me. He's Mrs Schofield's brother, actually, Eric Gill. He made a point of asking you not to send it to the office, where Sully can intercept it.'

'Goodness! I know Gill, of course. I wonder why he's writing.'

'It might be for the same reason we're having trouble: that Sully creature.' Christina explained about the previous day and night's events. Her hostess exclaimed several times, shocked that someone would dare do this, then sat frowning. Christina waited patiently.

At length Maud looked up. 'I think I'm going to send for Gerald right away. I'm certain he doesn't know that this has happened and he needs to. If you'll wait a minute, I'll go and telephone him.'

Christina heard her walk briskly into the next room, speak to the operator and get connected to her husband's place of business.

When the phone conversation ended, there was the sound of voices, then Maud came back, looking determined. 'I've sent the car for Gerald. I think some good is going to come of this. I've been trying to change a few things about how he runs his business. I don't need to tell you that he can be rather harsh with his poorer tenants and as for his slum properties, they're an absolute disgrace. I have a feeling that the presence of a Warburton here in his home – if you don't mind me being frank about that – not to mention him finding out about what Sully's been doing, will make a difference. He says he didn't send those men and had expressly forbidden Sully to trouble you.'

'We didn't think your husband did it, if only because he isn't stupid.'

'No, and my husband isn't a bad man either, Christina, not a really bad one. Because he was very poor as a child, he's been driven by a hunger for money. Now that he has enough money, he's equally hungry for acceptance by people like you. If you'll help me by agreeing to see him occasionally socially, I think we can persuade him to modify the way he runs his business, which will do a great deal of good in the town.'

'I prefer you to be frank.' Christina didn't beat about the bush about why she was accepting this idea. 'And I do enjoy your company, which is why I'm here.'

'I enjoy yours too.'

'I must say, I'd be very happy to help you do something about those dreadful slums.'

'Yes. I feel so sorry for the people who have to live there.' Maud gave a wry smile. 'My husband won't change overnight, of course, or become a philanthropist, but if we can just get rid of that horrible Sully creature, I'm sure things will improve. So . . . will you help me convince Gerald and continue nudging him in the right direction?'

'Come to dinner here as well as visiting you, do you mean?'

'Yes.'

'My sister and I will certainly give it our serious consideration. First, we'll have to see what he says and does about all this.'

There was the sound of a motor car outside and Maud looked up. 'Ah, there he is.'

When Christina had finished her account, Gerald couldn't hold back a grunt of anger. 'I hope you believe that I'd never, ever have sent men to attack your house, Miss Christina.'

'As I said to Maud, we didn't think you had done.'

He gave her a little nod, pleased by this, then looked down at the sealed envelope which was lying on the table next to him. 'I wonder if you ladies would excuse me for a few minutes? I'd better read this. It may have something to do with these matters.'

'Open it here and share it with us,' Maud said. 'After all, Christina's well and truly involved, isn't she?'

He hesitated, then, with a tightening of his lips that showed her he'd rather not have been pressed into staying, he ripped open the envelope, for once not bothering to slit it neatly. 'There's a letter and a list of figures.' He read the letter quickly then, as he studied the figures, gasped in shock. After rereading the letter, he studied the figures once more, his colour high and his anger quite visible to his companions.

By this time Maud could bear the silence no longer. 'Well? What does it say?'

'This is to go no further.'

'Of course not.'

'Gill has proof that Sully has been cheating me, taking my money on rather a large scale. I thought I was up to all such tricks, but he's managed to pull the wool over my eyes right from the start of our – um, association. If he'd suddenly changed what he was doing, I'd have caught it, but he's been keeping back some of my rent money from the very beginning so I didn't guess. I was so busy in the early days, I had to leave a lot to him.' He jerked to his feet and began pacing up and down the room, shaking his head from time to time, his thoughts clearly on other things.

'What are you going to do?' Maud asked after this had gone on for some time.

'Mmm? Oh, deal with Sully once and for all, of course. But I'd appreciate it if you could carry a message back to Gill from me, Miss Christina. And also, if you'll allow the car to wait for him behind the house. He can crouch down in the back and be driven here with no one the wiser.'

'Except your chauffeur.'

'He's very loyal. He's getting a bit past it now and knows I'll soon be paying him a pension if he doesn't upset me.'

'I'm happy to help you in any way I can.' Christina hesitated, looked at Maud and added, 'Friends should help one another, don't you think?'

Gerald looked from one to the other in surprise.

'Christina and I have quickly become good friends,' Maud said cheerfully, as if this weren't a momentous step.

He tried but failed to hide the pleasure this gave him. 'Excellent. I hope I'll soon be able to claim the same privilege. Now,' he glanced at his expensive, new-fangled wrist watch, 'I really must write that note to Gill. If you ladies will excuse me?'

When he'd gone, Maud said simply, 'Thank you.'

'This doesn't mean we shall ever sell him our house,' Christina warned.

'Oh, that. I hope you won't. I like it here, as I keep telling Gerald. It's much more convenient to be closer to town. He'll grow used to the idea eventually because I'll keep on about not wanting to move – and more importantly to him, not wanting to spoil our friendship.' She chuckled.

Christina relaxed. Maybe being friends with the Kirbys wouldn't be as difficult as she and her sister had feared. She did enjoy Maud's company – and her honesty.

But she did hope this revelation about Sully wouldn't lead to more trouble for the various people living at Fairview. She was growing so fond of them all. It was almost like having a family again.

After leaving his children in Vi's care, Joss went into town to consult his lawyer, who told him that Mrs Tomlinson had withdrawn her objections to him taking the children to live with him.

'Oh? When did she do that?'

'An hour or so ago. The magistrate's clerk popped in to tell me.'

'So there will be nothing to stop me going to pick up the children's beds and other possessions?'

Mr Graves pursed his lips. 'I think I should send my office boy with you. He can cycle back to fetch me if you have any trouble. He's very sharp for a lad his age. How are you going to transport the furniture?'

Joss sighed. 'I'll have to walk out to the farm to get a cart. Sully has stopped people in town dealing with me.'

Mr Graves permitted himself a tight smile. 'I think I can help there. I'll send the lad to hire a vehicle for me and he can lend you a hand with carrying things out of the house while he's there. No one will be any the wiser about who the cart is for until after the event.'

Joss leaned back in his chair. 'Thank you. It'll make a nice change to do something the easy way.'

'I'm happy to help and glad that your little misunderstanding with Mrs Tomlinson has been cleared up. I don't forget that men like you fought for us in France and I don't like to see you being treated badly. No one should ever forget the men from Drayforth who gave their lives. In fact, I'm about to start a fund to build a memorial for them.'

'I'd be happy to contribute. I can't afford much, but surely everything will help.'

'Indeed it will. I'm receiving a lot of promises of help. I shall co-opt you on to the committee.'

'Very well.' Joss glanced at the clock. 'I might just have time to nip along to the shop and let my family know what's happening while we're waiting for the cart.'

'You do that. If you're not back, I'll send the lad to fetch you. It's only a few doors away, after all.'

But Joss was back in time, relieved to see that business had picked up just a little at the shoe shop. Best of all, having his grandchildren to stay had shaken his father out of a depressed state, and his mother was looking far less strained and tired, with a daughter-in-law to help her around the house. Even the shop looked more cheerful and it took him a while to realise why. Someone had made a display in the window with a silk scarf, a lady's shoe and an artificial flower. 'That looks nice.'

'My Libby did it. She's got an eye for making things look pretty.' Wilf smiled. 'I like selling but I'm not good at fancying things up. Any road, it's all working out for the best. Sully did us a favour, chucking us out of our home, though he'd hate to think that.'

'No more trouble from him?'

'No. But there are nightly police patrols along the main streets now. You feel more secure somehow, just to know that. That new Police Sergeant has made a difference to the town already.'

When the cart drew up in front of Mrs Tomlinson's house, Joss asked the lad to come to the door with him, then wait on the cart till he was needed. 'I may be a few minutes getting the stuff ready. The old lady isn't what you'd call helpful.'

The lad grinned. 'I used to play with a friend who lives in this street. Old Mrs T used to come out and yell at us if we went anywhere near her place.'

Joss knocked on the front door, saw the curtain in the front room twitch and had to knock again before she'd open it.

'What do *you* want?'

'I'm here to collect the children's possessions and furniture. Mr Graves sent along his junior clerk to make sure there are no problems about that.'

She scowled at them both. 'What problems could there be? The stuff is yours, isn't it?'

Joss was shocked at how drawn and tired she looked, as if she'd suddenly aged ten years.

'You'd better come in and get the stuff ready then. I'm not doing it. And *he* isn't coming nosing about inside till it's time to carry the things down. I might have known you'd get a young lout like him to help you. He caused nothing but trouble in the street when he was a lad.'

As she led the way up the stairs, moving very stiffly, Joss sniffed. Surely that was – it couldn't be – yes, it was definitely gin. You couldn't mistake that smell. Surely she hadn't taken to the bottle? Or had she been drinking all along? He was astounded.

'What exactly came from my house?' he asked, looking round the bedroom.

'The beds and the chest of drawers between them were my Ada's, so I suppose they're yours now. The wardrobe's mine.'

'And the bedding?'

'Belonged to my Ada. Not up to much, is it? You kept her very short of money.'

'On the contrary, I gave her a decent amount, more than most young wives have, and she frittered it away.'

'She was young, deserved a bit of fun. And you had plenty of money in those days. That shop was a goldmine before the war. It was why I told Ada to—' She broke off and began fiddling with the door, wiping the part near the knob with the edge of her pinafore.

'—why you told her to marry me,' Joss finished for her. 'She said more than once that she wished you'd let her marry one of the other lads who were courting her, because they were more fun than I was.'

'You should have treated her better.'

'I treated her well and she was lying if she told you differently.'

'She never lied to me. Told me everything, she did.'

'Is that why you didn't take the baby as well as the children?'

'I'm too old to be doing with a baby. They're hard work when they're that young.'

'My mother said you never even went round to see Nora. Why not? She was Ada's too.'

Mrs Tomlinson pressed her lips together. 'None of your business.'

And suddenly, what she'd said earlier came back to him. She'd said Ada never lied to her. He put down the bundle he'd picked up and stared at her. 'You knew, didn't you?'

'I don't know what you're talking about.'

But her expression was guilty, so he said it, 'You knew Nora wasn't mine.'

The silence prickled with antagonism, then words burst from her as if a great dam had burst. 'Yes, I knew. But it was *you* who drove her to it. She'd not have done it else.'

'Who was he?'

'Wouldn't you like to know?'

'Not really. Better I don't know if I'm to raise the child, or it'd upset me every time I saw him walking down the street.'

He knew that bait would catch her, the miserable old devil.

'It was Sully.'

Joss felt bile rise in his throat. '*Sully!* But he's old enough to be her father. She'd never— I don't believe you.'

'You don't think she went to him willingly, do you? She got behind with the rent, didn't dare tell me and he *forced* her to go with him to pay it off. It went on for months before she told me. Then she put her head in my lap and wept, she did, when she found she was expecting his bastard. She'd waited too long to get rid of it, though. I wasn't risking her life. I wish I had done now! She might still be alive.' The last words were a wail of pure agony.

Joss couldn't say a word, was still trying to come to terms with this monstrous revelation.

'I was the one who told her to pretend it was yours, and now you'll never prove it isn't, because I shan't tell anyone else what I'm telling you now. You'll live with the knowledge that you've a cuckoo in your nest, a cuckoo fathered by that nasty old man.' She stared at him triumphantly, then turned and walked away.

He sank down on the bed, head in hands, groaning.

Sully. Nora was Sully's daughter. That thought made Joss feel physically sick. How could he ever bear to touch the child again?

Eric read Mr Kirby's note. 'Ah!' It was do or die now. Kirby would either listen to him and do something about Sully, or try to get rid of Eric. But his former employer would find himself in serious trouble if he did.

Getting into the car, Eric lay down on the back seat, letting the chauffeur cover him with a blanket. As the car drove off he wondered which way things would go. Was it a good sign that he'd got such a quick response to his letter?

When they slowed down and turned into Kirby's drive, he

started to sit up, but the chauffeur hissed, 'Stay where you are. You're to get out round the back. And even when we stop, don't move till I tell you. No one's to see you come here.'

A couple of minutes later he said, 'Get up now and follow me.'

They were in a garage, built specially by Kirby to house his cars. The big doors at the front were shut and the chauffeur led the way to a smaller door at the side, which looked on to the side of the house. He gestured to a door opposite. 'Go in there. It's his office.' When Eric didn't move he gave him a push. 'Go on. Don't bother to knock, just get out of sight as quickly as you can.'

Eric slipped inside the house and paused for a moment to take his bearings.

'Ah, there you are, Gill. Come and take a seat.'

He sat facing Mr Kirby, who didn't look best pleased with the world.

'Why didn't you tell me Sully was fleecing me?'

'I didn't know at first. When I found out, I thought I'd better get some evidence together before I spoke out, so I got hold of a back door key and went into the office at night a few times to check through the books. I knew what money I'd collected, you see, to the penny, but it was always entered in *your* ledgers as a lesser amount. I was still gathering evidence when I got sacked.' He scowled at his former employer. 'I'd expected you to support me there. You promised you would.'

Mr Kirby pinched the top of his nostrils and rubbed his nose in the way Eric had seen before when his employer wasn't happy about something. 'I was in a cleft stick. Sully knows too much about one or two things I did during the war.'

*One or two things*, Eric thought scornfully. Does he think I'm blind? But he didn't say that.

'I offered to pay for Sully's retirement elsewhere and he refused out of hand, said he enjoyed what he did, and would rather go to prison and take me with him than leave the town.'

'He was bluffing.'

'How can you be sure?'

'Because he's bought himself a house in Blackpool. I found

information about that in his office, too. Why would he buy that unless he did want to retire eventually?'

'Then why didn't he accept my offer?'

Eric thought hard and fast. 'I reckon he was planning to take more of your money before he went. He's a greedy bugger. You'd think he'd have enough by now. It's been the downfall of quite a few men that I've heard of, being too greedy. There was one in the papers the other week, sent to jail he was. But if he'd stopped embezzling money from his employer when he was ahead, he'd not have been caught.'

Mr Kirby stared at him as if he'd been punched in the guts and Eric wondered what he'd said to make the other look like that. He waited, not sure what to say or do next.

Kirby let out a dry sound, halfway between a cough and a laugh, then muttered, 'Out of the mouths of babes . . . and employees.'

'Excuse me, sir?'

'It means you're right. It doesn't do to be greedy. What do *you* want out of life, Gill? Will *you* know when to stop?'

Eric shrugged. 'I've got a dicky heart. I shan't have a long life, so no use aiming at the moon. If I've got a decent job and house, then I can get wed. What I want most is a son to carry on my name, to show I've been here.'

His employer gave him another of those hard looks, then took a deep breath. 'Well, only one way to find out if Sully is bluffing, eh? I'll have to give him the sack. Can you take over the rent side of the business from him if I do?'

'Easily. And run it more efficiently, too. But I shan't do it violently like he does, and I'd rather we did a few more repairs. Those houses in the Backhill Terraces are going downhill fast.'

'We've been paying for repairs. I have the accounts to— The old devil! He *was* taking extra money. I'll definitely sack him. I'll do it tomorrow, then send for you when he's cleared out.'

'Begging your pardon, sir, but I think you'd be wise to have some good, strong fellows with you when you see him. Not me, I'm no good in a fight. But I know one or two lads who've come back from the war and who'd be glad to earn an extra bob or two any way they can. And sir – you'd better threaten some drastic measures and sound as if you mean them. Sully won't really do anything to send himself to jail, he's not stupid, but he's a good card player, knows how to bluff.'

Kirby gave him another of those looks, then nodded. 'All right. You arrange it. I'll get my chauffeur to take you back now. Stay out of sight again. I don't want Sully knowing you've been here.'

Eric lay smiling beneath the blanket as he was driven back. The tide had turned and things were all coming together. Mind you, Sully would still cut up rough when he got the sack, he was sure of that. But Eric was going to take his own measures to protect himself.

He'd learned the hard way not to rely on Mr Kirby's protection.

# 25

Vi watched Joss arrive home. He was grim-faced, walking beside a small cart loaded with furniture and bundles. To her surprise, he made no attempt to come across to the kitchen, but carried things into the cottage with the driver's help.

Puzzled and quite sure something was wrong, Vi kept the children in the kitchen until the lad had driven the cart and its patient elderly horse away. Only then did she let them out and follow as they raced across the back yard.

They rushed inside the cottage, shouting for their father, who appeared at the top of the stairs. 'Come and help me sort out your things, you two scamps,' he said.

His smile was a travesty. To Vi he was like a man trying to seem cheerful when in reality he'd just received a bad blow. 'Do you want some help?' she asked. 'Nora's asleep and Miss Warburton's keeping watch on her.'

He hesitated, then nodded and waited for her to join him at the top of the stairs.

'Aren't me and Iris sleeping in the same bedroom, Dad?' Roy asked.

'I thought you'd like a bedroom each, for a change. You're getting a bit big to sleep with your little sister now, son. Besides, you won't want to go to bed as early as Iris, will you? You're growing up fast.'

The boy stood a little taller at this news, then looked round the landing and frowned. 'But there are only three bedrooms. Where's our Nora going to sleep?'

'I don't know. I suppose she'll have to stay with me for the time being.'

Vi heard his voice grow cooler as he spoke of the baby.

Roy nodded acceptance of this. 'When Nora gets a bit bigger, I s'pose she'll sleep with Iris, because they're both girls. Can I go and unpack my things, Dad? I've never had a room of my own before.' He clattered off, seeming full of energy today, in spite of his bruises and sore ribs.

Vi watched him go with a smile, then turned to Joss, her heart twisting at the wretchedness in his eyes. 'What's wrong, love?'

He pushed his hair back and said without looking at her, 'I'll explain later. Let's get the children settled. Those two should be happy from now on, at least.'

And what did that mean? she wondered, as she helped him make up the beds with clean sheets and carried the children's dirty clothes and crumpled escape sheets down to the scullery. *Those two*. He had three children, not two.

As they worked, Joss didn't speak unless he had to, didn't look at her even when she said, 'You need a washday.'

'Yes.'

'Want me to do it for you? I can do some of my own things at the same time, so it won't be an imposition. There's a good copper in the scullery if you'll bring me in some wood.'

'Thanks.'

'Have you any clothes that need washing, Joss?'

'A few things. But you don't need to do mine.'

'I might as well, once I've got the water hot. Go and fetch them so that I can see what needs doing. I start my new job next week, so I won't be able to help you as much then.'

'Right.' He vanished and brought a pile of clothing down to the scullery, then set to work filling and lighting the boiler.

She couldn't bear the silence, the pain emanating from him. 'At least there's a cold water tap so we don't have to fill the boiler with a bucket. And there's a tap to let the water out and a drain. Fairview might be old-fashioned but it was well planned for its day, even in the servants' quarters. The family must have been good employers.'

'Mmm.'

She couldn't drag more than a couple of words out of him, so in the end held her tongue and set to work on the washing, using hard soap to rub any stains, and soaking the sheets in cold water first in a battered enamel tub that had seen better days. She found a poss-stick to pound the clothes with, but had to clean the wooden circle with little legs at the end of the stick, before she could use it on the clothes. It looked as if it'd been gathering dust and cobwebs for years. And there was a mangle dumped carelessly in one corner, also dusty.

The clothes would have to be dried indoors at this time of year, but Joss offered to set up lines in the empty stables, which would be a big help. It seemed to Vi that he was relieved to have an excuse to get away from her.

A couple of times she went and peered out at him. He looked agonised, there was no other word for it, agonised.

What on earth had happened at his mother-in-law's?

When Eric arrived home a little later, he saw Vi pegging out washing in the stables. He slid out of the back of the car, unable to stop grinning as he turned and waved goodbye to the chauffeur.

'You look pleased with yourself,' she commented.

'I am.' He went straight up the stairs without explaining. Time enough for that when everything had been sorted out, as it would be tomorrow. He found young Harry kicking the skirting board, clearly bored to tears.

'Go and ask your mother if you can run some errands for me. You'll just have time before it gets dark. I'll give you a shilling if you do them quickly.'

Brightening up, the youngster ran off and reappeared a few minutes later with Tess behind him.

'I'm not having him going near Sully,' she announced, hands on hips.

'He'll be going nowhere near that sod.'

'Language. There are children present.'

'Sorry.' He sighed. Decent women made such a fuss about not

swearing, though 'sod' wasn't strong language in his book. 'He won't be going anywhere near Sully, Tess, and I'll give him a bob for going.'

She nodded and turned to Harry. 'And don't spend any of it. You know how short I am.'

The lad nodded, which showed he was a good kid, Eric thought. He wanted a son like that, alert and lively. That longing had grown to be a hunger in him. 'Right. It won't take me more than a few minutes to write a couple of notes and tell you where to take them.'

He went down and conferred with Joss about who to send for. Joss knew some of the lads who'd come back from the war better than anyone else would because everyone from the town had started out in a Pals Regiment. Eric didn't know whether to be sorry or glad he'd not been able to go with them. It'd have been better not to have a dicky heart and be able to do such things, but on the other hand, a fair few of them had been killed and he was still alive.

Ten minutes later he gave the boy three sealed envelopes with names and addresses written on them, making sure Harry could read them. 'Quick as you can, mind. And don't give them to anyone but the men whose names are on the envelopes, think on.'

Then he went to pace up and down the back yard until the cold wind drove him indoors, where he paced up and down the corridor instead. He always thought best when walking.

When Vi had finished the washing, doing rather a skimpy job of it, so that the whites weren't as bright as she would have normally got them, she went to find Joss. He wasn't in the cottage and Iris said he'd gone across to the house for Nora.

From the front doorstep Vi watched him come back across the yard, pushing the pram, shoulders slumped, the corners of his lips dropping. He didn't glance at the baby once.

She held the door open and he heaved the pram into the house, putting it at the foot of the steps.

Then he looked at the baby, glaring at her as if he hated her, making no attempt to pick her up.

Exasperated by this, Vi pushed him out of the way and lifted Nora out of the pram, carrying her into the kitchen. 'She can't lie in a dark passageway all the time.'

'She should be glad to have anywhere to lie, that one,' he snapped.

Before Vi could ask what on earth he meant by this, he went back into the hall and shouted up the stairs, 'Cook says if you're hungry she'll give you two your tea now.'

With yells of joy, both children clattered down the stairs and out of the house.

He returned to the kitchen and looked at Vi, mutely miserable.

'Tell me,' she said quietly. 'Whatever it is, for heaven's sake tell me.' She started changing the baby on the old armchair.

He went to stand with his back to her, looking out of the window at the darkening grounds, making no attempt to light the lamps.

Vi continued with what she was doing. You didn't need good light to change a baby's nappy and this one was only wet. 'Go on, Joss love. You'll feel better once you've told me.'

'I'll not. Nothing will make me feel better about it. But you have to know, to understand why I can't –' he indicated the baby – 'keep her. I just can't, Vi!'

She stared at him in shock, then listened as he explained, her heart going out to him. Fancy having all that happening when you were fighting for your country and didn't know whether you were going to live or die.

But her heart went out to the baby too. There was no one to love Nora now, no one at all. And she was a delightful baby, one of the prettiest Vi had ever seen, with a sunny nature to match.

When Joss had finished speaking, she put Nora back into the pram, then went to him. He hadn't moved, was still staring out of the window. She put her arms round him from behind and they stood there for a few minutes, not saying anything.

'What are you going to do?' she asked at last.

'Give her to Sully. He's her father.'

Vi pushed away, staring at him in horror. 'You can't mean that, Joss.'

He swung round, scowling at her now. 'Oh, but I do. You don't know what it's like. Bad enough that she's someone else's child, but to be the spawn of that villain! To think of *my* wife lying with him while I was out there, in that hell . . . It's beyond bearing. So I'm taking Nora to him first thing in the morning. He got her, let him look after her.'

Vi felt sick to the soul at the thought of that. 'Oh, Joss, love you can't.'

He took a step backwards, still looking at her as if he hated her. 'Why can't I?'

'Because Sully's a monster. I wouldn't give a dog to him, let alone a child.'

'*She* may be a monster too. She may take after him. Children often do. And whether she is or isn't, she's *not* my responsibility.' He laughed, a harsh, fractured sound. 'Even her grandmother didn't want her.'

'Mrs Tomlinson knows?'

'Yes. She taunted me with it, told me who the father was.'

'Then give Nora to me. I'll raise her.' Vi knew it was the right thing as soon as she said it and tried to explain. 'I've longed for children, Joss. You've no idea how sad it's made me not to have them, how many times I've wept about it. I'll take her and love her and—'

'If you do that, what about us?'

She wrapped her arms round herself for comfort and support. It took her a minute to work out the reasons for her instinctive offer. 'If you can't love that child, there is no us. I couldn't marry a man who'd give away a child as if she was just a parcel of old clothes. And to such a monster. I simply – couldn't.'

The threat hung between them like a dirty cloud and he took another step away from the pain of it. 'She belongs with her real father, Vi. I won't change my mind about that. I've lain awake night after night, fretting, trying to work out what to do. Only, I didn't know who he was then. Now I do.'

'Have you thought what people will say? What your own family will say?'

'Of course I have. Over and over I've wondered how to tell them. And there isn't an easy way. But what it comes down to is: I can't keep Nora. *She's Sully's daughter, not mine.*' The man had trampled on so many people, then planted a cuckoo in Joss's nest. He couldn't bear the thought of it.

'Roy and Iris are fond of their little sister. What'll they think? They'll never understand. How can you even begin to make them understand?'

'They're young. They'll soon forget her.'

'They won't! And I won't either. Give her to me.'

'Vi, don't do this. You said you loved me, now you're turning away just when I need you most.'

'I don't want to, Joss. Do you think the thought of it doesn't hurt me? But some things are so wrong they stick in your gullet. I couldn't live with it if you gave her to him. I just couldn't.'

He watched her walk away with what felt like tears of blood leaking from his eyes. Nora began to cry and he let her, couldn't bear to touch her. The crying went on and on, and still he didn't move.

Then Roy and Iris came in from the big house. Joss heard his son rock the pram and murmur to the baby. Iris's voice chimed in, gradually the wailing stopped and Nora fell silent.

The children came to peep into the kitchen. He managed to say, 'Can you get yourselves to bed now? I've got some things to do. You can play tiddlywinks or something for half an hour if you're very careful with the lamps.'

When they'd gone upstairs he went into the hall and forced himself to look at the baby, sleeping peacefully now. Could he? No . . . No, he couldn't. He felt tears roll down his cheeks and wished more than ever that he'd never set eyes on her. She'd just cost him Vi.

He went to stand in the garden, heedless of the cold.

It was dark outside, but it felt much darker inside his mind.

How could he bear to be without Vi just as he'd grown to love her so dearly?

Harry came back and claimed his shilling. A few minutes later a man came to Fairview and made his way round to the rear of the house. Tess peered out of the kitchen door, ready to slam it shut if this was trouble. 'Who are you? What are you doing here?'

The man raised his cap. 'Sorry to trouble you, missus, but I'm looking for Eric Gill.'

'He's up above the stables.'

Eric called, 'Come up the stairs and I'll meet you at the top. Sorry, Tess. I forgot to let you know I was expecting company tonight. There are two other men coming. Can you send them across to me if they come to the house?'

'If I see them. I'll be coming across soon myself to put the children to bed. Are they in your way?'

'No. We'll talk in my room.'

When the man reached the top of the stairs, Eric was waiting. 'Don, isn't it? Thanks for coming. I'll make it worth your while, but I'll wait to tell you why I need some help till the others arrive. No use repeating it all, is there? In fact, if you don't mind, could you go down and wait for them and bring them up? Thanks. I'm in the room at the end of the corridor. I'll leave the door open.'

Within ten minutes the other two men had arrived and joined them, to sit in a row on the narrow bed while Eric took a chair that just fitted in opposite them. Speaking in a low voice, he explained what he wanted them for and how much they could earn.

'I'd just about kill for that much money,' one said frankly.

'We don't want any killing,' Eric said quickly. 'Or any trouble, if we can avoid it. Now, I don't want anyone attacking me on the way into town so I want two of you to walk in with me very early tomorrow. The other can meet us at Mr Kirby's office. You can toss for it. When we get there, this is how we'll do it . . .'

* * *

Joss couldn't sleep that night. He tossed and turned, hearing again and again the disgust in Vi's voice. Twice he got up, lit a candle and went across to the cot to stare down at the baby. She looked so bonny and soft. Sometimes she nuzzled up against you like a puppy. He searched her features for any sign of Sully, but found none.

Could he do it? Raise that man's child?

Bile rose in his throat. No, he damned well couldn't.

But if he heard of Sully ill-treating her, he'd give the fellow what for or report him to the police or . . . something. He didn't want anyone to hurt her.

At about two o'clock Nora woke up and roared in pain, her legs twisting about in the bed. He knew what it was, wind, and how to deal with it quickly. Roy had been just the same sometimes in the middle of the night and Ada had always slept through it. Joss didn't want to touch her, but he couldn't leave her in agony, so in the end he snatched Nora up, lying her against his shoulder, and began to pace up and down, patting her back. She burped several times, then settled against his neck with a murmur, small and warm and trusting.

'Don't do that! I'm not going to change my mind.' He put her hastily back into the cot, wishing she didn't have such pretty eyes, didn't stare at you like that. He turned the lamp down and went back to bed. But he didn't sleep properly, kept waking up, thinking Nora was crying.

In the cold grey light of a very chilly dawn he got up and carried her downstairs, feeding her quickly and efficiently. He knew what she liked by now. He'd have to tell whoever next cared for her. Sully wouldn't do that himself, of course, but someone would have to.

After changing her nappy, Joss put all her things into the pram. He was writing a quick note for Roy and Iris when his son came down the stairs.

'What's the matter, Dad? Why have you got up so early? Is Nora not well?'

Joss tried to find words to answer him, but it was a minute

before he could speak. 'She's fine. But I'm taking her to live with another family.'

Roy looked at him in puzzlement. 'Why? We're managing all right, aren't we? I'll look after her more if you want. I know it's soppy boys doing that, but you can't help loving her, can you?'

Which floored Joss for a minute. Then he took a deep breath. Roy was old enough to understand, surely he was? 'Nora isn't my child, Roy. Your mother . . . went with another man and *he* is her father. So, she's going to live with him.'

His son stared at him in horror.

'Do you understand what I'm saying?'

Roy nodded. 'My friend Eddie's mam had a baby while their dad was away. But she kept the baby. Why can't we keep our baby?'

'Because she's not mine and I *don't* want her.'

Roy began to cry. 'Well, I do! She's my sister. I know how to make her laugh, she loves you to tickle her tummy. Me and Iris are going to teach her to play all sorts of games when she's a bit bigger. You *can't* give her away, Dad! I won't let you.'

He went to stand in the doorway, arms outstretched.

Joss hesitated, then an image of Sully rose before him and he shook his head. Moving the sobbing boy gently to one side, he edged the pram out of the house and set off.

The pram wheel squeaked and he looked up anxiously at the first-floor windows along the rear of the house. No lights came on and he breathed a little more easily.

Vi was woken by a squeaking sound and lay for a few seconds trying to work out what it was. She couldn't but as it went on she got up to peep out of the window. She saw a dark silhouette crossing the back yard, a pram with a man pushing it.

Where was Joss taking Nora at this hour of the morning? Surely he wasn't giving her away already?

It was none of Vi's business. He'd made it plain that he couldn't bear to keep the baby. Only, Vi couldn't bear to live with a man who'd put a child into Sully's power. She just – couldn't. Nor could she bear the thought of what might happen to Nora, whether Sully kept her – which seemed unlikely – or dumped her in an orphanage.

Then someone began to hammer on the kitchen door and a voice cried out for her.

'Vi, Vi! Come quickly!'

It was Roy. She went to slide up her bedroom window and call down, 'Shh. I'm coming. Wait there.' She grabbed her clothes and scrambled into them as fast as she could in the darkness, thankful that she always left them just so.

What did Roy want? Had he seen his father taking Nora away? The poor lad sounded so distressed. 'Oh, Joss!' She didn't realise she'd spoken aloud for a minute, then pressed the back of her hand against her lips to hold back more words.

It was worth one more try to stop Joss doing this, surely. If Vi adopted the child, Lady Bingram would help her find somewhere to live and work, she was sure, and then Roy and Iris could see their sister sometimes.

There had to be a way.

# 26

The damned pram squeaked all the way into town. Joss didn't notice it at first, then gradually became aware of it, a mournful sound in the grey world that was still waiting for the sun to rise properly. He should have oiled the pram, had been meaning to for a while.

He could see that Nora was still awake, looking up at the fading stars. Why did babies' eyes have this look of wonder? It made you feel— He broke off that thought abruptly. Soon be a thing of the past for him, babies.

It was a bit early but he knew where Sully lived and would knock the man up if necessary.

Only – he couldn't get the memory of Roy's weeping out of his mind, hadn't realised how much the lad cared for his little sister. And it sounded as if Iris felt the same. Oh, hell, he didn't want to hurt anybody, least of all his children.

He passed one or two people hurrying off to work but they didn't spare him a second glance. He felt alone in the world, wished Vi were here. She couldn't have meant it, could she? This wouldn't come between them, not once she'd got used to the idea.

But he remembered her determined expression and bowed his head, slowing down for a minute or two, hurting so much he didn't know what to do.

Was he to lose everything? Self-respect *and* the woman he loved?

It seemed a long time till he got to Sully's street, one of the better ones at the lower end of town, lined with three-storey houses that had basements as well. He stood for a long time at

Sully's gate, staring at the front door, strangely reluctant to take the final step.

Vi opened the kitchen door and Roy fell into her arms, sobbing still.

'Dad's taken her away. He's taken our Nora! He says she's not his. You've got to stop him.'

She cuddled the boy close for a minute and as she did so, she saw another figure come out of the cottage door: Iris, wearing only her long flannel nightie and with bare feet. She suddenly realised that Roy too was clad only in his pyjamas.

'Let's go into the cottage, eh? You and Iris will catch your death of cold standing here in your nightclothes.'

A light came on above the stables and she saw Tess looking out of the window at them as they hurried across to the cottage, so waved.

Inside, both children looked at her trustingly but she didn't know what to tell them, how to explain. She began tentatively, 'Your Dad is very upset and—' There was a knock on the cottage door and Tess came hurrying in, a coat over her nightdress.

'Is something wrong, Vi love?'

'Very wrong. Joss has taken Nora and – I think he's going to give her away.'

'Eh, why ever would he do that?'

Vi hesitated, looking at the children. 'This is a secret, but I may need your help, so . . . The fact is, Nora isn't his. He's quite certain he didn't father her. He's giv— Oh, Tess, he's giving her to her real father.'

Roy said fiercely, 'But she's still *our* sister and we should be living together. I'll never speak to him again if he does it.'

Vi pulled herself together for the children's sake. 'Well, you can't do anything about it in your nightclothes. Go up and get dressed quickly, both of you. Never mind about getting washed.'

When they'd gone, Tess said in a low voice, 'I never did like that Ada, but I'd not have thought her capable of that. The hussy!'

'Joss has known for a while. But he's only just found out who the father is.' After another hesitation, she whispered, 'It's Sully.'

There was silence, then Tess said quietly, 'He tried it on me once, the sod. Said he wouldn't charge me rent if I lay with him. I told him if he tried to force me I'd scream blue murder and tell everyone he was forcing me. He said I'd regret it, but I didn't.'

'Maybe he forced Ada.'

'He doesn't force them physically, he blackmails or bribes them and—' She broke off at the sound of footsteps clattering down the stairs.

'I'm going after Joss,' Vi said. 'And I'm taking the children. It's the only thing I can think of. Maybe they can help me change his mind. You won't say a word to anyone about this, Tess?'

'No, love. You know I won't.'

Vi gave her a quick hug and turned to take hold of Iris's hand. As they walked along, she felt Roy slip his hand into hers as well. She didn't say anything. Boys had their pride.

But though she walked as quickly as she could, she didn't catch up with Joss and when she got to the town centre she stopped, uncertain where to look first. Sully's house, probably. Everyone knew where he lived.

'When we get there,' she said to Roy, 'I want you to stay on the other side of the road and look after Iris. There may be trouble and I don't want her hurt.'

'But you will stop Dad?'

'I'll try. I'll do my very best, I promise you.' But when a man was hurting as much as Joss was, he didn't always think straight. She'd seen it many times with men bereaved or hurt during the war. It wasn't only men who were killed in the trenches but some families had been killed on the home front. She'd dealt with the case of a mother and two children blown to pieces. And others, like Joss, had found a cuckoo in the nest.

How could you explain to children what that sort of thing did to men?

* * *

Snug under his pile of blankets, Eric heard the noise and fuss, but didn't go out to investigate. He had his own plans for today and he didn't intend to let anything interfere with them.

Later, when his bodyguards arrived at the appointed time to escort him into town, he was ready and slipped quietly out of the stables without saying a word to anyone. He intended to get to the office really early, well before Sully. He still had the back door key and would go inside and wait to see what happened, whether Kirby really did sack that nasty sod. With three stout fellows to protect him, Eric would be all right, whatever the outcome.

'Not so fast, lads. I'm not a good walker,' he said as the others strode along too quickly for him.

He didn't try to talk to them as they walked along more slowly, because it still took all his breath to get into town.

Gerald Kirby also had a wakeful night. He would be putting all that he'd made of his life in jeopardy when he sacked Sully, and simply on the word of Eric Gill. What was he thinking of?

He eased himself out of bed, unable to bear lying there for one second longer.

Maud stirred. 'What's the matter?'

'Nothing. I just can't sleep. You doze off again.' He slipped into his dressing gown and wandered downstairs. The house felt different in the darkness, more comforting.

He went into his office and switched on the electric light, sitting at the desk, then standing up to go and stare out of the window at the darkness, before coming back to rearrange the ornaments on the mantelpiece.

The door opened and he swung round. 'Maud!'

'I thought I'd join you.'

He wasn't sure he wanted that. She was very keen for him to sack Sully, and if he changed his mind, he wanted to have free rein to do things his own way.

She took a seat and yawned hugely, fluffing up her hair and wriggling her shoulders. 'You're thinking of backing out of what we discussed yesterday, aren't you?'

He shrugged. He was definitely not going to be drawn into an argument.

'If you go on employing that horrible man, letting him do as he wishes, I'll leave you.'

It was the last thing he'd expected to hear and he couldn't believe what he was hearing. 'How would you live if you did that?'

'I do have a small income of my own, you know, Gerald.'

He couldn't help laughing. You'd not have enough to live on, not with your expensive tastes.'

'I'd have to cut back. I'd be able to get a room with the Warburtons, for a start. They're taking in all sorts of people these days.' She waved one arm to encompass their house, 'It's nice living in style here, I grant you that, but it's not nice being scorned by decent people because of the way *you* run your slums – or rather, Sully does.'

She looked at him through narrowed eyes, then stood up. 'I'll not nag you. I don't approve of nagging. But I mean what I say. You know me well enough now to understand that.'

He waited till she'd reached the door, then couldn't help saying, 'Maud . . .'

She swung round, her head cocked to one side, her expression hopeful, he could see that so clearly. But he couldn't finish his sentence because he simply couldn't promise what she was asking. The hope that had brightened her eyes faded quickly and he saw her shoulders slump.

'You must choose for yourself, Gerald. Sully or me. Staying a pariah or being accepted socially. I shan't change *my* mind.'

She walked out, graceful and elegant as ever, even in her dressing gown.

He stood very still, feeling a sense of great loss, then went to sit behind the desk again. It was all very well of Maud to say choose, but what if his choices landed him in prison for what he'd done during the war? He had only Gill's word for it that Sully wouldn't betray him to the police.

* * *

Joss knocked on the front door and heard footsteps shuffling towards it.

The old housekeeper, who'd been with Sully for a good many years, opened the door a crack and peered out.

'Yes?'

'I'd like to see Sully.'

'Can't.'

'I'm not going away till I've seen him.'

She cackled. 'Be standing there a long time, then. He's not here.'

'Where is he?'

'At work, where else? He don't lie abed all day.' She shut the door.

It took Joss a few seconds to pull himself together, because he'd been braced to do battle and felt suddenly let down.

Turning with a sigh, he set off again for Kirby's office. Surely that was where he'd find Sully? Nora was asleep now, her little face serene, one hand curled up beside her cheek. How had a brute like Sully created a pretty creature like this one?

It took longer than Vi had expected to get to Sully's house, because Iris was too little to walk fast. By that time, the child was flagging visibly.

Vi knocked on the door and got short shrift from the old housekeeper, who obviously knew who she was.

'He won't want to see *you*.'

The door was slammed in her face. But there had been no sign of a pram, either outside or in the hall, so Vi decided to go and check out Kirby's.

By now, Iris was trailing along so wearily, Vi said, 'I'm going to take you two to your Grandma Bentley's while I find your father,' she said.

Roy stopped dead in his tracks. 'I want to come with you.'

'Iris is too tired. Didn't you do much walking when you lived with your other grandma?'

'No. We came home from school and sat down, then we did

our piano practice. We went to bed soon after tea, even if we weren't tired. And I had to go to bed at the same time as Iris!' The injustice of this clearly still rankled.

'I see. Well, you two can wait for me at the shop.'

'I won't stay there. I'm coming with you.'

His tone was like his father's, utterly determined. So was his expression. 'I need you to look after your little sister.'

'She can stay with Grandma.'

'Roy, it's better if I do this on my own.'

'If you don't take me with you, I'll tell my uncle Wilf what you're doing, then *he* will want to come.'

'Roy, that's not fair.'

His chin was jutting out pugnaciously. 'It's Dad who's not being fair. And I'm *not* letting him take Nora away from us.' He turned to Iris. 'You're not to tell Grandma or anyone about Dad and Nora. Just say we were all going shopping and you got tired.'

She nodded.

'She's a bit small to remember that,' Vi protested.

'We had to learn to keep quiet at Grandma Tomlinson's. She won't say anything.'

What a bleak time they must have had in the last few months! Vi thought. How could anyone treat children that way?

The Bentleys were surprised to see them, but readily agreed to look after Iris while Vi did her shopping.

'We'll have a nice cup of tea waiting for you before you go back up that hill,' Wilf's wife said, giving her niece a hug.

Outside Vi stopped and looked Roy in the eye. 'If I say to keep back, you're to do it. Promise, or I'm not going any further.'

'I promise.'

When Eric arrived at Kirby's office, he was pleased to find the place still in darkness. He decided he would take Fred inside with him and told the others to stay hidden in the outhouses at the rear, ready to come to his help if they called. He probably wouldn't need all three men and it was costing him a fortune, but he wasn't going to risk being beaten up, which might kill him.

He let himself into the building, which was half lit by the grey light of early morning coming through the windows. He led the way upstairs to the room that had been his office. There was no sign that anyone else had been working there, the chair was still how he always left it and the desk was empty of papers. Most of the paperwork was kept in Sully's office, anyway, and Eric had had to get what Sully called the rough ledgers from there in the morning then hand them over at the end of the day. Then Sully would copy the totals into the other ledgers, the ones Mr Kirby saw. All papers were filed in Sully's office, too.

Hearing a sound downstairs, Eric put one finger to his lips. Rod, who'd come inside with him, grinned, his teeth shining white in the semi-darkness.

Footsteps clumped up the stairs and Sully's voice boomed out in the stair well. 'You can wait for me in there, Ted.'

The door of Eric's office began to open and he stiffened in fear.

'Not in there, you fool, in my room. Keep the door closed and whatever you hear, you don't come out unless I tell you.'

'Yes, Mr Sully.'

Eric closed his eyes in shuddering relief, then as Sully went downstairs again, he crept out on the landing, keeping an eye on the other office as he listened carefully.

Sully went downstairs into Kirby's office, whose door always creaked when opened, however much you oiled it. There was the sound of drawers being pulled out then slammed shut one after the other, papers rustling, Sully grunting.

What was he looking for?

The front door opened and someone came in. Mr Kirby. Eric grinned as he watched from above as the other hung his hat on the hallstand and put the fancy walking stick he always carried, the one with a silver falcon's head on the handle, into the umbrella stand. He twirled that stick sometimes as he walked along, but he certainly didn't need it to lean on. It was just for show, that stick was, like a lot of what Mr Kirby said and did in public.

Eric waited with bated breath. Now there would be hell to pay.

Mr Kirby didn't like anyone going into his office when he wasn't there, let alone searching through his drawers.

'What the hell are you doing here, Sully?'

'You're early.' The older man's tone was insolent, as if he was the one in charge.

Eric would never make that mistake. Mr Kirby liked you to be respectful.

'It's a good thing I was early. Do you make a habit of going through my drawers?'

Sully chuckled. 'How else would I find out what's going on?'

'Well, this is the last time you damned well do it. You're fired.'

'You wouldn't dare.'

'I mean it.'

'Well, we'll just see what the new policeman says about that. He's hell on black-market profiteers, they tell me, hates 'em with a passion.'

There was silence. Eric willed Kirby to stand firm.

'You'll go to prison too.'

'Better that than get turned out of a job I enjoy. Be very careful what you do to me, *Mr* Kirby, because I can do a lot worse to you. After all, I was only obeying your orders. *You* were the one in charge.'

The front door banged open before Kirby could respond and to Eric's amazement, Joss burst inside, holding the baby in his arms.

'Sully!' he yelled at the top of his voice. 'Where are you?'

Eric watched with great interest to see what this interruption meant. Even from up here he could see that Joss looked distraught, almost as if he'd lost his senses.

Sully came to the door of Mr Kirby's office. 'What the hell do you want at this hour of the morning, Bentley? Come back later, if you must. I'm busy now. Though I'm not letting you rent another house, if that's what you're after.'

'It's not. And what I have to say won't wait.'

Intrigued, Eric waited.

'Then say it quickly and get out.'

'I've brought you your daughter.' He held out the bundle.

There was dead silence, then Sully roared with laughter. 'That's *your* daughter, not mine.'

'I'd not been near my wife for over a year when the baby was born. You had. You forced her, you sod.'

Heavy footsteps walked across the hallway and Sully came into view. Eric watched him move the blanket so that he could see the baby's face. Then he looked at Joss and smiled again. 'You'd not have to force Ada. Everyone knew she was free with her favours. And I'm not paying out for every bastard brat someone claims is mine.'

'You know she's yours.'

'I'll deny it. How are you going to prove different now Ada's dead?'

'I'm not. I'm just going to leave her here for you.' Joss looked round the hall, then marched through the only open door into Kirby's office.

Eric heard Mr Kirby call, 'Hoy! What are you doing?'

Joss didn't answer, but when he came out, he wasn't carrying the baby.

Sully took the initiative, catching Joss by the arm and swinging him round, even as he threw a punch at the younger man's face.

Joss jerked his head away so the blow only grazed his chin, and quickly got in a punch of his own, a good right hook, Eric noted with approval.

Caught by surprise, Sully staggered backwards, tripped over the bottom step where it curved outwards and lay for a minute, winded. He was an experienced fighter, though, and rolled away when Joss approached him, as if expecting to be kicked.

But the baby had started to cry just then, a great wail of pain and anger, which distracted Joss for a moment. That gave Sully the chance to kick out from where he was still lying and knock his opponent's legs from under him. Then he began roaring for Ted to come down and help him throw this fool out.

Pushing past Eric on the landing, Ted tried to do just that. But Eric managed to trip him as he reached the top of the stairs and instead, Ted went tumbling down them, yelling and cursing all the way, to land on top of Sully.

Faced with two men lying in a tangle and still hearing Nora crying, Joss backed into the office.

Eric saw Sully scramble to his feet and follow Joss in. He moved along the landing so that he could see further into the office near the door.

Sully picked up the wooden chair which stood just inside the door and smashed it over Joss's head. The younger man fell as if pole-axed, with only his feet showing to the watcher above now. Eric kept away from the top of the stairs, not wanting to suffer the same fate.

Eric's bodyguard had come out of his office to watch the fight. 'Do you want me to do anything?'

'No. Give them a few minutes and see what happens. You know to yell through the window for the others if anyone comes after me.'

Vi entered the building in time to see Sully smash a chair over Joss's head. There was a man standing behind him in the hall, watching and rubbing one arm, wincing as if it hurt. As Sully raised his foot and kicked the fallen figure, she looked round for a weapon and grabbed a walking stick from the hall stand. Shoving the watcher aside she thumped the silver handle of the walking stick down on Sully's head, yelling, 'Get away from him, you bully!'

He spun round, his face a mask of fury. Then he gave a nasty smile as he saw only a small, furious woman. 'Are *you* going to make me, Vi bloody Gill?'

'No, I am.' Kirby who'd been staring open-mouthed, moved forward. 'Stop this at once.'

'I didn't start it.'

'If this man is right, you started it over a year ago,' Kirby said, disgust burring his voice. 'Now, get out of this building or I'll call in the police to remove you.'

Sully leaned against the door frame. 'You'll have to pay me if you want me to leave.'

'You've already embezzled a considerable amount of money from me, right from the beginning. Consider that your payment.'

There was dead silence as Sully took this in. 'Took you long enough to find out. Better be careful how you tread from now on, though. I'm not having you turning me in to the police. I've taken measures in case that happens.'

Kirby moved a step closer. 'Get out of this office and then get right out of town. If you do that, I might just forget you exist. If you're not gone in two days, I may remember some of the tricks I learned when I was making my fortune. I wasn't always a gentleman.'

Sully opened his mouth to argue. 'I won't—'

Kirby cut him short. 'Over the years, I've had my suspicions about a few incidents in which you were involved and heaven help me, I did nothing about them. Do the names Riley, Grendle or Burson mean anything to you?'

Vi stared at them in shock. Two of the men named had vanished completely and one had been found beaten to death.

Silence, then Sully spun round without a word, nearly knocking her over as he walked out. He was followed by Ted Fitch.

'Two days, remember,' Kirby shouted after them.

Vi went to kneel by Joss, who was groaning and trying to sit up. 'Lie still, love. He's gone and you'll feel better in a minute or two.'

Still lying on the armchair in Kirby's office, the baby began to cry again.

Vi looked up. Thank goodness. Nora was safe.

Roy, who'd not stayed outside as Vi had ordered, slipped through the office door and picked up his little sister. 'You're not giving her away!' he yelled at his father. 'I won't let you.'

Kirby looked from one to the other, puzzlement clear on his face. He winced as Nora gave them another demonstration of how well-developed her lungs were.

'Sit down and hold your sister,' Vi ordered sharply.

Roy looked at her then sat in the big armchair, cuddling Nora close, watching his father warily.

Joss tried again to sit up and Vi supported him.

Her love showed so clearly in her face that Gerald suddenly felt a pang of envy.

Footsteps on the stairs had him swinging round, alert to possible danger. But when he saw Eric he relaxed again. 'What are you doing here, Gill?'

'Just making sure Sully didn't attack you. I brought two friends with me to be on the safe side.'

Gerald threw back his head and laughed. 'I brought a couple of fellows with me too. They're waiting in the street. But I don't think we have anything further to fear from Sully, so you can pay yours off.'

'I'd rather keep them on till he's left town, sir, and you should keep yours too. Call it insurance, if you like.'

'He'll not dare do anything else.'

Eric opened his mouth, then shut it again. He knew Sully rather better in some ways than his employer did. Sully would be looking to leave a final mark on those who'd upset him. He always did. Eric's men would be keeping an eye on him, making sure he didn't.

'You'll take over from him here, Gill? You can manage the rents?'

'Oh, yes, Mr Kirby. I'll need a couple of men to work with me. I'll soon train them up. I'm not doing things violently, though. It doesn't pay.'

'Good. Do whatever you have to. And clean up those slums a bit. I don't mean spend lavishly, mind.' Suddenly he had an urge to go and see Maud, make sure she hadn't left him. 'I've got to go home and see my wife before I do anything else. I'll be back later.'

He looked at Vi and Joss. 'Take your time, Bentley. Don't try to leave till you've recovered.'

Joss was still leaning against Vi, eyes closed, and he didn't answer. Tears were leaking out of his closed eyes and trickling down his cheeks.

Gerald looked from one to the other, shook his head in bafflement and left.

* * *

When Kirby's footsteps had died away, Eric said, 'I'll go back upstairs now. I've things to sort out. Call me if there's any trouble, Vi. I don't think there will be today, though.' He jerked his head at Joss. 'He looks bad. Sully hits hard.'

'Yes. I'll give him a few minutes to recover.'

When Eric had left, Joss fumbled for her hand and held it without a word. A few minutes later, he looked at her, seeming more himself. 'I'm sorry, love. I must have gone mad, I think.'

'It was a hard thing to face.'

'Still, I shouldn't have used the baby like that.' He looked across at his son, who was still scowling at him. 'It's all right, Roy. We're keeping Nora.'

The boy stared at him, his expression lightening, then nodded and said in a thickened voice, 'Good.'

'What changed your mind?' Vi asked.

'The sight of Sully bending over her. It still hurts – that he fathered her, I mean – but it'd hurt a lot more to think of her in his power, being ill-treated or abandoned.'

She closed her eyes in relief for a moment. 'I'm glad. She's a lovely baby.'

'She kept smiling at me this morning. All the way into town, she smiled. It nearly tore me apart.' Another silence then, 'Vi . . .'

'Yes?'

'Thanks for saving me from Sully.'

She felt herself blushing. 'I just hit him with the walking stick.'

'And risked him turning on you. You're a heroine, you are.'

She shrugged. 'You don't think of things like that when there's a crisis.'

Joss pulled her to him and hugged her close, resting against her for a minute more, then moving away. 'I can't lie here all day.'

'If you're at all dizzy, you should stay where you are.'

'I'm not dizzy, though my head hurts.'

'I'll bathe it when we get you home. I think we should get a taxi from the station. You're in no fit state to walk anywhere.'

Without waiting for an answer, she turned to Roy. 'Leave Nora on that chair and fetch Iris, love. Tell your grandma we've met your dad and he's had a bit of an accident, hurt his head. Don't tell her anything else. Nora is our business and no one else's. When you and Iris get back, we'll find a taxi to take us home.'

Roy hesitated, staring from one to the other then smiling. 'Are you two going to get married? The lads at school say when grown-ups start to cuddle, it means they're courting and after that they get married.'

Joss chuckled softly. 'I hope so.'

'Would you mind, Roy?' Vi asked.

The boy beamed at her. 'I'd like it. Me an' Iris need a new mum, and Dad needs someone to look after Nora.'

'I need someone for more than that,' Joss muttered. 'I need someone to love.'

When the boy had gone and they were alone, Vi looked sideways at him, not knowing what to say.

'You have to make an honest man of me, after cuddling me so publicly,' he said with a loving smile, though he winced as he moved his head incautiously. 'Ouch! Is there anything you're afraid of?'

'Of course there is. I'm not a fool. But you can't let being afraid stop you doing things.'

'I do love you, Vi.'

The breath caught in her throat for a moment, then she smiled back at him. 'I love you too.'

'So you'll marry me?'

'Of course I will, you fool.' She gave a wry smile. 'Mrs Gilson will be pleased about that. They don't allow married women to work. I was looking forward to being a Health Visitor, too.'

'I'm sorry.'

'Don't be. Having a family will be just as good. I've wanted it for – oh, so long.'

'We may even add to it, have a baby or two of our own.'

She shook her head sadly. 'I'm a bit old for that. Len and I tried, but we never managed one. Does it matter?'

'No. What matters is you. Come on, help me get up. Let's go home.'

Gerald got out of the car as soon as it stopped, not waiting for the chauffeur to help him. He ran into the house, calling for his wife.

Maud came out of her sitting room, unsmiling. 'Well?'

'I've sacked Sully.'

She closed her eyes and let out a great sigh of relief. 'I'm glad.'

'Then show it, damn you.' He pulled her into his arms and gave her a kiss.

When they pulled apart, each breathing deeply, she said in a voice that wobbled slightly, 'That was the first real kiss you've ever given me, one that meant something.'

What she said was right, he realised in surprise. He pulled her closer. 'I think a lot of things are changing in Drayforth.'

'For the better, I hope.'

'I'll make sure of that.'

# 27

For the rest of that day there was a great deal of coming and going in Drayforth. One of the men Eric had hired came up during the early afternoon to ask if Vi could pack up her brother's things again, so that they could be taken back to Mayfield Place early the following morning.

'He says he won't be back till later, and you can move back in with him, if you like, missus.'

'I'll see him about that when he gets back tonight.'

She went across to the house to let the Warburtons know that Eric would be leaving the following day. 'I'm so grateful that you took him in. You've helped quite a few people.'

Phyllis smiled, then it faded. 'Are you leaving with your brother?'

'No. If you don't mind, I'll stay at the house for a day or two. Joss and I are getting married as soon as we can get hold of a special licence.'

'Oh, my dear, how wonderful!'

'And if it's all right with you, we'd like to rent the cottage.'

'It is all right.' Phyllis hesitated, exchanged glances with her sister, then said, 'We'd like to see Joss when he wakes – if he's well enough, of course. Perhaps the two of you would take tea with us?'

'I'm sure he'll be all right. His eyes seem clear and he doesn't seem concussed. I've seen men who were and they can't focus properly. Joss must have a very hard skull. He'll have a headache for a day or two, though.'

When Vi and Joss went across to the house later, having told the children about their plans, they were taken into the big drawing room, where a fire had been lit, and provided with dainty china cups and plates, plus tiny cakes.

Vi hid a smile as Joss tried to make the titbits last. She knew by now what a hearty appetite he had and these cakes would make only a mouthful for a man like him.

'Now,' Phyllis said once the refreshments had been taken away. 'My sister and I have been talking and we'd like to offer you a job, Mr Bentley.'

Vi saw him become instantly alert.

'Oh?'

'Yes. We'd like you to manage our estate for us, the house and land, selling items as necessary, supervising repairs, whatever needs doing. We're prepared to pay you two hundred pounds a year for this, plus the agreed percentage when you sell something for us.'

He looked at Vi and she gave him a tiny nod of encouragement, so he turned back to the ladies. 'I'll accept the job happily, but I'll only take the wages. If I'm working for you, I won't need paying to sell your silver and other precious objects.'

Both elderly ladies looked from Vi to him. 'That's very generous of you, Mr Bentley. In that case, we shall not charge rent on the cottage. But we do hope you'll allow us to see the children regularly. We've grown very fond of them, especially the dear little baby.'

On the way back Vi and Joss stopped to kiss one another. Roy, who had come to the doorway of the cottage, nudged his little sister. 'I told you. They're always cuddling. I'm not getting married if you have to keep cuddling girls.'

But Iris couldn't wait a minute longer and pushed past him to go running across to her father, who swung her round in his arms. After that she turned to smile at Vi and take hold of her hand.

It really was a dream come true, Vi thought, blinking her eyes furiously.

* * *

They got married three days later at the registry office, with all their friends and family there, even Arnie, carefully spruced up for the occasion by Doris. Sully had left town two days before and everything seemed to be settling down again.

As the wedding party were driven back up the hill in Kirby's two cars, and two taxis as well, the newly-weds exchanged another kiss.

Roy nudged Iris and pulled a face.

'I like to see them kissing,' she said. 'I like it when Vi kisses me, too.'

'Girls are so soppy!'

When they got to Fairview, however, it was to find the police wagon outside the front door and two men in handcuffs being shoved into it, while three others stood nearby, watching.

Joss was out of the car in a minute. 'What's happened?'

Rob Piper turned to him. 'These two were trying to break into the cottage. They'd got a bottle of lamp oil with them and some matches, so I reckon they were going to set it on fire.'

Eric and Mr Kirby got out of the other cars to join them.

'Good thing I set my men to keep watch, then, eh?' Eric said with a smug smile. 'I knew Sully would try something.' He looked at his employer. 'I always try to think ahead.'

'Keep doing it,' Kirby said.

Joss looked at the men. 'Sully must have arranged this. Who else could it be?'

Rob shrugged. 'I think so, too, but they deny any connection with him and apparently he's already moved to Blackpool. Of course I'll ring the police there and ask them to check where he was.'

'He'll have an alibi,' Eric said. 'He always does.'

Gerald gave a grim smile. 'I think I know how to make sure he doesn't try anything again.'

Rob turned to him. 'You won't do anything unlawful, will you, sir?'

Gerald continued to smile. 'Of course not, sergeant. I never do.'

Rob's expression of disbelief was eloquent but he didn't contradict Kirby.

'Well, if the fuss is all over, let's go inside,' Christina said. 'The sun may be shining but it's still a very cold day.'

Tess, who had also been at the wedding, had run round the back as soon as they returned to help Cook with the refreshments. Her children were waiting for her in the kitchen and told her about the fight.

As soon as the guests had assembled in the drawing room, Tess carried in a tray of glasses full of sherry, courtesy of old Mr Warburton's wine cellar, so that everyone could toast the bride and groom. After that she went dashing back to the kitchen to fetch Cook, and the two women stood in the doorway, having also been invited to join in the toast.

'Vi looks lovely, doesn't she?' Tess whispered.

Cook studied the bride. 'Not lovely, no. She'll never be lovely. Too thin. But when she's as happy as that, she's bonny enough for anyone.'

'Oh, you.'

Cook sighed. 'You should have seen Miss Christina when she was young. Now *she* was lovely.' After a minute, she added, 'As soon as they've finished these toasts, you go and fetch that wedding cake. I don't know where Mr Kirby gets his supplies but it was nice of him to think of providing the ingredients to make one, wasn't it?'

'It was probably Mrs Kirby who thought of it.'

Vi found herself standing in the bay window with her husband's arm round her shoulders while everyone toasted them. Then they insisted on the groom kissing the bride again.

She looked up into his eyes and couldn't see for happy tears.

He wiped one away with his fingertip. 'You'll have everyone thinking I'm ill-treating you if you cry.'

'I'm just – so happy.'

'Me too. I've not been this happy since I was a youngster. We'll make a good life together, Vi. I'll work hard, love you always.' He gestured to his children to join them and Phyllis passed over Nora, wrapped in a fancy lace shawl and trying her hardest to kick it off.

Then they all turned to pose for a family photograph by the town's chief photographer, which was the Warburtons' wedding present to them.

Vi felt as if the whole world was full of sunlight. She'd never expected to have a husband again, let alone children and a baby to raise. She looked up at Joss, her eyes still full of happy tears and saw that his eyes were similarly bright.

I hope you're looking down on this Mum, she thought and for a moment seemed to feel a gentle warmth on one cheek, the way she had when her mother had laid one hand there in a passing caress.

Vi was sure she and Joss would makes a good life together. Quite sure.

## CONTACTING ANNA JACOBS

Anna is always delighted to hear from readers and can be contacted:

### BY MAIL

PO Box 628
Mandurah
Western Australia 6210

If you'd like a reply, please enclose a self-addressed, business size envelope, stamped (from inside Australia) or an international reply coupon (from outside Australia).

### VIA THE INTERNET

Anna has her own web page, with details of her books and excerpts, and invites you to visit it at *http://www.annajacobs.com*

Anna can be contacted by email at *anna@annajacobs.com*

If you'd like to receive an email newsletter about Anna and her books every month or two, you are cordially invited to join her announcements list. Just email her and ask to be added to the list, or follow the link from her web page, part way down.